THE MILLION-DOLLAR WOUND

Books by Max Allan Collins

THE MEMOIRS OF NATHAN HELLER
True Detective
True Crime
The Million-Dollar Wound

NOLAN AND JON NOVELS
Bait Money
Blood Money
Fly Paper
Hush Money
Hard Cash
Scratch Fever

QUARRY NOVELS
The Broker (retitled: *Quarry*)
The Broker's Wife (retitled: *Quarry's List*)
The Dealer (retitled: *Quarry's Deal*)
The Slasher (retitled: *Quarry's Cut*)

IN THE MALLORY MANNER
No Cure For Death
The Baby Blue Rip-Off
Kill Your Darlings
A Shroud for Aquarius

NONFICTION/CRITICISM
One Lonely Knight: Mickey Spillane's Mike Hammer (with James L. Traylor)
Jim Thompson: The Killers Inside Him (with Ed Gorman)

COMIC STRIP COLLECTIONS
Dick Tracy Meets Angeltop (with Rick Fletcher)
Dick Tracy Meets the Punks (with Rick Fletcher)
The Files of Ms. Tree (with Terry Beatty; two volumes)

EDITOR
Tomorrow I Die (Mickey Spillane collection)
Mike Hammer: The Comic Strip (two volumes)

THE MILLION-DOLLAR WOUND

MAX
ALLAN
COLLINS

St. Martin's Press
New York

Library of Congress Cataloging-in-Publication Data

Collins, Max Allan.
The million dollar wound.

I. Title.
PS3553.04573M55 1986 813'.54 85-25091
ISBN 0-312-53252-0

First Edition

10 9 8 7 6 5 4 3 2 1

For George Hagenauer—
without whom Heller's world
would be much smaller

HOTEL
SHERMAN
RKO

Although the historical events in this novel are portrayed more or less accurately (as much as the passage of time, and contradictory source material, will allow), fact, speculation, and fiction are freely mixed here; historical personages exist side by side with composite characters and wholly fictional ones—all of whom act and speak at the author's whim.

Lucky indeed for America that in this theater and at that juncture she depended not on boys drafted or cajoled into fighting but on "tough guys" who had volunteered to fight and who asked for nothing better than to come to grips with the sneaking enemy who had aroused all their primitive instincts.

—Samuel Eliot Morison

History of the United States Naval Operations in World War II

Say a prayer for my pal
Who died in Guadalcanal.

—Commonest of inscriptions among the hundreds of crosses in a cemetery on that island

If you don't do like I say, you'll get shot in the head.

—Frank Nitti

There's no business like show business.

—Irving Berlin

Prologue

St. Elizabeth's Hospital

Congress Heights, Maryland

November 26, 1942

1

My name was gone.

When I woke, I didn't know where the hell I was. A small room with the pale green plaster walls and antiseptic smell of a hospital, yes, but *what* hospital? *Where?*

And then the damnedest thing happened: I couldn't remember my name. Couldn't remember for the life of me. It was gone.

There was nobody to ask about it. I was alone in the little room. Just me and three other beds, empty, neatly made, military fashion, a small bedside stand next to each. No pictures on any of the stands, though. No mirrors on the wall. How in hell did they expect a guy to know who he was without a mirror on the wall?

I sat up in bed, the horsehair mattress beneath me making an ungodly racket, working against itself like a bag of steel wool. My mouth had a bitter, medicinal taste. Maybe that was it; maybe I was so pumped full of medicine I was woozy. My name would come to me. It would come.

I stood up, on wobbly legs. I hadn't forgotten how to walk, exactly, but I wasn't ready for the Olympics.

Funny. I knew what the Olympics was. I knew all sorts of things, come to think of it. That the mattress was horsehair, pillow too. I knew what color green was. I knew that this brown, wool, scratchy blanket was government issue. But who was I? Where did I come from? *Who the fuck was I?*

I sat back down on the edge of the bed; my legs couldn't take standing up for long, and neither could the rest of me. Where did my memory begin? Think back. Think back.

I could remember another hospital. Yesterday, was it? Or longer ago? I could remember waking up in a hospital bed, next to a window, and looking out and seeing, goddamnit, seeing palm trees and *screaming,* screaming . . .

But I didn't know why palm trees would make me scream. I did know what palm trees were. That was a start. I didn't think seeing one today would make me scream. Shit, I needed some joe. That taste in my mouth.

Then I remembered looking at myself in the mirror! Yes, at the other hospital, looking at myself in the mirror, and seeing a man with a yellow face.

Fucking Jap! somebody said, and broke the mirror.

Still sitting on the edge of my rack, I lifted a hand to my forehead; felt a bandage there. The hand, I noticed, was yellow.

It was me. I broke the mirror. I was the one who yelled at the Jap. And I was the Jap.

"You're no fuckin' Jap," somebody said.

Me, again.

You're not a Jap. You think, you talk, in English. Japs don't think and talk in English. They don't know Joe DiMaggio from Joe Louis. And you do.

You know English, you know about Japs, you know about DiMaggio and Louis, but you don't know your own name, do you, schmuck?

Schmuck? Isn't that Jewish?

I'm a Jew. A Jew or something.

"Fuck it," I said, and got up again. Time to walk. Time to find another window and see if there are any palm trees and see if they make me scream.

I was in a nightshirt, so I dug in the drawers of the bedside stand and found some clothes. Skivvies and socks and a cream-color flannel shirt and tan cotton pants. I put them on; I remembered how to do *that,* anyway. And I about tripped over a pair of shoes by the bed; stopped and put them on. Civilian-type shoes, not the boondockers I was used to.

The adjoining room was a dormitory or a ward or something; twenty beds, neatly made, empty. Was I the only guy here?

I walked through the ward into a hallway, and at my right was a glassed-in area, behind which pretty girls in blue uniforms with white aprons were scurrying around. Nurses. None of them seemed to notice me. But I noticed them. They were so young. Late teens, early twenties. I hadn't seen a pretty girl in so very long. I didn't know why. But I knew I hadn't. For some reason it made me want to cry.

Held it back, though. Instinct said tears would keep me in here, longer, and already I wanted out. I didn't know where else I'd go, because I didn't know where the hell I belonged, but it wasn't here.

I went over to the glass and knocked; a nurse looked up at me, startled. She had light blue eyes, and blond curly shoulder-length hair showering from under her white cap. Petite, fine features. The faintest trail of freckles across a cute, nearly pug nose.

She slid a window to one side and looked at me prettily from behind the counter. "Ah—you're the new patient," she said. Pleasantly.

"Am I?"

She checked her watch, glanced at a chart on a clipboard on the counter. "And I think it's about time for your Atabrine tablets."

"What is it, malaria?"

"Why, yes. You've had quite a flare-up, as a matter of fact. You were just sent over from M and S after several days there."

"M and S?"

"Medical and Surgical building."

She got me the pills—small, bright yellow pills—and a little paper cup of water; I took the water and the pills. The aftertaste was bitter.

"Tell me something," I said.

She smiled and I loved her for it; tiny white teeth like a child. "Certainly."

"Do they have palm trees outside the window, over at M and S?"

"Hardly. You're at St. E's."

"St. E's?"

"St. Elizabeth's. Near Washington, D.C."

"I'm in the States, then!"

"Yes you are. Welcome home, soldier."

"Never call a Marine 'soldier,' sweetheart. We take that as an insult."

"Oh, so you're a Marine."

I swallowed. "I guess I am."

She smiled again. "Don't worry," she said. "After a few days, you'll get your bearings."

"Can I ask you to look something up for me?"

"Sure. What?"

"My name."

Her eyes filled with pity, and I hated her for it, and myself, but the feeling passed, where she was concerned; she checked on the clipboard chart and said, "Your name is Heller. Nathan Heller."

It didn't mean a thing to me. Not a thing. Not the faintest fucking bell rang. Shit.

"Are you sure?" I said.

"Unless there's been a foul-up."

"If this is a military hospital, there could sure as hell be a snafu. Double-check, will you? If I heard my own name, I'm sure I'd recognize it."

Pity in the eyes; more pity in the eyes. "I'm sure you would. But we're not strictly military here, and . . . listen, Mr., uh, sir, why don't you step into the dayroom and relax." She gestured graciously to a wide, open doorway just down and across from us. "If I can straighten out this snafu, I'll let you know."

I nodded and walked toward the dayroom; she called out after me.

"Uh, sir!"

I turned and felt my face try to smile. "I'm no officer."

"I know," she said, smiling. "You're a PFC. But that gives you plenty of rank to pull around here, believe me. You guys are tops with us, never forget that."

Pity or not, it was kind of nice to hear.

"Thanks," I said.

"Those palm trees you mentioned?"

"Yeah?"

"You were in Hawaii three days ago. At Pearl Harbor, in the naval hospital there. That's where you saw the palm trees."

"Thanks."

Only I had a crawling feeling Hawaii wasn't the only place I'd seen palm trees.

The dayroom stretched out like the deck of an aircraft carrier, eighty feet long by forty feet wide, easy. The same institutional pale green walls dominated, with an expanse of speckled marble floor where massive furniture squatted—heavy wooden tables, chairs, a piano, the smallest stick of this furniture would take two guys to toss around, and maybe not then. That was when I figured it.

I was in the nuthouse.

Hell, where did I *expect* to be? I didn't know my own fucking name, right? Of course, I knew who was singing "White Christmas," as the radio was piped in over an intercom system: Bing Crosby. I was no idiot. I knew the name of the song and the name of the singer; now, for the sixty-five-dollar question: who the hell was I?

If I had any doubt about *where* I was, the human flotsam sprawled across the heavy chairs cinched it. Hollow cheeks and hollow eyes. Guys sitting there shaking like hootchie-coo dancers. Guys sitting there staring with ball bearings for eyes. A few very ambitious guys playing pinochle or checkers. One guy sat in the corner quietly bawling. Made me glad I held my own tears back. I had enough problems just being minus the small detail of an identity.

Most of the guys were smoking. I craved a smoke. Something in the back of what was left of my mind told me I didn't smoke; yet I wanted a smoke; I sat next to a guy who wasn't shaking or staring; he *was* smoking, however, and he seemed normal enough, a tanned, brown-haired, round-faced man with distinct features. He was sitting along the wall over at right next to a window; this window, like all the other windows, looked out at a nearby faded red-brick building, through bars.

I was in the nuthouse, all right.

"Spare a cig?" I asked.

"Sure." He shook out a Lucky for me. "Name's Dixon. What's yours?"

"I dunno."

He lit me up off his. "No kidding? Amnesia, huh?"

"If that's what they call it."

"That's what they call it. You had the malaria, didn't you, Pops?"

Pops? Did I look that old? Of course Dixon here was probably only twenty or twenty-one, but somebody who hadn't been in the service might peg him for thirty.

"Yeah," I said. "I guess I still got it."

"I hear it's the ever-lovin' pits. Fever, shakes. What the hell, you got any other injuries?"

"I don't think so."

"What about that noggin of yours?"

He meant my bandaged head.

"I did that to myself. In some hospital in Hawaii."

"Yeah?"

"Yeah. Didn't like what I saw in the mirror."

"Know the feelin'," he said. Yawned. "That's most likely why you're on MR Four."

"What's that?"

"Men's Receiving, fourth floor. Anybody remotely suicidal gets stuck here."

"I'm not suicidal," I said, sucking on my cigarette.

"Don't sweat it, then. There's six floors in this joint. Worse off you are, higher your floor. As you get better, you get promoted downwards a floor or two. Hit MR One and you're as good as home, wherever that is for ya."

"Wherever that is," I agreed.

"Oh. Sorry. I forgot."

"Me too."

He grinned, laughed. "You're Asiatic, all right."

I understood the term; didn't know why I did, but I understood it. It described any man who'd served long enough in the Far East to turn bughouse. Subtly bughouse, as in talking to yourself and seeing the world sideways.

"You're a Marine, too," I said.

"Yeah. That much about yourself you remember, huh, mac? Not surprising. No Marine alive'd forget he's a Marine. Dead ones wouldn't, neither. You can forget your name, that ain't no big deal. You can't never forget you're a Marine."

"Even if you want to," I said.

"Right! Here comes one of those fuckin' gobs."

A medical corpsman in his work blues strolled over; he seemed cheerful. Who wouldn't be, pulling duty on a landlocked, home-front ship like St. E's?

"Private Heller," he said, standing before me, swaying a bit. Something about bell bottoms makes a Marine want to kill. If there was a reason for that, I'd forgotten it.

"That's the name they're giving me," I said. "But there's been a fuck-up. I'm no Nathan Who's-It."

"Whoever you are, the doctor would like to see you."

"I'd like to see him, too."

"Report to the nurse's station in five minutes."

"Aye aye."

He flapped off.

"Don't he know there's a war on," Dixon growled.

"I don't wish combat on any man," I said.

"Yeah. Hell. Me, neither."

"Is there a head in this joint?"

"Sure." He dropped his cigarette to the floor and ground it out with his toe. "Follow me."

He rose—he was shorter than I'd thought, but had the solid build that comes from boot camp and a tour or two of duty—and led me out into the hall, into the head, where finally I saw a mirror. I looked in it.

The face, with its white-bandaged forehead, was yellow-tinged, but it was American. I was not a Jap. That was something, anyway. But I could see why Dixon called me Pops. My hair was reddish brown on top, but had gone largely white on the sides. My skin was leathery, wrinkles spreading like cracks through dried earth.

"Do I look Jewish to you?" I asked Dixon.

Dixon was standing at the sink next to me, staring at himself intently in the mirror; he tore himself away to take a look at my reflection and said, "Irish. You're a Mick if ever I saw one."

"Micks don't use words like 'schmuck,' do they?"

"If they're from the big city they do. New York, say."

"That where you're from?"

"No. Detroit. But I had a layover there once. I put the lay in the word, lemme tell ya. Now, there. Look. Will ya look at that. That proves it. Once and for all."

He was covering one side of his face with his hand. Looking at himself with one eye.

"Proves what?" I asked.

"That I'm nuts," he said, out of the side of his mouth that showed. "Now, look."

He covered the other side of his face. Looked at himself with the other eye.

"They're completely different, see."

"What is?"

"The two sides of my face, you dumb sonofabitch! They should be the same, but they ain't. My goddamn face, it's split it in two. This fuckin' war. Oh, I got a screw loose, all right."

He turned away from the mirror and put a hand on my shoulder and grinned; there was a space between his two front teeth, I noticed. "We're in the right place, you and me," he said.

"I guess we are," I said.

"Semper fi," he shrugged, and strutted out.

I took a crap. That's something I hadn't forgotten how to do. I sat there crapping and finishing my smoke and thinking about how I wanted to get out of this place. How I wanted to go home.

Wherever the hell home was.

I flushed the shitter, went over to the sink, and threw some water on my face. Then I went out to meet the doctor.

He was waiting for me outside the nurse's station; he wasn't in military apparel. White coat, white pants. He seemed young for a medic, probably early thirties. Trim black hair, trim mustache, pale, kind of stocky.

He extended his hand for me to shake.

"Pleased to meet you, Private Heller," he said.

"If that's my name," I said.

"That's what I'd like to help you determine. I'm Doctor Wilcox."

Civilian, apparently. "Glad to make your acquaintance, Doc. You really think you could help me find my way back? Back to my name. Back to where I come from."

"Yes," he said.

"I like your confidence," I said, walking next to him down the hall. "But I always thought when a guy went bughouse, it was pretty permanent."

"That's not at all true," he said, gesturing with a hand for me to enter a small room where two chairs and a small table waited; not a straitjacket in sight. I went in. He went on: "Many mental disorders respond well to therapy. And those due to some intensely stressful situation, such as combat, are often easier to deal with."

"Why is that?"

"Because the trauma can be more or less temporary. Be grateful your problem isn't a physical one. That it isn't chronic."

I sat down in one of the chairs. "You going to give me truth serum?"

He remained standing. "Sodium amatal is one possibility. Shock treatments, another. But first I'd like to try to knock your barrier down with simple hypnosis."

"Haven't you heard, Doc? Vaudeville is dead."

He took that with a smile. "This is no sideshow attraction, Private. Hypnosis has often proved effective in certain types of battle neurosis—amnesia among them."

"Well . . ."

"I think you'll find this a less troublesome route than electric shock."

"It cured Zangara."

"Who's Zangara?"

I shrugged. "Damned if I know. What do I have to do, Doc?"

"Just stand and face me. And cooperate. Do exactly as I say."

I stood and faced him. "I'm in your hands."

And then I was: his hands, his warm soothing hands, were on my either temple. "Relax completely and put your mind on going to sleep," he said. His voice was monotonous and musical at the same time; his eyes were gray and placid and yet held me.

"All right, now," he said, hands still on my temples, "keep your eyes on mine, keep your eyes on mine, and keep them fixed on mine, keep your mind entirely on falling asleep. Now you're going into a deep sleep as we go on, you're going to go into a deep sleep as we go on."

His hands dropped from my temples, but his eyes held on. "Now clasp your hands in front of you"—I did; so did he—"clasp them tight, tight, tight, tight, tight, they're getting tighter and tighter and tighter, and as they get tighter you're falling asleep, as they get tighter you're falling asleep, your eyes are getting heavy, heavy . . ."

My eyelids weighed a ton; stayed barely open, his eyes locking mine, his voice droning on: "Now your hands are locked tight, they're locked tight, they're locked tight. Can't let go, they're locked tight, you can't let go; when I snap my fingers you'll be able to let go, when I snap my fingers you'll be able to let go, and then you'll get sleepier, your eyes getting heavier—"

Snap!

"Now your eyes are getting heavier, heavier, heavier, you're going into a deep, deep sleep, going into a deep, deep sleep, deep asleep, far asleep, now closed tight, closed tight, deep, deep sleep, deeply relaxed, far asleep . . . you're far asleep . . . far asleep . . . now you're in a deep sleep, no fear, no anxiety, no fear, no anxiety, now you're in a deep, deep sleep."

I was in darkness now, but his hands guided me, as did his voice: "Now just sit down in the chair behind you. Sit down in the chair behind you." I did. "Lean back." I did. "And now fall forward into a deep, deep sleep. And now falling forward, going further and further and further asleep. Now when I stroke your left arm it becomes rigid, like a bar of steel, as you go further asleep, further asleep."

My arm, as if of its own will, extended, rod straight.

"Going further, further, further asleep. Rigid."

I could feel him tugging at my arm, testing it.

"Cannot be bent or relaxed. Now when I touch the top of your head, when I touch the top of your head, that arm will relax and the other will become rigid. You'll go further asleep. In a very deep sleep."

His hand, lightly, touched the top of my head; my left arm relaxed, right one went sieg heil.

"And your sleep is deeper and deeper. Now when I touch this hand my finger will be hot. Now when I touch this hand my finger will be hot, you will not be able to bear it."

Searing pain! Like red hot shrapnel!

"Your arm is rigid. Now when I touch your hand you will no longer feel any pain there. Will be normal."

Pain was gone, no trace of it.

"Now your arm is relaxed and you're further and further and further asleep. Now you're deep asleep. Going back. Going back now. Going back to Guadalcanal. Going back to Guadalcanal. You can remember. Everything. You can remember everything. Back on Guadalcanal. You see everything now, clearly. You remember it all, now, every bit of it coming back. Tell me your story. Tell me your story, Nate."

One
The Island
Guadalcanal
November 4–19, 1942

2

Through the haze I could see it, the island, "the Island" we'd soon call it. A red-tinged filter of dawn, like a soft-focus lens on an aging movie queen, worked its magic on the cone of land ahead, seducing us into thinking a Pacific paradise reclined before us, a siren lounging in a cobalt sea, waiting, beckoning, coconut palms doing a gentle hula.

Even then we knew we were being lied to. But after a month of duty on Pago Pago—that grubby barren no-man's-land we'd come to call "the Rock," in honor of Alcatraz—the vista before us made us want to believe the come-on.

"It looks like Tahiti or something," Barney said.

Like me, he was leaning against the rail, sea breeze spitting pleasantly in both our faces. We, and the rest of B Company, 2nd Battalion, 8th Regiment, 2nd Marine Division, were so many sardines in a Higgins boat, a landing craft without a ramp, meaning soon we'd be going ass over tea kettle over the sides into the foam and onto the beach.

"Don't kid yourself," I said. "You've heard the scuttlebutt."

"Only it ain't scuttlebutt," a kid squeezed in just behind us said.

The tropical paradise beckoning us was, we all knew, the site of the bloodiest fighting to date in the Pacific Theater. We of the 2nd Marine Division were on our way to spell the battle-weary 1st Division, who since early last August had been struggling to hold on to and preserve Henderson Field, our only airfield on the Island, named after a Corps pilot who fell at Midway. Outnumbered and outsupplied by the Japs, the 1st had held on in the face of air attack, naval shelling, and jungle combat, the latter enlivened by mass "banzai" charges of crazed, drunken, suicidal Japs. We also heard about the malaria, dysentery, and jungle rot afflicting our fellow leathernecks; the sick were said to outnumber the wounded. Scuttlebutt further had it you couldn't leave the battle lines unless your temperature rose above 102.

That was no travel poster come to life, stretched out before us like Dorothy Lamour. It was green fucking hell.

I looked at Barney, an aging bulldog loaded down in battle gear. "Another fine mess," I said.

"Semper fi, mac," he said, grinning, not seeming nervous at all. But he had to be.

Like me, he wore a steel, camouflage-covered helmet, heavy green dungaree jacket with USMC stenciled on the left breast pocket, a web pistol belt (with a pair of canteens, Kabar knife, hand grenades, ammo pouch, and first-aid kit hooked on), green dungaree trousers tucked into light tan canvas leggings over ankle-high boondockers, and a bronze Marine Corps globe-and-anchor emblem on one collar, for luck. The heavy pack on his back no doubt contained, like mine, a poncho, an extra pair of socks, mess kit, boxes of K rations, salt tablets, twenty rounds or so of carbine ammo, a couple hand grenades, toothbrush, paste, shaving gear, and a dungaree cap. Barney also carried photos of his family and his girl, and writing paper and pen and ink, in waterproof wrappers. I didn't. I didn't have family or a girl. Maybe that's why, at age thirty-six, I found myself in a Higgins boat gliding toward an increasingly less beckoning beach.

Still, in a way, Barney really had gotten me into this fine mess. Mess kit, maybe I should say.

Oh, for the record: Barney is Barney Ross, the boxer, ex-boxer now, former world lightweight and welterweight title holder. We grew up on the West Side of Chicago together. The friendship stayed, as did we in Chicago, and in fact I was sitting with him in a booth in his Barney Ross Cocktail Lounge, across from the Morrison Hotel, on December 7, '41, when the shit first hit the fan.

We were arguing with a couple of sportswriters about how long Joe Louis would hold the heavyweight crown. The radio was on—a Bears game—and the announcer must've cut in with the news flash, but we were a little sauced and a little loud and none of us heard it. The bartender, Buddy Gold, finally came over and said, "Didn't you guys hear what happened?"

"Don't tell me Joe Louis busted his arm in training," Barney said, half meaning it.

"The Japs bombed Pearl Harbor!" Buddy's eyes rolled back like slot machine windows. "Jeez, boss, the radio's on, aren't you listening to it?"

"What's Pearl Harbor?" Barney asked.

"It's in Hawaii," I said. "It's a naval base or something."

Barney made a face. "The Japs bombed their own harbor?"

"It's *our* harbor, schmuck!" I said.

"Not anymore," Buddy Gold said, and walked away, morosely, polishing a glass.

From then on, or anyway right after President Roosevelt made his "day of infamy" speech, joining up was all Barney talked about.

"It's stupid," I told him, in one of God only knows how many arguments on the subject in his Lounge. Over beers, in a booth.

"So it's stupid to want to defend the country that's been so good to me?"

"Oh, please. Not the 'I came up from the ghetto to become a champion' speech again. You're not cutting the ribbon on some goddamn supermarket today, Barney. Give a guy a break."

"Nate," he said, "you disappoint me."

Nate. That's me. Nathan Heller. Onetime dick on the Chicago PD pickpocket detail, currently a fairly successful small businessman with a three-man (one-secretary) detective agency in a building owned by the very ex-pug I was arguing with. Actually, it was about to be a two-man agency—my youngest operative was going into the Army next week.

"I suppose," I said, "you think *I* should join up, too."

"That's your decision."

"They wouldn't even take me, Barney. I'm an old man. So are you, for that matter. You're thirty-three. The Marines aren't asking for guys your age."

"I'm draft age," he said, pointing to his chest with a thumb. Proud. Defiant. "And so are you. They're taking every able body up to thirty-five."

"Wrong on two counts," I said. "First, I turned thirty-six, when you weren't looking. Squeaked by the draft, thank you very much. Second, you're a married man. I know, I know, you're getting a divorce; but then you're going to marry Cathy, first chance you get, right?" Cathy was this beautiful showgirl Barney had taken up with after his marriage went sour. "Well," I went on, "they only take *married* men up to age twenty-six. And you haven't been twenty-six since you fought McLarnin."

He looked gloomily in his beer. "I don't intend to shirk my duty by using some loophole. As far as I'm concerned, I ain't married anymore, and even so, I'm joining up."

"Oh, Barney, please. You got dependents, for Christ's sake. You got family."

"That's just why I'm doing it. I got a special obligation to represent my family in the armed service."

"Why?"

He shrugged expansively. "Because nobody else was able to go. Ben's too old, Morrie's got back trouble, Sammy's got the epileptic fits, and Georgie's got flat feet and the draft board turned him down."

"That poor unlucky bastard, Georgie. Imagine goin' through life with flat feet when you could've got 'em shot the hell off."

"I take this serious, Nate. You know that. Think about what's happening overseas, would you, for once? Think about that cocksucker Hitler."

A word that harsh was rare for Barney; but the feeling ran deep. He'd gotten very religious, in recent years; and his religion was what this was most of all about.

"Hitler isn't your problem," I said, somewhat lamely.

"He is! He's mine, and he's yours."

We'd been over this ground many times, over the last three or four years. Longer than that, really. From the first news of persecution of the Jews in Nazi Germany, Barney had gone out of his way to remind me that I too was a Jew.

Which I didn't accept. My father had been an apostate Jew, so what did that make me? An apostate Jew at birth? My late mother was a Catholic, but I didn't eat fish on Friday.

"Okay, okay," I said. "You hate Hitler; you're going to whip those lousy Nazis. Fortunately for you, Armstrong isn't on their side." Armstrong was who Barney lost his title to. A little desperately I added, "But why the goddamn *Marines?* That's the roughest damn way to go!"

"Right." He sipped his beer, very cool, very measured. "They're the toughest of all the combat outfits. If I'm going to do this thing, I'm going to do it right. Just like in the ring."

I tried a kidney punch. "What about your ma? It was rough enough on her when you were fighting in a ring—now you want to go fight a *war?* How could you do that to her?"

He swallowed; not his beer—just swallowed. His puppy-dog eyes in that bulldog puss were solemn and a little sad. His hair was salt-and-pepper and he really did look too old to be considering this; he looked older than me, actually. But then I hadn't taken as many blows to the head as him. Very deliberately, he said, "I don't want to bring no more heartache to Ma, Nate. But wars have to go on no matter how mothers feel."

It was like trying to argue with a recruiting poster.

"You're serious about this, this time," I said. "You're really going to go through with it."

He nodded. Smiled just a little. Shyly.

I finished my beer in a gulp and waved toward the bar for another. "Barney, look at this place. Your business is going great guns. Ever since you switched locations, seems like it's doubled."

"Ben's going to take over for me."

"Aw, but you yourself are such an important part of it—the celebrity greeting his customers and all. No offense to your brother, but it'll flop without you."

Again he shrugged. "Maybe so. But if Hitler comes riding down State Street, I'll be out of business permanent."

Such a child. Such a simple soul. God bless him.

"How far have you gone with this thing?"

"Well," he said, smiling, embarrassed now, "they turned me down at first. Told me I was overage and should go run my cocktail lounge. Just like you did. But I kept swinging, and finally they sent a letter to Washington to see about getting me a waiver on the age rule. Took sixty days for it to come through. And today I got the word. All I got to do is sign on the dotted line, and pass the physical."

I sat there shaking my head.

"The recruiting office is in the post office," he said. That was just a few blocks away. "They're open twenty-four hours, these days. I'm going down tonight. Why don't you keep me company?"

"What, and join up *with* you? Not on your life."

"Nate," he said, reaching across to touch my hand. It wasn't something I remembered him ever doing before. "I'm not trying to talk you into any such thing. You have every right to stay here, doing what you're doing. You're past draft age, now, you got my blessing. Really. All I want is yours."

He didn't know I'd already given it to him. I just sat there shaking my head again, but smiling now. He took his hand off mine. Then suddenly we were shaking hands.

That's when we started to seriously drink.

It gets hazy after that. I know that my own mixed feelings—my own barely buried desire to get into this thing myself, my expectation of being drafted having turned to guilt-edged relief when the call-up missed me—came drifting to the surface, came tumbling out in confession to Barney, and, well, I remember walking him to the post office, singing, "Over There," along the way and getting strange and occasionally amused looks from passersby.

I remember studying a poster boasting the great opportunities the Marine Corps offered a man. There were three Marines on the poster—one rode a rickshaw, one was cleaning the wings of an airplane, one was presenting arms on a battleship. I remember, albeit vaguely, studying this poster for the longest time and experiencing what must have been something akin to a religious conversion.

I'm sure it would have passed, given time.

Unfortunately, time for sober reflection wasn't in the cards. The blur that follows includes a recruiting sergeant in pressed blue trousers, khaki shirt, necktie, and forest ranger hat (a "campaign" hat, I later learned). I remember looking down at his shoes and seeing my face looking up at me. I also remember saying, "What a shine!" Or words to that effect.

The conversation that followed is largely lost to me. I remember being asked my age and giving it as twenty-nine. That stuck with me because I had to concentrate hard, in my condition, to be able to lie that effectively.

I remember also one other question asked of me: "Any scars, birthmarks, or other unusual features?"

And I remember asking, "Why such a question?"

And I remember the matter-of-fact response: "So they can identify your body after you get your dog tags blown off."

One would think that would have sobered me up (and perhaps that question was the recruiting officer's attempt to do so, to not take undue advantage of my condition); but one would be wrong. It took the next morning to do that.

The next morning, by which time Barney Ross was in the Marines.

And so, when I woke up, was I.

BARNEY

3

We took a train at Union Station and left Chicago behind. Ahead, immediately ahead, was San Diego. Boot camp.

It was a three-day journey cross-country. Barney and I weren't the only ones aboard over thirty, and a fair share of these recruits were in their twenties; but the bulk of 'em were kids. Goddamn kids—seventeen, eighteen years old. It made me feel sad to be so old; it made me feel sadder that they were so young.

But so was the war, and, judging from the high spirits of its passengers, this train might've been headed for a vacation camp. Oh, it'd be a camp, all right; but hardly vacation. Still, the trip—particularly the first day or so—was filled for them with childish fun, yelling and pranks and waving out the windows at cows and cars and particularly girls.

These kids had never been west before. Both Barney and I had, but just the same we sat like spellbound tourists and looked out the window at the passing scenery. As the farm country gradually gave way to a more barren landscape, it seemed fitting somehow. I was leaving America slowly behind.

The kids knew who Barney was, and some of them razzed him, but mostly they wanted autographs and to hear stories. He'd humor them, fight Canzoneri again and again (which he'd had to do in real life, as well), and occasionally get the heat off himself by trying to make *me* out as somebody.

"Talk to Nate, here," he'd say, "if you want to hear about celebrities. He knows Capone."

"No kiddin'?"

"Sure he does! Frank Nitti, too. Nate was there the night Dillinger got shot in front of the Biograph theater."

"Is that so, Nate?"

"More or less, kid."

So word got around about the boxer and the private eye and we got paid a certain gosh-wow respect because of it. And our ages. We were the oldest aboard by a yard; nobody since that recruiting officer seemed convinced I was twenty-nine. Including me.

I had plenty of time on the train to reflect on the nature of my enlistment. Even before we left Barney had said, "You might be able to get out of it, Nate."

"I signed the papers."

"You were drunk, and you lied about your age. I had to get a waiver to get in, and I'm younger than you. Maybe you should . . ."

"I'll think it over."

Yet somehow, here I was, on a train cutting across a desert, on my way to San Diego and points God-knows-where beyond.

On the second day of the trip, sitting in the dining car, at a table for two, Barney looked across at me and said, "Why didn't you try, Nate?"

"Try what?" I asked. The meal before me was a hamburger steak and cottage fries and a little salad and milk and I was digging in, instinctively enjoying what I guessed would be one of the few decent meals of my foreseeable future.

"To get out of it," he said.

"Of what?"

"Don't play games, schmuck. Of the Marines."

I shrugged, chewed my food. Answered: "I don't know that I could."

"You don't know that you couldn't."

"I'm here. Let's leave it at that."

He smiled tightly and did. Never uttered another word on the subject.

I wasn't sure myself why I didn't try to worm out of it. I'd worked long and hard to build my little one-man show into a real agency. It'd be waiting for me when this was over—I'd left it in the capable hands of the sole remaining operative in the agency, Lou Sapperstein, a sober soul of fifty-three who was unlikely to get drafted, or drunk and enlist, either. But why leave at all?

I didn't know. I was a cop once. It hadn't worked out. It had been my dream since childhood to be a cop, to be a detective, but in Chicago the game was rigged, for cops, and to play it, you played along, and I'm no boy scout but there came a time I just couldn't play along anymore. So I went in business for myself, and I liked it, up to a point. But ever since December 7, something had been gnawing me. My old man was a union guy, an idealistic sap who never learned to play the game when it was straight, let alone rigged; you don't suppose I inherited something from him besides the funny shape of my toes? Who the hell knew. Not me. Not me. Maybe I was tired of following cheating husbands and cheating wives around and then coming home to read a paper filled with Bataan and Corregidor and ships going down in the Atlantic. Maybe the life I'd made for myself paled into something so insignificant I couldn't the fuck face it anymore and, well, folks, here I was in a dining car with that Damon Runyon character I called my best friend, on my way to war.

I wasn't the only one. Out the windows almost all the rail traffic we passed was military. Long trains consisting of flatcar after flatcar loaded with tanks, halftracks, artillery parts. Troop trains seemed constantly to pass us, going both ways. Army troops, mostly. We hadn't been Marines long enough to hate the Army yet, so the kids whooped and hollered at them as well, give 'em hell, guys, give 'em hell.

In Chicago, it had been late summer and felt like winter. The morning we arrived in San Diego, it was summer and felt like it, sunlight bouncing blindingly off the cement walkways of the terminal. We were wearing heavy winter gear, the only gear we'd thus far been given, lugging sea bags, sweating, immediately sweating. Falling into ranks just alongside the train, we watched a first sergeant amble up, seeming surprisingly cheerful, and inform the noncommissioned officers among us which of the waiting buses we were to board.

The first sergeant looked old to the kids, most likely; but I knew he was only a few years older than me, just enough so as to've made it into the previous war. His crisp green uniform bore campaign ribbons and a braided cord around his left arm.

"You people have some tough training ahead," he said, rather informally. "But it's gonna see you through, if you can see it through. Good luck. Now, fall out—board your assigned buses!"

On the bus, the kids were whispering about how nice the first sergeant was. Not at all like what they'd heard boot camp would be like.

Well, they weren't at boot camp yet, and being older than them, I didn't allow myself to be lulled into a false sense of security by the fatherly manner of a guy not much older than me. My cop's nose sensed trouble ahead.

And there was nothing wrong with my sense of smell.

As the buses rolled into camp, a.k.a. the Marine Corps Recruit Depot—a massive rambling assembly of cream-colored buildings with dark roofs—out the window I could see platoons of recruits rigidly marching to the individual cadence of drill instructors. Snappy as hell, had to admit. I was impressed, sure, but I'd been a guy on his own, a guy his own boss, for so many years that I couldn't keep from seeing this mindless regimentation as stupid and pointless. I was here on a stopover before going to kill some Nazis for Uncle Sam, right? I used a gun before; I killed before—I hadn't liked it, but I'd done it, and was prepared to do it again, for what seemed a just cause. Point me at Hitler and set me to shooting. Don't expect me to be a martinet, for Christ's sakes! I'm not one of these fucking kids . . .

Our bus's NCO, prior to this an agreeable sort, turned suddenly into that Nazi I'd been looking for; he stood at the front of the bus and all but screamed: "All right, you people, off the goddamned bus!"

The kids rushed off, and Barney and I got swept up with them. We lined up with men from the other buses and counted off into groups of sixty. A truck rumbled by, carrying in its open back a work party of seasoned-looking recruits. They laughed at us.

"You'll be *sor*-eeeee," one called, the truck leaving us behind in the dust.

A corporal in a campaign hat came walking toward us with a tight-lipped, somehow hungry smile. He was about five-ten and probably weighed 160 pounds; smaller than me by two inches and twenty-five pounds. But he was a muscular s.o.b., with massive arms and chest and a stomach flatter than day-old beer. His cold green eyes squinted and his hawk nose jutted and he clearly hated us, and just as clearly enjoyed doing so.

"All right, shitbirds, get in line," he shouted, from the gut, and the heart. He began walking up and down, like Napoleon inspecting his troops, giving us the once-over twice. "So you wanna make Marines, huh?" He sneered more to himself than at us, shaking his head. "What sad sorry sacks of shit. Where the fuck'd they dig you up?"

The kids were stunned by this; me, I smiled a little. I preferred this to the fatherly approach of the first sergeant back at the train station. This was bullshit, too, but at least it was amusing.

Only the corporal wasn't amused. He came over and looked me right in the face; his breath was hotter than the sun and bad.

"What in the fuck are *you* doing here?"

I knew enough not to say anything.

"Don't you know we don't take grandpas in the Marines?"

Then he noticed Barney.

"What did they do, empty out the goddamn old folks home?" He shook his head, walked back and forth in front of us. "Grandma and grandpa. And I'm expected to make Marines out of this shit."

Out of the corner of one eye I could see Barney starting to take this wrong; we were about half a second from Barney swinging on the guy, and starting his glorious patriotic service to his country in the guard house. I nudged him with my foot and his face went expressionless.

The corporal exploded but not, thankfully, at Barney in particular. At all of us in general: "*Patoon halt, teehut*. Right hace. Forwart huah. Double time, huah."

We didn't know what the hell that meant, but we did it. The s.o.b. ran us up and down the streets forever, and then a while longer, and then we were in front of the wooden hut that would be home, for a while. My guts were burning, my breath a slow pathetic pant; the former lightweight/welterweight champ didn't seem any better off. The corporal, who'd set and kept the pace, wasn't breathing hard, fuck him.

"*Patoon halt, right hace!*" He put his hands on his hips and rocked on his heels as he smiled tightly, oozing contempt. "You people are stupid. Now we know who *you* are. *I* am Corporal McRae. I am your drill instructor. This is Platoon Seven-fourteen. If any of you idiots think you don't need to follow my orders, just step right out here and I'll beat your ass right now." He began walking back and forth again. "You people are *shitbirds*. You are not *Marines*. You may not have what it takes to be Marines."

No one was moving; they were barely breathing. I did not hate this man before us. I did not even resent him. But I *was* scared of the fucker.

Before long we were in a chow line, trays flung into our hands, food flung from all directions onto the tray. One course flopped right on top of another, and if you didn't position your tray right as you passed, the food ended up on the floor or you or some goddamn where that wasn't the tray. The sweating cooks had done a real number on whatever this had been before it got to us.

"Hell of way to serve a meal," Barney said, under his breath, just loud enough for me to hear. "Good thing I don't keep kosher."

We didn't see him but, like God, Corporal McRae was everywhere, because he was right on top of Barney, saying, "Real wise guy, aren't you? Think you're in the fucking Waldorf?" Then something akin to thought seemed to pass across the corporal's face. "I've seen you before, shitbird. What is your name?"

Barney smiled a little; his smugness made me wince.

"Barney Ross," he said.

The corporal's face lit up like Christmas. "Whaddya know," he said, so everybody in the mess hall could hear. "Grandma here's a celebrity." Then his face went dark again. "Well, you're no fuckin' champ here, Ross. You're just another goddamn shitbird. You get no special favors and no special treatment."

"I didn't ask for—"

"We know you goddamn celebrities. You expect the red goddamn carpet. Well, you're gonna toe the mark, buddy. In fact, I think we'll give you a few *extra* things to do just so you're sure how you fit in here."

He strode off.

Barney stood there with the tray of food in his hands, steaming (both Barney *and* the food); a kid from Chicago standing nearby said, "Why don't you sock the bum, Barney?"

"Yeah, Barney," I said. "Sock him. Get us all off to a swell start."

He grinned crookedly at me and then we found our way to a table, joining some recruits who seemed seasoned, hoping to get some encouraging words about how the first day is toughest.

The main course on our trays was, apparently, beans and wieners, and I was about to apply some mustard to a wiener when one of the old-timers (who was probably twenty) said, "When you're through with the baby shit, pass it my way."

I swallowed and passed him the mustard without using it myself; I was more squeamish then than I am now. I've since asked somebody to pass me the baby shit on many an occasion.

Then, after lunch, like guys going to the chair, we had our heads shaved. To the skin. Now I knew how Zangara felt. You know—the guy that shot Mayor Cermak.

Anyway, most of the 714 seemed to be from Chicago, though Barney and I never met any of 'em before; but we did have a couple of Southern boys. That first night, Corporal McRae assembled us in our barracks and said, "All right now—any of you idiots who got straight razors or switchblades, throw 'em on the bunk next to me. I won't have you shitbirds cutting each other up. *I* draw the blood around here, people."

A kid from the South Side named D'Angelo—who told us he used to work for Capone crony Nicky Dean at the Colony Club on Rush Street—tossed a switchblade on the bunk. Two straight razors followed, and then some brass knuckles thudded on the thin horsehair mattress.

"You can't cut anybody with that, idiot," the Corporal said, and tossed the knucks back at the kid.

The Southern boys had apparently not seen any Chicago silverware before; their eyes were round as Stepin Fetchit's, although their complexions were considerably lighter.

Even for us Chicagoans, the chill San Diego morning came as a shock. That was Dago: freezing your ass off at dawn, and by noon you were roasting. The days were long and hard, brutally hard: calisthenics, close-order drill, marching, long hikes over rough terrain, bayonet training, judo, breakneck runs over obstacle courses, gas-mask drills, infantry training under combat conditions with live ammo whizzing overhead. McRae had his own special brand of sadism, unique to him among the Dago DIs: he'd double-time us to an area near the beach at San Diego Bay. There, while the beautiful, indifferent water watched, we'd drill back and forth on the hot, soft sand. My legs ached so, I would cry myself quietly to sleep in my rack on such nights.

McRae followed no pattern; we never knew what indignity or when it would be inflicted—in the midst of most any activity, we could take a break for rifle inspection, close-order drill, or a run in the sand by the bay. Sometimes in the middle of the night. It all seemed so chickenshit.

Barney was getting extra KP, garbage duty, and other dirty details, all because he was a "celebrity." And, since I was his pal, I caught some of that duty, as well.

My major run-in with McRae was on the rifle range, though, where I made the mistake of referring to my M-1 as my gun. Soon I was running up and down in front of the rows of barracks with my rifle in one hand and my dick in the other, shouting, "This is my rifle," as I hefted my M-1, "and this is my gun," as I gestured with my, well, my other hand. "This is for Japs," M-1, "and this is for fun," well.

Thirty-six years old, running around with a rifle in one hand and my dick in the other. Telling everybody about it.

Barney's moment came when McRae noticed him reading in his bunk before lights out; Barney was always poring over these books on religion and philosophy he lugged around with him. And he kept his mother's picture propped somewhere he could see it.

"The celebrity is religious, I see," McRae said.

Heads bobbed up, ears perked, all 'round.

"That's right," Barney said, bristling a little. All the religion and philosophy books in the world couldn't completely put his fighter's fire out.

"You pray a lot, celebrity?"

"Yes."

"Good. You better give your soul to God. Your heart may belong to mother, but your ass belongs to the United States Marines."

The corporal strutted off, leaving a trail of laughter behind. Not Barney's.

Eight weeks later, we were physically fit—even two old fogies like Barney and me—and mentally prepared for what lay ahead. Or as close to it as possible.

Wearing service greens—rifles and cartridge belts left behind—we each received three Marine Corps globe-and-anchor emblems, which we pocketed, and were marched to an amphitheater, to sit with other recruits.

Or I should say Marines. We were Marines, now. The short, friendly major on the stage smiled at us and told us so and we reached in our pockets and pinned an emblem on either lapel of our green wool coats and one on the left side of our caps. Then the major told us the one about the farmer's daughter and the three traveling salesmen, and we all laughed, and he said, "Good luck, men," and that was the first we'd been called men since we got here.

I passed McRae, later, and he nodded. I stopped and said, "Could I ask you a question?"

He nodded again.

"Why'd you get us up in the middle of the fucking night to go run in the fucking sand?"

Something nearly a smile touched his tight lips. "Combat allows sleep to no man, Private Heller."

I thought about that.

I thought about it on that Higgins boat, gliding toward a tropical "paradise" called Guadalcanal.

I sensed, even then, that McRae was wrong. Combat allowed sleep to just about anybody. Waking was something else again.

4

It was a peaceful landing, a beachhead having been long since established by the 1st Marines—many of whom were there to greet us as we waded ashore, hollow-eyed scarecrows with mud on their faces, oddly amused by our identifying shouts: "B Company here!" "A Company here!" The first 1st GI I encountered—just a kid, really, but older in his way than me—immediately asked me for a smoke, despite the gear I was shouldering. I told him I didn't smoke. He laughed in a curiously empty way and said, you will, mac, you will.

The palms lining the beach greeted us as well, bending to us as if in deference, when really they were just swaybacked seaward from the tropical winds, their fronds shredded from shelling; these evenly spaced, precisely aligned palms weren't, as you might assume, the handiwork of God on one of His more particularly inspired days—they'd been planted by Lever Brothers, on whose once (and, if the war went right, future) plantation grounds we were entering. This made our first approach, to Henderson Field, an easy one, the soap company having kept the ground in the groves cleared for harvesting purposes.

The crushed-coral airfield was the hub of activity, with two large air stations, machine shops, and electric-light plants, among other buildings inherited from the Japanese, fewer now than before the Nip bombing raids, of course. Repair sheds, hangars, and retaining walls had been built by American hands. And occasionally rebuilt.

The field, we were told, was shelled every night; its two airstrips were in understandably lousy condition, and under constant maintenance. Much of what had been crushed coral was filled in with dirt and packed down, and on hot dry days the runway swirled with dust, and on rainy ones sloshed with mud. No such problem on a humid sunny day like this one. The field was abuzz with warplanes, including F4F Wildcats, and it had been a long time since a Zero, Betty, or Zeke had dared try anything here in the daylight.

Night, however, was a different story; "Maytag Charlie," as one nightly Japanese visitor had been nicknamed due to his noisy, washing machine of an engine, dropped his 250-pound turds in an ongoing effort to keep the Marines on the Island awake, and to give them something to do the next morning.

Some of the battle-weary scarecrows of the 1st were filling in craters left by last night's raid, as we trooped in around noon, the transports at the beach having been unloaded of machinery, equipment, supplies. The living corpses halfheartedly jeered at us.

"We're safe now," a Southerner drawled, leaning on a shovel. "Here come the Howlin' Marines." Our division commander was General Holland "Howling Mad" Smith.

"Fuckin' A," a buddy of his said, shoveling. "Just in time for the Japs."

"I hear they're servin' tea today," said another.

I glanced at Barney; he smiled and shrugged. But I'm sure he was as unnerved as I was. Not by these lame, fairly good-natured jabs; but by the punch-drunk palookas throwing 'em. Would we look like they did, after a few months on this island?

We went through a chow line and received Atabrine tablets, a supposed malaria preventive, a corpsman flicking a tablet in our mouths and then peering down in to make sure we swallowed it. Later I learned this was because many had mutinied against the pills, suspecting them to be saltpeter. Whatever they were, they tasted bitter, but then so did our lunch, which was a bowl of captured Jap rice, to supplant our K rations. A few months on Spam and rice, and we no doubt *would* look like the skinny, grizzled 1st Marines. The deadness in their eyes, however, wasn't from something they ate.

Some of the 1st, preparing to be relieved, were bivouacked near Henderson, pup tents under coconut trees, nestled among the jungle growth—liana vines, twisting creepers, and smaller trees, many of them just overgrown weeds with bark, slanting skyward for no good reason, hogging space, making life tough for nearby plants, which assumed defensive postures, leaves fanning out into knifelike blades. In front of the tents were often bamboo makeshifts, racks to put things on and/or under, a pole to rest a helmet on. This was home to the 1st, though I doubted, having left, any of 'em would feel homesick.

"Ever seen combat?" one asked Barney and me; he was sitting out in front of his tent on a makeshift bamboo stool. He had light blue eyes, somehow very out of place in the tanned, mud-stained face. The eyes seemed more alive than some, albeit somewhat feverish. The most alive thing about him was the glowing tip of his Chesterfield.

We shook our heads no to his combat question; Barney added, "Nate here was a cop."

That same wry, weary smile the entire 1st seemed to share crawled onto his face. "You won't be writing any traffic tickets out here, Pops."

Barney got defensive, jerked his thumb toward me. "He was a *detective!* He's been in his share of shoot-outs."

I nudged him, embarrassed. "Please."

Barney gave me a disgusted look. "Well, you have."

"Any experience is better than nothing," the leatherneck granted.

"We just came from gettin' jungle training on Samoa," Barney said. "They told us how at night the Japs creep through the brush like ghosts and then all of a sudden jump right up in front of ya and blow your head off or slash your throat or cut off your . . . is that really true?"

"Fuckin' A a doodle de do," the leatherneck said. He smiled the wry, weary smile again, sucked on the cig. "Like some pointers?"

"Sure," we said.

He gestured to the ground, or anyway the brush and trees that clung to it. "Watch for trip wire. Those little bastards can set wires up in the jungle that can wipe out half a platoon."

It looked hopeless to me. I said as much: "How the hell do you spot a wire in undergrowth like this?"

"You either spot it or it spots you. And never go by a bunch of so-called dead ones without spraying the little fuckers. They like to play possum and then open up on you, when you walk on by."

"Thanks," I said. "Anything else?"

"The most important thing. If they capture one of your men, write the poor bastard off. They'll tie him to a tree and go to work on him. They're experts at it. You'll hear him holler, probably beg you to come rescue him. This is exactly what they want. They want your men to come running in like big-ass birds. 'Cause they're waiting for you and not a man one of you will survive, mac. Not a one."

Then he just sat there and smoked his cigarette.

"We appreciate the advice," Barney said, after a while.

"They feed you rice today?" he asked us.

"Yeah," we said.

He almost shivered. "I had a gutful of that swill. You know what winning this fuckin' war means to me? Never having to eat rice again." Wistfully, he added, "I could sure go for some of that Jap pogey bait, though. Hard and sweet—like the dame that ditched my Uncle Looie." Pogey bait was Marine for candy. "But you guys don't need to worry. You're gettin' the tail end of the rice, anyway."

"Why?" we asked.

He sucked on the cigarette, made a face. "The First's been cut off since we landed, the fuckin' Navy all but deserted us, what little supplies we got come in from flyboys and destroyers that broke the Nip blockade. If it wasn't for the food the Japs left behind, we'd've been eating roots and bark. But *you* ain't gonna have to eat no fish heads and rice; supplies and men are comin' in every day, now."

"The tide has turned, then," I said.

"It's turnin'. But you still got your work cut out for you."

"Henderson seems well secured," I said.

Barney, glancing back toward the busy airstrip—planes taking off, troops trooping in, supplies being unloaded—nodded.

"Boys—if you don't mind my callin' older gents like you 'boys'—my last piece of advice for ya is keep thinking like that and you'll be deader'n Mr. Kelsey's nuts by nightfall."

He was right, of course. The Nips were all around the perimeter, including Sealark Channel—or Ironbottom Sound, as it was informally known, referring to the sixty-five or so major warships resting there, about half-and-half American/Japanese. Nightly shelling from the Sound meant Henderson Field was virtually surrounded. Its security was as false as the orderliness of the plantation palms.

Soon we were moving up, past Henderson, toward the Matanikau River just five miles away, the west bank of which belonged to the Nips, and across which they weren't shy to come. Shells exploded all around us, shaking the earth and those creatures crawling on it, us included, on our bellies, inching through thick underbrush, thorns and brambles nicking us, marking us, shell smoke drifting over us like dark dirty clouds.

But we weren't the only crawling creatures. We crawled past snakes, and they crawled past us; we met bugs the likes of which the worst Chicago tenement never dreamed of, but is "bugs" the word when it's a spider the size of your fist, or a wasp three inches long? Lizards flitted by, forked tongues flicking; land crabs skittled along, like dismembered skeletal hands clawing frantically at the earth. And most of all mosquitoes. Ever-present, less than swarming, but so constant there soon came a point where you couldn't swat at them any longer.

Finally we reached the forward foxholes, where more of the 1st waited to be relieved. We did that, crawling in as they crawled out, into the two- and three-man holes. Barney and I and that kid from Chicago, D'Angelo, another veteran of Corporal McCrea back at Dago, shared a foxhole with the mosquitoes. Before us was a row of sandbags, stacked, beyond which was a double-apron barbed-wire fence. From our position you couldn't see the river, but I could hear it, and smell it. The smell of the jungle and the rivers and streams that cut through it was not nature's finest hour; it was a fetid perfume made from equal parts oppressive humidity, rotting undergrowth, and stink lilies.

The rest of the afternoon we stayed dug in, listening to and watching artillery shells explode, as our side traded fire with the unseen Japs across the river. It never became a passive experience—with every explosion, you knew that if the direct hit didn't get you, the flying red-hot shrapnel could, and if neither got you, it was getting some poor bastard just like you, down the line. And you knew most of all that you could be next.

In the lulls we'd talk and D'Angelo smoked; he was a thin, dark kid with a sensual mouth that the girls back in the Windy City no doubt loved, for all the good it did him here. We sat beating our gums, comparing bug bites and agreeing that Chicago was a pretty tame place to live, compared to this hellhole, anyway.

Then we watched a sunset paint the sky red and orange, in an impressionistic, tropical dream right out of Gauguin. The moment was a peaceful one; it was enough to make you forget bug bites and shrapnel and humidity, and darkness fell.

Generally speaking, I'm not afraid of the dark. But I'm here to tell you I'm afraid of the dark in a jungle. The rustle of leaves, the flutter of wings, the skittering of land crabs, indiscernible yet ominous shapes moving, looming out there. We'd been ordered not to shoot unless the Japs fired first, so as not to give our positions away. So we crouched in the foxholes with bayonets at the ready, and if I thought this was making *me* nuts, Barney was truly ready for a padded foxhole.

Seemed like every minute or two, he'd half rise and lunge forward, across the sandbags and barbed wire—a leaf moved in the wind, or an animal rustled in the brush, and Barney was out there slashing, stabbing, destroying imaginary Japs. Some of these nonexistent enemies would sneak up behind us, and Barney lunged to the rear, stabbed, slashed; you never knew when or from whence one of the yellow bastards was going to strike next.

It spread to the other nearby foxholes, and soon our whole platoon was going crazy slashing and stabbing little yellow men who weren't there. Finally I touched Barney's arm and said, "Take it easy. There's lots of sounds out there. If it's Japs, we'll know it."

I'd barely finished the sentence when an ungodly screech ripped the night apart, and I was on my feet, yelling, "*Banzai charge!*," bayonet flashing in the moonlight.

From a foxhole down the way, a voice that could only have belonged to one of the combat veterans of the 1st, a handful of which had stayed behind with us, whispered harshly, "It's a fuckin' bird, mac. A cock or two. Put a lid on it."

Cock or two? Oh. Cockatoo. Well. I was too scared and tired to be embarrassed. I sat down in the foxhole and pushed my helmet back on my head and the mosquitoes zoomed in for virgin territory.

They came at us the next morning. For real. They came up a slope of golden *kunai* grass, shoulder-high, the blades of which cut you like a knife, but the Nips didn't care. They were screaming, "*Banzai*," and they weren't cockatoos, either. They were savage little men in uniforms the color of brown wrapping paper. Many in the first wave weren't even carrying rifles; they had big mats in their little hands, rushing through the grass lugging those mats, screaming like hopped-up madmen, as were those coming up behind them with rifles in hand, firing past their mat-bearing brethren. Some had machine guns, chattering like a child's toy gun, but there was nothing childish about the bullets they were spitting at us, kissing the sand through the cloth of the sandbags nearby. There was mortar fire, too, ours and theirs—ours was landing amongst them, scattering them in the air like tenpins; where theirs was landing I couldn't say. Not near us, thank God.

Barney and I were side by side, firing our M-1s; D'Angelo, too.

We were cutting the Japs down like weeds, like they were the very *kunai* grass into whose spiky golden sea their bodies sank as our bullets hit the mark.

There was a moment when D'Angelo was firing and Barney and I both were pausing to reload our rifles, the barrels of which were red hot.

"What are those things those little bastards are hauling?" he asked.

"Mats," I said. "I think they plan to throw 'em over the barb wire, so the ones behind 'em can crawl over it and on top of us."

Then we were firing again, and they kept coming, shouting "*Banzai*," screaming, "Die, Maline!" They kept coming and we kept shooting and they kept dropping, disappearing, into the golden grass. A second wave tried; a third. We cut them down.

A kid named Smith—or was it Jones?—in the foxhole next to us, took a bullet in the head, in his forehead under his helmet. No mosquito bite, that. He tumbled over dead. I saw men die before, but never one so young. Seventeen, he must've been. Barney never saw a man die before, and turned away and puked on the spot.

Then he wiped off his face and started firing again.

When it was over, most of their dead remained hidden in the *kunai;* you could see the impression the bodies made, where they went in, but not the bodies, for the most part. A few were visible—those who'd gotten the closest to us, a few from the first wave, their mats spread out before them like offerings to their emperor or their gods or whatever. They seemed so small, rag dolls flung into the weeds by a spoiled child.

As the days wore on, they grew larger, puffing and swelling in that brutal tropical sun. A stench swept the area like a foul wind. But we got used to it. All of it. Dead, rotting flesh and kids like Jones (or was it Smith?) catching the one with his name on it and falling over dead, eyes blank as an idiot's gaze. Blanker.

The next attack came on the night of the following day. Shortly before 3:00 A.M. the sky lit just above us with a pale green glow—Jap flares—and coming up the hill in the darkness was the sound of chattering machine gun, mortar fire, and "*Banzai!*" It was an eerie moonlight replay of the previous attack, and we cut them down like so much cordwood.

Days stretched into a week; we ate K rations, smoked (me, too), talked about good food and bad women, took demeaning shits in the woods with flies swarming around our asses as we did the deed, turned into pitiful lowlife creatures who stank from the sweat of humidity and heat and killing. Even the rains, which came out of nowhere, like the Japs, didn't improve matters; it merely left us soaked and soaking in muddy foxholes. It made our K rations mildew—it didn't affect the canned Spam, but the chewing gum and biscuits just somehow weren't the same.

After two weeks they moved us off the line.

Back at Henderson Field, some Army infantry—the Americal Division—watched us troop in, looking like something the cat dragged in, I'm sure.

"How long you guys been on the Island?" a fresh-faced kid asked.

"Got a smoke?" I asked him.

5

The afternoon after we came off the line, the war took to the sea and to the sky. Like standing-room-only customers, we watched the show from the edge of the coconut palms lining Red Beach—Barney and me and just about everybody else from Henderson Field, Marine and Army alike. We could see them out there, battle wagons and cruisers and destroyers, from both sides, blasting away at each other with their big guns. Even from the shore the sounds of the sea war were deafening. Still, it seemed oddly abstract—like tiny ships, movie miniatures, battling out there on the horizon.

The air show seemed more real, and was certainly more exciting. Our Marine Grummans fought dogfight after dogfight with Jap Zeros and Zekes; dozens of the Jap planes went down, and not one pilot bailed out. Suicide was in their blood. I knew that from the *banzai* charges.

Whenever a Jap plane went spiraling into the sea, trailing smoke like drunken skywriters, the boys would whoop and cheer, like the crowd at one of Barney's fights. I never found myself doing that, cheering the battle I mean, and I noticed Barney didn't either. Maybe it was because we were older than most. Even at a distance this didn't seem like a game to us, or remotely fun.

The sea battle brought that home, finally. As we all watched silently while an American cruiser spewed smoke, burning orange against the sky, an obscene midafternoon sunset, Barney looked at me with those puppy-dog eyes gone wet in that battered puss of his and said, "Everybody's watching like it's a football game or a movie or something. Don't they know nice guys are getting blown up out there?"

"They know," I said, noting the wave of silence that had just washed up over the beach.

Before long, oil-splotched, water-soaked sailors were being brought ashore by rescue boats, among them the PT boats stationed on

NEAR HENDERSON FIELD

nearby Tulagi. The plywood torpedo boats bore an oddly cheerful insignia: a cartoon of a mosquito riding a torpedo, drawn by Walt Disney, so it was said. This Hollywood touch seemed perfect to me when I recognized the commander of the boat, who at the moment was helping usher a dazed seaman from the boat onto the narrow shore of Red Beach; his crew was helping similarly dazed, drenched, sometimes wounded gobs.

We were all moving out of the front row of trees to lend a hand, and I moved toward the familiar face.

"Lieutenant Montgomery," I said, saluting.

His smoothly handsome face streaked with grease, Montgomery didn't return the salute, his hands full. I could tell he didn't recognize me.

But he did say, "Lend a hand, would you, Private?"

I did, and as we unloaded the boat, pointing the soaked human cargo toward Henderson Field, other Marines pitching in to walk them there, Montgomery paused to look at me hard and say, "Don't I know you?"

I managed a smile. "I'm Nate Heller."

"The detective, yes. What in God's name are you doing here? You're easily past thirty-five, I should think."

"So are you. I got drunk and woke up the next morning in the Marines. What's your excuse?"

He smiled; even grease-streaked and in wartime, it was the sort of sophisticated, vaguely intellectual smile that had typecast him as British in the movies, even though he was as American as the next guy.

He didn't answer my question, but posed his own: "You know what we'd be doing right now, if we hadn't got noble and enlisted?"

"No, sir, I don't."

"Testifying to a grand jury, or getting ready to."

"What do you mean?"

"The Bioff/Nitti affair has really hit the fan, back home."

"No kidding. I wish they'd subpoena me back there."

"No such luck," he smiled. Looking past me, he said, "Isn't that Barney Ross, the boxer?"

"No," I said. "That's Barney Ross, the raggedy-ass Marine."

"Like to meet him sometime."

"Maybe you will. It's a small world, you know."

"Too goddamn, these days. Got to shove off."

We shook hands, and he climbed on board, and I turned back toward the beach, where Barney was guiding a wet, groggy sailor toward the airfield.

"Wasn't that Robert Montgomery you were earbangin' over there? The actor?"

"Nope," I said. "That was Lieutenant j.g. Henry Montgomery, the PT boat commander."

"Sure looked like Robert Montgomery the actor to me."

"That's 'cause they're one and the same, schmuck."

"What's a guy like him doing in the goddamn service, of all places?"

"You mean when he could be home running a cocktail lounge?"

The battle continued on through the night—flares and tracer bullets lighting the sky—and well into the next day. The Army guys, who were on the Island in force now, the brass getting ready to launch a counteroffensive, were mostly combat virgins, and these air and sea battles they'd witnessed from the beach were an education.

Marines are pretty notorious for mixing it up with the other branches of the service—the Army and Navy being ahead of us in line, where supplies and equipment were concerned—and a lot of resentment naturally developed; but the sailors who survived their ship going down were treated royally on the Island, and I don't know of a single fight between a soldier and a Gyrene on Guadalcanal. Maybe the jungle took the orneriness out of us. Maybe the Island was so all-consuming it reduced us all to common dogfaces and leave it go at that.

Or maybe what kept the peace was pogey bait.

The Army boys were Hershey-bar rich; we Marines had souvenirs up the wazoo to swap 'em. The bartering was intense and as all-pervasive as combat: Hershey bars and Butterfingers and Baby Ruths were traded for samurai swords and battle flags and Nip helmets. The Army had plenty of cigars and cigs, too—I swapped a rising sun battle flag for a couple cartons of Chesterfields and a quart of whiskey.

"Got any advice for somebody who was never in combat before?" an Army private asked me, after we swapped for something or other.

"Ever hear the expression 'watch your ass'?"

"Sure."

"It's got a special meaning in combat. See, the Japs know us Americans don't shit where we eat—we don't like to take a crap, or even take a leak, in or near our foxhole. So at dawn, when you get out of your hole to go looking for a bush to squat behind, stay low—that's when the snipers are really on the lookout for you. It's the most dangerous goddamn time of day."

"Thanks."

"Don't mention it, kid."

"Say, uh—are you feeling all right?"

"Never better. I'm in the pink."

"Okay," he said, smiling nervously. And went on his way.

But I wasn't in the pink. I was in the yellow, from the Atabrine tablets, despite which I had a fever. Goddamn malaria, no doubt.

"Check in at sick bay," Barney said.

"I already did," I said.

"And?"

"I'm only running a hundred and one degrees. And I can walk."

"So you'll be going back on the line with the rest of us."

"I guess so."

I guessed right. Late that afternoon we were moving past the native village, Kukum, to the dock complex we'd built there, a pontoon bridge having been thrown across the broad Matanikau days before. Some of the natives looked on—dark men in loincloths and the occasional scrap of discarded Marine clothing, faces tattooed, ears slit and bobbling with ornaments, frizzled hair standing eight inches and reddened by (so I was told) lime juice of all things, carrying captured Jap weapons: knives, bayonets, rifles. Several of them saluted me; I saluted back. What the hell. They were on our side.

On the sandbar nearby, as a grim reminder to the hidden enemy holding the river's west bank, lay the charred and/or water-logged remains of several Jap tanks, dropped dead in their tracks like great beasts gone suddenly extinct. A dead Jap soldier, bloating up, bobbled on the water as we crossed the pontoon bridge.

"One of Tojo's men who made good," the skipper commented, nodding toward the corpse as we passed. The skipper was Captain O. K. LeBlanc—we all liked him, but he was a hard-nosed fucker.

We pushed through the humid, pest-ridden jungle a few hundred yards and dug in for the night; digging foxholes through the roots of small trees and deep-tendriled weeds and brush was no picnic in the park. All I could think about was how nice it would be to be back in Chicago—indoors.

Barney was bitching about his knee—in that and other joints he had some arthritis setting in, and this sodden hellhole wasn't helping. He had to do all his shoveling without the bracing of a foot on the spade, and that made it tough; I told him not to worry about it—I could carry his weight, where the digging was concerned.

"Shit," he said, "you're half dead as it is. Your fever must be up to a hundred and three by now."

"You're the one's delirious," I said. "Just take it easy—I'll do the goddamn digging."

The next morning, after cold K rations, the Skipper got the platoon together and asked for a patrol to go scout up ahead. The patrol was to pinpoint the Japs' positions for the Army regiment that was coming up and taking over within hours.

I have to say, here, one thing: the number one Marine Corps rule is *Never volunteer*.

Barney volunteered.

"You dumb schmuck," I whispered to him.

"Fine, Private Heller," the skipper said. Whether he heard what I really said, or truly misunderstood me, I'll never know.

Whatever the case, his "fine" meant I was on the fucking patrol, too.

So was D'Angelo, and a big dockworker from Frisco named Heavy Watkins; also a short kid from Denver named Fremont and a Jersey boy we called Whitey, both of 'em right out of high school. There was also a big Indian guy named Monawk. I don't know where he was from or what he did for a living before the war.

And soon the seven of us were stalking into the daytime darkness of a jungle held by Japs.

We didn't crawl on our bellies, but we stayed low. Low enough for the bugs and scorpions to crawl on our clothes; low enough for *kunai* grass to cut us. The liana vines, with their nasty little fishhook barbs, reached down to try to hang us. There was no way to move quietly through underbrush and overgrowth like this and I kept thinking about that 1st Marine's advice about trip wires, knowing any given step could be the end.

"Hey, Ross," D'Angelo called out, in a harsh whisper. "Those bastards are real close."

We all looked over at him; the good-looking Italian kid from the South Side was bending down, holding a turd in the palm of his hand, like his hand was a bun and it was a sausage.

"It's still warm," he said, very seriously.

Barney and I exchanged glances, wondering if this kid had been on the Island too long, already.

Then, as we started pressing forward, D'Angelo said, in an effort to build support for his case, "It has to be Japanese. It *smells* Japanese."

Now we *knew* he was going Asiatic on us.

That was when we heard the machine gun.

It was nearby, but not aimed at us.

We settled in behind various fat-trunked trees or logs uprooted from artillery shelling, a man or two behind each; Barney and me together behind a massive tree.

"Who the hell's he shooting at?" I whispered.

"We're the only Americans this far forward on this side of the river," Barney whispered back.

"Well, he doesn't seem to be shooting at us."

The sound of it was growing louder, though.

A smile cracked my face. "He's fishing. He's sweeping the woods in a three-quarter circle, hoping to hit something."

"It's getting louder."

"I know," I said, and took a grenade off my belt.

When it seemed to me the machine-gunning had grown loud enough, I pulled the pin and leaned out and pitched.

There was an explosion and a scream, followed by silence.

We pushed on.

For a couple more hours, trudging through the dank jungle, the sun beginning to beat mercilessly down through the trees on us, we patrolled. We saw no more Japs.

Another guy from the platoon, Robbins, found us around four o'clock.

"Take another half hour," he said, "and then you're supposed to report back to the Skipper." And he headed on back.

We were just starting back when Monawk nudged my arm.

"Look," he said.

It was the first thing he'd ever said to me.

But it was a worthwhile comment: he was pointing to the advance patrol of Japs, at least double our number, moving toward us through the jungle.

"Let's get the fuck out of here," I said to Barney.

He waved back toward Heavy, Fremont, and Whitey, who were over to our right. Just parallel to the Jap patrol.

Who spotted them.

And opened up a machine gun on them.

Bullets danced across Whitey's chest and as if in response Whitey did a little dance himself and dropped into the brush, blood splurting out of his chest wounds like three or four men spitting tobacco. We ran to him, keeping low; the Japs hadn't seen us yet, and Whitey had fallen out of their sight.

Heavy, Monawk, and Fremont were right there with Whitey, too. I didn't know what the hell had become of D'Angelo.

"I'll be damned," Whitey breathed. "I'm still alive."

"You got the million-dollar wound, kid," I said, smiling at him, reassuring him. "You'll go home for sure."

"Looks like . . . the war's over for me," he said, smiling, his eyes cloudy.

"Let's make a stretcher for him," Heavy said, "out of our dungaree jackets."

"Yeah," Fremont said, "we can try and carry him back."

We improvised a litter, and Barney and I took all the rifles while Heavy, Monawk, and Fremont, bending low in the brush, carried Whitey. We moved slow, making as little noise as possible. No sign of the Jap patrol. Maybe they figured they got us. Maybe they moved on.

We'd got about fifty yards when machine-gun fire *bup-bup-bup-bup-bup*ed across our flank.

Heavy and Monawk screamed, one unified searing scream of pain—they'd taken the slugs across the legs, and the litter bearing Whitey capsized and Whitey spilled out into the spiky brush. Fremont drove for cover as another spray of machine gun chopped up the landscape. He howled sharply, and then was silent.

Barney and I were flat on our bellies, mosquitoes buzzing happily around our faces. Sweat was running in my eyes and my mouth, salty sweat. My mouth tasted as putrid as this goddamn jungle. Life was less than wonderful, but I resented the men with machine guns out there trying to end it for me.

They hadn't spotted us, I didn't think, but they were arcing their machine-gun fire around, bullets cracking, snapping all around.

I could see Heavy and Monawk, like cripples flung from wheelchairs, pulling themselves by the hands across the brambles and brush of the jungle floor, slowly, slowly, slowly finding their way to cover behind some trees. Then I saw Heavy slip down into a hole, a crater formed by an artillery shell. Barney and I edged over toward him, coming across Fremont on the way.

He was in bad shape: gut shot. He was whimpering, barely conscious, his stomach a black/red soggy mess into which he dug one hand, trying to hold his life in.

Above us, Jap bullets chewed up the landscape in a methodical arc.

Staying on our bellies, Barney and I each took one of his arms and dragged him toward the shell hole. We pulled him down in, by which time he was unconscious. Too many people for one small hole. I looked around, frantically; I was burning up, felt like I was looking out through red eyes.

Nonetheless, I saw it: another shell hole, ten yards or so away, a larger hole. In front of it, between us and the direction the Japs had been firing, was a fallen tree, dropped there by a bomb. Just beyond the shell hole, behind a tree, Monawk was slumped, legs shot to shit.

It was more than one machine gun now, and rifle fire was in there, too. Were they zeroing in on us?

Barney and I crawled to the hole, I slid in and he went on past and got Monawk and pulled him down in with us. We had that massive fallen tree between us and the Japs, whose bullets were hitting close enough to home that it was time to give up on keeping our position hidden, and start throwing it back at them.

About then D'Angelo crawled in the hole, grinning. "I told you that turd was warm."

"Shut up and shoot," I said.

"You'll have to prop me up," he said.

He'd gotten it in the leg.

"Not you too," I said.

"Thanks for the sympathy, Pops. Prop me up!"

I helped him sit up and he started tossing M-1 fire their way; our efforts seemed feeble compared to the barrage of bullets they were sending us. Barney started to throw Fremont's rifle and Heavy's BAR back to them, but they yelled from their shell hole that they were too weak, and in too much pain, to do any shooting.

"You guys can do more good with 'em than us," Heavy shouted. "Keep 'em . . ."

His voice trailed off.

"Hit?" I asked Barney.

"Sounds like he passed out," Barney said.

"He's got company," I said, nodding toward a barely conscious Monawk and a slumped D'Angelo.

"Christ! He isn't dead, is he?"

I checked D'Angelo's neck pulse. "No. Just unconscious."

Bullets continued to zing and whiz overhead.

I called out to Fremont and he didn't answer.

"Looks like we're *it*, buddy," I told Barney. "Everybody else is asleep."

I thought of Corporal McRae's remark, back at boot camp, about combat allowing no man sleep. He'd been wrong. So wrong.

"*They* aren't sleeping," Barney said, meaning those sons of bitches throwing machine-gun fire at us.

Neither was Whitey. I could hear him out there, not quite dead yet, yelling "Mother, mother—dad, dad, please help me!"

And then whimpering.

It was the saddest thing I ever heard, but I didn't cry. I was in that limbo world, that oddly detached place where men under fire go, to keep from going mad during the madness.

With cool desperation I fired my M-1 into the rain of bullets.

Wondering when sleep would next come for me.

And, when it did, if waking would follow.

6

Barney was leaning against the fallen tree, firing the BAR from within the shell hole. The big automatic rifle made him look like a grizzled, demented dwarf; maybe that look in his eyes was one his opponents in the ring were used to seeing from him—I'd known him a long, long time and never saw it before.

The barrel of my M-1 was getting hot as I fired clip after clip; I too was leaning against the tree, not able to see who I was shooting at, not really, an occasional shape moving in the denseness of the jungle, with only the bullets that were chewing up the jungle around us to prove anybody was really out there at all.

I heard a scream just behind me, and wheeled around and the nose of my M-1 thumped Mohawk in the chest like a bayonet. He'd come around, the big Indian had, screaming in pain. Scared the hell out of me, too, but the poor bastard could hardly help it.

Monawk would come in and out of it, like that, blacking out, then suddenly wake and start moaning and groaning and sometimes even screaming, bellowing like a big wounded animal. He was too weakened, too pain-racked, to help shoot or even reload. His legs were shot up real bad, way beyond anything we could do for him with the combat dressings in our first-aid pouches.

"That's all she wrote for the BAR," Barney said, lowering the big weapon.

"Watkins carries an extra fifty rounds on his belt," I said. "Want me to crawl over and get it for you?"

Barney shook his head. "I'll go. You're weak with malaria; you wouldn't be on your feet if you weren't leanin' on that log."

I didn't argue with him; he had a point—you could've fried an egg on my forehead. You could've fried a powdered egg on my forehead.

Barney continued: "Anyway, I want to stay over there awhile, and lay down some fire—let's make the Jap bastards believe they got a whole crowd of healthy Marines on their hands."

MARINES CROSSING MATINAKAU RIVER

MARINES CARRYING WOUNDED

"Why not. Get Fremont's extra rifle ammo, too, while you're at it. I'll lay some cover down for you."

I fired the M-1 over the log, emptying the rifle rapidly, then switching to another of the M-1s, to keep a steady barrage going while Barney crawled on his belly up and out of our hole and over to the one next door.

Then his BAR opened up, and damn near convinced me there *was* a whole healthy Marine platoon out here, giving the Japs hell.

I kept switching guns (*rifles*—this is my rifle, this is my gun, this is for Japs. . .) with the help of D'Angelo, who was groggy but awake, barely, and able to keep reloading for me. Even rotating six rifles, their barrels got so hot I was afraid they'd warp; the palm of my left hand was scorched black.

At some point, Christ knows when exactly, two soldiers—two young-looking, scared-shitless Army boys—came out of nowhere, crawling on their bellies and dropping into the hole. They were both wounded in the legs, and one in his side as well; they were sobbing with pain. They didn't have their rifles.

"Who the fuck are you?" I said, with all due sympathy, switching rifles again.

"We . . . we got detached from our infantry regiment," the less wounded one said. "We're lost."

"Join the club," I said. I fired off two rounds, looked back. D'Angelo was unconscious again. "You boys'll have to reload for me."

"Yes, sir." They were panting, but no longer sobbing. They reloaded for me.

"Don't call me 'sir.' My name's Heller."

They told me theirs, but I don't remember them.

Barney's BAR firing let up, about then. Soon he had crawled over and dropped down in with us, eyes going wide when he saw our two new tenants.

"The Army's here to start that mopping-up operation you been hearing about," I said. "They're just a little early."

Barney looked the boys' wounds over; applied a combat dressing to the wound in the one boy's side.

"What's the story?" I asked, no enemy fire coming our way at the moment.

Barney looked up from his medic duty and said, "Watkins said you and me should get the hell out of here—while we still got our legs to do it with, he said. Said they were trapped, couldn't hope to get out alive, but maybe we could."

"What'd you say to that?"

"I told him he was full of shit as a Christmas turkey. I told him we were sticking around, and not to give up. Help'll come."

"You really believe that?"

"Sure. Robbins was only a half hour ahead of us; the skipper knows by now we must've run into trouble. They'll come for us."

"I take it you're out of BAR ammo."

"Yup. But I got the extra rifle ammo. That'll help."

"What about grenades?"

"We'll have to go back for those, if we need 'em. Couldn't carry 'em in one trip."

"We'll be out of ammo before you know it, Barney."

"Maybe they're gone, those lousy Jap bastards. There hasn't been a round fired in three or four minutes."

I lit up a smoke. My mouth and throat were dry, my eyes were burning with the malaria and my head was pounding; a smoke was the worst thing in the world for me right now. But it was something to do. Which reminded me: "How's our water situation?"

He was finished with the dressing, now. He took his position down from me against the fallen log and looked at me glumly and said, "Not good. We had a bad break—both Watkins and Fremont's canteens got stitched by that machine-gun fire."

"Monawk's, too," I said. "I already checked."

The two Army boys did have canteens, and so did Barney and me, and D'Angelo. But the wounded men were going through the water fast. I craved it, or anyway my malaria craved it, but the poor shot-up bastards needed it worse.

Twilight.

The machine-gun and rifle fire had let up long enough, now, for the jungle to come back alive, birds cackling, land crabs skittering. Maybe the Japs were gone. Maybe we'd worn 'em down with the 350 or so rounds of ammunition we'd hurled their way.

The wounded men were sleeping, or in comas, who could say, and I began to think maybe we might just be able to last, just hide here, tucked away, and the American troops, Marines, Army, I didn't care if it was the fucking Coast Guard, would stumble across us, as the front moved forward.

Then machine-gun fire ripped open the night, whittling at the fallen tree, carving Jap initials in it, some bullets ricocheting wildly off the log, hitting my helmet, Barney's too, putting puckers in our tin hats. We ducked down.

"That fucker's close!" I said. Bullets flew over us, popping, snapping; tracers bounced off the log and rolled into our hole, sizzling like tiny white-hot rivets. It woke Monawk up with a scream, which dissolved into groaning.

"He's too damned close to keep missing," Barney said, over the gunfire and Monawk, "that's for sure."

"Hit the fucker with a grenade!"

"I can't stand up to do it! He'd riddle me to pieces."

I wasn't in the running for this event, standing or otherwise; the fever had weakened me too much. It had to be Barney. I mustered a pep talk: "You're a world's champ, you little schmuck; just throw 'em from where you are—body punches! Do it, man!"

Face bunched up like a bulldog's, he pulled three grenades off his belt and, one at a time, pulled the pin with his teeth and hurled. Each one in a slightly different direction.

He did it so quickly there seemed to be only one explosion.

And one high-pitched scream of terror.

And then Barney was standing up, bracing his rifle against the log, firing and screaming, "Got you, you dirty fuckin' bastard!"

Such profanity was rare from Barney, but he was right: he *had* got the dirty fuckin' bastard, only more machine-gun and rifle fire was coming our way—not from as close as the guy Barney just nailed, but coming and coming closer.

We started in firing again, and within fifteen minutes were running out of ammo. Soon we'd be down to the .45 automatics on our hips.

"One clip left," I said. Eight rounds.

"Cover me while I go over and get the rest of the grenades."

I used my eight rounds sparingly, but they were gone before Barney was back. D'Angelo, groggy but willing, was suddenly at my side, handing me a .45.

"It's Monawk's," the kid said. "He won't mind."

Monawk was out of it again.

By the time I'd emptied the .45, Barney had scrambled back in, dropping handfuls of grenades like deadly eggs into a basket.

"Gotta make another trip," he said, and scrambled back out.

I'd just taken my own .45 out of its holster when the mortar fire started in; I ducked down into the hole. The shells were landing close. White-hot shrapnel was flying, but it missed us.

It didn't miss Barney. He was on his way back to us with the rest of the grenades as the burning shrapnel ate into his side, his arm, his leg.

"Bastards, bastard, bastards!" he was screaming.

He stumbled back to the hole and I pulled him down in and put rough dressings on the wounds. The mortar barrage kept pounding on, and on. Like my feverish head. And everybody else but Barney in the goddamn hole was sleeping. That's war for you—you end up envying guys who passed out.

Then the shelling stopped.

We waited for the lull to explode away; half an hour slipped by, and the lull continued. Darkness blanketed us, now. We'd be hard for the Japs to find at night. But hard for anybody else to find, either.

"How are Fremont and Watkins?" I asked Barney.

"Watkins is conscious, or anyway he was. Fremont's got his finger in his stomach trying to stop the flow of blood."

"Jesus."

"Poor bastard doesn't stand a chance."

"I wonder if any of us do."

"I thought the infantry or B Company would've come to the rescue by now."

"There was a chance of that, till it got dark. They sure as hell won't try to advance at night."

He shook his head. "Poor Whitey's still lyin' where the boys dropped him. Dead by now. Poor bastard."

"Only difference between us and him is that we're already in a hole."

The mosquitoes were feasting on us, crawling in our hair. Barney was chewing some snuff to keep his thirst at bay—he'd given his water to the wounded men—and I was having a smoke, shaking, sweat dripping down my forehead in a salty waterfall. The fever seemed to keep me from getting hungry, that was something, anyway. But Christ I was thirsty, Jesus I could use some water.

It began to rain.

"Thanks for small favors," I told the sky.

Barney and I each had a shelter half along, and we covered the two shell holes with the camouflage tenting, or anyway Barney did. I was too weak even for that. The rain seemed to rouse the wounded men and boys to the point of being able to move themselves. We huddled together. As the shelter half collected water, I stuck my head out and tilted the tenting over and drank from its edge; Barney did, too, guzzling at it greedily. We drained the water into a canteen and passed it around to the wounded. Monawk was in especially bad shape, now, conscious, but moaning like a dying man.

The hole stayed fairly dry, but Barney and I would occasionally stick our heads out into the refreshing cloudburst; so did D'Angelo, who seemed in better shape than the others. Thirsty again, I drank from puddles near the edge of the hole.

Heavier and heavier, the rain came down, turning from blessing into curse; the shelter half began to leak, water running in along its sides, the earthen floor of our home turning into a muddy mess. I was starting to chill, now, hugging myself, shivering.

Barney was rubbing his knee.

"Nice weather for arthritis," I said.

"Ain't it."

Then, like all tropical downpours, this one ended as abruptly as it began. We sat under the shelter half, pigs in a wallow, listening to fat droplets finding their way down off the trees above, landing on the tenting like bird droppings.

The wounded, except for D'Angelo, were sleeping, or whatever it was they were doing. I was smoking. I lit one up for D'Angelo and passed it to him; he nodded thanks and sat quietly smoking. My chills had stopped. I felt the fever taking hold again, but by now that seemed only natural. I couldn't remember what it was like not to have a fever.

"I wonder if I'll ever see Cathy again," Barney said.

Did I mention Barney married his pretty blond showgirl just before we left San Diego? Well, he did. She was a gentile, so they had a civil ceremony. I stood up for him. He was writing her General Delivery, Hollywood, almost daily. But he hadn't got any mail from her, yet.

"Still not a single one," he said. "My God, d'you suppose maybe she was in an accident, knocked over by a hit-and-run driver or something?"

"She's fine. Service mail's always snafued, you know that."

He kept rubbing his knee, a little pile of grenades next to him. "If by some miracle I stay alive and get back to the States, back to Cathy, I swear the first thing I'll do is kiss the ground, and never leave the good old U.S.A. again."

The U.S.A. That sounded so far away.

It was.

"Ma and Ida and my brothers and my ghetto pals," he was muttering. "I'm never going to see 'em again, am I? Rabbi Stein'll read a funeral service over me, but who'll say *Kaddish?* I don't have any sons."

I wanted to comfort him, tell him not to give up, but the fever wouldn't let me. I was having my own thoughts, now.

"Funny thing is," he said, "I got into this to fight the Nazis, not Japs . . . I'm a Jew."

"No kidding," I managed.

"So are you."

I couldn't find a wisecrack; maybe one wasn't called for. Anyway, I wasn't up to it. I saw my father. He was sitting at the kitchen table with my gun in his hand. He lifted it to his head and I said, "Stop!"

Then Barney's hand was over my mouth; he was shaking, wild-eyed. His .45 was in his other hand. We were still under the shelter half. D'Angelo was awake, alert, automatic in hand; the two Army boys were too, similarly armed. Not Monawk—he was slumped, breathing hard.

His mouth right on my ear, Barney whispered: "You passed out. Be quiet. Japs."

We could hear them walking, twigs snapping, brush rustling. They couldn't have been more than thirty yards away.

Barney took his hand off my mouth, just as I was getting my .45 off my hip.

Then Monawk awoke, in pain, and screamed.

Barney clasped a hand over the Indian's mouth, but it was too late.

A machine gun opened up.

D'Angelo dove for Monawk as if to strangle him, but Barney pulled him off.

The machine gun chattered on, swinging in an arc.

That meant they'd heard us, but hadn't spotted us.

"Bastard's gonna get us killed," D'Angelo whispered harshly. Monawk, barely conscious, was confused, to say the least; then his eyes shut as he slipped away again.

Soon mortar shells began to land all around, and bullets zinged at us, as machine guns swept the area. It's all pretty hazy after that; images floating in a fever dream; one of the soldiers takes a hit in the arm but sucks in his howl and doesn't give us away; a slug creases Barney's ankle; bullets flying everywhere; Monawk starts to scream again, but then is quiet, a bullet with his name on it finds its way home.

More clearly, I remember: Barney, flat on his belly in the hole, starting to pitch grenades.

That was safe—it wouldn't give our position away; the enemy couldn't tell where the grenades were coming from, in this darkness. He must've thrown a couple dozen.

The sun was rising; I was burning up. They'd be coming any minute, climbing over the log, flowing over the edge of the hole, *banzai*, bayonets flashing, Barney saying the *Shema Yisrael* over and over, holding on to one last grenade to take the Japs with us when they came streaming over in and on us.

A mortar shell hit, nearby, rocking the earth.

"It's from behind us!" Barney shouted.

Our side firing . . . *our* side firing . . . another shell landed in front of us, in a crashing rumble, throwing up a huge cloud of smoke.

Hooray for our side.

"Nate, I'm going for help—the Japs won't be able to see me in all this smoke. Okay, Nate?"

I nodded. Nodded off. Slipping into a fever dream where things I never wanted to remember would teach me to forget them.

INTERIM

ST. ELIZABETH'S HOSPITAL

CONGRESS HEIGHTS, MARYLAND

FEBRUARY 1, 1943

7

"Nathan Heller," I said.

The captain smiled. He was a Navy man, the only uniformed doctor of the four on the panel. He seemed to be in his early forties—a doctor on his either side outranked him in age—and he was the only one who wasn't a little on the heavy side. One of the well-fed civilian doctors was Wilcox, my doc, sitting at the far end. But the captain was in charge. It took a Navy man to give you your walking papers, your Section 8.

"You know your name," the captain said, pleasantly. "That's a good start."

"Yes, sir."

"Dr. Wilcox feels you've done very well here. It's seldom a patient makes it down to the first floor so quickly."

"Sir, if I might ask a question?"

"Yes, Private Heller."

"It was my understanding that the program here is a three-month one, minimum. I've been here a little over two months. Now, I'm not complaining, mind you—I'm glad to be getting this consideration, but . . ."

The captain nodded, smiling again. "Your curiosity about this early Board of Review is a sign of your improved condition. I understand you were a detective before you enlisted."

"Yes, sir. I'm president of a little agency. It's waiting for me back in Chicago, when the Marines get through with me."

"You understand, Private, that returning to combat, to any sort of active duty, is out of the question."

It was the ultimate Hollywood wound, the jackpot million-dollar wound: if you cracked up in combat, there was no going back to it. Heller goes marching home.

"I've heard the scuttlebutt, yes sir."

"You'll be honorably discharged, when you're released from St. E's. You should feel no stigma about that."

"Yes, sir."

"You've served your country honorably. I understand you've been awarded a Silver Star."

"Yes, sir."

"You've acquitted yourself admirably, to say the least. Bravery under fire is no small distinction. But you're wondering why I haven't answered your question, about this early hearing."

"Yes, sir."

He gestured toward the wall behind me, which was lined with chairs. "Pull up a chair," he said. "Have a seat."

I did.

"There is a precedent for your early release, should we decide to do so, in response to the special circumstances that have come up. For example, many Army hospitals run an eight-week mental rehab program. So, Private Heller, you mustn't feel shortchanged by getting a 'rush job' at St. E's."

"Oh, I don't feel shortchanged, sir . . ."

He stopped me with an upraised hand. "Please relax. Consider the smoking lamp lit." He was getting out his own cigarettes, Chesterfields, and the other doctors joined in. He offered me one.

"No thank you, sir. I lost my taste for it."

His own cigarette in hand, the captain looked at me suspiciously. "That's unusual, under these conditions. There isn't much to do at St. E's but sit and smoke."

"Oh, they found some floors for me to scrub, sir. That kept me busy."

The doctors exchanged smiles, although one of them, a roundfaced man with thick glasses, asked, "Is it because you associate smoking with combat? Dr. Wilcox's report indicates you didn't begin smoking until you were on Guadalcanal."

I looked to the captain, rather than the doctor who posed the question. "May I be frank, sir?"

He nodded.

"Suppose smoking does remind me of combat," I said. "Suppose it does take me back to the Island."

They looked at me with narrowed eyes.

"Then I'd be crazy to smoke, wouldn't I? And put myself through all that."

Only the captain smiled, but then he was a military man; he could understand.

"I don't feel like a Marine, anymore," I said. "I don't feel like a civilian, either, but I'm willing to try to learn. I see no reason to dwell on what's happened."

The third doctor spoke for the first time. He had a small mouth, like a fish, and wire-rim glasses. He said, "You suffered amnesia, Mr. Heller. That, too, was an effort not to 'dwell' on your traumatic experiences."

"I don't want to forget what happened, or anyway I don't want to 'repress' it, as Dr. Wilcox calls it. But I do want to get on with my life."

Dr. Wilcox came to my defense, saying, "I think I've made it clear in my report that Private Heller quickly learned to regard his experience in its true perspective, as a thing of the past—something that no longer threatens his safety. I might add that it took only simple hypnosis, and no drug therapy or shock treatments, to achieve this effect."

The captain waved a hand at Wilcox, as if to quiet him on subjects better spoken about when the patient wasn't present.

But the doctor with the fish's mouth and the wire glasses picked up on Wilcox's little speech, taking offense, bristling openly, patient present or not: "I hope by that that you don't mean to imply anything derogatory about the use of drugs or shock by others here at St. Elizabeth's."

"Not at all. Merely that some battle neuroses are relatively minor compared to chronic cases we might encounter from within the civilian population."

"Gentlemen, please," the captain said. He looked like he wished he had a gavel to pound. Instead he looked at me and said, "We are going to have to ask you some questions, at some length, before we can reach a decision."

"Understood, sir. But before you begin, could you answer *my* question?"

"Private?"

"You said some special circumstances had come up, that made this early hearing necessary."

The captain nodded. "A federal prosecutor in Chicago wants you to give testimony before a grand jury."

"Oh." I thought I knew what that was about.

But the captain didn't realize that, and he shuffled through some papers, looking for the answer to a question I hadn't asked. "It involves racketeers and the film industry, I believe. Yes, here it is. The defendants include Frank Nitti, Louis Campagna and others."

"I see."

"You seem strangely disinterested, Private. Do you remember the incident this involves?"

I couldn't "repress" a smile. I said, "I don't have amnesia anymore, sir. But you can get amnesia permanently testifying against Frank Nitti."

For the first time the captain frowned; I'd overstepped my bounds—after all, I wasn't discharged yet. I was still in the service.

"Does that mean you're not interested in testifying?"

"Does it work that way? If I choose to testify, I'm sane and a civilian? And if I choose not to, I'm crazy and a Marine?"

The captain wasn't at all pleased with me; but he only said, calmly, "There are no strings attached to this hearing. We were merely requested to move it up a few weeks, to give a federal prosecutor—in Chicago—the opportunity to speak with you. Nobody's requiring you to do anything."

"Yes, sir."

"But I'm sure the government would appreciate your cooperation in this matter."

"Yes, sir."

"After all, it is one government. The same government prosecuting these gangsters is the one you chose to defend—enlisting, out of patriotic zeal."

Out of a bottle is more like it, I thought, but was smart enough to "repress" that, too.

"At any rate, we've been asked to consider your case, and we do have a few more questions for you."

The interview covered a lot of things—my memories and my feelings about what had happened on Guadalcanal. How and why I lied about my age enlisting. They even talked to me about the suicide of my father. One of them seemed to find it significant that I had carried the gun my father killed himself with as my personal weapon, thereafter. I explained that I had done that to make sure I never took killing too lightly, never used the thing too easily. But you killed in combat, didn't you? Yes, I said, but I left that gun home.

Anyway, it covered lots of ground, including how my malaria hadn't flared up since I first got here, and I didn't lose my temper anymore or crack wise and the captain seemed to like me again by the end of the interview. I was dismissed. There were chairs just outside the conference room, where I could sit and wait for the verdict. I sat and looked at the speckled marble floor. Part of me wanted a smoke, but I didn't give in.

"Hi."

I looked up. It was that pretty little nurse from the fourth floor; I hadn't seen her in weeks. She was a student nurse actually. Her name was Sara, and we'd struck up a friendship.

"Well, hello," I said.

"Mind if I sit down?"

"I'd mind if you didn't."

She sat, smoothed out the white apron over the checked dress; her blouse was blue, her cap white. And her eyes were still light blue, freckles still trailed across a cute pugish nose. She had some legs; you can have Betty Grable.

"I heard you were getting your Board of Review today," she said. "I just wanted to come down and wish you luck."

"Too late for that. I already said my piece."

"I wouldn't worry. You've made remarkable progress. I don't know of anybody ever getting a Board of Review after only a couple of months."

"Uncle Sam has something else in mind for me, that's all."

"Pardon?"

"Nothing. Just a federal grand jury they want me to testify to, for some stupid extortion racket that dates back before the war."

Her tight little smile crinkled her chin. "It all seems so . . . unimportant, somehow, doesn't it? What happened before the war."

"Yeah. It all kind of pales, that life back there."

"You'll be going back to it."

I shook my head. "It's all changed. Haven't you heard, lady? There's a war on."

"Nate. Are you sleeping better now?"

I put a smile on for her. "Oh, yeah. Sure. Fine. No problem."

"You had some rough nights on the fourth floor."

"I graduated to the floors below, remember? I'm the wonder boy, or I would be if I were younger."

"You weren't sleeping much at all. And when you did . . ."

When I did I had nightmares of combat and I woke up screaming, like Monawk.

"Not anymore," I said. "Ah, you know, that Doc Wilcox is a whiz. He put my head back together, piece by piece. I feel great."

"You have dark circles under your eyes."

I was glad she wasn't on the Board of Review.

"I'm fine, honestly. If I wasn't sleeping, how could I be so bright and cheery today?"

"You get plenty of rest sitting around the dayroom. You seem able to catch naps, sitting there, not knowing you're sleeping. But at night—"

At night, sleep refused to come, until I was so tired it and the nightmares sneaked up on me, like a Jap with a knife in the dark.

"It's not a problem, anymore. Really. Gosh, Sara, it was nice of you to stop down and wish me luck."

"I know you're still not sleeping. I know you're still having the nightmares."

"Sara, please . . ."

"I'm not going to say anything. I know you're keeping it to yourself so the doctors won't keep you in here. You want to go home, don't you?"

"Yes," I said, and suddenly my goddamn eyes were wet. What is this shit!

She slipped her arm around my shoulder. "Come 'ere, big boy."

I wept into her blue blouse, and she patted me like a baby. Another woman did that once, babied me while I bawled; I'd seen somebody I cared for die, violently, and it had rocked me, and Sally had helped me through that.

"There, there," Sara said.

I sat up, glancing around, hoping nobody saw me. After all, I wouldn't want to look like a nut in a mental ward; people would talk.

"I'm sorry," I said.

"It's okay," she said. "I'm not going to say anything to the doctors. You'll be better off back in Chicago, anyway. Do you really know some of the people you say you know?"

"Yeah. What's wrong, haven't you ever met anybody famous?"

"Oh sure. Napoleon, for instance, and a guy who thinks he's Hitler."

"Did you ever consider that if you had the genuine articles they'd be in the right place?"

She smiled broadly, showed me those pretty childlike teeth. "Good point." She stood. "If you're ever in Washington again, try and look me up."

"Are you implying you'd go out with a former mental patient?"

"Sure," she said. "There's a man shortage."

"Some compliment. Say, how's Dixon doing?"

Her cheerful expression faded and she shook her head; sat back down. "Not so good. He's up on the sixth floor. No early Board of Review for him."

"Damn. What about that Navy guy who wasn't talking, the uh, what did you say his condition was called?"

"Catatonic," she said, and started to giggle.

"What's so funny?"

"I shouldn't laugh. You remember the fuss he made, when we fed him with a tube?"

I had helped her, on several occasions, her and the corpsman, feed the guy his mixture of tomato juice, milk, raw eggs, and puréed meats and stuff; if they won't eat, they get this concoction in a tube down the throat, but this guy—completely clammed up otherwise and placid as glass—would go berserk when you tried to put the tube in him.

"He's started to talk," she said. "He's had some shock treatments, and he's talking now. He told us why he squirmed so when we tube-fed him."

"Yeah?"

"He thought it was an enema and we were putting it in the wrong end."

We sat and laughed and laughed and pretty soon I was crying again, but it was a different kind, a better kind.

She stood.

I stood.

"Good luck," she said. She touched my face. "Get some sleep."

"I'll do my best," I said. Sat.

She swished off; pretty legs. I'd spent hours here beating my meat, thinking about those legs. There's not much to do in a mental ward.

I wiped some residue of moisture off my face, thinking what a sweet cunning little bitch she was. She knew I was holding back; she knew, hypnosis or not, there were things I hadn't told Wilcox.

Hell, there were things I *couldn't* tell Wilcox. There were doors that just wouldn't open. Or was that jumble of events, that rush of images in the shell hole, simply the fever that had gripped me then?

How the fuck *did* Monawk die, exactly? He was shot. Who shot him?

Well, the Japs, of course. Don't be stupid.

Then why did he have black, scorchy powder burns on his chest, where he was shot? Why was the hole in his goddamn back big enough to drive a Mack truck through?

Close range; somebody shot him close range.

With a .45, that had to be it, like the .45s we all had, Barney, D'Angelo, those Army boys, me.

Me.

Like the .45 I had in my hand when I noticed the powder burns on Monawk's dungaree jacket . . .

I bent over, covered my face with my hands. No, I hadn't told Wilcox about that. I hadn't told anybody about that. I hadn't told anybody that I thought I'd seen it happen, Monawk's murder, but I, goddamnit, I repressed it, it's stuck back here someplace in my fucking head but I can't, I *won't* remember.

Did I kill you, Monawk? Did you scream and endanger us all and I killed you?

"Private Heller?"

It was the captain. In the doorway of the conference room.

"Please step in."

I did.

"We've reviewed your case," the captain said, sitting back down behind the table. I remained standing. "We're quite impressed by your recovery, and are convinced that you are in every way ready to rejoin society." There were some papers in front of him, with various signatures on them; he handed them to me.

My Section 8.

"And here's your honorable service award," he said, handing me a little box.

I didn't bother opening it; I knew what it was: my Ruptured Duck, the lapel pin all armed forces vets got upon their discharge—so called because the eagle within the little button spread its wings awkwardly.

"Check with the front receiving desk, and they'll help you arrange transportation. You should be able to make train reservations for this afternoon, if you like. You're going back to Chicago, Mr. Heller."

I smiled down at my discharge. Then I smiled at the captain. "Thank you, sir."

He smiled too and stood and offered his hand and I shook it. I went down the line shaking all their hands. I lingered with Wilcox, squeezing his hand, trying to convey some warmth to this heavy-set little man who'd brought me back to myself.

"Good luck, Nate," he said.

"Thanks, Doc."

Just as I was leaving, he said, "If your trouble sleeping persists, check in at the nearest military hospital. They can give you something for it."

I guess I hadn't fooled him so good, after all.

"Thanks, Doc," I said again, and headed back to my ward, to pack my sea bag.

It didn't matter what happened back there in that shell hole; that was over, that was history. What mattered was not that Monawk died, but that some of us had lived through it. Fremont and Whitey hadn't, of course, but Watkins did and D'Angelo and the two Army boys and Barney, hell, Barney was a hero. They said he killed twenty-two Japs with those grenades he was lobbing. They also said he was still over there, on the Island. Still fighting. How could he still be over there?

And me here?

I sat on the edge of my rack and thought about how screwy it seemed, going back to Chicago to see some federal prosecutor about Frank Nitti and Little New York Campagna and the Outfit bilking the movie industry. What did that have to do with anything, today? Who cared? Didn't they know there was a war on? It seemed another world, Nitti's Chicago—a lifetime ago.

Not three short years . . .

Two

Nitti's Town

Chicago, Illinois

November 6–12, 1939

ILLINOIS BELL

8

The deli restaurant on the corner was calling itself the Dill Pickle, now, and the bar next door was under new management. Barney Ross's Cocktail Lounge had moved to nicer, more spacious digs, across from the Morrison Hotel, where Barney kept an "exclusive" suite. I lived at the Morrison myself, in a two-room suite, not so exclusive.

Which was still a step up from the days, not so long ago, when I slept in my office, on a Murphy bed, playing nightwatchman for my landlord in lieu of rent. My landlord, the owner of the building, was then, and was now, one Barney Ross.

Who had walked over from the Morrison with me on this brisk Monday morning, back to the former site of his cocktail lounge, above which was—or anyway had been—my one-room office. He wasn't the only one who was expanding.

"I'm anxious to see what you've done to the place," Barney said, working to be heard over the rumble of the El.

I stepped around a wino and opened the door for him and he started up the narrow stairway (Barney, not the wino). "No permanent improvements," I said to his back as we climbed. "I wouldn't want your investment to appreciate."

"Ever since you started paying rent," he said, grinning back at me like a bulldog who spotted his favorite hydrant, "you just ain't your charming self."

Actually, I was feeling very much my charming self this morning. Very much full of my charming self. Life was good. Life was sweet. Because business was good. And that's sweet in my book.

I was a small businessman, you see. But not as small as I used to be. I was coming up in the world.

You couldn't tell that based upon Barney's building, however; this block on Van Buren Street, the hovering El casting its shadow down the middle of the street, remained a barely respectable hodgepodge of bars and hockshops and flophouses. And our building wasn't exactly the Monadnock. We had a couple of cut-rate doctors, one of whom seemed to be an abortionist, another of whom purported to be a dentist; anyway, they both made extractions, including from wallets, and even an old pickpocket-detail dick like me couldn't do anything about it. We also had three shysters and one palm reader and various marginal businesses that came and went.

And one detective agency, now proudly expanded to a suite of two offices, count 'em, two. At the far end of the hall on the fourth floor was my old office, now partitioned off and used by my two freshly hired operatives, whereas the office next door, looking out on Plymouth Court and the Standard Club (a scenic view of the El now denied me), was mine and mine alone.

Almost.

I opened the door, the pebbled glass of which bore the fresh inscription A-1 DETECTIVE AGENCY, NATHAN HELLER, PRESIDENT (I was afraid if I touched it, it'd smear), and Barney and I entered my outer office. My outer office! Hot damn. All I needed was a stack of year-old magazines and there wouldn't be a waiting room in the Loop that had anything on me.

I also had Gladys.

"Good morning, Mr. Heller," she said, smiling with no sincerity whatsoever. "No calls."

I glanced at my watch. "It's five after nine, Gladys." We opened at nine; Pinkerton never slept—Heller did. "How long have you been here, anyway?"

"Five minutes, Mr. Heller. During which time there were no calls."

"Call me Nate."

"That wouldn't be correct, Mr. Heller." She stood from behind the small dark beat-up desk Barney had given me from downstairs, when he moved his cocktail lounge. "If you'll excuse me, I'll just keep working on straightening out your files."

My four wooden file cabinets were in the outer office here with Gladys, now, and she was putting them in order, something which hadn't been done for a couple of years. Gladys, by the way, was twenty-four years old, had brunette hair that brushed her shoulders, curling in at the bottom, a fashion a lot of girls seemed to be wearing. None more attractively than Gladys; right now, as she stood filing, in her frilly yet somehow businesslike white blouse and a black skirt that was tight around the sweet curves of her bottom and then flared out, she was any lecherous employer's dream.

Unfortunately, that dream was unlikely ever to come true. I had hired her for her sweet bottom and her delicately featured face—did I mention the dark brown eyes, their long lashes, the pouty puckered mouth? That sulky mouth should've tipped me off; some goddamn detective I was. Anyway, I hired her chiefly for her rear end, noting that her secretarial background (letter from former employer, secretarial school diploma) looked pretty good, as well.

But she double-crossed me. She was turning out to be an intelligent, efficient, utterly businesslike secretary, without the slightest personal interest in her boss.

Barney nudged me.

"Uh, Gladys. This is my friend Mr. Ross. He's our landlord."

She turned away from the filing cabinet and gave Barney a smile as lovely as it was disinterested "That's nice," she said.

"Barney Ross," I said. "The boxer?"

She'd already turned back to her filing. "I know," she said, tonelessly. "A pleasure," she added, without any. She had the cheerfully cold cadence of a telephone operator.

Barney and I moved past her, past the dated-looking "modernistic" black-and-white couch and chairs I'd bought back in '34, in the art-deco aftermath of the World's Fair, and opened the door in the midst of the pebbled-glass-and-wood wall that separated Gladys from my inner office. My old desk was in here, a big scarred oak affair I'd grown used to. I had sprung for a new, comfortable swivel chair so I could lean back and not fall out the double windows behind me. Barney got it wholesale for me. There was a secondhand but new-looking tan leather couch from Maxwell Street against the right wall, on which hung several photographs, including portraits of Sally Rand and a certain other actress. Both photos were signed to me "with love." Something that personal has no business in an office, but the two famous female faces impressed some of my clients, and gave me something to look at when business was slow. Against the other wall were several chairs and some fight photos of Barney, which he'd given me, one of them signed. Not with love.

"She's a sweet dish," Barney said, jerking a thumb back in Gladys's direction, "but not a very warm one."

"I knew it when I hired her," I said, offhandedly.

"The hell you say!"

"Her looks didn't mean a damn to me. I looked at her qualifications and saw she was the right man for the job."

"You looked at her qualifications all right. She was friendlier when she interviewed for the position, I'll bet."

"Yup," I admitted. "And it's the only position I'll ever get her in. Oh, well. How's *your* love life?"

He and his wife Pearl were separated; he'd gone east, briefly, to work in her father's clothing business and it hadn't worked out—the marriage *or* the business arrangement. Back to the Cocktail Lounge for Barney.

"I got a girl," he said, almost defensively. "How about you?"

"I'm swearin' off the stuff."

"Seriously, Nate, you're not gettin' any younger. You're a respectable businessman. Why don't you settle down and start a family?"

"*You* don't have any kids."

"It's not for lack of trying. Aw, it's probably for the best, since it didn't work out with Pearl and me. But Cathy, she's another story."

His chorus girl.

"Out of the frying pan," I said. "When you're in my business, it's hard to have much faith in the sanctity of marriage."

He frowned sympathetically. "Doing a lot of that sort of work these days, are ya?"

"I have been. Divorces keep many an agency afloat, this one included. But from here on out I'm leaving as much of that horseshit as possible to my operatives. When you're the boss, you can pick and choose your cases."

"Speakin' of your ops, why don't you take me over to their office and introduce me? Haven't met either of 'em."

We walked back out through the inner office, nodding and smiling at Gladys, getting back a nod as she filed on, and went next door, to my old office, the pebbled glass on the door of which said simply: A-1 DETECTIVE AGENCY, PRIVATE. I went in without knocking, Barney following.

It had always seemed such a big room when I'd been working in it; partitioned off into two work areas, desks with extra chairs for clients, it seemed tiny. The plaster walls were painted a pale green, now. Only one of the desks was filled, the one at left. The man behind it, a bald fellow with dark hair around his flat-to-his-skull ears, wire-rim glasses sitting on a bulbous nose, fifty-one years of age, rose; his suitcoat was off, hung on a nearby coatrack, but he still looked very proper, in his vest and neatly snugged solid blue tie.

"Barney," I said, "this is Lou Sapperstein."

Sapperstein grinned, extended a hand across his desk, which Barney, smiling, shook. "You made me some money last year," Sapperstein said.

"How's that?" Barney said.

"He bet on Armstrong," I said.

Barney laughed a little. "What a pal," he said, meaning me.

"I wasn't referring to that," Lou said, a little embarrassed. "Actually, after you lost, I bet a friend of mine you would quit. Which you did, of course."

"How'd you know I'd quit and *stay* quit? I had plenty of comeback offers, you know."

"I can imagine. I couldn't collect the bet till a year from the day of your Armstrong defeat. That was part of the deal. It was fifty smackers, too. Thanks, Mr. Ross."

"Make it 'Barney,' please."

"Lou retired after twenty-five years on the force," I said. "We were on the pickpocket detail together."

"I was his boss," Lou told Barney. "Hiring me is just Nate's idea of revenge."

"Hiring you is my idea of being a nice guy," I said. "Working your ass off is my idea of revenge. Where's Fortunato?"

"Late," Sapperstein shrugged.

"On his first day?" I asked, a little stunned.

Sapperstein shrugged again.

"I wanted him to start right in on those credit checks," I said, pointing over to some paperwork on the other desk, which from where Lou was seated he couldn't see, anyway.

The door opened behind us and Frankie Fortunato came in; he was small, thin as a knife, with dark widow's-peaked hair and sharp features. He would've looked sinister, but his smile was bright, white and wide. His suit was brown and snappy and his tie was yellow and red.

"Hey, I'm late," he said. "Off to a flyin' start."

"You don't have to be here till nine o'clock," I said. "Is it asking too much . . ."

"You looking for quality, or punctuality?"

"Actually, I was looking for both."

"Heller, you're turning into an old man. You don't remember what it was like to be young. I had a hot date last night." He was over behind his desk, now, dialing his phone.

"That better be a credit check," I said.

"Sugar?" he said into the phone. "It's Frankie." He covered the phone, waved us off. "Do you mind? Little privacy."

I went over to the phone and took it from his hand. I said, "Hi, sugar. Frankie just called to say he was unemployed." I handed the phone back to him.

"Talk to ya later, sugar," he said into it, and hung up. He grinned. "Just testing the waters, boss. Mind if I get started on these credit checks now?"

"Go right ahead. This is my friend Barney Ross, by the way."

"Listen," he said to Barney, by way of greeting. "There's dough in a comeback. It don't have to be Armstrong. Hey, Canzoneri's still fighting; a third Ross-Canzoneri fight'd make some tidy dough. We should talk." He glanced at me and smiled on one side of his face. "After business hours of course."

I nodded to both Frankie and Lou and we went out.

Barney said, "That kid's cocky, but I bet he's bright."

"Safe bet. I'll get him straightened out. Much as possible, anyway."

"What's his background?"

"He was fired off the force in his first year for rubbing Tubbo Gilbert the wrong way."

Captain Daniel "Tubbo" Gilbert was, even in Chicago terms, a notoriously corrupt cop. A notoriously powerful corrupt cop, at that.

"Aw," Barney said. "No wonder you like the kid. You see yourself in the little son of a bitch."

"Hey," I said. "I see admirable qualities in a lot of sons of bitches. I've even been known to hang around with washed-up ex-pugs."

Barney's expression turned suddenly thoughtful. "You're liable to lose that kid to the draft, you know."

I shook my head. "It'll never come."

We were standing just outside my office now.

"I think it's going to *have* to come, Nate. We might get caught up in it, too, you know."

"*That* I guarantee you will never happen."

"I might go whether they ask me or not."

"Don't be foolish," I said.

"Don't you know there's a war on?"

"In Europe. We been snookered into fighting their battles before—never again."

"You really believe that?"

"Sure."

"But, Nate, you're a Jew . . ."

"I'm not a Jew. That doesn't mean I don't sympathize with what's happening to the Jews in Germany. I don't like the idea of military seizure of property happening anywhere to anybody. But I don't feel it has anything special to do with me."

"You're a Jew, Nate."

"My pa was a Jew, my ma was Irish Catholic, and me, I'm just another mutt from Chicago, Barney."

"Maybe so. But as far as Mr. Hitler's concerned, you're just another Jew."

Well, he hadn't scored a knockout punch, by any means, but Barney had made his point. It wasn't the first time, and was hardly the last.

So without even trying to crack wise, I sent him on his way, while I went in to get to work. I made several calls on an insurance matter before I noticed the morning was nearly gone.

Then Gladys stuck her pretty, impersonal puss in my office and said, "Your eleven o'clock appointment is here."

I'd almost forgotten.

Which considering the stature of the client—potential client, as we hadn't talked, he'd merely called for an appointment—was stupid of me.

"Send Mr. O'Hare in," I said, straightening my tie and my posture.

But Mr. O'Hare wasn't the first person in. A striking-looking woman was, a rather tall, dark woman who strolled in as if out of an Arabian dream (or was it a Sicilian nightmare?), regal in her camelhair swagger topcoat with padded shoulders, open to reveal a mannish, pinstripe suit beneath. Beneath the suit, any good detective could deduce, was not a mannish body; the lapels of *my* suit didn't flare out like that. She wore a gray pillbox hat atop long black shining hair pulled back in a bun; a large purse was slung over her shoulder on a strap—she could've carried a change of clothes in the thing. She glanced at the portraits of actresses on my cream-color wall and seemed faintly amused. Then she smiled at me, nodded; there was no warmth in it, but there was sensuality and smarts: a wide mouth, with dark red lipstick, a patrician Roman nose, dark, dark eyes, and ironic arching brows.

O'Hare, shorter than her, was on her heels, helping her with her coat, like she was the queen and he was her foot servant.

Which was ridiculous, whoever she was, because Edward J. O'Hare—a small but powerful-looking man in his own natty pinstripe suit, a diamond stick pin in his red, spotted-black tie, a black topcoat over his arm, black fedora in his hand—was a big man in this city, a millionaire with connections in both city hall and the underworld. Especially the underworld. His face was handsome in a lumpy way, dark bushy black eyebrows hanging over piercing dark blue eyes, a sharp, prominent nose, strong features undercut by a small chin riding a saddle of flesh.

He hung her coat up, and his own, and smiled at me, the smile of the professional glad-hander. "Mr. Heller, I hope you don't mind my bringing my secretary, Miss Cavaretta, along . . . to take some notes during our visit. It's my practice at business meetings."

I was standing, gesturing to the chairs along the nearby wall. "Not at all," I said. "Such charming company is always welcome."

She smiled, tightly, holding something back, her eyes alive with things she knew I didn't, and she sat down and crossed slender, shapely legs, getting a steno pad and a pen from her purse.

O'Hare was standing across from me, offering his hand, still smiling like a politician. I shook the hand, smiled back, wondering why he was so eager to please. This was an important man. I was nobody in particular. Did he always come on this strong?

"It's a real pleasure, Mr. Heller," he said. "I've heard good things about you."

"Who from, Mr. O'Hare? Frank Nitti, possibly?"

His smile disappeared; I shouldn't have said that—it just blurted out.

He sat. "My associations with that crowd are exaggerated, Mr.

Heller. Besides, you can make money through such associations and run no risk if you keep it on a business basis, and are forthright in your dealings. Keep it business, and there is nothing to fear."

He sounded like he was trying to convince himself, not me.

I said, "I didn't mean to be rude, Mr. O'Hare."

"Call me Eddie," he said, getting out a silver cigarette case. He offered one of the cigarettes to Miss Cavaretta; she took it. He offered me one and I politely refused, though I eased an ashtray toward Miss Cavaretta. Our eyes met. She smiled at me with them. She had long legs. They were smiling at me, too.

"We've just closed the season out at Sportsman's Park," Edward J. O'Hare said, lighting Miss Cavaretta's cigarette with a silver lighter shaped like a small horse's head. He put the cigarettes and lighter away without lighting one up himself.

I said, "You've had a good year, I understand."

Sportsman's Park, of which O'Hare was the president, was a 12,000-seat, half-mile racetrack, converted from dogs to nags back in '32. It was in Stickney, very near Cicero. In other words, right smack in the middle of mob country.

"Yes. But we have had a few problems."

"Oh?"

Miss Cavaretta was poised, ready to write something down; she'd written nothing as yet, not even a doodle. She wasn't the doodler type.

"As you may know, at a park like ours, some of our clientele is less than savory."

"Sure," I said. "Ex-cons, thieves, bookmakers, whores . . . excuse my French, Miss Cavaretta."

The faintest wisp of a smile.

"Particularly on the weekdays," I went on, "when working stiffs can't get away from the salt mines."

"Precisely," O'Hare said, sitting forward, striving to be earnest. "We've done our best to keep out the hoodlums and deadbeats and troublemakers. But there's only so much we can do, in our business. That's where you come in, Mr. Heller."

"I do?"

"We've been having pickpocket trouble. A regular epidemic. We don't mind our customers getting their pockets emptied, it's just that we prefer to do it ourselves."

"Naturally."

"I understand that you have a certain expertise in that area. Pickpocket control, I mean."

"That's my police background, yes. And, since going private, I've done a lot of security work in that area, that's correct."

He smiled—patronizingly, I thought. "I understand you even handled the pickpocket problem at the World's Fair."

"The Chicago one, back in '33," I said. "They didn't invite me out to New York for the new one."

"They're holding it over, I hear," someone said.

Surprisingly, it was Miss Cavaretta—who was now in the midst of actually taking a few notes—putting in her two cents, in a lush, throaty voice that was like butter on a warm roll.

"Maybe they'll invite you there next year," she said.

O'Hare laughed at that, a little too loud I thought. Was he trying to get in her pants? Was that what this was about? And since when did a millionaire have to try so hard to get in his secretary's panties? Then again, on the other hand, I kept in mind my own situation with Gladys. Of course, I wasn't a millionaire.

"Maybe they will invite me," I said, feeling like the unwanted chaperone on a date.

"What I would like," O'Hare said, "is for you to instruct my own security staff in the art of spotting and catching pickpockets. I will want you to spend some time at the park yourself, when the next season opens, supervising. You'll need to come out, as soon as possible, and take a look around the facility, of course."

"Just a moment, please," I said, and I picked up the phone and called next door.

In a few moments Lou Sapperstein, wearing his suitcoat, looking spiffy as a hundred bucks, entered, nodding, smiling, eyes lingering just a second on the enticing, enigmatic Miss Cavaretta. I made introductions all around, ending up with Lou: "He was my boss on the pickpocket detail. And he's my top operative, now. I'll put him on this for you, Mr. O'Hare."

O'Hare's face turned pale; weird as it might seem, his expression was tragic as he said, "But that simply won't do. I must have *you*, Mr. Heller. I must have the top man."

I laughed just a little, a nervous laugh. "You don't understand, Mr. O'Hare. Lou's *my* top man. He was my boss. He taught me everything I know about dips. You couldn't be in better hands."

O'Hare stood. "Perhaps when it comes to the supervision of my people, he would be satisfactory. But I'm afraid I must insist that you come out to the park and have a look around personally. I only deal with the top man, understand?"

"Mr. O'Hare, with all due respect, *I* am the top man in this agency, and I delegate work as I see fit . . ."

O'Hare reached in his inside coat pocket. He withdrew a checkbook. Leaned over the desk and began to write. "I'm leaving you a thousand-dollar retainer," he said. "On the understanding that you will come out to the park tomorrow afternoon to inspect the plant, personally."

He tore off the check and held it out before me, the ink glistening wetly on it.

I took it and blotted it and put it in my desk.

"You want Nate Heller," I said, "you got Nate Heller."

"Good man," O'Hare beamed. He turned and all but bowed deferentially to his secretary. "Miss Cavaretta?"

She stood; smoothed her dress out over long, presumably lush thighs. Why is a woman in mannish clothing such a perversely attractive thing? Maybe Freud knew; personally, I didn't give a damn. I just knew I would've liked to see the lacy things underneath Miss Cavaretta's pinstripe suit.

She extended a hand with long, clear varnished nails, which I took; was I expected to kiss it? I didn't.

She said, "It's been very interesting meeting you, Mr. Heller."

"Same here, Miss Cavaretta."

He helped her with her coat, and got his own coat on; he left his hat on the rack. Lou was about to point that out to him, but I raised a finger to my lips and stopped it. I'd been watching O'Hare closely; he'd left that hat on purpose.

I stood and waited and then O'Hare ducked in again, calling back to Miss Cavaretta, "Forgot my blamed hat, my dear," and went to the hat rack and got it and said to me, very quietly, his face sober and without a trace of the glad-hander's smile, "Come alone."

He closed the door and was gone.

Lou and I looked at the door, our brows furrowed.

Lou sat down and so did I. He said, "What the hell was that all about?"

"I haven't a clue."

"That guy's connected up the wazoo, you know."

"I know."

"He was Capone's front man for the old Hawthorne dog track. He's been an Outfit front man for years."

"I know."

"Why'd he bring his secretary along?"

"So she could take notes, he said."

"Did I miss something? All I heard him do was ask if he could hire us—hire *you*—to do some security work at his lousy racetrack."

"That's right."

"What did he need to bring a secretary along to take notes for, if that's all he wanted? Hell, why didn't he just call you on the phone, if all he wanted was to hire you for some pickpocket work?"

"I don't know, Lou," I said.

And I didn't know.

Nor did I know why he felt he had to impart his final message to me out of his dark, lovely secretary's earshot.

But I was detective enough to want to find out.

9

E. J. O'Hare was a lawyer, but he hadn't practiced law since he moved from St. Louis to Chicago in the late '20s, to begin overseeing various of Al Capone's business interests, specifically horse- and dog-racing tracks. And not just in Illinois: O'Hare also looked after the Outfit's tracks in Florida, Tennessee and Massachusetts. He was a stockholder in all of those parks, having gotten a foothold via owning the patent rights on the mechanical rabbit used in dog racing. From that he'd built a financial empire that included extensive real estate holdings, an insurance company and two advertising agencies. According to Barney, O'Hare was also a heavy investor in the Chicago Cardinals pro football team, though that wasn't widely known.

He was unquestionably a wheeler-dealer, and a financial wizard; the mob's "one-man brain trust," the papers called him.

But today, as I entered his office at Sportsman's Park in Stickney, he was just a nervous little heavy-set man in a gray vested suit and blue-and-gray-speckled tie, sitting at his big mahogany desk atop an elaborate Oriental rug, cleaning and oiling an automatic pistol. A foreign make, I'd say.

"Nate Heller!" he said, with a big grin, standing behind the desk to extend a hand, like I was an old friend, an unexpected and welcome guest who just happened to drop by. Never mind that I'd known him since yesterday and was here at his paid request.

I shook his hand; the other one held the automatic. There was a little 2-in-1 oil on the hand that firmly gripped mine, and when I took a handkerchief out of my pocket to wipe off my palm, he apologized for this uncharacteristic messiness.

"Sorry," he said. "A man can't be too careful." He meant the gun, which he now lay gently on the desk.

"I've already had a walk around your facility, Mr. O'Hare," I said, hanging my topcoat and hat next to his on the tree in one corner. "I hope you don't mind my taking the liberty."

E. J. O'HARE

"Not at all, and I asked you yesterday to call me Eddie."

"Fine, Eddie. Call me Nate." He already had, actually.

"Pull up a chair," he said, and I did, glancing around the office, which—like O'Hare—was small but plush. Dark wood paneling, a wall of framed photos to my left, a built-in bookcase at right. The wall of photos—from which I took a chair—showed O'Hare in the presence of various civic leaders and Chicago celebrities, here at Sportsman's Park, lots of big smiles and arms around shoulders, his Outfit associates conspicuous in their absence. My favorite picture was one of him with Mayor Cermak at the opening of the park, His Honor and O'Hare standing on either side of the winning jockey who was atop his horse, with a huge floral horseshoe draped around them all. Behind him at his desk was a gigantic framed photograph of Sportsman's Park, from a slightly overhead angle that got both the grandstand and the track in, in color, pastel tints. On the desk, at either side, were clusters of framed family photos. The bookcase at right was brimming with volumes, some leather-bound, interspersed with an occasional fancy crystal glass piece and various busts of various sizes of Napoleon.

He must have noticed me taking in the Napoleon busts curiously, as he smiled, rather proudly, and said, "An interest of mine. Those books, all of them, are on the Little General. A small sampling of what I daresay is the largest collection of Napoleonana in the United States."

"Really?"

He had a distant expression as he looked at the wall of Napoleon stuff. He said, "Napoleon was a little man."

"Uh, yeah. So I heard."

"But he was the biggest general history ever saw."

"No argument there."

He turned his attention back to the gun he was cleaning; he had a pipe cleaner stuck down the barrel at the moment. He said, "He always made the right decision when it counted."

"Who?"

A little crossly he said, "Napoleon." Then wistfully: "Once he had to decide whether to carry fifteen hundred prisoners of war or have them killed."

"Really."

He gestured with a fist, suddenly firm. "He had them shot, making the decision in five minutes."

What decisions had Eddie O'Hare been making in this office, of late?

"Mr. O'Hare. Eddie. I've looked over your plant, and can see no insurmountable problems, assuming your security staff numbers twenty or more."

"Few problems regarding what?"

"Your pickpocket situation. The grandstands themselves are too large to effectively control, but I doubt the dips would hit there much, anyway. It's down by the cashier windows that they'll make their move. And at your concession stands."

He nodded, a strained look on his face, as if the relevance of all this was something he couldn't really grasp.

"At any rate," I said, "I think a few weeks before the next season begins, we can give your staff some pointers, and not just the security people. Ushers and concessionaires and all. Do you have any questions?"

"How did you come?"

"What?"

"Did you drive out here?"

"No. I took the El to Laramie and hopped a streetcar. One of my other operatives needed my car. Why?"

"Good." He smiled, but more to himself than to me. "I'll give you a ride into the Loop."

"That isn't really necessary." Just as this trip out to Sportsman's Park wasn't really necessary.

"No! I insist."

A knock came at the door.

"Yes?" O'Hare said.

A small, boyish, nattily dressed man with graying hair entered, smiled pleasantly, said, "Excuse me, gentlemen. Is this a private conference?"

"Not at all, Johnny," O'Hare said, half rising, gesturing for him to come in with one hand, continuing to clean his automatic with the other.

I stood and shook hands with the little man.

"This is Nate Heller, the private detective," O'Hare said. "Nate, this is—"

"I recognize His Honor," I said, trying not to sound tongue in cheek.

I had recognized him at once, though I'd never met him: Johnny Patton, the boy mayor of Burnham. The "boy" mayor was well over fifty now, but he'd supposedly been fourteen when he opened his first saloon and wasn't yet twenty when first elected mayor of Burnham, another of the mob-dominated southwest suburbs like Stickney and Cicero. Once upon a time he'd been Johnny Torrio's boy; in recent years he'd been snuggled comfortably in Frank Nitti's pocket.

He was also O'Hare's chief partner in Sportsman's Park. That is, excluding the silent ones.

"Oh yes, Nate Heller," Patton said, nodding for me to sit back down, but not taking a seat himself. "You're going to help us lick our pickpocket problem."

"I'm going to try," I said.

"I'm sure you'll come through for us. I've heard good things about you."

Nitti again? I wondered to myself. I had presence enough of mind, this time, not to blurt it out.

He turned his attention to O'Hare. "Could you step in my office, E.J.? Bill and I have the last of that publicity material ready—you need to take a look at it."

"Certainly," O'Hare said, and rose. "Wait here a moment, will you, Nate? I'll give you a lift back to the Loop."

"Fine," I said.

Patton said, "You'll be riding back with E.J.?"

"Yes," I said.

"I see," he said.

Then, slipping an arm around O'Hare's shoulder, Patton and O'Hare exited.

Not long after, Miss Cavaretta came in; she was in another mannish suit, and it fit her curves snugly, in a most unmannish manner. An attractive woman, all right, although she had a certain West Side hardness, and she'd seen the last of thirty-five. She seemed a little startled to see me; or anyway as startled as a cool customer like her could seem.

"Well hello," she said. In that throaty purr.

"Well hello," I said.

"I didn't know you were here."

"I seem to be. I'm surprised this is the first I've seen of you today. I expected you'd be taking notes while Mr. O'Hare and I spoke."

"Yes, uh—Ed *has* been having me keep minutes of his business meetings of late. But I just got back from lunch."

In the midst of the wall of photos was a square clock with roman numerals.

"Mr. O'Hare must be a pretty soft touch, as bosses go," I said, nodding toward the clock. "Here it is a quarter till two and you're just back from lunch."

"I didn't leave till one," the secretary said, not at all defensively. She walked to the coat tree, near the wall of books and the solemn Napoleon busts, where O'Hare's topcoat hung, as did mine. She stood digging in one of his pockets, her back to me; her seams were straight, despite the curves in the road they traveled.

Then she turned and shrugged and displayed two open hands to me and said, "I was looking for his keys. I'm missing some papers that I thought might be in his car."

She didn't have to explain herself to me; I wondered why she bothered.

"Tell Mr. O'Hare I'm back from lunch, will you?" she said, and left.

Curiouser and curiouser.

I got up and looked around a little. In the midst of the framed photos on the one wall, just under the clock, was a framed poem, in flowery lettering:

The clock of life is wound but once
And no man has the power
To tell just when the hands will stop,
At a late or early hour.
Now is the only time you own:
Love, live, toil with a will.
Place no faith in tomorrow,
For the clock may then be still.

Having absorbed that bit of philosophy, I sat back down. The faces in the framed photos on O'Hare's desk—a boy and two girls who, in the various photos, grew into a handsome young man and two attractive young women—seemed as confused about being here as I was.

They were innocent faces, out of place here, ill at ease, sharing the desktop with the foreign-looking automatic.

O'Hare came back in and smiled, not in his glad-hand manner, and said, "I see you're admiring my kids."

"Nice-looking family."

"Separated from my wife. I'm getting married again, when . . . when everything's straightened out." He was behind the desk again, cleaning the gun. "I think my kids understand." He put the gun down and turned one of the photos to me: the boy, in a Naval uniform.

"He's a pilot," O'Hare said, beaming. And to himself: "I'd do about anything for Butch. Or Patricia Ann or Marilyn Jane, for that matter."

"Your secretary came in while you were out."

He looked up sharply; put his boy's picture back in place. "I didn't realize she was back from lunch."

"Well, she is, and said to tell you so."

"Oh. Anything else?"

I gestured back to the coat tree. "She was looking in your coat, for your car keys, she said."

Something like relief crossed his face. "Oh. There were some papers of hers in the car. Anyway, my keys weren't in my topcoat pockets."

"I gathered as much."

"It can wait." He stood; dropped the gun in his suitcoat pocket. "Let me get you back to the Loop."

"Mr. O'Hare—"

"Eddie."

"Mr. O'Hare, what is this, anyway? You haven't said two words to me about your pickpocket problem, and now you're hustling me back to the Loop."

He waved that off, getting into his black topcoat and fedora. "We'll talk in the car."

I got my own coat and hat and gloves on and followed him out. We entered directly onto the betting area, two rows of cashier's windows facing each other across a wide expanse of unpainted cement. No Oriental carpets here.

We rounded a corner and Patton was talking to another little man, pale, slight, bespectacled, conservatively dressed, and both men stopped talking as we approached, smiling and nodding at us.

"I won't be back in till tomorrow, Johnny," O'Hare said as we passed. And to the other man: "See you later, Les."

Les said, "See you later, E.J."

As we were going out onto Laramie Street, into the crisp overcast November afternoon, I said, "Who was that little guy?"

"The park's accountant."

"He looks familiar."

O'Hare said nothing, moving toward an expensive-looking, shiny black late-model Ford coupe.

"What's his name?" I asked.

"Les Shumway."

"Shumway." Familiar.

He unlocked the door for me on the rider's side and I climbed in. "Shumway," I said.

He got behind the wheel, started her up, pulled out onto Laramie. Awkwardly, he withdrew the automatic—a .32, I'd say—from his suitcoat under his topcoat and placed it on the seat between us.

"Wait a minute," I said. "That's not the same Shumway that testified against Capone, is it?"

O'Hare said nothing, glancing behind him as he drove. A railroad yard was on our left; Sportsman's Park stretched along our right.

"That's who it is, isn't it?" I said. "The accountant from the Hawthorne Smoke Shop who identified Capone as his boss? Without him, the feds couldn't have made their tax case."

"Yes, yes," O'Hare said, irritably.

"What's he doing working for you? Better still, what's he doing alive?"

"Les's a good man," O'Hare said, as if that explained it.

"Capone's getting out in a few days," I said. After seven years and some months. "He and Les'll have a lot to talk about. Old times and all."

"Capone's sick."

"So I hear," I said. "Syphilis. The papers say the docs gave 'im malaria, to induce a fever. Some cure."

We were in Cicero, now, having passed out of a thumb of Stickney that stuck into Cicero's pie; this was a working-class neighborhood of single-family dwellings, an occasional two-flat, mostly wood-frame structures.

"Never mind that," he said, looking nervously behind him. "We don't have all that much time."

"For what?"

"For me to tell you why I hired you."

"Oh. Somehow I figured it didn't really have much to do with picking pockets. But why the elaborate show in front of your secretary and everybody?"

We were passing by a nice little park, now. O'Hare turned right onto Ogden, which was a well-traveled four-lane thoroughfare, a diagonal street, making each major intersection a three-way one. For now, the railroad yard was on our left, more frame dwellings on our right. And lots of neighborhood bars. This was Cicero, after all.

"I don't know who I can trust," he explained. "Every person in my life, with the exception of my kids, is tainted by those hoodlums. Even my fiancée."

"Who's your fiancée?"

Vaguely sad, he said, "Sue Granata."

I'd seen her before; a beautiful young woman with dark blond hair and a brother who was a mob-owned state representative.

I said, "And you figure you can trust me?"

"You have that reputation. Also, we have a mutual friend."

"Besides Frank Nitti, you mean?"

"Besides Frank Nitti."

"Who, then?"

He looked back over his shoulder. Then he said, flatly, "Eliot Ness."

"How do you know Eliot?"

"I was his inside man with the Outfit."

I felt my jaw drop. "What?"

O'Hare had a faint, sneering smile. He was gripping the wheel like it was somebody's neck. "I've always detested the hoodlums I've been forced to deal with. Their loud dress, their bad grammar, their uncouth manners."

"Yeah, their grammar's always been one of my chief complaints against 'em."

"This is hardly amusing, Mr. Heller."

"What happened to 'Nate'?"

"Nate, then. All I ask is that you ride along with me, into the city, and listen to what I have to say."

"I'll listen, but I don't appreciate being brought out to your track on false pretenses."

He shook his head, the firm little chin contrasting with the quivering flab it rested on. "The security work for which I've retained you is legitimate. But I have a second job for you—a matter that must stay between just the two of us."

"I'm listening."

"Some years ago, I was a conduit of information for your friend Mr. Ness, as well as Frank Wilson and Elmer Irey."

Jesus. That was a laundry list of the federal agents credited with "getting" Capone.

"Then this *is* about Capone getting out," I said. "You're nervous he may've found out you were an informer."

"That is a part of it. And I've been told as much, that Capone's been making noise about me in Alcatraz. But I'm valuable to the Outfit, and am as powerful in my way as any of them." He sighed. "It's all rather complex. With Capone's release, various factions within the Outfit will be jockeying for position."

We were moving up over a tall traffic bridge, over the railroad yard; then we came down into Chicago, into a factory district.

"What do you want of me?" I asked him.

"I haven't been an . . . 'informer,' as you put it . . . in years. And my racing interests are quite legal, now. But recently federal agents have tried to contact me, left several messages at my office, asking for information about a small-time thief from my St. Louis days. Apparently somebody told them I'd be willing to talk. This comes at a very bad time indeed!"

We were in a residential area now; occasional bars, mom-and-pop groceries.

"With Capone's return imminent," I said, "it's a very bad time to be renewing your federal acquaintance. Say—the recent problems Billy Skidmore and Moe Annenberg have had with the feds could also be laid at your doorstep—"

Skidmore, scrap iron dealer and bailbondsman, had run afoul of the Internal Revenue boys; and Moe Annenberg's nationwide wire service—on Dearborn, around the corner from my office—had just been shut down for good.

"Precisely. And I had nothing to do with either. But I'm afraid some people suspect I may have."

"Oh?"

"I fear for my life, Nate. I'm being followed. I'm being watched. I've taken to staying in a secret little flat in a building I own on the North Side."

We crossed Pulaski and 22nd Street—renamed Cermak Road, though nobody seemed to call it that yet—into a commercial district. A black Ford coupe, a similar make to O'Hare's, pulled out from the curb and fell in behind us.

I said, "If it's a bodyguard you want, I'm not interested."

"That's not what I want of you. I wish that simple a remedy were called for. What I want is for you to go to them, the feds in question. Woltz and Bennett, their names are."

"I don't know 'em."

"Neither do I! But you're Ness's friend. He'll vouch for you."

"He's not a fed anymore; and he hasn't been in Chicago in years."

"I know, I know! He's in Cleveland, but he'd vouch for you, with them, wouldn't he? There's such a thing as telephones."

"Well, sure . . ."

"Tell them I'm not interested. Tell them *not* to call me. Tell them *not* to leave messages for me."

"Why don't you tell them?"

"I've had no direct contact with them as yet, and I want to keep it that way."

We were now in what had been Mayor Cermak's old turf—some of the storefronts even had lettering in Czech. I'd grown up not far from here, myself—we were just south of Jake Arvey's territory, where Czech gave way to Yiddish.

"Okay," I said. "I suppose I could do that."

"There's more. I want you to go to Frank Nitti and tell him what you've done."

"Huh?"

He was smiling and it was the oddest damn smile I ever saw: his upper lip was pulled back across his teeth in a display of smugness tinged with desperation. And what he said was everything his smile promised: "As if you're going behind my back, out of loyalty to him, you go to Nitti and tell him that somebody's trying to make it look like O'Hare's informing the feds, but that in fact O'Hare *isn't* informing, that he went so far as to instruct you to tell the feds he is *not* about to do *any* informing."

I hate it when people talk about themselves in the third person.

"Why don't you just go to Nitti yourself?"

"Coming from me, it would be dismissed as self-serving. I might be lying to him. Coming from you, without my knowledge, it can prove my loyalty."

We went under the El.

"Will you do it?"

"No."

"No?"

"I don't want anything to do with Nitti."

"Nitti likes you. He'll believe you. He respects you."

"I don't know that any of that is true. I've had dealings with him from time to time, and he's been friendly to me in his way, but I always wind up in the middle of something bloody."

He took one hand off the wheel and reached over and grasped my arm with it. "I'm being set up, Heller. Only somebody on the outside can save me."

I shook the arm off. "No."

"Name your retainer."

"No."

We crossed Kedzie into Douglas Park. I used to play here as a kid; I wondered if the lagoon was frozen over yet. Probably not.

"Five thousand. Five grand, Heller!"

Judas Priest. For running a couple of errands? Could I say no to that?

"No." I said. "No more Nitti. Five grand is five grand, but it ain't worth getting killed over. Now, pull over and let me out."

"Somebody's following me."

"I know. They have been since Twenty-second Street."

The park was empty of people; the faded green of it, its barren trees, leaves blown away, seemed oddly peaceful. O'Hare was picking up speed, going forty, now, and the Ford was a few car lengths behind, keeping right up.

"Do you have a gun?" he sputtered.

"In my desk drawer in my office, I do. Pull over."

"Use mine, then!"

"Okay."

I picked up his automatic and pointed it at him. "Pull over and let me out."

His cheeks were blood red. "I'm not stopping!"

I put the gun in his face.

He swallowed. "I'll slow down, but I'm not stopping!"

"I'll settle for that."

"At least leave me the gun!"

He slowed, I opened the door, stepped onto the running board, tossed the gun on the seat and dove for grass.

The other black coupe came roaring up, and then it was alongside of O'Hare, both cars going fifty at least, barreling through the park, and then a shotgun barrel extended from the rider's window of the coupe and blasted a hole in the driver's window of O'Hare's car, the roar of the gun and the crash of the glass fighting over who was loudest.

O'Hare swerved away from the other coupe, then back into it, nearly sideswiping them; they were riding the white center line of the four-lane street. I could see them, barely, two anonymous hoodlums in black hats and black coats in their black car with their black gun, which blew a second hole in O'Hare's window, and in him, too, apparently, for the fancy coupe careened out of control, lurched over the curb, sideswiping a light pole, its white globe shattering, and then shuttled down the streetcar tracks like a berserk sidecar and smashed into a trolley pole and stopped.

The other black Ford coupe cut its speed, stopping for a red light at Western. I couldn't make out the license plates, but they were Illinois. Then it moved nonchalantly on.

I was the first one to O'Hare's car. The window on the side I'd been sitting on was spiderwebbed from buckshot. I opened the door and there he was, slumped, hatless, the wheel of the car bent away from him, his eyes open and staring, lips parted as if about to speak, blood spattered everywhere, one hand tucked inside his jacket, like the Little General he'd patterned himself after, two baseball-size holes from close-up shotgun blasts in the driver's window just above him, like two more empty eyes, staring.

The .32 automatic was on the seat beside him.

I had to find a phone. Not to call the cops: some honest citizen would've beat me to it, by now.

I wanted to call Gladys and tell her if she hadn't already deposited O'Hare's check, drop everything and do it.

10

The two dicks from the detective bureau knew who I was, and called my name in to Captain Stege. So I ended up having to hang around waiting for Stege to show up, as did everybody else, four uniformed officers, the two detective bureau dicks, a police photographer, somebody from the coroner's office, three guys with the paddy wagon that O'Hare would be hauled off to the nearby morgue in. The captain wanted to see the crime scene, including poor old Eddie O'Hare, who accordingly had spent the past forty-five minutes of this cold afternoon a virtual sideshow attraction for the gawkers who'd gathered around the wrecked car, which was crumpled against a trolley pole like a used paper cup. Ogden is a busy street; and several residential areas were close by, as was Mt. Sinai Hospital, a pillar covering the corner of California and Ogden. So there were plenty of gawkers.

Lieutenant Phelan, a gray-complected man in his forties, asked me some questions and took some notes, but it was pretty perfunctory. Phelan knew that Stege would take over, where questioning me was concerned. Stege and me went way back.

The captain was an exception to the Chicago rule: he was an honest cop. He'd helped nail Capone—his raid on the Hawthorne Smoke Shop, where O'Hare's accountant Les Shumway had once worked, provided the feds with the ledgers that allowed them to make their income tax case against the Big Fellow. Later Stege (rhymes with "leggy," which he wasn't, being just a shade taller than a fireplug) had been the head of the special Dillinger Squad.

His one bad break was getting unfairly tarnished in the Jake Lingle affair. Lingle, a *Tribune* reporter gunned down gangland style in the pedestrian tunnel under Michigan Avenue, had been thick with both Al Capone and the police commissioner—the latter being the bloke who appointed Stege chief of the Detective Bureau. Guilt by association lost Stege that job. And being even vaguely linked to Capone was a bitter pill for one of the Chicago PD's few good men.

But that was almost ten years ago. Now he was the grand old man of the force, a favorite of the Chicago press when an expert quote on the latest headline crime was needed.

There was a time when Stege despised me. He had me pegged as a crooked cop, which was true to a point but by Chicago standards I was a piker; all I did was give some false testimony at the Lingle trial (in return for a promotion to plainclothes), so the patsy the mob and the D.A.'s office selected could take the fall and put a sensational story that refused to die in the press finally to rest.

Plus, I'd later testified, truthfully, against Miller and Lang, the late Mayor Cermak's two police bodyguards who had attempted to assassinate Frank Nitti for His Honor, and failed (which Nitti's hit on Cermak, less than two months later, had not). Testifying against those cops, dirty as they were, still made two black marks against me with Stege: I'd embarrassed the department publicly; and I'd tarnished the martyr Cermak's memory. Stege, you see, had been a Cermak crony.

Still, in recent years, Stege seemed to have earned a grudging respect for me. We'd bumped heads in the Dillinger case and a few times after and found, despite ourselves, we often saw eye to eye. Considering how much shorter he was than me, that was an accomplishment. Anyway, he no longer seemed to despise me.

Or that's what I thought, until I saw the look on his face when he climbed out of the chauffeured black-and-white squad car, which had come up with siren screaming, as if there was any rush where O'Hare was concerned.

Stege was a stocky, white-haired little man with a doughy face and black-rim glasses. He looked like an ineffectual owl. Looks can be deceiving.

"Heller, you lying goddamn son of a bitch," he said, striding over on short legs to where I stood, on the grass, away from the gawkers and the crumpled car and dead Eddie O'Hare. He wore a topcoat as gray as the overcast afternoon and a shapeless brown hat and half of a grayish-brown cigar was stuck in the corner of his tight mouth. He poked my chest with a short, thick finger not much longer than the cigar. "You're out of business. You overstepped yourself this time, you cagey bastard. You're going to jail."

"I'm glad to see you're keeping an open mind," I said.

"Stay," he said, as if to a dog, pointing to the ground where I stood.

He went over and had a lingering look at O'Hare. Then he allowed the paddy-wagon cops to pull the body out of the car onto a sheet. Lieutenant Phelan bent down and frisked the corpse; emptied its pockets. I couldn't make out the contents from where I stood. The crowd was wide-eyed as the cops wrapped the body in the sheet and tossed him in the paddy wagon with a *thunk* and, with no more ceremony than that, Edward J. O'Hare exited public life.

The car had already been searched; I'd seen Phelan find a steno pad in the glove box of the car—O'Hare's secretary's steno pad, perhaps? Had that been the "papers" she wanted to get out of his car? At any rate, Phelan was showing the pad to Stege, who was thumbing through it; he stopped at a page and read, then glanced over at me.

Stege came over and said, "Give me your story from the top."

"O'Hare approached me to handle a security matter at Sportsman's Park," I said. "He had a pickpocket problem there. I went out today and had a look at his plant. Then he offered to drive me into the Loop and I took him up on it."

"That's it? That's your story?"

"Every word is true, Captain."

"A witness—a guy who was painting windowsills on a ladder over on Talman Avenue—saw the whole thing. And he says you jumped from the car, seconds before this went down."

I'd seen a guy in work clothes being questioned, earlier, by Phelan. I'd noticed them looking over at me, too, so this revelation came as no real surprise.

"Yes I did jump from the car. I noticed we were being followed, and I noticed too that the car behind us was picking up speed. I asked O'Hare to let me out, he refused, and I jumped."

Stege grimaced; then he spoke, with a formality filtered through sarcasm: "And what made you think the car following you presented a danger great enough for you to risk injury by jumping from a moving vehicle?"

I nodded over at the wreck that had been O'Hare's car. "Gee, I don't know, Captain. For the life of me."

His cigar was out; he looked at it, as irritated with it as with me, and hurled it off into the park. Then a stubby finger was pointing at me again: "You jumped because you knew they were going to shoot O'Hare."

"It was a reasonable assumption on my part."

"That's all it was? An assumption?"

"O'Hare was acting jumpy, nervous. He was cleaning a gun in his office this afternoon, when I went to see him. He had it on the seat next to him while we drove."

"And why is that?"

"Haven't you heard, Captain? Al Capone is getting out of jail in a few days. Not that he would ever think of having a respected community leader like E. J. O'Hare murdered . . ."

Stege reflected on that for a moment. More to himself than me, he said, glancing over at O'Hare's smashed car, "There's no one on earth Capone wouldn't send to his death if he thought his interests would be served."

I shrugged. "I've heard rumors O'Hare was an informant, and that Capone's known about it for some time."

He didn't confirm or deny that; his putty face looked at me blankly, only the hard dark blue eyes behind the round dark rims of his glasses betraying his dislike for me as he said, pointing at me again, less forcefully now, "You fingered him."

"What?"

"You fingered O'Hare. You set him up, I was right about you the first time; you *are* a bent cop."

"I'm a private bent cop, I'll have you know."

"You've been known to have audiences with Nitti himself. Are you still for sale, after all these years? Are you Nitti's man, now?"

"I kind of like to think of myself as my own man, Captain. Are you going to charge me with anything, or maybe just haul me into the basement of the nearest precinct house and feed me the goldfish for a few hours?"

Red came to the white face. "I wouldn't waste a good rubber hose on you."

"You could always use a lead pipe. Can I go?"

He was lighting up another cigar, the wind catching the flame of his match and making it dance. "You can go," he said flatly. Puffing. Pointing the cigar at me, now. "But I'm going to investigate this killing myself, personally. And if you were Nitti's finger man in this nasty little episode, you'll spend Christmas in the Bridewell, and eternity at Joliet. That's a promise."

"That's funny. It sounded like a threat. What did it say in that steno pad?"

"What?"

"The steno pad. It's O'Hare's secretary's steno pad, right? Her name's Cavaretta. I don't know her first name."

The hard blue eyes squinted at me from behind the owlish glasses. "It's Antoinette. Toni."

"I see. Did she take notes on O'Hare's visit to my office yesterday?"

His lips were pressed together so tight, it was a shock when they parted enough to emit: "Yes."

"And does it confirm my story about O'Hare wanting some pickpocket work done?"

"Yes. Very conveniently, too."

He was right about that. Was the steno pad left there on purpose, to explain away my presence? To let the cops tie off the loose end called Heller?

"You met this Cavaretta woman?" he asked.

"A couple of times, yes. Briefly."

"Any impressions?"

I shrugged. "Handsome woman. Pretty hard-looking, though. Calculating."

"What makes you say that?"

"Just an impression. She's in her mid- to late thirties but she isn't married. Yet she's not bad looking. Nice shape on her."

"By which you mean to imply what?"

I shrugged again. "A dago gal from the West Side working for somebody like O'Hare, unmarried. She must be somebody's sister or mistress or something. Both, maybe."

Stege was nodding. "I'll keep that in mind when I question her."

"You see this as something Capone ordered from inside, Captain?"

He looked over at the wreck again. "Well, it's more Capone's style than Nitti's."

"True. Nitti doesn't like to fill the headlines with blood."

"Nitti would've arranged it much less spectacular," Stege agreed. "Nitti has more finesse. His boys would've taken Mr. O'Hare at their leisure and dumped him in a spot from whence he would not emerge, till Gabriel blew his horn."

The crowd was thinning. With O'Hare gone, there was nothing much to see but the wreck. Some reporters had arrived, but Phelan was holding them off.

I said, "This does seem a strange place for a hit to go down. A major thoroughfare like Ogden, with Cook County Jail a stone's throw away, ditto for the Audy detention home for juvies. There's always cops all over this area."

"Imported killers," Stege said, nodding again. "Local boys wouldn't have done this this way."

Stege was right, although I failed to point out that using out-of-town help was the way Nitti usually went, when he veered from his normal low-profile use of force. It helped keep the heat off the Outfit, if the killers were seen as out-of-towners, where their actions could be written off as having been the bidding of Eastern gangsters.

"It's the Maloy hit all over again," Stege said suddenly.

"By God, you're right," I said. It hadn't occurred to me.

Tommy Maloy, the movie projectionists' union boss, had been driving one February afternoon in 1935 on Lake Shore Drive just opposite the abandoned buildings of the World's Fair, when two men in a car drew up alongside his, poked a shotgun out the window and blasted the driver's window, blowing a hole in it, then blasted again, blowing a hole in the driver.

"That was supposed to be imported talent, too," I said.

Stege studied me for a moment, then, impulsively, he took something from his pocket and showed it to me, saying, "What do you make of this?"

It was a memo. It read: *Mr. Woltz phoned and he wants to know if you know anything about Clyde Nimerick. He said you are to call Mr. Bennett*. It was signed *Toni*. The secretary had graceful, feminine handwriting; but there was strength in it, too.

"Where did you find this?" I asked.

"In his topcoat pocket."

Talk about convenient. "There's your motive."

"Yes," Stege nodded. "Woltz and Bennett are FBI agents. And Clyde Nimerick is a small-timer from O'Hare's shyster days in St. Louis. A bank robber."

"So O'Hare was up to his informing tricks again, and the Outfit rubbed him out."

"Or some St. Louis hoodlums connected to Nimerick did."

It was a setup, of course. Another sweet setup with Nitti's crafty name all over it. O'Hare hadn't been informing again; but Nitti, for some reason, had wanted to make it look like he was. Five'll get you ten Toni Cavaretta had planted that note in O'Hare's topcoat pocket, in front of me, when she pretended to be looking for his keys. To bring O'Hare's federal connection out in the open.

I didn't mention any of this to Stege. It just wasn't any of my business. At least it wasn't any business that I wanted to be mine.

"You know what else he had on him?" Stege asked, smiling humorlessly. "A crucifix, a religious medallion, and a rosary."

"Sounds like he was getting his house in order."

Stege shook his head, flicked cigar ash to the grass. "Here's a guy who owns a yacht, who's got an ocean villa, a four-hundred-acre farm, a house like a palace in Glencoe, and your occasional spare penthouse on the side. Who hangs around at the Illinois Athletic Club with the sporting crowd and the money boys. Who chums with judges and mayors and governors and respected people. Who says publicly he will have no truck with gangsters and yet he's in bed with 'em and ends up this way."

"Welcome to Chicago, Captain."

He smiled again, just a little. Then it faded. His eyes became slits. "Were you part of this, Heller?"

"No."

"I'd like to believe you."

"Go right ahead and believe me, then."

"Would you like a ride back to your office?"

"Please."

He jerked a thumb over his shoulder. "You can catch the El at Western and Eighteenth."

I did.

11

It was after six when I got back to the office, and everybody was gone for the day. I found a stack of memos Gladys had left on my desk, all of them calls that had come in in the late afternoon, in the aftermath of the O'Hare shooting, from reporters wanting a statement. I made a big wad out of them and dropped it in the circular file. Then I fished my keys out of my pocket and unlocked the bottom left-hand drawer of my desk and got out the automatic, the nine-millimeter Browning I'd had since my police days, all tangled up in its shoulder holster. I untangled the gun, took it out of the holster, put it on the desk; then I got out of my topcoat, slipped off my suitcoat, slung on the holster, sat and cleaned and oiled the gun like O'Hare had before me, an irony not lost on me I assure you, loaded it, stood, put on my suitcoat, put on my topcoat, slid the gun not under my arm but into my deep right-hand topcoat pocket, keeping my hand on the gun, rose from my desk and locked up and left.

It was dark now. A cold, nearly freezing rain was spitting at me; I kept my hand in my pocket gripping the gun. I felt tired—the evening may have been young, but the day and I felt old. Cutting down Plymouth, I thought for a moment about stopping in at Binyon's, a favorite restaurant of mine that fortune had put just around the corner from my office. I was hungry enough, despite what I'd witnessed; being close to death doesn't necessarily kill your appetite—matter of fact, it can make you appreciate life all the more, including such simple, taken-for-granted pleasures as good eats.

Instead I walked on to the Morrison, going in the main entrance on Madison, through the plush lobby with its high ceiling and inlaid marble and dark wood and overstuffed furniture and potted plants. To the left was a bank of elevators, but I stopped first at the marble-and-bronze check-in desk.

"Any messages?" I asked the assistant manager, a pockmarked young man named Williams, whose neatly tended slick black hair and tiny mustache complemented his pointlessly superior attitude.

"That's an understatement," he said, with more disgust than humor. He turned to his wall of boxes and withdrew a fat handful of notes; I glanced at them—phone messages from reporters. Davis of the *Daily News* had called half a dozen times, alone. Some journalistic joker, frustrated in not reaching me it would seem, had left the name Westbrook Pegler. Very funny. Pegler, of course, was a star columnist for Hearst, and hadn't worked the Chicago beat in years.

I pushed the stack back at Williams, said, "Toss those for me, would you?"

His tiny mustache twitched with momentary displeasure, but he did it.

"And hold all my calls," I said. "Unless it's somebody from my office—that would be my secretary or my two operatives."

He jotted their names down; at least he was efficient. Then he smirked at me. "I suppose you realize you have a guest."

"A guest?"

"Yes," he said, a little surprised that I was surprised. "An attractive woman. She said she was a friend and I gave her a key."

My right hand was still in my pocket, gripping the automatic; with my left I pointed a finger at him like a gun, almost touching his nose. His eyes involuntarily crossed for a moment, trying to focus on the finger.

"Never do that," I said.

"Well, I'm sorry . . . I just assumed . . ."

"Never let anybody in my room. Never give anybody my key."

"She's a very attractive woman, Mr. Heller. She said she was a friend, a close friend."

"Never do that. Never let anybody in my room. Never give anybody my key."

I was still pointing the finger at him.

He swallowed, his mouth obviously gone dry on him. "I assure you it will never happen again."

"Good."

I got on the nearest elevator; I wasn't alone: in addition to the red-uniformed operator, there was a mustached midget in a gaudy yellow suit. The little man was smoking a big cigar and reading *Variety*. He got off on the fourteenth floor, and, when he was gone, the operator, a Swedish kid, said, "He's a World's Fair midget." And I said, "What?" And the operator said, "He's a World's Fair midget. We have a troop of forty-five of them visiting from the New York World's Fair. Appearing in town someplace." I said, "Oh."

He took me up to the tower. The Morrison was the tallest hotel in the city, its main building twenty-one stories high, a nineteen-story tower sitting on top of that. My suite (which is to say my apartment) number was 2324. The operator let me off at the twenty-third floor and I walked toward a room that almost certainly had an uninvited somebody waiting inside for me.

Probably not the attractive woman, though. Who wasn't my girlfriend, or even *a* girlfriend, because I hadn't been seeing anybody lately. Most probably this dish was sent to con a key out of the clerk, said key then being turned over to a male accomplice or accomplices with a gun or guns. And that's who'd be waiting for me inside my room.

So, the Outfit considered me a stray thread from this afternoon; well, I didn't feel like getting picked off.

I could have called the cops, or the house dick, but fuck it, I was a cop, I was a dick, and I had a gun and this was my apartment and the goddamn Outfit, goddamn Nitti who was supposed to have all this respect for me, had very nearly killed me this afternoon. If I hadn't hopped out of that car, I'd be as dead as O'Hare right now. Deader.

So I got out my keys and I got out my gun and I worked the key in the door and when I swung it open, I was down low, lower to the ground than that goddamn midget, and I was pointing the gun directly into the sitting room of my small suite, where Sally Rand was sitting on my couch reading *Collier's*.

Sally had the biggest blue eyes in creation, but they were bigger right now than I'd ever seen them; she had her long light blond hair back in a bun and was wearing a light blue blouse and a darker blue skirt and silk stockings and she'd kicked off her heels and made herself at home, already.

I hadn't seen her in over five years.

"Some greeting, Heller," she said.

I let out a major sigh. Stood and shut the door behind me and latched it and tossed my gun, lightly, on an easy chair nearby.

"I had kind of a rough day," I said, slipping out of the topcoat, tossing it on another chair. The room we were in wasn't large, though there was a kitchenette at the far end by a window overlooking North Clark Street; the walls were papered in yellow and tan stripes, like a faded tiger. There was a console radio, a servidor, a standing bookcase.

And Sally.

She wasn't a large woman, and, as I stood before her, she looked almost like a child sitting there, a child who'd tried to please and now was afraid of being scolded.

"I didn't think you'd mind," she said. "I flirted with the desk clerk and he gave me a key."

"That answers a mystery I hadn't been able to solve," I said.

"What's that?"

"Whether that guy likes girls or not."

She smiled, now, her wide, unabashed smile, and she stood slowly, smoothing her dress, shoulders back so that I could see how nice her body still was, as if there was any doubt, and she said, "Why don't you kiss me?"

"Why don't I?" I said.

And I took her in my arms.

She was such a sweet fit, in my arms, Sally was. She was a sweet fit elsewhere, as well.

But that had been a long time ago, and the spontaneous kiss at first reminded us how well we'd known each other once but by the time we broke our clinch we remembered how very long it had been, and then it was awkward, then we were sitting next to each other wondering what to say next.

I broke the ice. "What in hell are you doing here?"

"You're such a sweet talker, Heller."

"I'm known for my smooth line with the ladies. It's great to see you again. It's wonderful. That goes without saying."

"No it doesn't. Say it."

"It's great to see you again. It's wonderful."

"That's better." She leaned over and up and kissed me again, softly, briefly. But comfortably.

"It's been over five years, Helen."

Her smile turned into something sad. "It must be," she said. "Because it's been at least that long since anybody called me Helen."

She'd been born Helen Beck; when I'd met her, in the summer of '34, when she hired me to check up on a would-be suitor, I'd taken to calling her by her real name, at least some of the time. In bed, for example.

She laughed a little. Not much humor in it. "Even my mother calls me 'Sally' now."

"Well, you're a famous girl."

"I'm not really a girl, anymore."

"You could've fooled me."

"I'm a woman past thirty, Heller. Never mind how far past thirty."

"Yeah, you're a wreck all right."

Now the smile went crinkly. "Stop it, you. I'm . . . well preserved; it's my job to be. But I do have a few miles on me."

"Don't we all."

She did look her age, though, close up at least; I was sure with makeup and lighting, on stage, from a distance, she still looked like the Sally Rand who was the hit of the Chicago World's Fair in the summer of '33 (with her fan dance) and '34 as well (with her bubble dance). She was still a top box-office draw, although she hadn't played Chicago in some time.

Anyway, she looked her age, but a beautiful woman of, say, thirty-five who looks thirty-five is hardly over the hill. In fact, one of the oddities about being in my thirties myself was that women about my age seemed more attractive to me now than the sweet young things.

"Why the gun?" she asked, a little concerned, nodding over at the automatic that was sitting on the chair.

"It's a long story," I said.

"I like long stories."

I told her about O'Hare. Unlike my report to Stege, I told her everything. The summer I'd spent with her had been a rough one—I'd been involved in the Dillinger case up to my ass, and she'd seen some of the rough stuff go down, or anyway saw the aftermath of the rough stuff, and had taken it in stride. She was a tough cookie, Sally, without being hard; and she was a good sounding board, had helped me figure some things out. She was smarter than me, I'd discovered. Probably still was.

"Frank Nitti," she said, shaking her head. "After all this time. You told me you intended to steer clear of him, for once and forever."

I shrugged. "It's his town. In my line, I'm bound to bump up against his interests from time to time."

"He almost bumped up against *you*, this time."

"You're telling me. He told me he owed me one, once. Maybe he forgot the debt." I thought back. "Or maybe he remembered I forgave it without exacting payment."

The wide eyes narrowed. "You thought Nitti might have sent someone here, to your hotel suite, to . . . ?"

Another shrug. "Definite possibility."

"Why?" she said, indignantly. "What did *you* do?"

"I spent time alone with O'Hare just before he died. They may think he told me something damaging, something I could carry to the cops or the papers."

"You talked to Captain Stege already, didn't you? And told him nothing?"

"Yeah. And Tubbo Gilbert will see Stege's report, and Tubbo will tell the Outfit that I either don't know anything, or chose to keep my mouth shut. And the morning papers will show I haven't talked to the press. So if I can just last the night, I may be all right."

She slipped her arm in mine; sat very close to me. "We'll just stay inside your cozy little place, then, just you and me. Have you had supper?"

"No."

"I checked your Frigidaire. All you have is eggs and beer and half a loaf of bread. Is there an all-night grocery I could slip out to, and . . ."

"You know what I'd like, Helen? One of those breakfasts you used to make me. Nobody makes an omelet better than Sally Rand."

"You're right. It's not exactly what I'm famous for, but you're right."

Soon she was serving me half of a big fluffy omelet, serving herself the other half—like the Kingfish says on "Amos 'n' Andy," she even gave me the "bigges'" half; she also toasted up some bread and managed to round up some butter somewhere. We drank beer out of glasses. Real elegant like.

We were midway through the meal when I finally asked her again.

"Helen, what the hell are you doing here? I saw your bags near the bedroom door as I came in."

She ate some eggs. Between bites, blandly, she said, "I'm bankrupt."

"What?"

"I've gone bankrupt. It'll be in the papers soon enough."

"That's crazy. You're one of the top nightclub draws in the country!"

She nodded. "Right after Sophie Tucker and Harry Richman. And nobody can touch me in vaudeville and the picture houses."

"So what happened?"

She cocked her head; it was a shrug of sorts, but her expression was reflective, the big blue eyes searching. "Got too big for my britches, I guess."

"Helen, you don't wear any britches in your business."

Now her smile was wistful. "You should've taken me up on my offer that time, and been my business partner. You're more conservative than I am. You'd have stopped me."

"Stopped you from what?"

"Overdoing. Maybe you heard, I put together a thing called Sally Rand's Nude Ranch. We played the San Diego and Forth Worth fairs. Set record gates at both. Then for this San Francisco Exposition—which is trying to compete with the New York World's Fair, you know—I went all out. Top-flight costumes, lighting, scenery, the works. Built and paid for my own buildings to house the show. Hired forty girls. Overextended myself."

"It could happen to anyone."

She shook her head. "Never thought it would happen to me. I have the reputation of being a savvy businesswoman, you know. Me and my shows have generated over three million bucks' worth of business, the past six years, starting with the Century of Progress. I was making forty-five hundred a week, not so long ago."

Her weekly wage was a yearly wage many men would've killed for. And here she was broke.

We'd finished eating now, but we stayed at the table. City lights winked at us through the adjacent window. She pushed the plates aside and reached out and held my hands in hers. "I had to let my girls go," she said, as if apologizing to them through me. "I have to start over, as a single. The natural place to do that is Chicago, I got the right connections, I could find a top club easy enough. But I couldn't even afford a room while I went about it."

"So you thought of me."

"I thought of you. Oh, I had a room lined up with a girl who used to be in my chorus line at the City of Paris, but it fell through 'cause she suddenly shacked up with some guy. Which recalled that summer when you were sleeping in a Murphy bed in your office, and how on so many nights you slept with me instead in my soft round bed in that fancy-ass suite at the Drake. I thought maybe you'd return me the favor."

I nodded toward the small sitting room. "This isn't exactly your suite at the Drake."

"No, but it'll do quite nicely, thanks. You do seem to be doing well, Nate. Business is good?"

"It's good. I don't make forty-five hundred a week for dancing in my nothin' at all, but . . ."

"Neither do I, at the moment. And maybe I won't be able to. I wasn't appearing with the revue, you know."

"Sally Rand herself wasn't in Sally Rand's Nude Ranch?"

"No. I staged and directed and, obviously, financed the show. But I wasn't in it. I'm getting older."

"You're afraid you won't be able to make a comeback, huh?"

"A little."

"You know what I think?"

"What?"

"I think you'll still be strutting around in your birthday suit when I'm in the old-age home. Looking good, and getting paid the same way."

"You're sweet. You never married, Nate?"

"Not yet. I've had a few close calls."

Her smile was tinged with sadness again. "Like me, for instance?"

"Like you, for instance. You aren't married, are you, Sally?"

"Other than to my work? No. And I wish you'd keep calling me Helen."

"I think I can manage that."

Somebody knocked at the door.

"Get on the floor," I told her.

"Don't be silly."

"Do it! Get under that table."

She made a face but she did it.

I got up and got the automatic and unlatched the door and, standing to one side of it, reached over and flung it open.

And shoved my gun right in the chest of a short but massive man in a brown suit and hat; the eyes in the lumpy face were dark and cold and unimpressed. He had an envelope in his hand, and, while I sensed he might be playing messenger, he sure wasn't Western Union.

I was pointing my automatic at Louis "Little New York" Campagna. Frank Nitti's right-hand man. A powerful man in every sense of the word—a killer who had moved up the ranks into management in the business of crime.

I backed off, but my gun was still pointed at him.

"That's something you don't want to do," he said, pointing a finger at me gently. His finger seemed far more menacing than my gun.

I lowered the gun but kept it in hand. I did not ask him in.

I said, "I was almost killed today."

"I know. That's why I'm here." He handed me the envelope.

I took it; I peeked out into the hall, to see if he was alone. He seemed to be.

"Put the rod away," he said, "and look in the envelope."

I let some air out. I stuck the gun in my waistband and looked in the unsealed envelope. Ten fifty-dollar bills. Five hundred dollars.

"Is this what Nitti thinks my life's worth?" I said. Anger made my voice tremble. Fear, too.

"No," he said. "Who could put a price on a life?"

"Some people do it everyday."

He lifted his shoulders and set them down again. "Some people put a price on death. That's different."

Now I was arguing semantics with Little New York Campagna. Well, it's an interesting life.

"Frank would like to thank you for showing such good sense," he said, "where the cops was concerned."

Tubbo had acted fast.

"And if you could keep your story simple for the papers, Frank would be grateful. Can you manage that?"

He touched his hat by way of bidding me good-bye and started off.

I stepped out into the hall. "Don't you want my answer?" I said. Stupid question.

Campagna turned back and smiled at me; it was like a crack in a stone wall. "I got your answer. I got your number, too, Heller." He turned and walked away. Then he turned back and, almost reluctantly, said, "Uh, Frank said to say he's pleased you are still amongst us."

"Well. Thank Frank for his concern."

"Sure. Beats being dead, don't it?"

And then he was gone.

I shut the door, latched it, put the gun back on the chair. Seemed as good a place as any.

Sally crawled out from under the table, straightening her clothes. "Sounds like you're going to be okay, where the boys are concerned."

"Sounds like," I nodded, tentatively. "Campagna isn't an errand boy, anymore. Sending him was a gesture from Nitti of how serious he takes this."

"Is that a good sign or bad?"

"You got me. Look, Sally. Helen. You're welcome to stay. You're most very welcome to stay. But there's no, uh, rent here. No strings. No obligations. By which I mean to say, you're welcome to my bed and I'll sleep out here on the couch."

"Shut up," she said, and began unbuttoning her blouse.

12

I didn't make it into the office the next morning till almost ten-thirty. We'd had another breakfast, Sally and I, and I don't mean anything racy by that: simply that I bought her some breakfast, this time, in the Morrison's coffee shop. And we sat drinking orange juice and putting pancakes away and then cup upon cup of coffee as we filled each other in on our lives for the past five years. Then she noticed the time and remembered she had an eleven o'clock appointment with the manager of the Brown Derby and was off.

And I walked to the office, where Gladys greeted me, if "greeted" is the word, with a disgusted expression and a hand outthrust with another stack of memos.

"Reporters," I asked, only it wasn't really a question.

"Reporters," she said. She had on a pale blue blouse and a navy skirt with a wide black patent leather belt and was everything a man could want in a woman except friendly. "Do you realize Westbrook Pegler's been trying to call you?"

"Yeah, right," I said. I went on through to my office.

I was sitting behind the desk, glancing at some insurance adjusting reports that Gladys had typed neatly up, when herself was standing in the doorway—never leaning, that wasn't her style—and saying, "He really has been calling. Three times already today."

"Who?"

"Westbrook Pegler! The columnist!"

"Gladys, my dear, you're mistaken—you've apparently never read him. Pegler's no Red."

She did a slow burn. "I said columnist, not communist."

I kept trolling for a sense of humor with the girl and coming up old rubber tires.

"My dear," I started again, and she reminded me humorlessly that she wasn't my dear. She reminded me further that she preferred "Miss Andrews," to which I replied, "Gladys—that's Hal Davis of the *Daily News* calling, needling me."

"Are you sure?"

"Why would Westbrook Pegler be in Chicago, for Christ's sakes, and if he was, why would he be calling about some Chicago racetrack tycoon getting pushed?"

"Pushed?"

She hadn't been affiliated with the detective business long.

"Killed," I explained. "Shot. Rubbed out. Liquidated. Mob style."

"If you say so," she said, disinterested but lingering.

"Shoo. Go file."

"Yes, Mr. Heller."

God, what I wouldn't have given for even some *sarcasm* out of that kid. She was cute as lace panties but not nearly so much fun.

A client kept an eleven o'clock appointment, the office manager from the Swift Plant; he was white collar, but he brought the fragrance of the stockyards with him. He had a recurring pilferage problem—desks, lockers, cabinets forced open, pocketbooks gotten into. I explained how we could plant valuable articles in obvious places, as decoys to invite theft, articles to which thief-branding dyes would be applied. I was explaining how I preferred dry dyes of the sort that didn't immediately stain, but that perspiration would soon bring out, when Gladys leaned in and interrupted.

"He's here."

It wasn't like her to interrupt; most unbusinesslike.

"Who?" I said.

"Mr. Pegler."

I shook my head, smiled; Gladys hadn't met Davis yet. "Tell him to go to hell."

"I will not."

"Then tell him it'll cost him a C-note if he wants a quote. That'll get rid of him."

She pursed her lips; she wasn't blowing me a kiss. "What is a C-note?"

"A hundred dollars. Go."

She went.

"Excuse me," I said to my client. "Where were we?"

"Dry dyes," the stockyard office manager said, looking bewildered.

The door flew open and I could hear Gladys saying, "Please," and a big red-faced man was in the doorway. I yanked the automatic out from under my arm and yelled, "Up with 'em!"

Gladys screamed, the office manager dropped to the floor and the big man's face whitened. He swallowed, thickly. He was very well dressed; double-breasted gray pinstripe suit with stylish wide lapels, a flourish of a hanky in his breast pocket, a wide, thick-knotted, dark blue tie patterned with white abstract shapes. He put his hands slowly in the air, narrowing his eyes, which hid under shaggy, cultivated-to-points satanic eyebrows.

"Put that ridiculous thing away," he said. The words were strong, but the tenor voice had something of a quaver. The voice wasn't as big as the man, that's all there was to it.

I came around the desk, saying, "Just keep 'em up," and patted him down. He stood for the frisk, but scowled all the while. He had on heavy, masculine lotion; pine needles.

He was clean. Which is to say no weapon, but also well tailored and freshly bathed. This guy had money and I didn't think it came from the rackets. Not of the Nitti variety, anyway.

"Who the hell are you?" I asked, lowering the gun but not putting it away.

"Who the hell do you think? Westbrook Pegler!"

"Oh." Now I was swallowing. "I'll be damned if I don't think you are." I turned to the stockyards office manager who was crouching on the floor, looking up like a big bug. "We about had our business taken care of, didn't we, Mr. Mertz?"

He got up, brushing himself off, said, "Yes," and I told him my secretary would call him and set up an on-site meeting with one of my operatives as he scurried out. I closed the door on Gladys's pretty, glowering face.

"Won't you sit down, Mr. Pegler?"

"I'm not sure I'm staying. I'm not delighted with having guns pointed at me."

"But then, who is? Please," I said, smiling nervously, pulling up a chair for him.

He cleared his throat, in a grumbling manner, and sat and I got behind the desk. Slipped the gun away, under my shoulder, feeling embarrassed and trigger-happy.

"Mind if I smoke?" he asked.

"Not at all."

He took a gold, FWP-emblazoned case from his inside suitcoat pocket and a cigarette from the case and lit it up and I pushed the ashtray his way, saying, "This wasn't a story I expected someone of your stature to be interested in covering."

"What story is that?"

"The O'Hare shooting."

"Oh. Afraid I just glanced at the headlines, this morning; he was a racetrack promoter, wasn't he? Why, were you involved in that?"

"If I might explain," I said, and briefly I told him about yesterday's incident, and my fears about mob retaliation and my reluctance to talk to any newshound.

"I didn't believe for a minute that Westbrook Pegler had called me," I said.

"Admittedly Chicago isn't my beat," he granted. "But they do carry my column here."

That they did. I often read Pegler, who was basically one of those journalistic attack dogs who latched onto whichever side of an issue grabbed him by the seat of the pants. He was the king of the "meatball" journalists, always on whichever side was the most entertaining and/or controversial, the side most likely to get the loudest cheers, or boos, from the grandstand. You couldn't peg Pegler for the left or the right, politically; one day he was praising a lynch party for ridding the world of a killer, and the next he was bemoaning poverty in the slums. Champion of the underdog, on Monday, he might be defender of the rich, on Tuesday.

"Do you know a man named Willie Bioff?" he asked.

Willie Bioff? Why in hell would Westbrook Pegler be asking about that fat little creep?

"I used to," I said.

"What do you know of him?"

I shrugged. "He used to be a pimp. He was a union slugger, too. He's still involved in union organizing, isn't he?"

"That's an understatement. Ostensibly, he's the bodyguard of a man named George Browne. In reality, he runs . . ." And here he paused, in order to spit each of the following words out like distasteful seeds: ". . . the International Alliance of Theatrical Stage Employees."

"The Stagehands Union," I nodded. "Yeah, I know Browne. He's a drunk, and a blowhard. But when you prop him up he can make a speech and get the rank and file stirred up. He's got patriotism and mom and apple pie and ten other kinds of baloney, for any occasion."

"But you see him as a figurehead."

"Yeah, sure. Bioff's been the brains behind Browne for a long, long time. They say Browne drinks a hundred bottles of beer a day. He better have *somebody's* brains behind him."

Pegler drew on the cigarette; smiled a little. Just being polite, I thought. He said, "I met . . . or rather, encountered Willie Bioff once, many years ago. 1913, I'd say. That was the last time I worked a Chicago beat steadily. My father was the star rewrite man for the *American,* at the time, and they took me on as a favor to him."

"You must've just been a kid."

"Seventeen," he said, his elaborate shrug not masking his pride. "And working for the United Press at the same time. I may live in the East, Mr. Heller, but I'm of the Chicago school of journalism. The New York school represents . . ." And these words, too, were distasteful seeds to spit. ". . . ethics and manners. Reporters on rival papers actually cooperated with each other in gathering facts when working on the same story." The thought of it was beyond him, and he smiled as he described the Chicago school: "We, on the other hand, sanctioned the commission of any crime short of burglary in pursuit of an exclusive, and wouldn't've helped a rival reporter if he was bleeding in the street. Ha! We fought and tricked and, to be honest about it, hated each other."

He seemed lost in nostalgia; what this had to do with Willie Bioff or George Browne, or Nathan Heller, for that matter, was lost on me.

Then he answered my unasked question: "I saw Bioff when I was covering the police stations and police courts. I did a little bit of everything in those days—chased fires, took pictures, held down City Hall on weekends, where I lost at poker to the likes of Ben Hecht and Jake Lingle. The Harrison Street police court was perhaps the most eye-opening of my experiences . . ."

It would have been. West Harrison Street gave its name to a precinct that included one of the most depressed sections of the city, immigrants and colored and Chinese seeking the dream of America and finding the reality of tenements. And a red-light district second to none, the prostitutes a dreary rainbow of races and colors.

"The court enjoyed a steady diet of stabbings, shootings and sluggings," Pegler said, pretending disgust at a memory he relished. "Judge Hopkins would get bored with the violence, and would shout, 'Bailiff, bring me in some whores!' The judge enjoyed badinage with the girls; he loved it when a girl would say she hadn't the wherewithal to pay his five-dollar fine. 'Oh, I think you do, dearie,' he'd say, and give her time to earn the money. But he wasn't a bad judge, just the same. It was a grim atmosphere, and gallows humor, especially from a judge, was to be expected. Winos, ginsoaks, stewbums, hopheads and lesser delinquents were a constant parade before the bench. And the ever-present ladies of the evening."

"And where there are whores," I said, "there are pimps."

He smiled, not just being polite now, showing some teeth this time. "You anticipate me. I like that. Yes, it was in one of the police courts—Harrison Street, perhaps, though my memory isn't exact on that account—that I first saw young Willie Bioff. It made an impression on me, barely eighteen myself, seeing a panderer who was younger than me, *years* younger. The judge asked him his age and he said, 'Thirteen,' proudly. He was fined and released. But I remembered him."

"Why?"

"As I said, his age. Younger than me, but eons older. The street had done it to him, the liberals would say, and perhaps they're right to a point. But even at his age he had a gleefulness about who he was and what he did. And cold, piglike eyes that bore no human compassion."

"You had this impression just from a court appearance you were routinely covering?"

He shrugged facially; the bushy eyebrows danced. "Well, I saw Bioff again, a few months later. His name had stuck with me; I'm a literary man myself, after all, and the Dickensian name, 'buy off,' made its mark on my memory. Have you ever heard of the old Arsonia Cafe?"

"Bit before my time, but wasn't that Mike Fritzel's saloon?"

Nodding, the memory obviously a fond one, Pegler said, "Yes, back before the Great War, and a wild place it was. Fritzel's gal Gilda Gray would allow herself to be hoisted up onto the bar for an impromptu performance of her well-known shimmy."

Judging from the gleam in his eyes, the shimmy had made its mark on his memory as well.

"At any rate," he continued, putting out his cigarette, getting the gold case back out again, "we reporters would occasionally congregate at the Arsonia, which was frequented by prostitutes and their panderers, and other denizens of the night."

"And that's where you saw Bioff again."

"Precisely. Like any good reporter, I observed these creatures closely—it was an education of sorts for a lad like myself. I happened to spot Bioff, the teenage pimp, wearing a silk shirt, talking with some older examples of his ilk; there he stood, gesturing with his mug of beer, its contents sloshing onto the floor as he bragged." This memory seemed anything but a fond one, but it was vividly recalled: "I assumed a spot at the bar nearby, and soon discovered Bioff was regaling his fellow panderers with his technique for 'keeping his girls in line.' Do you have a strong stomach, Mr. Heller?"

"I've lived in Chicago all my life, Mr. Pegler."

"Sound answer. Here, more or less, is what I heard him say: 'If you slug a girl half silly and then tie her down, you can stuff her . . .'" He paused, shook his head. "'. . . her cunt with powdered ice. They tell me it's so cold in there it feels like fire. You got to gag the girl, she screams so loud, but you don't really hurt her permanent. But after ten minutes of that, she will get down on her knees to you any time you say the word *ice*.'"

He lighted a new cigarette; his hand was shaking. I didn't blame him. It was an ugly story.

"You have a memory any reporter would envy you for, Mr. Pegler."

"Is it any wonder I remember it?" he said, a bit defensively. "I was an impressionable lad of eighteen, and I was hearing detailed and horrid descriptions of sexual perversion from a boy four or five years my junior. A boy whose polished nails caught the light, shining his financial success in my ten-dollar-a-week face. Is it any wonder I viewed it as an insult?"

I didn't point out that Pegler had in fact been eavesdropping, that Bioff hadn't intended to impress anybody but his fellow pimps. Still, I could see this man, as a boy, taking it as an insult.

"I saw him again, years later, in another bar," Pegler continued, "on the North Side. He looked familiar, and I asked my drinking companion if he knew the fat, dapper little man, and my friend said, 'Why, that's Willie Bioff—the union slugger and pimp.'"

"And of course the name rang a bell. When was this?"

"Nineteen twenty-seven, perhaps," he said.

"I didn't know you were in Chicago then."

"I didn't live here. I was working for the Tribune Syndicate, however, and touched bases often. Working a sports beat, traveling all over. Got here quite often."

"I see."

"Let me bring you up to date," he said, sitting forward. "If you've indeed read my columns, you must know that I've waged something of a war against the crooked unions."

"Yeah."

He was getting wound up, his eyes staring, not looking at me, as he said, "The newspaper guild soured me on unionism once and for all, you see; it was a hotbed of Reds, and as for the AFL, that great, arrogant, corrupt, hypocritical, parasitic racket, well, I . . ."

"I've read your column," I said. He was starting to irritate me, now. My father was an old union man, he gave his heart and soul to the movement, and while Pegler's opinions weren't entirely baseless, they still rubbed me the wrong way.

He sensed it. "Let me stress that the idea of unionism is something I can admire; what it is rapidly degenerating into is something I can only abhor."

"Understood."

"At any rate. I usually make two or three cross-country jaunts each year, looking for material for my column. I think of myself as a reporter, and while I'm paid handsomely to air my opinions, those opinions mustn't be formed in a vacuum. I need to get out and be a newspaperman from time to time. Last week I was in Los Angeles, that modern Babylon, and I found a *real* story." He drew on the cigarette, relishing the moment. "I was at a party given by Joe Schenck, the Twentieth Century-Fox film executive. Across a wide room, filled with Hollywood stars and directors and producers, with all the fancy trimmings, cocktails and caviar, I spied a familiar face."

"Bioff?"

Pegler nodded, smugly. "Oh, he was older than a teenager, now, by some distance. As was I. But that fat round smiling face was the same, and, as I drew nearer, the hard little pig's eyes, behind wire-rim glasses now, were as cold and inhuman as ever. Oh, he was handsomely turned out, in the Hollywood style, double-breasted pinstripe suit, a handkerchief with a monogram, WB."

Except for the initials, Pegler might have been describing his own wardrobe.

"I asked my host if that man's name wasn't Bioff," Pegler said, "and he replied, 'Yes it is—that's one of our most illustrious citizens. Would you like to be introduced to him?' I said I wouldn't shake hands with Willie Bioff if I were wearing gloves."

"I wasn't aware Bioff was in Hollywood; I didn't know what became of him, frankly." I shrugged. "I guess I assumed he was still involved with Browne and the Stagehands Union. Browne moved his office to the East Coast years ago."

A humorless smile made a slant on Pegler's fleshy face. "Well, it's in Hollywood, now, and has been since 1935. I did some checking. I talked to Arthur Unger, the editor of the *Daily Variety*, and he informed me that the Stagehands Union now controls some twenty-seven different unions. Browne, or in reality Bioff, controls not just the stagehands and the movie projectionists, but ushers, treasurers, porters and hatcheck concessionaires in legitimate theaters coast to coast, and movie studio mechanics, sound technicians, laboratory technicians, virtually everyone involved in the manufacturing end of the film industry. A hundred and seventy-five thousand dues-paying members."

"That's a lot of power for our fat little former pimp."

"It is indeed." He straightened up in his chair and smiled tightly, smugly. "Mr. Heller, I intend to expose Willie Bioff for the panderer he is."

"That should be easy. He's been arrested enough times."

"Yes, but has he been convicted?"

"At least once that I know of."

"You're sure of that?"

"I was the arresting officer," I said.

He smiled. "That was a rumor we heard, but we've not been able to verify it."

So that's how my name got picked out of the hat to be the dick Pegler pegged for his legwork.

"I'm not sure I want to be involved in this," I said. "I hear Browne is tied in with Nicky Dean, and Dean's an Outfit man. If this is an Outfit operation, my future health precludes my involvement."

"You don't need to decide this instant. Have you ever been to California?"

"No."

He reached in his inside pocket and produced an envelope, which he handed to me.

I took it.

"Look inside," he prompted.

I did. Two one-hundred-dollar bills and an airline ticket.

"Your flight to Hollywood leaves at six-twenty this evening," he said.

13

Train travel I was used to; plane travel was something new, and a little frightening. Truth be told, I slept through a lot of it. Twenty-five other hearty souls and I sat within the DC-3 "Flagship," a noisy, rattling projectile that churned through the night sky like a big kitchen mixer. The businessman I sat next to actually read *Fortune* magazine, as if this sort of travel was an everyday thing to him. Maybe it was. We spoke a few polite words, but, sitting over the wing, fighting the sound of the propellers, there just wasn't much to be said. I was relieved when the thing sat down in Dallas, sometime after one o'clock in the morning, and was surprised to find I could make my stomach accept a little something in the airport cafeteria, where oddly enough the people working had Southern accents. Within an hour I was on a sleeper plane, within which two facing seats in a sort of train-type compartment were converted to a berth by a good-looking blond woman in a vaguely military outfit, a "stewardess" she was called, who then shut the curtains and I got awkwardly undressed, hanging my clothes in the netting provided, and slipped under cool sheets and I'll be damned if the sound of the props and the up-and-down motion didn't put me to sleep. Some hours later the stewardess woke me to let me know the airliner was landing—at Tucson, Arizona, which, unlike my present confusion, was a state I'd never been in. I dressed, and then helped her turn the berth back into two seats, into one of which I was strapped, and we landed. Another airport, another cafeteria. Soon I was sleeping again, in my pants atop the blankets this time, and before long it was eight o'clock in the morning in Los Angeles (ten o'clock in the real world, but never mind).

But this wasn't the real world, it was Glendale, where I caught a cab, despite the six-mile ride I was in for. All expenses were paid on this little jaunt, after all; that was the deal: two hundred bucks, all expenses, no strings. I could enjoy the trip to sunny California,

ROBERT MONTGOMERY

pocket the two C's, and head back for the windy city, even should I refuse the job.

Which well I might, but I didn't see how I could turn down this preliminary offer. Besides, I was going to meet a real-life movie star, unless that was a contradiction in terms.

"Where to?" the cabby said. He was a blond handsome kid of about twenty, who'd been sitting behind the wheel at the curb reading something called the *Hollywood Reporter*.

"One forty-four Monovale Drive," I said.

"That's in Beverly Hills," he said, matter of factly.

"If you say so."

I climbed out of my raincoat, folding it up and easing it into my overnight bag; anticipating warmer weather here, I'd taken the lighter coat, but was already warm in spite of it. The sun was bright in a blue sky, bouncing off the asphalt, slicing between the fronds of palm trees. This was California, all right.

"What street is this?" I asked, after a while. This seemed to be a central business and amusement district—shops, movie houses, office buildings, some of the latter approaching skyscraper stature (if not Loop skyscraper stature).

"The Boulevard," he said. He wasn't friendly; he wasn't unfriendly.

"Hollywood Boulevard?"

"Right."

I'd thought people might sleep till noon out here, but I was wrong. Either side of the Boulevard was busy with folks sauntering along looking at each other and themselves, reflected in the shop windows, where fancy displays showed manikins wearing expensively informal clothing, the latest polo shirts and sport jackets for men, sporty blouses and slacks for women, earlier examples of which the window-watchers were already wearing, white their predominant color. A few years before, I'd been in Florida; this seemed much the same, and not just because of the sun and pastel art-deco look—the spirit here was similarly that odd combination of sophistication and naivete I'd noticed in Miami.

Not that I wasn't impressed.

"That's the Brown Derby," I almost shouted, pointing over toward the east side of Vine Street, where a great big hat squatted. Chicago's Brown Derby was just a building.

"Sure is," the cabby said, blasé.

Pretty soon he turned off on a side street, into an area of stores, taverns, small hotels, motor courts, drive-in markets, apartment houses. We passed green parkways, pepper trees, palms. A pastel rainbow of stucco bungalows, white, pink, yellow, blue, with tile roofs, often red.

Then we turned onto a major thoroughfare. "What's this?"

"Sunset Boulevard."

Soon, he condescended to inform me, we were on the "Strip": he pointed out such movie-colony night spots as the Trocadero and Ciro's and the Mocambo. Many buildings along the Strip were painted white with green shutters, housing various little shops with windows boasting antiques or couturiers or modistes and other French-sounding, expensive-sounding nonsense, and restaurants with Venetian blinds protecting patrons from the glare of sun and passersby.

Hollywood was every bit as strange a place as I'd expected. Later that day, in another cab, I'd pass a small independent movie studio where chaps in chaps and sunglasses and Stetsons, and girls in slacks and sunglasses and bright kerchiefs (protecting their permanent waves) were standing at a corner hot dog stand either flirting or talking shop or maybe a little of both. The hot dog stand, of course, looked like a great big hot dog. Giantism was big out here: fish and puppy and ice cream cone buildings, mingling with papier-mâché castles. It was like the '33 World's Fair, but screwier. People ate in their cars.

Right now, however, I was in a cab winding its way through the rolling foothills of Beverly Hills, on which were mansions, luxuriating behind fences in the midst of obscene green lawns, two stories, three stories, white Spanish stucco, white English brick, yellow stucco, red brick, you name it. The rich north suburbs of Chicago had nothing on these babies.

"This is Robert Montgomery's house," the cabby said, breathlessly, pausing before entering onto the private drive.

"So what?" I said, unimpressed.

After all, what was it to me? Just another rambling two-story Colonial "farmhouse," white frame and brick, surrounded by a rustic rock garden, perched on a hill against a horizon of more hills. Hell, there's one of them on every third corner back in Chicago.

He took me up the winding drive, up the sloping lawn. Plenty of trees, too, and not a palm in sight. Clearly this Montgomery was a guy with dough who wasn't afraid to spend it. Clearly, too, this was a guy who'd rather not be in Hollywood, to the point of reinventing the place into New England.

I got out of the cab and handed in a sawbuck to the guy, saying, "Keep it."

"Thanks," he said. "Do you *know* Robert Montgomery?"

"We're like this," I said, holding up crossed fingers.

"I'm an actor, too," he said, earnestly.

"Aren't we all," I said, and turned my back on him and went up the sidewalk.

I knocked on the polished white door, and soon it swung open and a small, attractive woman in her thirties, with light brown hair and a fine smile, greeted me, smoothing her crisp print dress, blue on white, as she spoke.

"You'd be Mr. Heller," she said.

I had my hat in my hands. All I could think of was I hadn't brushed my teeth since that goddamn sixteen-hour plane ride.

"Yes I am," I said, the soul of wit.

"I'm Mrs. Montgomery," she said.

I hadn't taken her for a servant.

"Pleased to meet you, ma'am."

She offered me her hand and I accepted it, a smooth, cool hand which I gently grasped rather than shook.

"Please step inside," she said, taking my overnight bag (although I could use the toothbrush therein about now) and she stepped graciously aside and then I was in.

The hall was knotted pine, and the smell of pine was in the place too; it brought to mind Pegler's aftershave, which was fitting I suppose, since Pegler brought me here. Mrs. Montgomery paused to gracefully point toward an elaborately framed picture that seemed a little out of place, amidst the otherwise early American trimmings of the place: a bunch of royal-looking dopes in a carriage.

"This picture is a special prize," she said. "We were in England at the time of the Silver Jubilee, and this is a signed copy of the Jubilee picture. Painted by Munnings."

"By Munnings. Really."

"Yes. That's Queen Mary and King George V on their way to Ascot. And there in the carriage are the Prince of Wales and his brother who became, of course, King Edward VIII and King George VI, respectively."

"Of course."

A stairway curved gently to the left; also opening to the left was the open-beamed dining room, where dark mahogany early American furniture was surrounded by wall paper brightly depicting scenes from the Revolutionary War, redcoats and bluecoats cheerfully fighting. I guess I knew who Queen Mary and King George V would've rooted for. At a bay window, next to sheer ruffled curtains, sat a small oval table. At the small oval table sat Robert Montgomery. He was reading the *Daily Variety*, a cup of coffee before him.

"Mr. Heller's here, Bob," Mrs. Montgomery said, and Montgomery rose and smiled. It was the same urbane smile I'd seen in any number of light comedies; it was also the same urbane smile of the killer in *Night Must Fall*.

He was about my size, six foot, and weight, one-seventy, casually attired in white shirt and brown slacks; and, like me, was in his mid-thirties or so. His eyes were blue and his hair brown, and he wasn't strikingly handsome, exactly—it was one of those faces that seemed soft and strong at once—but you knew you were in the presence of somebody.

We shook hands. He had a solid, strong grip, and his hands were not the smooth movie-star hands I'd expected; this man had, at some time in the not too distant past, worked a real job.

"Please join me," he said, gesturing to the chair opposite him at the small oval table, and he sat down, and I sat down.

"We waited breakfast for you. Is French toast all right? Orange juice and coffee?"

"Sure. That's very gracious of you."

He folded the *Variety* and put it to one side of his place setting; only his coffee cup was before him—he really had waited to have breakfast till I got there.

"I knew what time you were getting in," he said, shrugging, smiling just a little. "And I know what those flights are like. You've grabbed a random bite at this airport cafeteria and that one. And, despite sleeping on the trip, you're very tired, aren't you?"

I was. I hadn't noticed it, really, but I was bone tired.

"I guess I am," I said.

"Well, you can relax some, while you're here. You're to stay at least overnight. I've made reservations for you at the Roosevelt."

"Yes, that was my understanding. Thank you."

"Thanks for coming out here on such short notice."

His wife brought the food in and served it; again, no servants, at least none in sight.

"It looks delicious," I told her, and it did.

"Breakfast is usually a one-man affair at our house," she said. "I'm sure Bob will appreciate the company."

They smiled at each other, quite warmly, and she left. This was a civilized house, that was for sure. Of course with dough like this, they could afford to be civilized.

Well, the breakfast tasted as good as it looked, the orange juice everything fresh-squeezed California orange juice is supposed to be including pulpy, and we didn't talk about the pending case, rather talked about my flight and other general small talk. At one point he asked me what I thought about FDR seeking a third term; and I said, I didn't know it was official; and he said it wasn't, but that it was going to happen; and I said, I'd probably vote for the guy again.

"I worked for him in '33 and '37," he said, thoughtfully, seriously, "but it goes against my grain to support *any* President for a third term. We stop short of royalty in this country, thank God."

Jubilee painting or not.

"I liked you in that movie where you played the killer," I said.

He smiled, but it wasn't the killer's smile. "It was the role I liked best," he admitted.

"You got an Academy Award nomination for that, didn't you?"

"Yes." He laughed to himself. "Do you know what the Academy of Motion Picture Arts and Sciences *really* is?"

"Uh, not exactly, no."

"A company union." Now he smiled the killer's smile. "A *failed* company union. You see, Louie B. Mayer wanted to fight any *legitimate* unionization of actors and directors. The Academy was to be the contract arbitrator between the studio and the guilds. You can imagine just how impartial that arbitration would be. Well, we put a stop to that."

"That's good."

After breakfast he ushered me into the nearby "study," which was bigger than my entire suite at the Morrison: fireplace, built-in shelves of leather-bound books, hunting prints on pine walls, tan leather furniture (none of it patched with tape, either). He settled at one end of an absurdly long leather couch and helped himself to the pipes and tobacco on a small round table before him. He nodded to an overstuffed leather chair opposite him and I sat down in it, and I mean down, in, it.

"Smoke, if you like," he said, lighting up the pipe.

"I don't smoke."

"I thought all private eyes smoked."

"Nope. And my secretary isn't in love with me, either."

That amused him. "So the Hollywood clichés don't apply in real life, hmmm? Well, some do."

"How's that?"

"Let's just say, Jimmy Cagney, Eddie Robinson, and George Raft seem to be drawing from life."

Well, Raft, anyway.

"By that you mean," I said, "there really are gangsters in this wicked old world."

"Precisely. And in this wicked old Hollywood as well."

"Pegler told me Willie Bioff has muscled into the unions out here. And that that's what you wanted to talk to me about."

He nodded sagely, puffing at the pipe, getting it going. "I'm one of the people who got SAG off the ground. A three-time past president."

"SAG?"

"Screen Actors Guild. We aren't under Bioff's thumb—yet. He's been making some moves in that direction. Now, I invoke Bioff's name, but in fact the president of the IATSE is Browne."

"But Browne's just the figurehead."

"Right. Do you know a man named Circella?"

"Uh, isn't that Nicky Dean's real last name?"

"Yes it is. He and Bioff and Browne are all but inseparable, out here."

"That's bad, Mr. Montgomery."

"Bob."

"Bob. And if you'd call me Nate, that'd be just swell, too, but I don't think I'm going to take this job. I hate to have taken your money and your plane ride and breakfast and all, only to turn you down, but . . ."

"But what, Nate?"

"Nicky Dean is an Outfit man."

"Syndicate, you mean. Crime Syndicate."

"Yes. He's one of Frank Nitti's people. And I'm from Chicago. I live in Chicago. I work in Chicago. And I can't do either of those things, particularly the first, if I get on Frank Nitti's bad side. It's his town."

"So will this be, if something isn't done."

I started to rise. "That's very noble, and I hope you can do something about it. I just ain't going to be part of it."

Patiently, he gestured for me to sit. "Hear me out."

"Mr. Montgomery—"

"Bob. Hear me out. You came this far, after all."

"Well. Yeah, I did come a distance. Okay. I'll hear you out. But I'm afraid I'll be wasting your time on top of your money."

He sat forward, tapped his finger on a manila folder on the little table between us. "Bioff's got one foot in the figurative grave already. Evidence gathered by an investigator, a former FBI man whom I hired with SAG's approval, has already been turned over to the Treasury Department." He pushed the folder toward me. "Those are your copies."

I picked the folder up and looked in it. Photostats of letters on IATSE stationery from Browne and Bioff both; statements from disgruntled union members; nothing much. Except for one thing: a photostat of a check made out to Bioff for $100,000. Signed by Joe Schenck.

"Isn't Schenck. . . ?"

"Vice president of Twentieth Century-Fox," Montgomery said, smiling like an urbane killer again.

"How did your investigator get this?"

He shrugged. "There are rumors of a break-in at the IA offices."

"That's illegal."

"So is extortion."

I flapped the folder at him. "Is that what you think Bioff's doing? Extorting money out of the movie executives? Selling them strike-prevention insurance?"

He shrugged again, puffed at his pipe. "It would certainly be cheaper for the studios than paying their help what they're worth."

"Yeah," I said, looking around. "It's a tough life."

He sat up straight; bristled. "Don't judge Hollywood by these standards. I'm a lucky, lucky man. The rank-and-file union members in this town—in whose behalf Bioff and Browne are supposedly fighting—are average working joes and janes. They deserve better than being sold out."

"But is that little pimp powerful enough to blackmail somebody like Schenck?"

Nodding forcefully, he said. "Or Thalberg or Mayer or Jack Warner or anybody else. Remember, Bioff has under his thumb the movie projectionists, who alone can shut down every theater in every major city in the country. And a few such dark days would deliver a blow to the industry that the studios couldn't recover from."

"If the Treasury Department has this evidence, they should be able to prosecute Bioff."

"Perhaps. On income-tax evasion, which is fine, but I need to show Bioff for what he is. His drunkard friend Browne is a convincing public speaker; and conditions for workers were so wretched prior to unionization that Bioff and Browne can sell the working man out and he won't even know it."

"So you'd like to see Bioff smeared, to keep him and Browne and the union they represent from attracting any converts. Specifically, to keep the actors out from under their greasy thumb."

"Yes. But 'smear' isn't the word." He pointed with the pipe. "*Expose.*"

"Yeah. That's why you linked up with Pegler."

"Certainly. He's a yellow journalist; a muckraker. But that's what's called for in this situation."

"You have Pegler. You don't need me."

"I need a good man in Chicago. So does Pegler."

"You've already hired a private detective."

"He's an L.A. man. Nate, the SAG board authorized me to spend five thousand dollars to investigate Bioff. You see, I assured them if the investigation didn't prove that Bioff is a very sour apple, I'd personally refund the five thousand."

"Five grand, huh? Uh, how much have you spent so far?"

"Let's just say I'm prepared to offer you a thousand-dollar retainer, on top of the two hundred dollars you've already received, plus expenses, and if your daily fee eats up the thousand, I can authorize you up to another thousand."

My mouth felt dry. "That's a lot of money." It wasn't the most money I'd been offered for a case this week, but then again, unlike Eddie O'Hare, Montgomery was alive.

Montgomery gestured with his pipe, quietly convincing; he could've sold Ford a Buick. "You are reputed to be street-smart, where Chicago and especially the Nitti Outfit are concerned. You would in this instance work essentially undercover. Just talk to people you know, find out what you can, and prepare a confidential report for me. You wouldn't have to appear in court. Your name would never be revealed. But the information would be shared with federal agents, the SAG board and, possibly, probably, leaked to the press."

"And my name wouldn't be attached to any of it?"

"Well, with one exception. We understand you once arrested Willie Bioff."

"That's a matter of public record."

"It is?"

"Sure. He was convicted of pandering. I was the arresting officer."

Montgomery smiled. "So we heard. It's nice to have it confirmed."

"Where did you hear all this stuff about me? How the hell did you and Pegler get a line on me in the first place?"

"Is that important?"

"Ness! Damnit, of course. You've been talking to Treasury agents, and your private dick's an ex-FBI man. You asked them for a reliable, Mob-savvy Chicago private cop, and they checked with somebody they knew who'd know that sort of thing about Chicago, which was Eliot, and Eliot mentioned me. My old friend Eliot probably remembered hearing me ranting and raving about how much I hated that little fat prick pimp Bioff, remembered me saying I arrested him once, and passed that along to you!"

"Mr. Heller. You are a detective."

"Mr. Montgomery. Goddamnit. You just hired one."

GEORGE BROWNE

NICKY DEAN

14

A little after nine that evening, dressed to the nines in a rental tux Montgomery had sent around, I strolled out of the Roosevelt Hotel into a balmy breeze with a touch of ocean in it and climbed in a cab.

"Eighty-six ten Sunset Boulevard," I told the cabbie, and we rolled off into a night made day by neon.

Montgomery was picking up the tab for this night on the town, which with luck might turn into work. He wanted me to hit the Trocadero, one of the swankier joints in Hollywood, because Bioff, Browne and Dean frequently held court there. It seemed the "Troc," as it was affectionately known, was owned by William "Billy" Wilkerson, an enterprising gent who had made the Strip what it was today, which is to say a gaudy, expensive trap for tourists, and stars and would-be stars looking for publicity, as the Trocadero and the Vendome (Wilkerson's luncheon-only complement to the Troc) were gossip-columnist haunts. This was partly due to Wilkerson also being editor and publisher of the *Daily Reporter*, and, as Billy was eager to stay in Bioff and Browne's good graces, no negative stories about the Stagehands Union and the Unholy Trinity who ran it should ever be expected to appear therein.

"Thank God for Arthur Unger," Montgomery had said.

"You mean the guy who tipped Pegler to Bioff's racket," I said, recalling the columnist's mention of the *Variety* editor. "But why would a big-shot newspaperman like Wilkerson be intimidated by Bioff and company?"

"Because he and Browne have the power to call Wilkerson's restaurant employees out on strike. About the only story Billy's ever run on Bioff is one in which he called the little pimp 'the type of man the IATSE should be grateful for.'" Here Montgomery had paused, thoughtfully. "Although the winds may be blowing differently now," he went on, "because there was a story in the *Reporter* just yesterday criticizing, however mildly, the IA's labor methods. I'm surprised it got through."

I resisted the notion of having any contact with Bioff, Browne and/or Dean while I was in Hollywood, but Montgomery suggested it would be safer than not.

"Let's bring your trip to California out in the open, and not risk anyone finding out about it and reading something in. Develop a cover story, an invented reason for being here. And then you can run into the gentlemen from the Stagehands Union, casually, and perhaps they'll invite a fellow Chicagoan to sit at their table, in which case maybe they'll spill something more than Browne's latest bottle of imported beer."

"Bioff knows I hate his guts," I said, shaking my head. "Browne I barely know. Dean I've had some contact with, but we're by no means chums; hell, I used to see his girl friend Estelle from time to time, before she was his girl friend, that is. I admit it might be smart for me to try to mend some fences with Bioff, if I'm going to be nosing around . . . but no matter how you slice it, I wouldn't count on them rolling out the red carpet."

"We'll see. At any rate, it will give you a firsthand chance to see how high on the hog these union officials are living. Did I mention the two percent 'income tax' they've assessed all their members?"

"No . . ."

"Since 1936 they've been getting two percent of all their union members' salaries. We estimate their take in this regard alone is a million a year."

"Jesus! This is no small operation."

"No. And if they get their hands on SAG, it will mushroom further. Check out the Trocadero. You'll see how union officials of the IA spend the rank and file's hard-earned dues."

The Troc was a long, low, rambling building, white-frame Colonial with a red-tiled roof with a large central gable and a couple of smaller ones on either side, lorded over by an incongruously folksy weathervane. A striped canopy ran across the long front of the building, and at right, just over the canopy in squat art-deco neon, the words CAFE TROCADERO were tacked on like an afterthought; underneath the pastel glowing letters a smaller neon said PHIL OHMAN'S MUSIC. Potted plants stood like World's Fair midgets along the front of the building. This hodgepodge of architecture and oddball trimmings didn't add up to anything much in particular, and like a lot of structures out here it looked like one you could put your foot through without half trying. Hollywood's idea of swank was just another plasterboard fantasy.

A colored doorman in a white linen double-breasted uniform with gold salad on the shoulders let me in; I wouldn't have tipped the guy in Chicago, but this was Hollywood so I gave him a dime out of embarrassment; he said thank you sir, but didn't show me his teeth. Maybe opening a door was worth a quarter out here. Inside the dark, vaguely Parisian place I smiled at the hatcheck girl, who I would have rather given the dime to. She had short dark hair and a nice smile, was wearing peach-color Chinese pajamas, and made me sorry I was out here alone. I wondered what she was doing later, but I had no hat to check so I stopped at the velvet rope where the captain asked if I had a reservation and I said I did if Robert Montgomery called one in for me like he said he was going to.

That didn't impress anybody of course, including me, but I did have a reservation, although it would be fifteen minutes before my table was ready, so I made my entrance down a stairway designed for making entrances, into the bar. This was a Thursday night but crowded, the patrons at the bar standing two-deep; since there was just the one of me, I soon found a place to stand and had some rum, and nibbled at a bowl of parched corn, and took the place in. The French decor gave way to American colonial, here, red-and-black plaid, hanging copper utensils; either way, I sure wasn't in Chicago. I didn't see a lot of movie stars, though; somebody who might have been Cesar Romero was having cocktails with a little starlet over in the corner, but that was about it.

Finally I was shown to a table upstairs; most of the patrons were in evening dress, tuxes on the men mostly, an occasional white jacket, the women in slinky gowns, black sequins and silver lamé, velvet trimmed with feathers, silk touched with fur. You'd have to check in at a nudist colony to find more female flesh unembarrassedly exposed. I wasn't complaining.

It was almost ten o'clock before I ate, and since a movie star was paying I had the lobster, only it wasn't as good as I could've got at Ireland's at Clark and Ontario. I was wiping the butter off my chin when somebody tapped me on the shoulder.

When I looked up it was a honey-haired blue-eyed blonde in a black dress with her tits hanging out. That's an inelegant way to put it, perhaps, but that's what went instantly through my mind, a thought most any man this side of the limp-wrist set would've had.

"Could you join us?" she asked, in a chirpy, innocent voice.

I turned around in my seat and suddenly figured out that

Montgomery must have requested a table in this specific area; because not far away, in a corner booth, sat Nicky Dean and George Browne and another girl, a stunning redhead, in a white dress with her . . . you finish it.

Dean smiled a little—very little—and waved me over. He was a round-faced man in a snazzy white evening jacket, with slicked-back black hair, a better-looking Edward G. Robinson. Even seated, the incongruously tall, slim frame below the balloon puss was evident. He had a single drink before him, and a cigarette rested regally in the hand he was motioning with. Next to him in the booth was the redhead, and next to her was George Browne, in a tent of a tux, double-chinned, wire-rim glasses, fat, bland-looking; what distinguished him was the array of beer bottles before him, half a dozen of them, various foreign labels. He was pouring one into a glass.

"Nate Heller," Nicky Dean said, appraising me with the dark, matinee-idol eyes that were his best feature. The blonde was sliding in next to him; I was just standing there, rum cocktail in hand.

"Nicky Dean," I said. "Who's minding the store?"

By that I meant the Colony Club, his Rush Street joint, which had a restaurant and bar downstairs and a casino upstairs, a pretty fancy layout.

"My girl Estelle," he said, without any apparent concern for, or effect on, the bosomy little blonde next to him who was smiling at him with considered affection, running her fingers idly through his slick black hair. "You remember Estelle, don't you?"

So Estelle had mentioned me to Dean.

"I knew her back in my pickpocket detail days," I said, smiling nervously, shrugging the same way. "Cute kid. Smart as a whip."

"Cute. Smart. She sure is. I miss her. Sit down, Heller. Slide in next to Dixie."

I did. "Hi, Dixie," I said.

"Hiya," Dixie said, just barely looking at me, but she was the kind of girl who could load an hour of promise into a split second of glance.

Browne was drinking his latest beer. A barmaid in black and white with her legs showing came over and brought him three more bottles with three other labels and piled the empties on her tray while Browne handed her a hundred-dollar bill and said, "Let me know when that's gone. Keep the last five for yourself, honey."

She thanked him, and was gone, and he looked over at me. "I

know you," he said, bloodshot eyes narrowing on either side of a bloodshot nose. "You're that dick."

The two girls looked at me.

"That's right," I said. "I have my own little agency on Van Buren."

The girls looked away.

Dean blew a smoke ring and said, "What brings you to Tinseltown?"

"Business. What brings you boys here?"

Dean smiled at Browne, but Browne wasn't looking; he was pouring his next beer.

Dean said, "We work out here. For the Stagehands Union."

"Really? Is that a good racket?"

Browne belched into his hand. "It's not a racket," he said, having to reach for the indignation. "We serve the working man. Without us, they'd be out on a limb. You can trust an employer just so long as you're shaking hands with him. When he relaxes his grip, you're had, unless *we're* on your side. Excuse."

Browne had chosen the outside seat for a reason; he was up and gone.

"Little boy's room," the redhead explained to me. "He does that every half hour."

"You could set your watch by it," the blonde said.

"Girls," Dean said, and that meant they were to be quiet. "What kind of business you out here on, Heller?"

"Wandering daughter job. A Gold Coast swell hired me to find his little girl. She's out here trying to make it in the movies."

"I'm an actress," the blonde said.

The redhead chose not to declare herself.

"You'll find there's lots of actresses out here," Dean said. "Any luck?"

"Yeah. The father had an old address on her, which I checked out. Found she'd been doing a little work as an extra. Tracked her through SAG."

Mention of the Screen Actors Guild didn't raise a ripple out of Dean. He merely said, "The girl going back home?"

I shook my head no. "I didn't expect her to. They had me give her some dough, which'll underwrite another six months out here."

This story was more or less true, by the way, should Dean go checking—only the job dated back a couple months and had been handled by me over the phone from Chicago. This afternoon I'd called the moneybags papa long distance and asked if he wanted me to look in on his daughter, while I was out here, and see how she was doing; he'd said yes, and to write her a check up to five C's if she needed money, for which he'd reimburse me and then some. The bit about finding her through SAG was baloney, though—she'd left her new address with her old landlady—but Montgomery had checked for me and she did carry a card. The story would hold.

"If she's a good-looking kid," Dean said, "she won't need their money."

The blonde sipped her drink; the redhead lowered her eyes—I thought I saw contempt there. Whether for Dean or herself or the world in general, I couldn't say.

"You may be right," I said, "but she took the dough."

Dean shrugged. The orchestra was starting up, across the room. They were playing "I'll Be Seeing You."

Browne returned, sidled his heft back in the booth. "Where's that waitress? I'm down to one beer."

Nobody answered him.

Dean said to the little blonde, "Do you want to dance, Dix?"

"Oh, sure, Nicky."

He turned his dark gaze on me. "Dance with her, Heller, would you." It wasn't a question.

"My pleasure."

I threaded Dixie through tables to the crowded dance floor and held her close. She smelled good, like new hay. I hated the thought of the kid being in Dean's arms.

However, the first thing she said was, "Isn't Nicky sweet?"

"He's a peach."

"Inn't he, though? Ooh, look. There's Sidney Skolsky."

"Who?"

"You know, Sidney Skolsky, the columnist! I wish you were somebody. I could get in his column."

"I was somebody last time I looked."

She looked at me, with melting embarrassment. "I'm sorry. I didn't mean that to sound like that."

"It's okay, Dixie. Is it okay if I call you Dixie?"

"Sure. How should I call you?"

"Any time you want."

She giggled and snuggled to me and we moved around the small packed floor awhile; we danced three or four numbers. It turned out Dixie was her stage name—the last half of which was "Flyer"—but she didn't want to say what her real name was.

"Oooh, look! There's Barbara Stanwyck and Robert Taylor!"

I looked over and there they were, at a little table together. They looked small.

"Inn't it nice," she said, "that people leave them alone here? I hope when I'm famous people aren't all the time bothering me for autographs."

"There's worse problems in the world," I said, looking at Dean looking at us from the booth. Browne wasn't; he was just drinking his current beer.

"There sure is! Hey, you're kind of cute. What's your name again?"

I told her, and the orchestra let up, and we made our way back. I waited for Dixie to slide in next to Dean, then slid in next to her.

"You two make a cute couple," Dean said.

"Thanks," Dixie said.

I didn't say anything.

"We must have similar taste in dames," he said, with a cold little smile. "Where you staying?"

"Pardon?"

"While you're in town. What hotel you staying?"

"Roosevelt," I said.

Dean's faint smile now seemed honestly amused. "Ha. Joe Schenck's joint."

"What do you mean?"

"Guy at Twentieth we know," he said, glancing at Browne, who didn't glance back. "He owns that hotel, him and some other guys."

Montgomery had a wry sense of humor, I'd give him that much.

"Mr. Dean?" somebody said.

I looked over and a mustached, dapper little man in evening dress was standing, almost bowing, before the booth; he seemed nervous, even frightened.

"Hello, Billy," Dean said. The words were like two ice cubes dropping in an empty glass.

"I'm relieved to see you back at the old stand tonight," he said. "I was afraid we'd seen the last of you for a while."

"We're funny people, in this day and age," Dean said. "We believe in staying loyal to our friends."

The man stepped closer. "Allow me to explain."

Dean said nothing.

"For whatever mistake I have made, I stand willing to do anything you dictate, to make it up," the man said, his voice barely audible, trying, it would seem, to keep the humiliation of this scene from being broadcast. "There was an unfortunate circumstance, caused by a new man on the desk covering union news."

"Aren't you the boss?" Dean said.

"I have to take responsibility for it, I know. That story got through, which to you says I broke my word. But please believe there was no intention not to take care of you, as you have of me."

Dean said nothing.

"It was a horrible mistake," the man continued, filling the awful silence, "and I stand willing to rectify it. Please. Command me."

"Forget it. All is forgiven."

The little man smiled, almost crumpling under the humiliation, and said good evening, and moved quickly away.

"Who was that?" I asked.

"Billy Wilkerson," Dean said. "He owns the joint."

And the *Hollywood Reporter*. That had been about the negative piece on the IA that Montgomery mentioned had run in the *Reporter* yesterday. These boys did have clout.

Half an hour on the second and Browne was getting out of the booth again, saying, "Excuse."

"Anyway, Heller," Dean said. "You must not have a car out here. Maybe we can drop you off at your hotel?"

I didn't think there was anything sinister in that; and, if there was, I couldn't think of a graceful way out, so I said, "That'd be swell."

"Maybe you'd like to show Dixie your etchings."

Dixie, whose fingers were working in Dean's hair, smiled at me shyly. Maybe she did have a future as an actress. As for whether or not I took Dean and Dixie up on this, I'm not going to say. You might be disappointed in me, either way.

Browne came back and settled his fat ass in the booth and said, "Willie wants to see you while you're out here."

I didn't know that was directed toward me, at first; then Browne repeated it, saying he'd phoned Willie at home to say Wilkerson had eaten crow, and I said, "Bioff's out here, too?"

"Sure," he said. "Kind of unofficially these days, but he's out here."

"Willie and I go way back."

"Yeah," Dean said. "You hate each other's goddamn guts."

"I don't hate anybody," I said, smiling, sipping some rum. "I haven't seen Willie in years. If he's making good, more power to him."

"He's making good," Dean said.

"Anyway," Browne said, wiping some foam off his face, "he wants to see you."

"Why would he want to see me?"

"I don't know. When I called him, I mentioned we run into you. He wants you to come out to his place."

"I'm leaving tomorrow afternoon."

"Go out to his place at Bel Air tomorrow morning. Hell, I'll drive you out there myself. He says to tell you it's worth a C-note minimum."

The thought of George Browne driving a car was a sobering thought.

But I said, "Call him back and tell him sure," anyway.

"In half an hour I will," Browne said, and lifted another bottle.

WILLIE BIOFF

15

Browne driving was no problem: he picked me up in a chauffeured limo, a big shiny black Caddy. I tried not to make anything out of the fact that the last big shiny black car I went riding in was E. J. O'Hare's. Besides, that was overcast, chilly Chicago and this was warm, sunny Hollywood.

There was plenty of legroom, despite the extra passenger that sat between us on the floor: a tub of ice and beer. It was ten o'clock in the morning and Browne was already at it. Maybe the tale about him putting away one hundred bottles of imported beer a day wasn't an exaggeration; maybe it was an understatement.

Probably it was the constant drinking that did it, but he showed no signs of the night before having taken any effect; he was wearing a baggy brown suit and had a glow in his cheeks, not to mention his nose. We were on our way to Westwood, on the other side of Beverly Hills, and we had plenty of time to talk.

"You have any idea why Willie wants to see me, George?"

"Not a clue," he said, cheerfully, bottle in hand. "But Willie always has his reasons."

"You guys been partners a long time."

Swigging, nodding, he said, "Long time."

"Even before the soup kitchen?"

In 1932 the Stagehands Union, which is to say Browne and Bioff, had opened up a soup kitchen in the Loop, at Randolph and Franklin Streets to be exact, two blocks west of City Hall. The 150 working members of the local would pay 35 cents a meal, which—along with the donations of food from merchants and money from theater owners—helped ensure that the 250 unemployed members could eat free.

"Oh yeah, sure," Browne said, "before that. Willie was running a kosher butchers union, similar to what I was doing with the gentile poultry dealers."

"You were already head of the Stagehands local, though."

"Yeah, sure. My 'Poultry Board of Trade' was just a sideline. No, the soup kitchen was what taught me to listen to Willie, what taught me Willie had brains. That was a sweetheart idea, that soup kitchen."

"Made you a lot of friends," I said agreeably. "Nice publicity."

Browne's smile was a proud fold in his flabby face. "We served thirty-seven hundred meals a week, most of 'em free. The biggest actors in the land passed through our portals—Harry Richman, Helen Morgan, Texas Guinan, Jolson, Cantor, Olson and Johnson, everybody."

"So did a lot of politicians and reporters."

Browne swigged and swallowed and grinned. "Being close to City Hall didn't hurt. It's like Willie always says: never seen a whore who wasn't hungry or a politician who wasn't a whore. So we let the politicians eat for nix. And the reporters."

That bought the boys a lot of good will—particularly considering the Bioff-Browne chefs maintained a deluxe menu for celebrities and politicos and press, including such first-rate fare as orange-glazed roast duck, prime rib, and porterhouse steaks. What the hell—even a cynical soul like me had to hand it to 'em: the out-of-work stagehands ate the majority of the meals, in a time when otherwise God knows where or how they'd have eaten at all. Still, I always suspected Bioff and Browne were squeezing more out of the deal than just the means to keep the newspapers and politicians friendly.

Three beers later we were in Westwood, which was just more of the Beverly Hills same except less rolling, and Bioff's estate, which we pulled into the driveway of, was an impressive sprawling double-story wood-and-stone ranch-style which (Browne informed me) Bioff had dubbed "Rancho Laurie," after his wife. Compared to Montgomery's mansion, it came in a fairly distant second; next to a room at the Morrison Hotel, it was paradise. The little pimp from South Halsted Street had gone Hollywood, all right.

I followed Browne around the side of the perfectly tended, gently sloping grounds, an occasional tree throwing some shade on us, and there, reclining on a lounge chair, next to a kidney-shaped pool somewhat smaller than Lake Michigan, was Willie Bioff.

I'd always thought of him as fat, and I guess he was fat, but not in the dissipated George Browne way. His barrel chest was covered with tight curls of black hair as were his muscular arms and legs; he was neckless, stocky but hard, like a wrestler—he had once been a union slugger, after all. Under the black body hair, the flesh I remembered as Illinois pasty was California tan. He wore money-green bathing trunks and blood-red house slippers—not a bead of water on him; my guess was he didn't swim much—and sunglasses and had a cigarette in one hand and a glass of ice water in the other.

He rose quickly as we approached and smiled broadly and extended a hand to me. "Thanks for coming out here, Heller."

We shook hands. His was a strong grip. Stronger than mine.

"I was surprised to be invited, Willie. We aren't exactly pals."

He waved that off, taking a lime monogrammed crushed velvet robe off a nearby lounge chair and belting it around him. He exchanged his sunglasses for clear rimless octagonal ones from a pocket of the robe. "I told you once, we should let bygones be bygones. I meant it then, I mean it now."

"Okay."

He turned a hard, hooded gaze on Browne and said, "I want to talk to Heller alone."

"Sure thing, Willie. I'll just sit here by the pool."

"Why don't you go down to the office?"

"Friday's a slow day. You know that."

"You should be there."

"Look, Willie, I'll just sit by the pool. Could you send your houseboy out with some beer?"

"Why don't you sit in your car and drink your own?"

Browne seemed more sad than embarrassed by this exchange, wandering off without another word, as Willie showed me inside, through glass doors into a big white modern kitchen.

"You'll have to pardon my lush of a partner," Bioff said. "He can be a real cluck. You care for anything to drink?"

"No thanks."

"I gave the help the morning off," Bioff said, as if needing to explain the emptiness of the kitchen, and the house beyond. "My wife and kids are at our place in Canoga Park—I'll be joining them this afternoon for the weekend. But I wanted to see you first."

"Why, Willie?"

"I'll get to that. Come with me."

For a place called Rancho Laurie, where you'd expect rustic to be the word, it was pretty posh. We padded across a plush carpet, past a formal dining room, and various antique furniture, none of it early American, and paintings in the manner of Old Masters, and Chinese vases seemed to be set on anything that wasn't moving.

I never imagined I'd find myself in Willie Bioff's bedroom, but neither did I imagine it would be an elegant Louis XV affair. He led me into a walk-in closet where dozens upon dozens of tailored suits hung; the back of the door was heavy with racks of ties, dozens of ties, every color, every pattern in creation; snappy snap-brim hats sat on a long shelf in a row, as if supervising. Shoes polished like black mirrors lined the floor. I thought he was going to change clothes, but that wasn't the point of this.

"What do you think of my ties?" he said, running a caressing hand over some of them.

"They're real nice, Willie."

He sucked on the cigarette, smiling with immense satisfaction. Then he said, "How about those suits?"

"They're swell. Hats, too. Like your shoes."

He looked at me and smiled, just a little. "I'm not showing off. I just wanted to share this with you. You were a poor Chicago street kid yourself. You can appreciate how sweet my life is, compared to what shit it was once."

"Sure."

He led me out of the closet and I sat down while he changed into slacks and a short-sleeved white shirt in the adjacent bathroom, losing the cigarette. Then he led me back down the stairs and we were soon in a knotty-pine library that was uncomfortably similar to Montgomery's study. About the only difference was the lack of hunting prints—Willie had instead some handsome tinted photos of outdoor landscapes ("I took those," he said proudly, as I looked at them)—and the leather furniture here wasn't oversize, and was black not tan. On the couch, spread open face down, as if to save a place, was a book: *Das Kapital* by Karl Marx. I didn't think I'd have found that at Montgomery's; of course I didn't expect to find it here, either.

I sat down next to the book. "Are you reading this, Willie?"

"A great man wrote that book," he said defensively. "We'll be living that way sometime in the future."

And then we'll all have closets full of suits and ties and hats and shoes. "Why am I here, Willie? Besides to look at your suits and ties and hats and shoes."

He sat beside me. "You still think I'm a low uncouth man, don't you?"

"The question isn't whether you own Chinese vases, Willie. The question is how you paid for 'em."

He sneered, and looked more like I remembered him. "Are you sure you're from Chicago? Jesus, Heller, I come up the hard way, you know that. I slept in my share of doorways, stomach growling like a stray dog; like the man said, bread is expensive when your pockets are empty. I learned to earn a buck any way I could. But I'm legit now. I'm doing good work for the unions out here, lookin' after my members."

"Why do you feel you have to justify yourself to me, of all people? I'm just an ex-cop who busted you once."

"*That's* why. I want you to understand I don't hold any grudge against you. You were doing your job. I was doing mine. Hell, they were the same job, really."

"How do you figure?"

He shrugged. "We were both maintaining law and order. I just happened to be maintaining it in a whorehouse."

"Slapping women around."

"I never slapped a woman in my life. I got great respect for women. I have slapped some whores in my time. Of various sex. Like the man said, most businessmen are nothing but two-bit whores with a clean shirt and a shine." The moon face beamed. "Only now I know more subtle ways of slapping them around than just plain slapping."

"I guess greedy people just rub you the wrong way."

"Be sarcastic if you want, but I'm a union man. I look out for the little guy!" Unconsciously or not, he was pointing a thumb at his own barrel chest as he said that.

"Why am I here, Willie?"

"To maybe do a job for me."

"Aren't there any detectives in California?"

"Sure. But not the Chicago variety. When Georgie called me from the Troc last night, I thought, this is *perfect*. Just the ticket."

"What is?"

"You being here. You know what irony is?"

"We've met."

"Well, then you can appreciate this. You know who Westbrook *Pegler* is?"

My mouth went dry.

"Irony's sister?" I said.

"You know who he is. He's in Chicago right now. He's looking for dirt on me. To spread in his column."

"I know," I admitted.

It was the only way to play it.

The hard dark pig eyes behind the rimless glass squinted. "You know?"

I shrugged. "Yeah. He stopped by my office the other day. He wanted to know if I was the arresting officer on your pandering charge, years ago."

He went a little pale, sat up. "What did you say to him?"

I shrugged again. "I said yes."

"Shit. Did you give him any details?"

"No. It was a long time ago, Willie. He just asked if the rumor that I arrested you for pimping, once, was true, and I said it was. He asked if you were convicted, and I said you were."

He didn't like that. He stood, paced; wandered over to a writing desk decorated with framed pictures of his brood of kids and lit up a cigarette and began smoking nervously. But soon he said: "I can't expect you to have said otherwise. Thanks for telling me straight out."

"No thanks needed."

He sat next to me again, cigarette in hand, his expression painfully earnest. "You got to understand, Heller—the feds have been breathing down my neck for months. I had to step down as the IA's representative, not long ago, 'cause of this federal heat. Oh, I'm still running things. But from the sidelines; I can't even go in my own goddamn office, can you picture it?"

So that was why he bitterly bit off Browne's head for not being at the office: he was jealous he couldn't be there himself.

"Now, this Pegler shit. Comes at a bad time. I know who put him up to it, too."

"Who?"

"That bastard Montgomery. The smart-ass actor."

This irony guy got around.

"Robert Montgomery, you mean?"

"Yeah, him. That smart-ass, no-good, double-crossing bastard . . . after all I did for him."

Here was a new wrinkle.

"Why?" I asked. "What did you do for Montgomery?"

He scowled, not looking at me, but at an image of Montgomery fixed in his mind, I'd guess. He said, "Couple years ago SAG—Screen Actors Guild—serves notice on the studios that they now consider themselves a legitimate labor union, and want to be so recognized. You know—they wanted to enter into collective bargaining, like the big kids. So we, the IATSE, *me*, went to bat for 'em."

"Really."

"Yeah, I told that prick L. B. Mayer if he didn't recognize SAG, he'd have an IA strike to play with. My movie projectionists can shut this industry down overnight, you know."

"So I hear."

The round face was reddening. "Thanks to me, Mayer recognized their lousy little Guild, and Montgomery thanked us publicly, but now, fuck him! We're not *good* enough for him and the fags and dykes and Reds in his club."

So much for Karl Marx; Willie seemed more interested in the brothers Marx, or anyway their union dues.

"I'll tell you whose fault it *really* is. Frank. Frank's getting too greedy."

He meant Nitti. It was Bioff's first admission that he was working for the Outfit. He let it escape casually and I didn't react to it as any big deal. All I said was: "How so, Willie?"

"He wants to expand, and it just ain't the right time. There's this rival group, a CIO bunch called the United Studio Technicians, and they're spreading dissent among the IA rank and file. We got *them* to deal with, we got plenty to do, rather than try and kidnap a union that don't want anything to do with us, anyway."

"Why such a fuss, over show business? Aren't there bigger fish to fry, better unions to go after?"

As if speaking to a slow child, he said, "Heller, no matter what anybody tells you, people do not have to eat. Like the man said, there's only two things they really got to do—get laid, and see a show, when they can dig up the scratch."

The philosophy of a pimp turned Hollywood power broker.

"Listen," he said. "You've got a reputation of being a straight shooter. Frank speaks highly of you."

Nitti again.

"That's nice to hear," I said.

"You're known as a boy who can keep his mouth shut."

Actually, I was known in at least one instance for singing on the witness stand—when I helped bring the world crashing down on Mayor Cermak's favorite corrupt cops, Lang and Miller; but I had indeed kept some secrets for Frank Nitti. That was more important, where somebody like Bioff was concerned.

"I appreciate the vote of confidence," I said.

"How would you like to earn a couple of grand?"

The money was sure flying this week; I wondered if I'd live to spend any of it.

"Sure," I said. "What's your poison?"

"Pegler," he said.

It would be.

He was asking, "When are you heading back?"

"This afternoon," I said, somehow. "I'll be in Chicago tomorrow morning."

"Good. There are some people I want you to see."

"About what?"

"About me. I want you to find out if Pegler's been around to see them, and if he has, try and worm out of them what, if anything, they spilled."

Oh my.

"If he hasn't been around," he continued, "warn them him or somebody he's hired *may* be around. And tell them if they talk they'll go to sleep and never wake up."

I shook my head no. "Willie, I'll do some checking for you. Gladly. But I won't threaten anybody for you. And I don't want to know about that end of it, understood?"

He smiled, friendly as Santa Claus. "Sure, Heller. Sure. They can figure that out for themselves, anyway. Like the man said, when you eat garlic, it speaks for itself. Shall we say a grand down, a grand upon your reporting back to me? By phone is fine."

"Okay."

"You want this on your books, or should I give you cash?"

"Cash'll do."

"Sit tight and I'll get you some. Oh, and Heller. Don't tell anybody about this. Not Nitti or anybody. As far as Nick Dean is concerned, I had you out here to ask you about that O'Hare killing. I knew Eddie, you see, and as a matter of fact I would like to ask you a few questions about that before you go."

"All right."

"Anyway, I don't want Nitti to know I'm nervous about this Pegler deal. It wouldn't look good. I'm on the spot enough with this federal tax heat. So be careful—like the man said, when you play both ends against the middle you risk getting squeezed."

You're telling me.

He got up and went out and came back shortly with a thousand in hundreds in an IATSE envelope. I put it in my suitcoat pocket, answered his questions about the O'Hare shooting in a similar manner to the way I'd handled Captain Stege's, and soon he was walking me out of the house, an arm reached up around my shoulder, two old buddies from Chicago.

"Let me tell you about the time Little New York came out to visit," he said.

Louis Campagna; now *there's* a house guest.

"I had my sprinkler system going," Bioff said, gesturing to his expansive green lawn, "and Campagna—you know, he's a nature lover—"

"I didn't know that."

"Oh yeah, he's got a farm in Wisconsin, goes fishing all the time, loves the great outdoors. Anyway, he sees my sprinklers, dozens of 'em, turning in full circles, and he asks me what the hell they are, and I tell him, and he says, that's great! Get me six hundred."

I laughed.

"So I told him that six hundred of those things could irrigate all the city parks in Chicago. And that they'd freeze up in the cold weather. But he insisted, and he said I should charge 'em to the union. So I called the Waiter and asked him to talk Louie out of it."

The Waiter was Paul Ricca, rumored to be second in the Outfit only to Nitti.

"What happened?" I asked.

"Ricca wanted three hundred of 'em," he said, and walked me to the limo where his partner sat in back drinking beer.

On the way he told me who to see in Chicago.

16

The Southern belle, hoop skirt flouncing, parasol atwirl, a vision in white and pink and lace, strolled coyly to the settee and, with a leisurely grace, took off her red slippers. Then she removed her bonnet. The languid strains of "Swanee River" filling the air began to pick up tempo, build in volume. The belle, who was blond, shoulder-length curls tumbling to lacy shoulders, was rolling down a knee-length silk stocking from a leg extended from under the hoop skirt, foot arched; another slowly peeled stocking fell, and then she stood, stepping ever so ladylike out of her hoop skirt. She was about to step out of her lacy pantaloons as well when somebody tapped me on the shoulder.

"You pay to get in or what?" Jack Barger asked. The balding little Jew with the gone-out cigar in the corner of his mouth and the expensive but slept-in-looking brown suit was the owner of the theater, so he had a right to ask.

"No," I said. I was standing in back, next to a bored, uniformed usher who was looking at something he'd just picked out of his nose. "I told the girl at the box office I was here to see you."

Barger put a disgusted look on a puss that was naturally sour anyway, nodded toward the light. "Is that me?"

Across the darkened theater and its bumpy sea of male heads, I could tell at once that the stripper, who was now parading across the stage in lace panties and blue pasties before a cheesy plantation backdrop, was not Jack Barger.

"I'd say no," I said.

"You ain't kidding when you claim to be a detective, are you?" he said, typically. Barger was one of those guys whose kidding always seemed to be on the square; I'd known him, casually, for years, but sensed no affection in his sarcasm. If so, it was deep down.

He crooked and wiggled his forefinger at me in a "come along" motion. Though he was barely ten years my senior, he treated me like a kid. But I had a feeling he treated everybody that way.

I followed him through the small, rather bare lobby, with its seedily uniformed ushers and well-stocked concession stand and embarrassed uniformed girl behind it and all-pervasive popcorn smell, toward some stairs. The Rialto, which was on State Street just up the block and around the corner from my office on Van Buren, was the Loop's only burlesque house. The exterior was flashy enough, with the bright lights and usual promises—CHARMAINE AND HER BROADWAY ROAD SHOW, 25¢, GIRLS GIRLS GIRLS, with the window-card cheesecake displays and life-size standees to prove it, and of course, on the Rialto screen, this week's cinema masterpiece, *Sinful Souls*, ADULTS ONLY. And the promises were pretty much kept, even if the interior was decidedly unracy looking, more along the lines of an unadorned, smallish neighborhood theater. The patrons didn't mind; like the congregation of a spartanly appointed Protestant church, they didn't begrudge the lack of a cathedral as long as they could get to heaven.

Judging from how fast and loud the pit band was belting "Swanee River," now, heaven was well within view.

But not to me. I was following Barger up the jogs of the stairs to the level of purgatory housing his office, a cubbyhole next to the projectionist's booth.

The office was, like the theater itself, stark—a dark-wood desk and some metal file cabinets and a few framed photos of strippers and baggy-pants comics on one of the pale cream pebbly plaster walls; each and every one of the photos hung crooked.

"You look like something the cat drug in," Barger said, sitting behind his cluttered desk, lighting up a new cigar. It smelled like wet leaves trying to burn.

I sat across from him, topcoat in my lap. I still had on the suit I'd traveled in, and I didn't just have bags under my eyes, I had valises. I hadn't slept well on the plane; the flight had been bumpy, and so were my thoughts regarding my two conflicting clients, Montgomery of SAG and Bioff of the IATSE.

"I been out of town," I said.

"So I gathered from what you said on the phone," he said, picking some tobacco off his tongue. "I'm disappointed in you, Heller. Taking work from a rat bastard like Willie Bioff. Don't quote me."

"Don't worry. I'm on Bioff's payroll, not president of his fan club."

He shook his head. "Who'd have thought Nate Heller'd be another of Willie Bioff's whores."

"Who'd have thought Jack Barger would."

He laughed humorlessly. "Fair enough," he said.

"Speaking of Pegler," I said, "Fair Enough" being the name of his column, "that's why I'm here."

He squinted at me. "Westbrook Pegler? The big-shot columnist? What would he want with a minor-league Minsky like me?"

Barger's humility was false; while he was certainly no Minsky, he was the king of the local grind circuit. And in a convention town like Chicago, that meant money.

"He's looking to smear Bioff," I said.

"I've seen Pegler's stuff," Barger nodded, unimpressed. "He makes a living out of hating the unions, and Bioff's as good a place as any to start giving unionism a bad name."

"This has to do with the power the Stagehands Union is building in Hollywood, you know."

He expressed his disinterest with a wave of the hand in which the cigar resided, embers flying. "Don't give me history lessons on Willie Bioff and George Browne. I been around that block so many times your head'd spin. No, far as I know, Westbrook Pegler ain't been in my establishment. Not unless he likes young tits and old jokes."

"He doesn't seem the type," I admitted. "But he might send somebody around to pump you."

"Nobody pumps Jack Barger for information."

"It might not be direct; somebody might come around under false pretenses and—"

"Do I look stupid to you, Heller? Do you think I'm going to advertise what those bastards done to me? That'd make me look like a schmuck, and if Frank Nitti found out I'd been vocal, which he would, I'd wake up with a hole in my head in a goddamn ditch."

He was talking to me like I was an insider; if I handled this right, I could open him up like a clam.

"I'm not working for Nitti," I said. "I'm working for Bioff. And I'm only in it for the dough."

He pointed the cigar at me. "Be careful who you go whoring for, my friend. Those sons of bitches are murderers and thieves. Grow up."

I knew Barger primarily from the occasional drink he'd have with

Barney and me in Barney's cocktail lounge, when it was still below my office, and just around the corner from the Rialto. He and Barney were friends, hit it off fine, but Barney's more Jewish than I am. I always felt Irish around guys like Barger.

So I gave *him* the needle for a change. "You say you're surprised to see me, Jack. Hell, I was surprised to get *your* name from Bioff. I didn't know they had their hooks in you."

He stirred in his chair. "What'd you think, I don't have stagehands? Not that I should pay those lazy bastards anything for what little they do. Move some scenery here, carry a prop there. They should pay *me* for the privilege of working here, the ass they get. Only it don't work that way. And, fuck, the IA's got me coming and going, 'cause I'm a moviehouse, too, I got projectionists to deal with. Shit, I've had to put up with that beer-guzzling slob Browne longer than Bioff himself!"

The best way to keep Barger talking was to make him think I already knew more than I did. This required some calculated guessing, which as sluggish as I was from the sixteen-hour plane ride was going to be a good trick.

But I jumped right in—casually: "Browne must've been a phantom on your payroll since the Star and Garter days."

He didn't hesitate in confirming that: "To the tune of a hundred and fifty smackers a week, the drunken bastard."

The Star and Garter, a burlesque house at Madison and Halsted, had been Barger's mainstay prior to the success of the Rialto, which the "minor-league Minksy" opened during the World's Fair in '33; the Rialto's Loop location was closer to the fair, and less threatening for tourist trade, than the Star and Garter's Skid Row neighborhood.

"Of course a hundred-and-fifty's cheap," I said, "compared to what Bioff's hitting you for, these days. By the way, he said, 'Give my regards to my partner Jack.'"

Which Bioff had in fact said, and which proved to be what opened Barger's floodgate: "That arrogant little pimp! Partner! The first time I ever talked to him, what, must've been four years ago anyways, he walked in here with Browne and said, 'Kid,' called me *kid*, the condescending little bastard, 'kid, everybody's paying to keep the unions happy. So you have to pay.' What the hell, this is Chicago, I expect that, so I say, 'How much?' And Bioff says, 'Let's say twenty-five grand to start.' And I damn near fall off my seat! I say fuck you, go to hell, I ain't got twenty-five grand, and Bioff says, 'You want to stay in business, that's how it's gotta be.' I told 'em to get the hell out and they did."

He smiled to himself, pleased with the memory of getting tough with Bioff and Browne, then noticed his cigar had gone out and was relighting it when I said, "Yet here I am, Jack, giving you a message from your partner Willie."

His expression turned as foul as the cigar smoke. He said, "The fat little pimp came back alone, next time. No Browne, just the two of us, in this same office, and he said, 'How's tricks, partner?' And I said, 'I ain't your goddamn partner, and I suggest you leave.' And he said, 'I already talked to the Outfit about our partnership.' And I told him I'd close my show down before I got in bed with the mob."

Barger was shaking, now; whether with anger or fear or just the intensity of the memory, I couldn't say. But he went on speaking, and it seemed more for his own benefit than mine.

"The bastard Bioff says, 'You're already in. There's no getting out. You're partners with me, and I'm partners with the Outfit.' He said it'd be foolish for me to close down my show 'cause a man's gotta work, a man's gotta eat." Then with harsh sarcasm he added, "'Like the man said,' he said, 'don't throw away the blanket because you're mad at the fleas.'"

He sat smoking, his eyes glowing like the cigar's tip.

"That's Willie Bioff," I said. "A proverb for every occasion."

Very softly, with what I felt to be self-hate, he said, "And then he said, 'And just think, if you close the show, there's always the fact that maybe the mob wouldn't like it. They're sensitive people.'"

"And you went along with it," I said, with a tiny matter-of-fact shrug. "What else could you do?"

He slammed a fist on the desk and the clutter there jumped. "I *didn't* go along with it. Not till . . . aw, fuck it."

I made an educated guess, based on past experience: "Not till Little New York Campagna invited you on a certain suite at the Bismarck Hotel."

Where Frank Nitti himself would've waited.

Barger only nodded.

Then he sat up, pointed with the cigar. "Some friendly advice, kid. If you can get out from under Bioff, do it. That's bad company you're in. I like you, Heller. Any friend of Barney's is a friend of mine. This is no good for you."

I had a card left to play. On two occasions, in Barney's cocktail lounge, I'd seen Barger approached by Frankie Maritote, also known as Frankie Diamond, Al Capone's brother-in-law, a big ape with a broad homely mug and thick eyebrows like grease smears over beady eyes. It had stuck with me, and, when Bioff mentioned Barger as one of those I was to warn about Pegler, I remembered the mob connection the earlier Barger/Diamond encounters seemed to indicate.

Anyway, I played the card: "How long was it before Frankie Diamond came around?"

Barger shrugged. He seemed defeated. "Not long. They thought I was monkeying with the books, because I said business was off, and they heard we did standing-room-only, which was true, when the fair was in town. Since then it's weekends and conventions; we die during the week."

"So they sent a Syndicate bookkeeper over."

"Yeah. This guy Zevin. He's the Stagehand Union's bookkeeper, for this local anyway. He found I was giving myself a salary of two hundred a week. They made me fire myself and take Diamond on as manager. Only he never came around except to collect money from me, me who was doing the actual managing. Then, on one of the happiest days of my life, Diamond leaves town, for some other Syndicate deal, and I figure I'm rid of the leach. And this guy Nick Dean—you know him?"

I nodded. "He's a cold one."

He almost shivered. "Freezing. He brings Phil D'Andrea around. Phil D'Andrea!"

D'Andrea was the Capone bodyguard infamous for attending the Big Fellow's trial armed with a revolver, and getting caught at it. Contempt of court and six months in jail.

Barger was shaking his head. "Now D'Andrea's the 'manager.' That girl down in the box office is his goddamn sister."

Silence and cigar smoke filled the air.

"I appreciate the words of advice," I said, rising. "I'll finish this job for Bioff, and be done with him."

"You do that. The bastards've damn near drained me dry. I had to sell the Star and Garter for a lousy seven gee's, just to pay my goddamn taxes, and when they found out, they took half of *that!* Stay the hell clear of 'em, Heller."

"I'll do that. And you stay clear of Pegler, or anybody he might send to sniff around."

"Yeah, yeah. They won't get word one out of Jack Barger."

The baggy pants comics and a couple of girls from the pony line were doing the "Crazy House" routine on stage, when I came downstairs, leaving Barger behind. I watched from the back of the house; watched another stripper. Good-looking dame with black hair and somebody tapped me on the shoulder.

Barger again.

"You pay yet?" he asked.

"No."

"You must still think you're a cop. Everything's a free ride. Is it true Sally Rand's in town?"

"Yeah."

"You think you'll see her? Barney says you two were an item, once."

"I might see her."

"I hear she's broke."

"For the moment."

"If she'll stoop to a grand a week, I'll cancel my next booking and make room for her."

"I'll tell her if I see her. But I don't think she does burlesque."

"She will. She's not getting any younger."

Then he disappeared, and soon so did I, around the corner to my office.

Two other names on Bioff's list, Barney Balaban of the mighty Balaban and Katz chain, and James Coston, who managed the Warner Brothers chain in Chicago, were not receptive to visits by me. When I called from my office to make appointments, they insisted instead on taking care of our business over the phone.

"Willie Bioff wants you to be aware that Westbrook Pegler is in town," I told Balaban, "asking embarrassing questions."

After a long pause a confident baritone returned: "Tell Mr. Bioff that no one has been around to see me, and that should anyone do so, no embarrassing answers will be forthcoming from me. Good afternoon, Mr. Heller."

Coston was also inclined toward brevity: "Tell Willie not to worry. I won't talk."

These distinguished representatives of the Chicago motion picture community had, in their few short phrases, spilled as much in their way as Barger had in his.

They both knew Willie Bioff, and they both shared secrets with him they Had no intention of revealing to the press, or anyone else, for that matter.

Coston had told me volumes by simply repeating a typical Bioff aphorism; as a parting shot, I'd said, "Willie said to tell you if you got cornered, somehow, to lie, lie, lie."

"Tell Willie it's like he told me, once, when he threatened me with a projectionist's strike: 'If the only way to get the job done is to kill Grandma, then Grandma's going to die.'"

Now, only one name remained on Willie's list: my old flame Estelle Carey.

Nicky Dean's girl.

ESTELLE

17

She was wearing a skin-pink gown with sequins on the bosom, cut just low enough to maintain interest, her curled page-boy barely brushing her creamy shoulders. Tall, almost willowy, her supple curves and picture-book prettiness made her look twenty, when she was thirty. At least she did in the soft, dim lighting of the Colony Club, Nicky Dean's ritzy Rush Street cabaret, where Estelle Carey was overseeing a battery of "26" tables—numbered boards about three feet square at which mostly male customers shook dice in a leather cup and "threw for drinks." Each table was in turn overseen by another young woman, a "26 girl," a breed as much a Chicago fixture as wind or graft, pretty birds sitting on high stools luring homely pigeons. Here at the Colony, with its upstairs casino, the girls were on the lookout for the compulsive customer ready to graduate from the 26 table to "some real action" on the second floor, roulette, craps, blackjack.

Estelle was the acknowledged queen of the 26 girls; she even rated mention as such in the gossip columns, where the story was often told of her having taken ten grand from one high-roller in two hours.

She wasn't playing tonight; these days, that was for special occasions only. She was milling, chatting, glad-handing—she was a Chicago celebrity herself, in a minor way; a bush league Texas Guinan. She'd come far from her waitress days at Rickett's.

Not that Rickett's was a shabby place for a girl just twenty, at the time, to work. It was the Lindy's of Chicago, your typical white-tiled lunch room but open twenty-four hours, a Tower Town mainstay famous for attracting bohemian types and show people and your occasional North Side gangster. Rickett's was also known for its good, reasonably priced steaks, which was what brought me there, in my early plainclothes days. What kept me coming back, though, was the pretty blond waitress.

Nick Dean must've met her there as well, but that was after I'd stopped seeing her. We only lasted a couple of months, Estelle and me. But they were some months.

I'd run into her occasionally since, but we'd never more than had coffee, and not that, in five or six years.

So now I was edging through the packed Colony Club—this was Saturday night after all—with its art-deco decor, all chromium and glass and shiny black and shiny white, its crowd of conventioneers and upper-income types whose recreation in better weather was sailing skiffs and larger craft in Lake Michigan, the muffled sounds of ersatz Benny Goodman from the dine-and-dance area adjacent mingling with the noise of dice-and-drink, wondering if she'd recognize me.

Then I was facing her.

She gave me her standard, charming smile, one to a customer, and then it sort of melted into another kind of smile, a smile that settled in a dimple in one cheek.

"Nate," she said. "Nate Heller."

"I'd forgotten how goddamn green your eyes are."

"You know what you always said." Her eyes tried to twinkle, but the effect was melancholy.

"Yeah. That all they lacked was the dollar signs."

"Maybe you just didn't look close enough."

"You mean if I had I'd've seen 'em?"

She tossed her blond curls. "Or not."

Somebody jostled me—we were holding up traffic—and she took me by the arm and led me through the smoky, noisy bar to a wide open stairway, which was fitting for this wide open place. It separated the bar from the restaurant and wound gently up to two shiny ebony doorways overseen by a bouncer in a white coat and black dress pants and a shine he could look down in to check how mean he looked. She and the bouncer nodded at each other, and he pushed the doors open for us and I followed her on through.

We threaded our way through the crowded casino, a big open room with heavily draped walls and indirect lighting and action at every table, noise and smoke and the promise of easy money and easy women. Some of the men here had brought a date or possibly even a wife; but many of these girls in skin-tight gowns were from the same table as the 26 girls downstairs.

At the bar in back, Estelle approached a fleshy-faced man with wire glasses who stood near, but not quite at, the bar; he wore a white jacket and dress pants and was keeping an eye on the casino before him, arms folded, patrons stopping to chat and him smiling and nodding, occasionally dispatching directions to other, lesser white-jacketed employees.

We waited while he did that very thing, and then Estelle introduced us.

"Sonny, this is Nate Heller."

He smiled automatically, the professional host's twitch, but the eyes behind the glasses were trying to place me; as we were shaking hands, his grip moist and unconvincing, they did: "The detective."

"That's right. And you're Sonny Goldstone. I remember you from the 101 Club." Which had been a Rush Street speakeasy not so long ago, where—like here—he'd been floor manager. Now as then, Goldstone was one of Nicky Dean's partners—his front man, the ostensible owner of the Colony Club.

"I understand you've done some favors for the boys from time to time," he said in his hoarse, toneless voice.

"That's right." That wasn't exactly true, but it wasn't the sort of thing you went around denying, especially not to anybody connected.

"Pity about Eddie O'Hare," he said, impassively.

"Pity," I said, not reading him at all.

Estelle said, "Sonny, Nate's an old friend. I haven't seen him in years, seems like. I'm going to go upstairs with him for a while."

"The front two suites are in use."

"All right."

"Will you be long, Estelle? It's Saturday night, you know."

"We're just going to chat for half an hour or so."

"The people come here to see you, you know."

She patted his cheek like he was a naughty child for whom she held a certain reluctant affection. "The people come here to throw away money and their cares. I'm just window dressing. I'm sure you can keep the cash register ringing for a while without me."

"Have fun," he said, flatly; it might just as easily been "so long" or "fuck you."

We threaded back through the casino into the entry area, where we rounded a corner and found a door that said "No Admittance," which proved its point by being locked. Estelle unlocked it, and we were in a little hallway, off of which were a few doors and a self-service elevator. We took the elevator.

The third floor seemed to be offices and conference rooms and, as promised, a few suites.

Ours wasn't a lavish suite, just the like of a room in a typical Loop hotel, maybe a touch bigger, in shades of blue, small wet bar, bed and bath. Bed is what she was sitting on, kicking off her shoes, stretching out her million-dollar legs to relax, and show off.

"You want a drink, Nate?"

"When I knew you, you didn't drink."

"I still don't," she said, tossing her pageboy again. "I don't smoke either. But when I knew you, you sure did. Drink, I mean. Rum, as I remember. Has that changed?"

"No. I still don't smoke, though."

"You sound like a regular all-American boy."

"You're an all-American girl, all right. Horatio Alger in a skirt."

She frowned, just a little. "Why are you angry?"

"Am I?"

She patted the bed next to her. "Sit down."

I sighed, and did.

"You're angry because I'm so successful."

"No! I think your success is swell. It's what you wanted, isn't it?"

"Exactly what I wanted. And you've got what you wanted, all those years, don't you? Your own business. Your own detective agency."

I shrugged. "We are expanding," I said, not being able to help myself from bragging it up a little. I told her how I'd added two operatives and doubled my office space and even had a secretary, no more hunt-and-peck on the typewriter.

She smiled, both dimples. "I bet she's cute as a button, with a great big crush on her boss. Taken advantage of her yet, Nate?"

"Your psychic powers are failing you on that one, Estelle. I'm sorry I was a grouch, before."

She touched my shoulder. "I understand. It's just the same old argument, isn't it?"

"I guess."

"We don't need to have that, anymore, do we?"

"No we don't."

"We can't ever be an item again, so we should live and let live, right? No reason not to be pals, huh?"

"None at all."

Then I kissed her, and she put her tongue in my mouth, and the sequined dress was coming loose in my hands and then my mouth was on her breasts, frantically switching from one to the other, not able to get enough of either, her nipples startlingly erect, each a hard sweet inch, and her soft generous ass was in my two hands and my trousers were falling to the floor with the thud of a fainting man, and then I was in her, to the hilt, hating myself, hating her, loving her.

The old argument—the dispute that had killed us—had of course been back in her waitress days. We quickly fell headlong in love, or anyway I did, and whenever I wasn't working we were together, and most of the time had been spent in bed. She was only the third woman I'd ever been with, and the first one I'd ever had a real affair with. And I loved her till I thought my fucking heart would break, which, sure enough, it did.

She always asked for money. Not like a whore. Not right after the act. But before I left her, she'd say she was a few dollars short. Her rent was due. Her mother was sick. Her machinist stepfather was out of work. If I could just help out . . .

And I would.

But I wasn't alone. One night they changed my shift on me, and I had a night free I hadn't anticipated. I went to surprise her, to her little apartment on the near North Side and knocked, and she came to the door, cracking it open, and looked out at me with her wide green eyes and her wide white smile and said, "Nate, I'm afraid I have company."

I stood outside in the goddamn rain half the night before I gave up the vigil. Whoever he was, he was staying till morning, so fuck it.

The next day's confrontation was in Rickett's, where she was behind the gleaming white counter, and I almost lost her her job.

"What was his name?"

Softly, she said, "I see other people, Nate. I never said I didn't. I got a life besides you."

"You see other men, you mean."

"I see other men. Maybe I see women, too. How do you like *them* apples?"

I grabbed her wrist. "Do they *all* give you money?"

She smiled at me through gritted teeth, a hateful, arrogant smile. "Only when I ask them to," she said.

Now, ten years later, here I was in bed with her again. Or, anyway, on top of a bed with her. A fast frantic fuck, my pants off, my shoes and shirt and tie on; her dress pulled down and up and a jumble around her middle, panties caught on one ankle. We must've been a sight.

I pushed off her, embarrassed, ashamed. I couldn't look at her. I couldn't look at myself.

"I'm sorry," I said. "I'm sorry."

She was touching my shoulder. I wanted to shrug her hand off, violently, but I couldn't. I wanted to ask her to slip her arm all the way around me, but I couldn't.

"It's all right, Nate. I wanted it."

"You're Nicky Dean's girl."

"I'm my own girl, honey. Nicky's not one to talk. He's out in Hollywood cheating on both of us."

I looked at her. "What do you mean, 'both of us'?"

She shrugged, shot me a crinkly smile. "Me and his wife."

"I didn't know he was married."

"Neither does he, most of the time. She's a little chorus-line cutie he married back in the early twenties. She's still pretty cute, for an older broad. Real sickly, though."

There was no jealousy in her voice. Very matter of fact.

"You mind if we put our clothes on?" I asked.

"Yes I do," she said, rolling one of her stockings down; the Southern belle at the Rialto had nothing on her. "I want you to strip down and I'm going to do the same and then we're going to slide under these cool sheets and turn down the lights and cuddle and chat and see what comes up."

I looked into that cute, mischievous face, trying to see the cold cynical heart that had to dwell behind it somewhere; but I couldn't find it.

I could only smile back and sit unprotesting as she undid my tie and my shirt, and soon we were two cool bodies between cool sheets in a dark anonymous room.

I thought of Sally (Helen in bed), and wondered if I was a bastard. Well, perhaps I was a bastard, that was almost certainly the case, but Sally had left town this morning, before I even got back. She was on a sleeper plane to California this very minute, flying the same sky that I crawled down out of this morning. There'd been a note of thanks on the bed, saying she'd made her Brown Derby booking and would be back in town next month; she'd try to see me then. That "try" browned me off. But what the hell—Sally was just a sweet memory I'd had a chance to momentarily relive; there was no future for us.

Just as there was no future with the memory I was holding in my arms now. Like Sally, Estelle was the past. But since there were no women in my present to speak of, the past was better than nothing. Let the future take care of itself.

"Aren't you even interested why I came around?" I asked her.

"To see me, of course."

"That's true. But I came looking for you for a reason. I'm working."

She snuggled against me. "You mean, you're getting paid for this? Why, Nate Heller, you little whore."

"You're more right than you think," I said. "I'm here on an errand. Willie Bioff sent me."

She pulled away to have a look at me and her smile was open-mouthed and her green eyes amused but mostly she was just surprised.

"But you *hate* that little pimp! I remember when you busted him . . ."

"You remember that?"

"Sure! You were ranting about how he slapped some woman around. You were quite the knight in shiny armor in those days."

"Hardly. It was pretty tarnished even then. You forget how I moved from uniform to plainclothes."

She waved that off with a friendly smirk. "So you lied on the witness stand. You know anybody who hasn't?"

She had me there.

She pulled away from me, just a little, to lean on a pillow and half sit up and appraise me. "Willie Bioff, huh? If he's in town, why didn't he stop up and see me personal?"

"He isn't in town. I just got back from a couple days in California."

Her laugh was a grunt. "He's making hay while the sun shines out there, that's for sure. What put the two of *you* in bed together? Pardon the expression."

Briefly, I told her about Pegler investigating Bioff's past and present; that she should be on the lookout for Pegler himself or somebody Pegler might send around.

"Nobody's been around yet," she said. "And I don't think anybody'd get a single word out of me. But I appreciate the tip. Willie must be afraid his phones are tapped."

"Or that yours are."

"Possible," she said, nodding. "These FBI and internal revenue boys are hard to bribe. They seem intent on doing their goddamn jobs."

"You never met Eliot Ness, did you?"

"Actually, I did a couple times. He raided the 101 more than once. He was cute. You two boys were thick, later on, I hear. The tarnished knight and the boy scout. Quite a combo."

"Let's just say he did his goddamn job. I can respect that; can't you?"

"Why not? What became of him?"

"He's public safety director in Cleveland."

She mock-yawned.

"It's not really all that dull," I said. "He's done his share of gang-busting in those parts. He's the guy that ran the Mayfield Road Mob out of Cleveland."

"I just love civic progress." She shook her head, smiled wryly. "You and Willie Bioff. That's a match made in hell."

"He's not such a bad guy," I lied. Again, I played a surmise of mine like it was a fact, saying, "So what if he's hitting up the movie moguls for some strike-prevention insurance? He's done okay by the rank and file . . . going back as far as that soup kitchen he and Browne started."

She started laughing and I didn't think she was going to stop.

"Estelle, cut it out, you're gonna bust a gut . . ."

"The soup kitchen!" Tears were rolling down her face. "Yeah, yeah, the soup kitchen . . . couple of philanthropists, that's Bioff and Browne." Laughing throughout.

"Okay, okay, so I'm a naive jerk. Let me in on the joke, why don't you?"

She leaned on her elbow, shaking her head, smiling ear to ear. "That soup kitchen was the biggest scam Willie Bioff ever ran on this burg. That's what got him and Browne started."

"How do you mean?"

"They used the joint to launder money, you cute impressionable little hick. They went to Barney Balaban of the B and K chain . . ."

"I talked to him today, for Bioff. Giving him the same warning about Pegler as I gave you."

"How is he in bed?"

"Cute, Estelle. Very cute."

She snorted. "Well, it wouldn't be the first time he got screwed. See, after the crash, Balaban got the Stagehands Union to let him get away with a twenty-five percent pay cut. You know, hard times and deflation and all. Then all of a sudden the World's Fair came in and every kootch show on the midway was needing stagehands and show business in general around here was booming. This next part I love. Balaban is in the hospital for his ulcers, and Willie and George go visit him. They take him flowers and smile at him and ask him how he's feeling and he says better and smiles back and they inform him that if he doesn't restore the twenty-five percent pay cut immediately they will call their men out on strike. This would close every one of his four hundred movie theaters. Some treatment for stomach ulcers, huh? Anyway, Balaban said his company couldn't afford it, and Willie reminded him about the soup kitchen. How there were good Samaritans who donated to it. And Balaban offered 'em a hundred and fifty a week for the soup kitchen, if they'd forget this strike business."

"And Willie and George grabbed it."

She gestured with an upraised, lecturing finger. "No. They asked for *fifty thousand a year* for the soup kitchen."

"Jesus Christ. Did they get it?"

Knowing chuckle. "They settled for twenty grand. Of course, Browne did use some of the dough for supplies for the kitchen. He bought four cases of canned soup for two dollars and fifty cents each."

"I always suspected that soup kitchen was some kind of racket."

"Sure! What else? They sold votes to politicians out of there, too—all those stagehands and their families would vote any way Willie told 'em. That brought in a pretty penny in soup kitchen donations."

I was impressed. "Estelle, you are one knowledgeable girl. Dean must really trust you to let you in on all this stuff."

"Ha! What little spider do you think led Bioff and Browne into Nicky's web in the first place?"

"You?"

Another wry smile. "In case you hadn't picked up on it, Detective Heller, Browne drinks."

"Really? My, you *are* knowledgeable."

"Shut up, Nate. But *Bioff* doesn't drink, not as much anyway. He's not used to holding his liquor."

"So?"

"So the night after they took Barney Balaban for twenty grand, they went out on the town. That afternoon they'd bought themselves fancy foreign sportcars, and spiffy new clothes. Bioff likes to look good, good as he can, the fat little greasy bastard. Anyway, guess where they go to celebrate? The 101 Club. Nick's club. Guess how they choose to unwind? With a little game of twenty-six. Guess who the twenty-six girl was? Little ole me."

I laughed softly. "And guess who started bragging about being in the dough?"

"Exactly right," she said, green eyes smiling. "I motioned to Nicky and he came over and joined us. Before the night was out we had the whole story."

"I think I can guess the rest. Nicky told Nitti."

"Ricca, actually. Little New York and Frankie Rio picked Willie and George up the next day, hauled 'em to the Bismarck. Nitti was in on it, by that time, I'm sure. I don't know what was said, but the upshot was the Outfit cut themselves in for half."

"How'd Willie and George take that?"

"The same way they took it when Nitti upped the Outfit's share to two-thirds, a few years later. Without any fuss, how else do you take something like that? But it paid off for 'em in the long run."

"It was bound to," I said. "Nitti's a financial mastermind, and about as shrewd a planner, as skillful a chessplayer as you could find in the board room of the biggest corporation in town."

"Nate, he *is* in the board room of the biggest corporation in town."

"My mistake."

She elaborated: "First thing they did for those union Katzenjammer Kids was get Browne elected national president of the IA. He ran once before and lost. Before he had the Outfit's support, I mean. This time when they held the election, in Columbus back in '34, there were more gunmen in the room than voting delegates. Lepke Buchalter was the guy in charge."

"That could sway a fella's vote."

"Like Capone said, you can get more with a kind word and a gun than with just a kind word. Anyway, those two horses' asses have been on the gravy train ever since. They were in New York awhile, where the studios have corporate headquarters—and then they were going to move their office to Washington, at the president's request, but Nitti vetoed it."

"What president's request?"

"You know. *The* president. The guy with the glasses and funny cigarette holder and dumpy wife? He wanted George and some other union leaders to be close at hand, to be advisors on domestic affairs."

Maybe Montgomery was right about that third term.

She seemed to be winding down, now. "Three years ago they moved the office to Hollywood, and Nicky went with 'em, to keep an eye on them for the boys. He comes back a lot, though. This club's his first love."

"I get the feeling Nitti doesn't trust Willie and George."

"It's not George. George is just a tub of fat, guzzling beer all day long. Willie's the one who might pull a fast one someday."

"Well, when Willie sent me here to warn you, he hoped it wouldn't get back to Nitti. Which means I'd appreciate it if you didn't tell Nicky about this."

"Sure, honey. You can trust me."

"I guess Bioff figures he's on the spot enough, with this income-tax scare."

Her expression was thoughtful, businesslike. "Willie Bioff could be about to get caught. A lot of money's been pouring through his chubby fingers. They been getting brown paper bags of cash for years now, from every major studio you can think of—MGM, Twentieth Century-Fox, Paramount, Warner Brothers, you name it. Willie's latest scam, Nicky says, is making the studios make him their 'agent' for buying raw film stock. He gets a seven percent commission on all film stock the studios buy."

"A money laundry again?"

"Yeah. But that's a new idea, and there's a lot of money to wash out there. Anyway, don't give me this song-and-dance about Willie Bioff looking after the rank and file. He's been selling out his own union members, agreeing to wage cuts and longer hours, for as long as he's been a union boss."

"How do you feel about that, Estelle? You used to be a working girl."

She shrugged. "I still am. Willie's just doing what we all gotta do,

Nate. Looking out for himself. You *got* to look out for yourself; nobody's gonna do it for you."

"My old man gave the best years of his life working for the unions."

"What'd it get him?"

"Nothing. Heartbreak."

"See? Enough of this. Let's kick Bioff out of bed and keep it to just the two of us."

Part of me wanted to be a million miles away from this sugar-sweet, hard-as-nails dame; part of me, and not just the part you're thinking, didn't ever want to leave. "Don't you have to be getting back downstairs?" I asked her, half looking for an out. "Won't you get in trouble with Sonny?"

Short deep laugh. "Don't be silly, Nate. Sonny works for me. I own a third of this place, and he owns jack shit. I can stay up here and screw my brains out all night long, if I like, and who's to stop me?"

"Must you be so romantic, Estelle?"

"Be quiet. I'm a whore, Nate. I can't remember ever saying it right out like that, before, but it's true, isn't it? I'm Nicky Dean's little whore. And you're Willie Bioff's little whore. Well, fuck them both. And fuck us."

And we did. Repeatedly.

18

Sunday I slept in till noon. I was in my own bed in my own room at my own hotel, having left the Colony Club around 4:00 A.M., getting the fish eye from Sonny Goldstone but not much caring. I knew there was no way to approach Estelle without Nitti and company learning. But Estelle was an old flame of mine, and besides, any man who ever saw her wouldn't question my motives for spending six hours in a suite with her.

I'd asked the desk to hold all calls, but on my way to lunch I picked up my messages and found that Pegler had been trying to call me all morning. Why wasn't he in church, praying for an end to unionism? Anyway, I stopped at a pay phone and called him; he was staying at the Drake.

"I must see you at once," he said.

"I'm going to get something to eat and then I have some things to do. Meet me at my office around four."

"Heller, I have a train to catch."

"When?"

"Eight this evening."

"Meet me at my office around four," I repeated, and hung up.

I could have done without meeting with Pegler at all, but I didn't see any way around it; Montgomery was a client, and he expected me to cooperate with Pegler, to a degree at least. But being seen with Pegler at this point could prove embarrassing, maybe even fatal, which made me glad he was coming up on a Sunday-afternoon, not a business day. Of course, if he were to be seen entering my office on a Sunday, that might be interpreted as a secret meeting, and . . .

What the hell. I felt reasonably secure, and not just because I had an automatic under my shoulder. I'd pulled it off—done my job for Montgomery by doing my job for Bioff. Slight conflict of interest, there, of course, but who was to know? Still, as I walked the Loop on a quiet Sunday afternoon of a winter day that had me turning up my

PEGLER

collar and stuffing my gloved hands deep in my topcoat pockets, I felt a little jumpy, looking behind me, seeing if I was being tailed.

I didn't seem to be, and I had a leisurely solitary luncheon at the Brevoort Hotel dining room—breast of guinea hen, corn fritters, fresh mushrooms. Two cups of hot black coffee, declining a third to keep the jumpiness at bay. The wear and tear of the California trip was starting to fade; the glow of last evening's sexual adventures still warmed me; and I was comforted by the thought that I would soon be at my office typing up a confidential report to Robert Montgomery, after which I would phone Willie Bioff, and finally dispense with Westbrook Pegler, putting this risky but neatly profitable affair behind me.

It was one-thirty-something when I climbed the stairs to the fourth floor of Barney's building, my footsteps making hollow notes in the otherwise silent Sunday-afternoon symphony the empty building was playing. My keys were already in my hand, I'd fished them out on the stairs, so even that didn't add a sound.

But something inside my office did.

Through the pebbled glass, at left, adjacent to the door, I could make out a shape, rising, and heard a grunt.

Quietly, quietly, I slipped the gun out from under my arm.

Pegler? No. Not two and a half hours early. Or was Pegler's hotel phone tapped? Did someone know about our meeting at four, and was waiting to do the both of us in, a Sunday afternoon two-for-one sale? From the sound of it, whoever it was was making some effort in there, not expecting me here this soon, tossing the office, maybe, looking for something or staging a fake robbery to drop some bodies into and, well, that was enough of that.

The gun tight in my gloved hand, I smashed the pebbled glass, with a powerful swing of the forearm, gun barrel leading, shattered the glass and shards went flying as I thrust my arm, gun in hand, through the jagged teeth where the panel of glass had been and pointed it at where the shape had been as a woman screamed and a man said, "Oh, *shit!*"

There, on the couch, on my old modernistic black-and-white World's Fair couch, was Frankie Fortunato, with his bare hairy ass, his bare hairy everything, showing, as he looked back at me with eyes that managed to be narrow and wide at the same time. Under his skinny naked body was a beautiful naked girl.

Specifically, Gladys.

"Whoops," I said. Lowering the gun.

"Mr. Heller," Frankie said, and it was the first time he ever used "mister" in front of my name, "I can explain."

He was crawling off Gladys, leaving the poor girl there to do an embarrassed, impromptu "September Morn" imitation, and not a bad job for somebody lying down. She wasn't screaming anymore, but her mute humiliation killed the fun of learning that the body under her clothes lived well up to expectations.

I unlocked the door and went in, and Frankie was almost in his pants, and Gladys had reached for her dress, and was sitting now, covering herself up with it, looking scared and ashamed.

"We didn't have anywhere else to go," Fortunato explained, lamely, zipping up. "Gladys lives with her mom and I live with my uncle and aunt."

"Don't," I said. Embarrassed myself. Putting the gun away. "Not necessary."

"Are we fired, Mr. Heller?" Gladys managed to say. Her big brown eyes showed white all around.

I went over and sat on the edge of her desk; assayed the damages. Glass fragments littered the floor like huge misshapen snowflakes. The hole in the pane provided a scenic view of the abortionist's office across the way.

"Nobody's fired," I said. "Get dressed, Gladys. Pick up your things quick like a bunny, I won't even look, and duck in my office and dress. Shoo."

She shooed. But I watched out of the corner of my eye. Only the memory of last night with Estelle enabled me to live with the sure knowledge that the only time Gladys's perfect pink body would be naked in my inner office would be today, putting her clothes back on at my request.

"Jesus, I'm sorry, Heller," Frankie said. He was fully clothed now. Snugging his tie in place.

The "mister" hadn't lasted long.

"It's okay," I said. "I know how it is. Get it while the getting's good."

"You're not mad?" Smoothing a hand up over his dark widow's peak.

"I'm jealous."

Gladys emerged, dressed in a blue-and-white Sunday frock with a virginal bow at the neck. She said, "I'll pay for the window."

I looked at Frankie.

He shrugged. "We'll go dutch."

"Frankie," I said, "as long as you're around, chivalry is not dead. In a coma, maybe, but not dead. *I'll* pay for the window. It was my fault."

"How could it be your fault?" Frankie wondered.

"I'm jumpy today. And, also, some dangerous things have been going on and I haven't bothered to clue you people in. That's *my* mistake, and it comes out of working alone for so long."

Frankie slipped his arm around Gladys, supportively. "We'll go now," he said, "if that's okay."

"Sure. I got some work to do, or I'd let you use the couch."

Fortunato grinned, but Gladys, still embarrassed, looked away from me. But she let him keep his arm around her.

"Oh," I said to them. "One of you could get the broom from the closet and sweep up that glass, before you go, but be careful. Of course judging by those, I can see you already are . . . pick them up, too, would you?" I was referring to, pointing to, a package of Sheiks that lay on the floor next to the couch.

Gladys was crying a little, or trying to.

I put a finger under her chin and lifted her head and looked into her wide brown eyes. "I don't mean to make you feel bad. I'm just jealous, understand?"

And then she did the most remarkable thing, which made the whole embarrassing, expensive encounter worthwhile: she smiled at me.

I went into my inner office and pulled my typing stand around and began pecking out Montgomery's confidential report. After while I heard glass being dumped into the wastebasket and, surprisingly, it wasn't Fortunato but Gladys who opened the door and looked in.

"I'm sorry, Mr. Heller."

"Nothing to be sorry about. Can I ask you a question, though?"

"Sure."

"Why him?"

She shrugged. "He's cute."

And then she was gone, and I was pecking at the report. I put it all in, every rumor, every anecdote, every slip of the tongue that

Browne, Dean, Bioff, Barger, Balaban, Coston and Estelle had handed me. But I stated clearly that it was all hearsay, and should be used only as background, or as the starting place for a real investigation. None of these people was likely ever to go public with their knowledge. It took over two hours and I made some corrections in ink and then folded the six single-spaced pages and put them in an envelope, with Montgomery's home address typed on it. I included no cover letter and no return address. He had promised to keep my name out of it, after all; why not remind him?

I put my feet up on the desk and called Willie Bioff at the number he'd given me, which was his eighty-acre ranch in Canoga Park. A colored maid answered and it took a few minutes for him to come to the phone; calling long distance and hearing silence for several minutes is like watching dollar bills float out the window, but considering I'd wrapped Bioff's two-grand assignment up in as many days, I could stand to watch a few of 'em float.

"Heller," Bioff said.

"I talked to your friends."

"Good. Any problems?"

"No."

"Any of them say anybody's been around asking?"

"No."

"Think they'll keep mum?"

"I couldn't say."

"That's a fair answer. I'll send you a cashier's check for the second grand. We don't want to trust that much cash to the mails. Those guys ain't union—yet."

He hung up, and so did I.

At ten to four I heard somebody enter the outer office. I slipped my gun out of the holster and leaned back in my chair and waited.

Pegler came in.

"You're early," I said, gun in hand.

He frowned and waggled a finger at me. "Aren't we past that?" Then he waggled the finger back where he came from. "And what happened in your outer office? It's a goddamned mess."

Not a "goddamn" mess. A "goddamned" mess. Ain't we grand.

I put the automatic back under my shoulder. "I thought somebody was in my office lyin' in wait for me, so I broke the glass, but it was just one of my operatives humping the secretary."

Pegler made a disgusted face, pulled a chair up and sat down. "Very amusing, I'm sure. What have you got to tell me?" He wore another expensive, beautifully tailored suit with lapels wide as wings, light brown this time, with monogrammed pocket kerchief and a dark brown tie touched with white.

"Nothing, really," I said. "I'm making a confidential report to Robert Montgomery. If he wants to share any of it with you, that's up to him. But nothing I discovered is anything you'll be able to easily prove. Nobody who talked to me is going to talk to you, or anybody, not openly."

"*You* could be quoted," he said, with a shrewd little devilish smile. "My column is not a court of law; I'll admit hearsay evidence, gladly."

"No. It wouldn't be healthy to."

"I see. I didn't take you for a coward, Heller."

"I didn't take you for a jackass. I've been risking my life, poking into this. This is Frank Nitti's business you're nosing in, and if you really did play cards with Jake Lingle, once upon a time, you'll know that the Capone mob *has* been known to kill reporters—so you're not immune, either."

He took his cigarette case out of his coat pocket and selected a cigarette and lit it up. "Is it a matter of money?"

"No, it's a matter of life and death. I don't want you for a client, Mr. Pegler. I have enough clients already."

He shrugged elaborately, blew out smoke. "Do what you please. I don't need your paltry gossip, anyway. You've *already* helped me, Heller, whether you know it or not, whether you *want* to or not."

"Really?"

His smile, the tilt of his head, turned coy. "I've just spent the last several days looking through old police records. With the help of a local officer, a Lieutenant Bill Drury, and several others, I've made some interesting discoveries."

Bill Drury and I had started out on the pickpocket detail together; he was an honest, ambitious cop who hated the Outfit almost irrationally. He'd rousted every major mob figure in the city, numerous times, just for fun—Nitti, Guzik, Ricca, all of them. Why he was still alive was a mystery it would take a better detective than yours truly to ever solve.

But I meant it when I said, "Bill is as good as they come."

"He spoke highly of you," Pegler conceded. "If I hadn't dropped your name, in fact, I don't know that he would have devoted the time to this he did. He helped me locate a number of brief jail terms Bioff served, dating back as early as 1922. But more importantly we tracked down the record of *your* arrest of Bioff. There it was—a lonely faded index card—with your name and Shoemaker's, as arresting officers."

"Old Shoes"—another honest cop, a legendary police detective, dead now.

"So what?" I said. "I already told you Bioff got a conviction off that bust."

Smugness was in every line of his face, every pore. "We needed verification. But we found much more; we hit the proverbial jackpot. You see, Willie Bioff's *never served* his six-month sentence for pandering."

I shrugged. "I could've told you that. He clouted his way out of it."

"Perhaps. But I don't think you understand—it's on the records as an 'open' conviction—Willie Bioff *still* owes the state of Illinois *six months*."

I sat forward. "Maybe you really do have hold of something. You're sure about this? My understanding was he appealed it and bought his way out."

"Money no doubt exchanged hands," Pegler said, blowing out smoke but not hot air, "and William Morris Bioff did appeal the sentence, and was released pending the decision of the higher court. But when I placed a simple phone call to the clerk of the Supreme Court in Springfield, Illinois, I learned that the appeal had never reached there. The case had been purposely sidetracked in Cook County, somewhere, and conveniently forgotten."

Jesus. In 1930 I'd been part of a raid on a sleazy South Halsted Street brothel and we'd caught the stocky little pimp slipping out the back with the brothel's tally sheet in hand; later he'd slapped one of the whores who said the wrong incriminating thing about him, and I'd sworn to myself the little bastard would serve time in the Bridewell for it, Chicago or no Chicago. Now, almost ten years later, it looked like maybe he would.

"I've laid the information before State's Attorney Thomas E. Courtney," Pegler said grandiosely, "who informs me he'll request Bioff's extradition to Illinois."

"By God, I think you've got the little bastard."

"I've got the little kike, all right."

Silence.

"Watch that, okay, Mr. Pegler?"

Amused little smile. "You're offended?"

"Nothing much offends me. But sometimes I get pissed off awful fierce. You remember me—the guy with the gun?"

Pegler smirked at that and said, "At any rate, your friend Lieutenant Drury has come up with the goods on George Browne, as well. In 1925 Browne was involved in a gangland shooting, in a restaurant; he was shot in the seat of the pants, and his companion was killed. Browne was quoted as telling the police at the scene, 'I'll take care of it, boys.' Four weeks after he got out of the hospital, the man who fired the shots was himself shot to death, his assailant never found."

"That's not as good as an unserved jail sentence," I said, "but it'll play in your column. It'll paint Browne as a union man with a gangster past."

"They're both finished," he said, with quiet glee. "And so is the Stagehands Union."

"I wouldn't count on that. Maybe they'll clean house. Maybe if Bioff and Browne and the Outfit are tossed out, it'll be a *real* union again."

He looked like he had a bad taste in his mouth, as he said, "A real union, what is that? An inert rank and file who go to meetings only when something's in it for them. And a union boss who's part ham actor and part Tammany chief, who knows enough not to show too much respect for their intelligence."

"I don't want to talk unions with you, Pegler. I'm for exposing Bioff and Browne and Dean and the rest, because they're perverting something that *should* work. But your anti-unionism offends me, it's bullshit. My father—"

"Your father. He was of that particular tribe, I take it?"

"What?"

Pegler rose. Stabbed his cigarette out in the glass tray on my desk. "Nothing. It's too bad you're unwilling to put your convictions on the line and tell me what else you've discovered, in your own investigation. You'll be a hero in my column, nonetheless, as the surviving arresting officer, as the man whose hard work ten years ago made possible bringing Willie Bioff to justice today."

"Spell my name right and mention the agency and I won't sue you."

"How generous of you. Are you certain you wouldn't care to share any further information with me? There's money in it. A man of your persuasion can appreciate *that*, I'm sure."

"My persuasion?"

His lip curled in a patrician sneer. "You're a Jew, aren't you? Mr. *Heller?* You don't look it, but you are."

"So fucking what?"

He didn't like being cursed at; his face reddened and his satanic eyebrows twitched and he said, "Listen to me, you foul-mouthed little hebe—if I didn't need you to make this story float, I'd paint you for the kike coward you are . . ."

I was out from behind the desk before he could finish and grabbed him by the wings of his suitcoat and dragged him out of my inner office and dragged him through my outer office and hurled him out into the hall, where he bounced up against and off the abortionist's office, almost shattering *that* glass.

"I could break you," Pegler said, sitting in a pile, breathing through his nose like a bull.

"I could kill you," I said.

He thought that over. I was, after all, a guy who'd pointed a gun at him more than once. And I was breathing hard, too, and looked like I meant it. I did.

He pushed up and straightened himself and walked off without another word.

That evening, in Barney's Cocktail Lounge, I sat in a rear booth with my ex-boxer pal and said, "I never felt this Jewish before. I never felt particularly Jewish at all. Anyway, not since I was a kid."

Barney hadn't been surprised by my Pegler story.

"There's a lot of it goin' around," he said, shrugging.

I knew what he meant.

"Don't start with me, Barney. Please don't start."

He didn't. But for the first time I think I understood him, and his concerns. I knew that something was loose in the world that was worse than the Chicago Outfit.

For the moment, however, the Outfit was bad enough.

Because suddenly there was Little New York Campagna standing by the booth with his cold dark eyes and impassive putty face trained on me.

And without saying a word, he clearly conveyed to me that somebody in a suite at the Bismarck Hotel was waiting to see me.

19

Nitti didn't have an office in the Loop. He did his business out of several restaurants and various hotels—most frequently the Bismarck, on the corner of LaSalle and Randolph, just across from City Hall. I'd met Nitti here before, in this very suite—the *Presidential Suite,* the little gold plate on the door said. The room was at the dead end of the seventh-floor hall, down at the left after you stepped off the elevator, and I was presently standing in a vestibule facing Louis Campagna.

We'd walked here from Barney's cocktail lounge; a gentle snow falling. Sunday night in the Loop, and the concrete canyons were strangely peaceful. Like church. My heart was a trip-hammer.

And it hadn't slowed yet; which was fine with me, since having a heart that was still beating was something I valued. Campagna hadn't said two words to me on the way here—he hadn't said one word, either—but he was keeping two eyes on me, rarely blinking, perfecting a cold dark stare that made me wonder just how much trouble I was in.

If I was in serious trouble, wouldn't I be dead in an alley by now? Or did Nitti merely want to talk to me, first? He'd sent Campagna after me, tonight, just as earlier in the week he'd sent him to deliver a message; and Campagna was beyond that sort of thing—he was in the inner circle, now, not just a bodyguard or an enforcer. Yet Frank had sent *him,* not some flunkie. What did that mean?

The door opened and Johnny Patton, in a dapper gray topcoat with a dark fur collar, exited, looking back, smiling, saying, "A pleasure as always, Frank," a black homburg in one gloved hand.

What was Patton—the "boy mayor of Burnham," Eddie O'Hare's business partner at Sportsman's Park—doing here? And why had Nitti let me see him?

Patton put his hat on and walked by without a word, not recognizing me, or not choosing to.

NITTI

Campagna jerked a thumb toward the door, which Patton had left ajar.

That meant I was to go in.

There were no bodyguards in the suite, at least in the living room that I entered into, the same white-appointed, gold-trimmed room I remembered. A bedroom off the entryway, to my right, had its door cracked open and a light was on; someone was rustling around in there. Whether a bodyguard or a woman or what, I couldn't say. And I sure as hell didn't ask.

As for Nitti, he was seated on a white couch, feet on a glass coffee table on which were several stacks of ledger books; he was thumbing through one, reading one of the large, awkward-to-hold books like the latest popular novel. He was wearing a brown silk dressing gown, black dress pants and brown slippers. There was no monogram on the robe. A glass of milk, about a third drunk, was making a ring on the coffee table, next to some ledgers.

He looked heavier than the last time I'd seen him, and older, but good. The mustache he'd had when I first met him was long gone; he was a smooth executive now, despite his rough features, a strong, almost handsome face with flecks of scar tissue here and there, most noticeably on his lower lip. His hair was longer, brushed back with less of that slick look I remembered, a little gray in it, and the part in his hair had wandered from left to right. Maybe he was cutting his own hair, now—I'd known him to be dissatisfied with other barbers. I say "other" barbers, because he'd begun as a barber himself (his first such job in Chicago had been in the same shop as Jake "The Barber" Factor, who later helped Nitti frame Roger Touhy, but that's another, if typical, Nitti tale) and even before he began to effect the look and style of a business executive, he'd been immaculately groomed.

"Forgive me if I don't rise," he said.

I tried to find sarcasm in the words, but couldn't quite do it. Couldn't quite rule it out, either.

"Sure, Frank." Was it still okay to call him that? "Mind if I sit down?"

Still reading the ledger, his eyes having not yet landed on me, Nitti waved one hand with mild impatience, saying, "Sit, sit."

I sat in a high-backed, gold-upholstered chair near Nitti. I was up higher than him, in this thronelike chair; and he was a relatively small man, perhaps four inches shorter than me. None of which kept me from feeling intimidated, and very small indeed.

After what seemed forever, and was probably a minute, Nitti put the ledger on top of some other ledgers and pointed to his glass of milk. "Care for something? Just 'cause I gotta drink this goddamn stuff doesn't mean you can't enjoy yourself."

"No thanks, Frank."

"Not a drinking man?"

"Sometimes. Not during business. I assume this isn't a social call."

He shrugged, ignored the question, saying, "I'm not a drinking man myself. Some occasional vino, that's about it. My apologies for bothering you on a Sunday, a Sunday night at that."

"No, that's fine," I said, "it's good to see you," trying not to let it sound like a lie.

He gestured with both hands, a very Italian gesture, or in his case Sicilian. "I usually don't work on Sundays," he said. "I like to spend Sunday with the family. Go to Mass. Play with my boy. Hey, you want to see something?"

I swallowed. "Sure, Frank."

He dug under the robe. I remembered the story about the night Capone threw a testimonial banquet for Scalise and Anselmi and was toasting them when he reached behind him for a baseball bat and splattered their brains.

But Nitti was only getting his wallet. He opened it, grinning, pushed it in front of me.

It was a picture, in a plastic compartment in the wallet, of Nitti, smiling, his arm around a little boy. Hugging the child; the child was smiling, too, obviously loving his father. As that's what this obviously was: a snapshot portrait of father and son.

"He's big for six," Nitti said, beaming; he withdrew the wallet and looked at the picture himself. "You know, I'm a little guy."

Right.

"My son's gonna be a bigger man than me. The men in his mama's family are six foot, some of 'em. He'll stand taller than his old man."

There seemed to be no irony in his words.

"Handsome lad," I said.

Nitti nodded in agreement, smiled at the picture, and put the wallet back in his pocket.

"Now," he said, "what's this about you nosing around in the Outfit's business?"

I hadn't *seen* any baseball bats when I came in; maybe one was behind Nitti's couch . . .

"What do you mean, Frank?"

"Don't shit me, kid."

I wasn't a kid anymore, but I didn't point that out to him; I'd been young enough for him to call me that when we first met, and it was clear I'd be a kid to him till the day he died. Maybe that was a saving grace; maybe his looking on me that way was keeping me alive.

"I did a job for Willie Bioff," I said. Hoping that was what he wanted to hear. Hoping to Christ he didn't somehow know about Montgomery. That was the job that would get me the testimonial banquet.

"I know," Nitti said. He reached for the glass of milk, sipped it; brushed away a small milk mustache with a hand that then extended to point a blunt finger at me. "You shouldn't try keeping things from me."

I gestured with two open hands. "Bioff didn't ask me to keep anything from you, exactly. He just didn't want this situation advertised. He seemed to think he was in the doghouse enough with you fellas, over the income-tax trouble he was in."

Nitti's eyes weren't narrowed; they seemed as casual as two eyes could be. But I knew they were studying me; watching my every movement. Looking for me to betray myself.

"I sometimes think it was a mistake," Nitti said, reflective all of a sudden, "letting that pimp represent us. But he was in on the ground floor, on the IA deal, so it only seemed fair."

"He seems to have done a good job for you."

"He's got himself rich, is what he's done, and I don't begrudge him. That's what we're in it for, all of us, our own financial well-being. How the hell else are a bunch of immigrants like us gonna make it in this world, if we don't look after ourselves?"

"Right," I said. He seemed to be including me in that, so I didn't remind him I was born here.

"Tell me what you did for Bioff, exactly."

I did. From Barger through the phone calls to the movie circuit bigwigs to Estelle. No details about my method of dealing with the latter party, but Nitti smiled at the mention of her name, anyway.

"Nice work if you can get it," he said.

"She's who told you, isn't she? I mean, Sonny Goldstone obviously reported seeing me at the Colony Club, but then you talked to Estelle, and she spilled about me and Bioff, right?"

"Never trust a whore, kid. Haven't you learned that yet?"

"I guess not. But, then, I'm tempted to say the same thing to you about pimps."

"Point well taken," he said, nodding.

"I, uh, didn't feel I was working behind your back, Frank. Bioff's one of yours, after all."

For the first time this evening, his expression seemed thoughtful, not offhand. "I asked around a little. I hear you hate Bioff. Why would you take work from somebody whose fuckin' guts you hate?"

Shrug. "Money's money. And I don't hate Willie. I don't feel much about him one way or another."

"I hear you arrested him once."

Batter up.

"Uh, Frank, that was a long time ago. I haven't been on the force since '32, remember?"

He cracked his knuckles; it sounded like a firing squad warming up. "This guy Pegler," he said, back to his deceptively casual tone, "this big-deal columnist that Bioff was havin' you issue the warnings about. You had any contact with him?"

Straight was the only way to play it; pretty straight, anyway.

"Twice," I said. "He came around early this week asking if I ever arrested Bioff. I said yes, but gave him no details. He came around to my office this afternoon, looking for more information; I didn't give him any. In fact, I threw him out of my office. And I mean *threw* him out—bodily."

He took another slow sip of milk. "Why?"

"He called me a hebe."

"Why, are you a hebe?"

"My father was Jewish. Does Heller sound Irish to you?"

He liked that small bit of impertinence. He said, "If he called me a wop, I'd have him talked to."

"I'll bet."

"I wouldn't kill him. I'd like to have him hit, right now, for the trouble he's drumming up for me, but he's out of bounds."

"Hitting a newsman like him would really stir up the heat."

"Like Al used to say," he added, with a private smile. He meant Capone. "I hear this Pegler's found out that Bioff still has six months to serve."

Nitti knowing that was no surprise: little went on in the police department that wasn't known to the Outfit.

"He told me as much this afternoon," I said, confirming it.

"You'll be made a hero," he said, still smiling, faintly.

"It'll stick in Pegler's craw," I said. "Hebe that I am."

Nitti laughed. "That is kinda sweet. He needs to build you up to help tear Willie down."

"I'm not going along with it, Frank."

He waved a hand at me. "Don't worry about it. It's not your fault you busted that little pimp a hundred years ago. It also ain't your fault that this old unserved sentence caught up with him. He shoulda served it, or bought his way out, or something—not just let it hang."

"If I had it to do again," I said, "I'd still bust the bastard. He was a mean pimp; he hurt his girls."

"Sometimes I think you're still a cop at heart, Heller."

"Sometimes I think I am, too."

"Then why do I trust you?"

"Because I'm afraid of you, Frank."

He laughed; it was a booming laugh. I'd never heard him laugh that way before; and I never did again.

He said, "I like you, kid. You got chutzpah, you got integrity, you got brains. Why don't you close down that little shop of yours and come to work for me?"

"I really am too much a cop, Frank. I respect you. You're the best man in your world. But the Outfit does a lot of things that make me . . . uncomfortable."

"Fair enough," he said, and I couldn't help thinking again that that was the name of that goddamn Pegler's column, "but I got to ask you a favor."

"Sure."

All humor, all good will, left his face; like a sudden change in the weather, Nitti rained on me: "Stay out of the Outfit's business. You turned up twice this week in my business. You almost got killed once because of it. I would've regretted that. I would've sent flowers. But dead is dead, my friend, and that is how you will be if you continue to put your nose in my affairs. *Capeesh?*"

"*Capeesh,*" I managed to say.

He leaned back; his face and his voice softened a bit. "You can't be faulted for taking on a client who offers money. I understand that. I understand the temptation when an O'Hare, a Bioff, comes around and says I will give you money. But next time such a person comes to you, *think,* next time, *remember:* Frank Nitti offered you a job. I offered you a job years ago, in a hospital room as a matter of fact, not long after you saved my life from Cermak's maggots and I don't forget that, not a second do I forget that, but in truth you turned my offer down. And you turned me down just now, again. From that I take it to mean that you aren't interested in my business. So stay the hell out of it. I mean this in a friendly way. Final warning."

I swallowed. "I appreciate your frankness, Frank. I appreciate the warning."

"Right. Some people wake up dead in the alley. They didn't rate no warning. You, I figure, got that much coming."

"I'm glad you feel that way, Frank. I apologize for—"

He waved a hand again. "No apologies. Clients hired you; that's what you're in business for. But that was before the law was laid down. Henceforth, stay the fuck out of my affairs."

I couldn't think of anything to say, except: "Yes, Frank."

"Now, you saw some things at O'Hare's."

What was he talking about?

"Frank, I don't know . . ."

"I want you to forget it. All of it. Anything O'Hare said to you, before he was killed. Anything you saw there, at his office. You just put that out of your mind."

And as he said that, I put it together: the very thing he didn't want anyone to put together. Because as he sat there looking at ledgers—fresh from a conference with O'Hare's partner Johnny Patton—I recalled who was the accountant at Sportsman's Park: Les Shumway, the witness who helped put Capone away. And who was O'Hare, but the federal informer who helped put Capone away? Yet O'Hare had prospered, in the wake of Capone's fall, and even Shumway had found refuge, right under Frank Nitti's nose. *Why wasn't Shumway dead?*

Perhaps he *was,* now, like his boss O'Hare. Or he was out of town, or he was being well taken care of.

Because the man sitting across from me was the *real* man who put Capone away. It wasn't Stege or Ness or Irey or Frank J. Wilson or Uncle Sam.

It was Frank Nitti.

I knew, with a certainty that chilled me, something that the papers for all their theorizing had not guessed, something that the feds for all their investigating had not even considered, something that few people living knew, few people but for the handful of conspirators themselves, one of whom, Edward J. O'Hare, was freshly dead.

That Frank Nitti had, through O'Hare and Shumway, set Capone up for the federal fall.

To vacate the throne for himself.

"Well," he said, "I won't take up any more of your time. It's been a busy week for all concerned."

"I would imagine," I said, casually I hoped, "what with the big boss coming back in a few days."

He laughed again; not the booming laugh, but loud enough. "Al's not getting back in the business, kid."

"Would I be out of line asking why?"

Matter-of-fact shrug. "We heard rumors, but till they let his own doctor examine him at Lewisburg the other day, we couldn't be sure."

"Sure of what?"

His smile stopped just short of gloating. "Kid, Al's crazier than a bedbug. The syph's eaten away half his brain. He just didn't live right, you know."

And he finished his milk.

I rose. My knees felt weak, but I could stand. I could even walk, and did, out the door.

Campagna, waiting, said, "You want a ride home? Snow's comin' down. I got a car."

I could hear the muffled sound of Nitti talking to a woman, in the entryway back of the closed door behind me.

"No thanks," I said.

After all, the day might come soon enough when Louis Campagna, or someone like him, took me for a ride at Nitti's behest.

20

On November 22, the first of Pegler's columns exposing Bioff and Browne appeared in hundreds of papers nationwide. For once, Pegler submerged his quirky, alternately folksy and pompous writing style into a flat, clear, straightforward reporter's voice that helped make his union-busting series something that was taken seriously.

The first column specifically exposed Bioff's unserved sentence for pandering; later Pegler bared Browne's gangster-tinged past.

In February 1940, due to public pressure created by Pegler's columns, Bioff was returned to Chicago and, on April 8 of that year, the clang of a cell door swinging shut at the House of Correction marked the start of his actually serving that long-forgotten six-month sentence. Word was he had a private office-like cell with a fresh tub of iced beer each day, the latter a luxury more suited to Browne than Bioff; and he was sometimes released on a good-conduct pass, and was seen out-and-about in Chicago. What the hell—I was pleased that the bust I'd made so long ago had finally resulted in a jail sentence being served at all, iced beer, private office, good-conduct passes or no.

On May 4, 1941, Pegler was awarded the Pulitzer prize for journalism, for "articles on scandals in the ranks of organized labor."

Twenty days later, Bioff and his co-defendant Browne were charged in a federal court in New York under the Federal Anti-Racketeering Statute on the film-industry extortion. Shortly thereafter, so was Nick (Dean) Circella. Dean and Browne each received eight years; Bioff ten. All three went to prison without uttering a word about Nitti and the Outfit.

Dean, however, was a fugitive for some months prior to his trial, until FBI agents arrested him in a roadhouse known as Shorty's Place, in Cicero. He was hiding out with Estelle Carey, who had dyed her hair black and posed with Dean (himself posing as a workman) as his little homebody housewife; it must have been a masquerade Estelle enjoyed not in the least.

The murder of E. J. O'Hare remained (and remains) unsolved.

Me? I went about my business, watching all this from the sidelines, keeping what I knew about the Nitti-directed murder of O'Hare to myself. That week never quite faded from my memory, however, if for no other reason than it was the single most financially rewarding week I had in those early years, and for some time thereafter. Between O'Hare, Nitti, Montgomery and Bioff, I brought in enough mazuma to pay the entire yearly salary of my secretary with some left over toward one of my ops. At the same time I knew the risks I'd taken earning that dough could never be properly compensated. I could still be killed for what I'd done, and for what I knew.

Nonetheless, I thought all this movie-union crap was behind me. I had not been called to testify in the Bioff/Browne/Dean proceedings, and Pegler had in his columns played down my role as much as he could; he probably thought he was getting back at me, but I considered it a favor. I took Nitti's advice and stayed out of his Outfit's business—as much as I could, anyway, in a town he owned.

When I came back to Chicago in February 1943, Guadalcanal weighed more heavily on my mind than Willie Bioff and company, and I had no intention of allowing myself to get drawn back into that sordid affair. Nitti's "final warning," after all, to stay out of his business, still went—and, battle fatigue and amnesia not withstanding, I clearly remembered that Frank Nitti was not to be taken lightly.

And then Estelle Carey came back into my life, and everything went out the window.

Three

The Ruptured Duck

Chicago, Illinois

February 2—March 20, 1943

21

I got a cab at Union Station just before noon, sharing it with two sailors, and sat in the rear holding on to the strap and looking out the window at snowy, grimy streets. I was back in Chicago, all right. It had been less than a year, but the world had changed. Service flags were in every storefront window—one star for each son at war, and most flags bore at least two stars; horse-drawn wagons ("This Wagon replaces a truck for the duration!") mingled with autos, while cabbies caught behind the wagons turned shades of patriotic red, blue and white, swallowing their irritation. The autos all had ration stickers prominently displayed in their windshields, B stickers in evidence mostly, and an occasional C, like my cabbie's. The sidewalks seemed filled with lovely young women, the edges of their skirts under their winter coats flapping, the city's famous wind intent on exposing pretty, nylonless legs; but if you had a nickel for every guy under forty you saw on the street, you wouldn't have busfare—unless you counted the boys in uniform.

Me, I wasn't in uniform, unlike the gobs I was sharing the cab with, and I wasn't a boy, either. I was a gray old man in a gray woolen overcoat I'd picked up in D.C. yesterday—under which I was wearing the suit I'd worn to San Diego last year, and it seemed a little big for me, like it belonged to somebody else. Maybe somebody I used to be. I sat there craving a cigarette, but for reasons I couldn't explain, not giving into it.

The cabbie dropped me in front of the Dill Pickle, the rumble of the El greeting me, making me feel at least a little at home. Up in the window of the A-1 Detective Agency a service flag bore a single star. I wondered if it stood for me, or Frankie Fortunato, who was in the Army. Probably Frankie.

Sea bag slung over my shoulder, I stepped around a wino (4-F or over forty? Hard to say) and started up the familiar narrow stairs; passed some people there, older men, younger women, coming down for lunch, nobody I recognized. I set foot on the fourth floor, feeling like my own ghost. Walked down the familiar hall with its wood and pebbled glass and paused at the door that still had NATHAN HELLER, PRESIDENT, on it. I touched the letters; they didn't smear.

I turned the knob.

Gladys was sitting behind her desk, on which was a rose in a slender vase. She looked lovely, her brown hair in a slightly longer page boy, now, her white blouse slightly more feminine and ruffly than I remembered ever seeing her in. She was a little heavier, but it looked good on her—made her bustier. She gave me a big smile.

"Hello, Mr. Heller," she said.

She stood and came around and hugged me. I hugged her back. It felt good, if a little awkward.

A banner made from a bedsheet said WELCOME HOME, BOSS in crude yet oddly graceful red letters; it was tacked on the wall over that World's Fair couch where I'd caught Gladys and Frankie humping, years ago.

"You shouldn't've made a fuss," I said.

"Not that big a fuss," she said, shrugging.

"No ticker-tape parade?"

She narrowed her eyes; she didn't get it. Gladys still didn't have a sense of humor. "This is the extent of it," she said, gesturing to the banner, which I felt sure she'd made herself. "Except for we have some champagne chilling."

"That's fuss enough," I said. "Lead me to it."

"You got it," somebody said.

I turned and saw Lou Sapperstein, looking haggard and wearing a black arm band on one sleeve of his brown suitcoat, standing in the doorway of my inner office, pouring me a Dixie cup of champagne out of a big bottle.

I went over and took the cup with my left hand and shook hands with Lou with my right and drank the champagne and said, "How's business?"

He was a touch thinner; more lines in his face. He'd switched from wire-rim glasses to tortoise shell, bifocals now; gray tinged the dark hair around his ears. His skull hadn't lost its shine.

"Business is not bad," he said. "Let's have lunch at Binyon's and I'll fill you in."

"Fine. Why the, uh . . . ?"

He lifted the arm with the armband, gently. "My little brother. Fighter pilot. Silliest goddamn thing. Died in the States while still in training."

"I'm sorry, Lou."

"I am, too. Hell of a thing." He looked at Gladys. "Care to join us? We can make it a celebration."

Gladys was already back behind her desk. "No. Somebody has to hold down the fort."

Gladys had loosened up, considerably, over the years; but she was still business first.

"Where shall I put this?" I said, referring to the sea bag, currently residing on the couch.

"Why don't you stick it in the office next door?" Lou said.

"For now," I said. "But I got to find a place to stay. I should've made arrangements while I was still at St. E's, but it was hard to think that far ahead . . ."

Gladys said, "They called us, Mr. Heller."

"For Christ's sakes, will you call me Nate."

"Nate," she said. It was hard for her. "Anyway, one of your doctors called several weeks ago, and we've been looking for a room ever since. I'm afraid there's nothing at the Morrison."

"Quite a housing shortage," Lou said, with a fatalistic shrug.

"So we took the liberty of rearranging the office next door," she said.

"With both you and Frankie gone," Lou said, "we haven't been using that office at all. I've been working out of your office, of course . . ." He nodded to my inner office, his expression apologetic.

"That's as it should be," I said.

"So we had the partitions taken out next door," he went on, "and put your desk in there, as well as some of the personal items you'd put in storage. Some furniture from your old suite at the Morrison. You remember that old Murphy bed of yours that's been stored in the basement, for years?"

I sat down on the couch, put a hand on the sea bag. "Don't tell me."

"We had it hauled back upstairs. It's in there. You can have that whole office to yourself, and live in it, too, temporarily, till you find something else."

"Full circle," I said.

"What?" Gladys said.

"Nothing," I said.

Lou said to her, "He lived in his office when he started out. *That* office."

"Oh," Gladys said, not getting it. Irony wasn't her strong suit.

I stood. "I appreciate you going to that trouble."

"If you like," Lou said, gesturing with two open hands, "I'll use that office, and you can use the one in here, and just sleep in there. I just figured, with clients used to dealing with me, it wouldn't hurt to have a transition period, where . . ."

"Don't say another word. You stay put, Lou. It's going to take me a while to get into the swing of things again. For the next few weeks, at least, consider yourself the boss."

"Am I wrong in assuming you'll be wanting to get right back to work?"

"No. Anyway, I don't think you are."

"Mr. Heller," Gladys said, her brow knit. I didn't bother correcting her; "Nate" was just not in her vocabulary. "You do look a little peaked, if you'll excuse me saying."

"Gladys," Lou said, harshly.

"It's okay, Lou," I said. "She's right. I look like hell. But I just spent sixteen hours or so sitting on a train, with no place to sleep, and . . ." The train had been filthy, crowded; I was lucky to find room to stow my sea bag and plant my butt. The saddest thing had been the pregnant women, of whom there had seemed to be a batallion, and gals with small children in tow, trying to diaper 'em, feed 'em, in the most cramped god-awful conditions, all of these young mothers present and future on their way to see their overseas-bound husbands one last time, or coming back from having seen 'em off.

Lou and Gladys were both staring at me, pity in their eyes, as I'd trailed off in mid-sentence and got lost in thought, thinking about the train ride. That was going to happen; me going in and out of focus like that.

"You might as well get your minds set," I said. "I'm going to be out of step for a while. Not long ago I was on a tropical island getting shot at. The comparative peace and quiet of Chicago is going to take some getting used to."

Lou stepped in my, or his, office and got into his overcoat. "Binyon's okay?" he said.

"Binyon's is fine," I said.

As we were leaving, Gladys called out, "Should I tell people you're in, if they call?"

I stopped, the door open; Lou was already out in the hall. The abortionist was still in business.

"Why should they even know I'm back?" I said.

"Your friend Hal Davis on the *News* did a story about you. Or rather it was about your friend Mr. Ross, with you in it. How you're a couple of heroes who are coming back to Chicago."

"That cocksucker!"

"Mr. Heller!"

"Gladys, I'm sorry. Forgive that. I've got a bad case of serviceman's mouth, and I'll try to get over it quick."

"Yes, Mr. Heller."

"Good girl."

"Mr. Heller—did, uh, did you see Frankie over there?"

"Uh, no, Gladys. Sorry. It's a big war. Why, is he in the Pacific?"

"He's on Guadalcanal, too, didn't you know?"

"I'm sorry, I didn't. He must've been one of the Army boys who came in to spell us. Is he with the Americal Division?"

"Why, yes," she said. The concern on her face was easy enough to read. Specifically, she was looking at gray, skinny, hollow-eyed me and had to wonder about how her husband was faring. She was Mrs. Fortunato now, you see; they'd gotten hitched just before he joined up.

"Will he be all right, Mr. Heller?"

I knew enough not to assure her of that, but I could in good conscience say, "The Island's a mop-up operation, now, honey. He should be fine. Barney and me did the hard work; all he's got to do is clean up after us."

She liked hearing that; she even smiled. For a girl with no sense of humor, she had a great fucking smile. Nice tits, too. It made me feel good to know I could still appreciate the finer things.

Like Binyon's. My appetite at St. E's had been lousy, but the corned beef platter (albeit a smaller serving now) in the familiar male-dominated restaurant with its wooden booths and spare decor, reminded me of the simple pleasure of good food. In fact, I attacked the plate like a Jap whose bayonet I'd taken away and was using on him. I think I embarrassed Lou. He didn't say a word through the meal.

I wiped my face off with a cloth napkin. A cloth napkin; ain't civilization something. I said, "I didn't eat on the train ride. No dining car, and if you got off when they made a stop you could lose your seat."

"No explanation necessary, Nate. This is Lou, remember? We go way back."

Somebody laughed; me, apparently. "I guess two guys who got falling down drunk together as often as we did, in the old days, ought to cut each other some slack."

"That's how I see it."

"I'm goddamn sorry about your brother." I couldn't keep my eyes off his arm band.

"It's okay," he said.

"But it isn't," I said.

"No it isn't, but it's not something I can talk about. I thank God *you* made it back. I was afraid I might never see you again, you dumb son of a bitch. You were too old to go in the service, what were you thinking of?"

"Ya talked me out of it," I said. "I'm not going in."

The waiter brought us each a second beer.

Lou shrugged, smiled. "I understand the impulse. I'm older than you and I thought about it, too."

"When your brother enlisted," I said, beer at the ready, "you went down the next day and took the physical. If you hadn't flunked, you'd be in right now."

Wide-eyed, smiling, he said, "How do you know that?"

"I'm a detective." I took a sip of beer. "Anyway, I used to be. How much play did Davis give me in the *News?*"

"'Barney Ross's Private Eye Pal.' Pretty corny. All the Cermak and Dillinger and Nitti stuff, dredged up. The Pegler bit, too. But just one story. Yesterday."

"Fuck. Did I understand Gladys to say Barney's coming back to town?"

"I believe so. His malaria flared up, and he was off Guadalcanal before New Year's; he's been in the States for—"

"I know," I said. "They let us read the papers in the bughouse. It's just sharp objects they kept from us."

"No offense meant, Nate . . ."

"Me neither. Anyway, I know about Barney. I talked to him on the phone once, even. Did you know Roosevelt pinned the medals on him, personal?"

"We get the papers here, too," Lou said, smiling faintly.

"But he didn't say anything about coming back to Chicago, on this extended furlough they're promising him. He said he was going out to Hollywood, to be with his girl friend. Wife, I mean."

"Well," Lou said, "he's changed his mind, apparently. My guess is he's needed to pump some business into his cocktail lounge. His brother Ben just isn't the manager that Barney was."

"Shit—Barney was a terrible manager, Lou. But he was a draw. A celebrity."

Lou shrugged facially. "Now that he's a war hero, they'll flock there to see him."

For some reason I didn't like to hear that. I didn't know why, exactly, but I could feel anger behind my eyes.

Lou said, "Do you want to hear about *our* business, or not?"

"Sure. How have I been doing?"

"You're not getting rich, but you're no pauper. Business is off slightly—divorce work is way down—but there's still too much for one op to handle. If Frankie were here, one of us might be featherbeddin', but there's plenty here for the two of us."

Why didn't I care? I tried to look interested and said, "Such as?"

"Half a dozen suburban banks are using us for investigating loan applicants and credit; also some personnel investigation, and inspection of property and businesses. We got plenty of retail credit-risk checks to do, and four lawyers are now using us to serve their papers . . ."

I couldn't listen. I tried. I swear I tried. But after while I was just looking at his face and his mouth was moving but I couldn't make myself listen.

This is your business, a voice in my head was saying, *this is what you worked so hard to build, once upon a time, so jump back in, jump back in,* but I didn't give a shit.

"Nate?" he said. His change of expression, to concern, made me tune his words in. "Are you all right? You seemed . . . distant, all of a sudden."

"I know. I'm sorry." I sighed. Sipped the beer. "You just drop a stack of work on my desk and I'll get to it. I promise you."

"You're the boss," he said.

"In name only. You got to run the show till I get back on the ball. I had amnesia, did you know that?"

"No," he said. Trying not to show his surprise. "We were told . . . battle fatigue. Shell shock . . ."

"I blocked it all out," I said. "Forgot everything I could. My name. Who I am. Who I was. I don't know if I can remember *how* to be a detective, to be quite honest with you."

He smiled a little, swirled his beer in its glass. "Nate Heller with amnesia is still twice the detective of any other man I can think of."

"That's horseshit, Lou, but I do appreciate it."

He looked in the beer, not at me, as he said, "I took the liberty of setting up an appointment for you this afternoon."

"Really? I don't think I'm in any mood to see a client just yet, Lou—"

"It's not a client, and this is something you might just as well deal with right away, 'cause they're not going to let loose of you till you do. They been calling for weeks, trying to set something up."

"Oh. The federal prosecutor. That grand jury thing."

"Yeah. Treasury and Justice Department investigators been swarming around town for weeks. Months. They're really trying to put the screws to the Outfit. For whatever good it'll do 'em. The prosecutor's name is Correa, by the way."

"Don't know him."

"He's out of New York. That's where the grand jury will eventually meet. But much of the investigation's going on here. Most of their witnesses, and those they indict, will be from here, so Correa keeps a local office. And there's an Illinois-based grand jury in the works, as well. Same subject—the Syndicate infiltrating the unions."

"Aw shit."

"They want to talk to you, bad."

"Can't it wait?"

"There'll be somebody to talk to you, informally, at the office at two this afternoon. If you don't want to face it, duck out. Me, I'd suggest you get it out of the way. You won't get any rest till you do."

"Shit."

"Correa won't be there; he's in New York at the moment. But a couple of old friends of yours *will* be."

"Such as?"

"Such as your favorite cop, for instance."

"Stege?"

"Stege?" Lou shook his head, grinned. "You're behind the times, Nate. Stege retired months ago, while you were overseas."

I felt a strange pang; a sense of loss. Funny.

"I'm talking about our buddy from pickpocket-detail days," Lou said. "Bill Drury."

Drury. That lovable hard-ass.

"I should've guessed," I said. "He always has had a hard-on against the Outfit. He *would* get involved in something like this. You said two old friends."

"What?"

"You said two old friends were going to meet with me about this grand jury deal. Drury, and who else?"

He smiled on one side of his face. "If you were Uncle Sam, and you wanted to convince Nathan Heller to testify, who would you send?"

"Oh, no," I said.

Lou toasted me with his beer.

"That's right," he said. Drank some beer. "Mr. Untouchable himself."

Eliot Ness.

ELIOT

22

Eliot was fifteen minutes early.

He walked into the big single-room office—into which he'd walked so often, years before—and the sight of the Murphy bed against the wall, in its long-ago position, and me sitting behind my big old scarred oak desk in my long-ago position, made him smile.

"Isn't that a Murphy bed?" he said.

"Yeah," I said. "There's a housing shortage. It's been in all the papers."

I got up from around the desk and I thought I could make out a slight tightening around his eyes as he got his first good look at me, skinny, gray, sunken-eyed me. I put the sore into sight for sore eyes.

He, on the other hand, looked much the same; a slight salt-and-peppering around the ears was the only noticeable difference. All else was familiar: a comma of dark brown hair falling down on his rather high forehead, a ruddy, handsome six-footer who was pushing forty and didn't look it, partly due to the trail of freckles across his nose that kept him looking boyish in the face of time.

We shook hands, exchanging grins. His topcoat was over his arm, hat in hand; his gray suit with vest and dark tie was nicely tailored, giving him an executive look. I took the coat and hung it on the tree by the door.

"You look good, Nate."

"You're a liar, Eliot."

"Well, you look good to me. You crazy SOB, what's a grown man doing fighting a young man's war?"

SOB was about as blue as Eliot's language got.

"I'm not fighting it anymore," I said, and got back behind the desk, gesturing to one of the two waiting chairs I'd placed opposite me in anticipation of my visitors. "What are you doing in Chicago, anyway? Who's minding the store?"

"If you mean Cleveland," Eliot said, crossing his legs, resting an ankle on a knee, "I resigned."

That was a shock; the public safety director slot—which was essentially like being commissioner of both the police and fire departments—was perfect for Eliot. He'd had a lot of glory, a good salary, and accomplished plenty. I thought he'd die in that job, an old bearded public servant.

"First I heard of it," I said.

"It was while you were away."

"I knew you'd had that trouble . . ."

In March of '42 Eliot had been involved in an auto accident that had found him, wrongly, briefly, accused of a hit-and-run; as a public safety man known for taking a tough stand on traffic violators, Eliot caught a lot of public heat.

"The press never left me alone after that," he said, his tone matter-of-fact but his expression just barely revealing a buried hurt.

"Fuck 'em! You've been their fair-haired boy for *years*. You were cleared, weren't you? Goddamn newspapers. Why couldn't the bastards give you a fair shake . . . ?"

He shrugged. "I think it was the fact that Evie and I had both been drinking. We weren't drunk, Nate, I swear—but we had been drinking, and, well, you know my reputation as the big-shot prohibition agent. It made me look like a hypocrite."

"How *are* you and Evie?"

Evie was his wife; his second wife.

"Not so good," he admitted. "A little rocky. I'm traveling a lot."

I was sorry to hear that, and said so. He just shrugged again.

Then I said, "What *are* you doing these days? Since you're here to quiz me for the grand jury, I assume you're back in the law enforcement business. So what is it? Treasury or Justice or what?"

"Nothing so glamorous," he said, with a chagrined grin.

"Come on. Spill."

"Actually," he said, sitting up straight, summoning his self-respect, "it's a pretty important job. I'm working for the Federal Security Agency. Specifically, the Office of Defense Health and Welfare."

"What's that mean?"

"Well," he said, shrugging, "I'm the Chief Administrator of their Division of Social Protection."

"What's that mean?"

"We're dealing with social problems of the sort that inevitably develop when there's a rapid expansion of a work force in a community, or a large concentration of armed forces."

"What are you talking about?"

He pursed his lips, mildly irritated, or was that embarrassment? "I'm talking about safeguarding the health and morale of the armed forces and of workers in defense industry. What do you think I'm talking about?"

"I think you're talking about VD."

He sighed; laughed. "I am talking about VD."

"I think I saw some of your movies while I was in the Corps."

That did embarrass him, and he waved it off. "That's only a small part of it, Nate. I'm supervising the activities of twelve regional offices, and what we're primarily doing is trying to help the local law enforcement people cut back on prostitution, especially in areas close to military and naval bases, or industrial areas. And in cities where military and naval personnel are likely to go on leave. That's why they brought an old copper like me in to be in charge."

"I see."

"You can sit there and grin if you like. But VD's a big problem; in the first war, soldiers suffered more cases of venereal disease than wounds in battle."

"I think you're right. What we need in this world is more killing and less fucking."

He smiled wearily. "Only you would look at it that way, Nate. *I* look at it as important work."

"You don't have to sell me, Eliot. I know enough to wear my rubbers when it rains."

"You haven't changed much."

"Neither have you. You're still with the goddamn Untouchables."

He laughed and so did I. It was a nice moment. But then the moment was gone, and silence filled the room, somewhat awkwardly. An El rumbled by and eased the tension.

"You know why I'm here," he said, tentatively.

"Yup. I don't know why they sent the top VD G-man to do a grand jury prosecutor's job, though."

"I am still a G-man, and that's why I'm in town, doing a joint workshop with the FBI over at the Banker's Building. We got cops from all over the city and the suburbs coming in."

I bet I knew the conference room they were using—the one next to the old FBI HQ, that big room whose windows faced the Rookery across the way, windows from which agents like Melvin Purvis and Sam Cowley hung suspects out by their ankles till they talked. At least one suspect had been dropped. It made a splash in the papers. And on the cement.

Now Eliot Ness was using it to teach cops about whores. Wasn't law enforcement a wonderful thing?

"Let me guess," I said. "The steel mill district on the east side must be hooker heaven about now."

He nodded. "The Pullman plant, just west of there, is another key area."

They were Pullman Aircraft, for the duration. Electromotive was near there, too; even before I joined up, it was rumored they were making tanks.

He got up and got himself a Dixie cup of water from the cooler over by the bathroom. "The cops in these industrial districts never had a prostitution problem the like of this before; it's an epidemic. We're helping 'em out."

"You and the FBI."

"Yeah." Sitting back down, sipping his water.

"So if they ask *you* to help *them* out, by talking to a contrary cuss name of Heller, you say, why sure."

"Do you resent that, Nate?"

I shook my head. "I could never resent you, Eliot. Not much, anyway. But it's been ten years now that you've been trying to turn me into a good citizen. Won't you ever give up?"

"What are you talking about? I've heard you tell the truth on the witness stand before. With my own ears. Saw it with my own eyes."

"Who else's were you planning on using?"

"Well, you did do it. You told the truth."

"Once. That doesn't make me a saint."

"Nate, you're not on Nitti's side. You never were."

"That's right. I'm on my own side."

"Which is whichever side is safest, you mean."

"Or the most profitable."

He crumpled the paper cup in a fist and gestured with it. "The Outfit is strangling every union in this town. Can you honestly think about your father, and what he gave to unionism, and sit back and let that happen?"

I pointed at him, gently. "Eliot, you're my friend, but when you bring up my old man, you're pushing it. And when you suggest that I could in any way single-handedly clean up union corruption that goes back years, decades, you're screwier than the guys I was bunking with back at the bughouse."

He tossed the crumpled cup at the wastebasket by my desk; it went in. "The investigation is centering on the IA movie extortion racket, you know."

"So?"

"So you were involved in Pegler's initial investigation of the racket."

"Something you dragged me into, by the way, giving my name to your federal pals. I never thanked you for that, did I?"

"I guess you didn't."

"That's because at the time I felt like kicking you in the slats."

He ignored that, pressed on: "You know plenty about that racket, Nate. You had contact with most of the principals."

"I don't know anything firsthand. All I did was talk to some people."

"One of whom was Frank Nitti."

Shit.

I said, "Nobody knows that for sure."

"Federal agents have a record of you going to see him several times, over a seven-year period, including in November 1939. At the Bismarck Hotel?"

"Christ."

"The Grand Jury is going to want to know what was said in those meetings. Going way back, Nate. Back to Cermak."

I sat up and gave my friend as nasty a grin as I'd ever given him. "What about back to Dillinger? How would the FBI like to have what I know about the Dillinger hit go public? How at best the feds aided and abetted crooked Indiana cops in a police execution, and at worst shot the wrong man? If what I knew came out, Hoover would shit his fucking pants."

He shrugged elaborately. "That would be fine with me. Hoover's overrated anyway. All I care about is the truth."

"Oh, Eliot, please. You're not naive. Don't pretend to be."

"Your testimony could be very valuable. You are the only non–mob-tainted party known to have had frequent private meetings with Nitti. Your testimony would have credence well beyond that of Bioff and Browne and Dean."

"So the Three Stooges are talking, huh?"

He nodded. "They didn't talk at their first trial, but when those stiff sentences came down, and they found out how much different prison life was than the El Mocambo, they started fishing for a deal."

"It was the Trocadero where they hung out in Hollywood, Eliot, but never mind. I still don't want to play."

There was a knock at the door and I said, "It's open."

Bill Drury came in.

He wasn't a big man, really—perhaps five-nine, a hundred and sixty pounds—but he was broad-shouldered and he had great energy, and a physical presence that could overwhelm you. He hung his camel-hair topcoat next to Eliot's, and his fedora, too, revealing his typically dapper attire, a black-vested suit with gray pinstripes and a colorful blue-and-red-patterned tie and a fifty-cent shine. Bill was the best-dressed honest cop I ever met.

And one of the friendliest, unless you were part of the Outfit. He strode over to us with his ready smile, shaking my hand first, then Eliot's. His dark thinning hair was combed across his scalp to give an impression of more but the effect was less. His dark, alert eyes crowded a jutting nose under which a firm jaw rested on the beginnings of a double chin.

"Heller," he said, cheerfully, sitting down next to Eliot, "you truly look like death warmed over."

"An honest man at last," I said. "You look fat and sassy."

"When your wife works," he said with an expansive gesture of one hand, "why not?"

I had no argument with that.

"I presume Eliot has filled you in," he said.

"Somewhat."

"We were asked, because we're old friends of yours, to pave the way for the federal prosecutor. They'd like you to be a witness."

"Then I presume they'll subpoena me."

"They'd like you to be a *friendly* witness."

"You know me, Lieutenant. Friendly as the day is long."

"And the days are getting shorter, I know, I know. And it's 'Captain,' now."

"Really? How the world does change when you go off on a pleasure cruise."

Eliot turned to Bill and said, "I get the feeling Nate feels we're imposing upon his friendship."

"If we are," Bill said to me, flatly sincere, "I apologize. I think you know what sort of stranglehold the Outfit's had on the unions, here, and we're finally getting a chance to break it. Your inside knowledge could play a major role in that."

"I doubt it," I said.

"The IA's extortion racket is going to blow the lid off. We're talking about ending gangster control of not just the IA, but the laborer's council, which includes twenty-five local unions, twenty-thousand members, street cleaners, tunnel workers, streetcar company employees, you name it. Then, beyond the laborer's council, there's the sanitary engineers union, the hotel employees, the bartenders, the truckers, the laundry workers, the retail clerks —"

"I get the point, Bill."

"Then cooperate with the grand jury."

"Let me ask you something. Both of you. You keep talking about the IA's movie 'extortion' racket. What extortion is that? As I recall, it was collusion between the movie moguls and the mob. Since when is strike prevention insurance 'extortion'?"

Drury finally bristled. "I don't know what else you'd call it."

I put my feet up on the desk and leaned back in my swivel chair. "I tell you what. I'll come testify. I'll come spill my guts about every secret meeting I ever had with Nitti. I'll tell you and the grand jury things that'll make the hair on your head curlier than the hair in your shorts. I'll tell God and everybody things that'll guarantee me ending up in an alley with a bullet in my brain. But first you got to assure me of one thing. You got to assure me that those movie moguls are going to be indicted right alongside Nitti and company."

Eliot had given up; he was staring out the window. Drury sat up in the chair, straight as his principles. "I don't know anything about that," he said. "I only know this is our chance to put Nitti and Campagna and Ricca and that whole sorry crowd away."

"And then the next crowd'll step in, and will they be any better? What are we talking—Accardo? Giancana? That'll be swell. Nitti, at least, has kept the bloodshed to a minimum."

Drury shook his head. "How in God's name can you find anything good to say about that evil son of a bitch?"

"Nitti's no worse than the next guy in his slot, and possibly a damn sight better. I remember the Capone days, and so do you, Bill."

"Nate, I'm disappointed in you."

"I told you I'd testify. I'll sing like Nelson Eddy sitting on hot coals. But I want to see Louie B. Mayer and Jack Warner and Joe Schenck sitting in cells next to Nitti and Campagna and Ricca."

"Schenck did time."

"On income tax, and not much."

Eliot looked at me, glumly. "They can subpoena you anyway, Nate. You know that."

"Haven't you heard? I'm battle-fatigued. I'm shell-shocked. I got amnesia, remember? Just ask the medics."

Eliot shook his head, looked at the floor.

Bill sat there, dumbfounded. "I don't get you, Heller."

"Bill, those Hollywood schmucks Bioff and Browne and Dean plucked were just trying to get off cheap where paying the help was concerned. And the rank and file knew they had gangsters in their union but figured all that muscle was getting 'em some extra bucks, and looked the other way accordingly. So I say screw 'em. Screw 'em all."

Drury started to say something, but the phone rang. It was Gladys, next door; for Drury.

"I left my number," he said, taking the phone. "Hope you don't mind."

I waved that off.

Drury was mostly listening, so I said to Eliot, quietly, "No hard feelings?"

He smiled wearily again. "None. I'm just glad you're back from that hellhole in one piece. Why don't I buy you dinner tonight?"

"Why don't you?"

Drury barked, "Jesus Christ," into the phone, and we looked at him. Then he said, "Right away," and handed me the receiver, and stood.

"Why don't you come with me, Heller," he said, his face ashen. "There's something you might be interested in."

"Oh?"

"Yeah. A good example of your theory how Nitti and company soft-peddle the bloodshed."

"What are you talking about?"

"Grab your coat and we'll go over to Addison Street, in Lakeview. You might be interested in seeing what's become of Estelle Carey."

23

She was naked under her red silk housecoat, but she wasn't much to look at. Not in the way she had been, once.

She lay on the plush carpet partially under a straight-back chair in the dining room of her third-floor five-room apartment at 512 West Addison in an upper-middle-class neighborhood of wall-to-wall apartment buildings near the lake on the North Side. She'd been living well. Dying had been something else again.

Her hair—she'd dyed it red since I saw her last—was a fright wig, clumps of it torn away from or possibly cut off at the scalp, scattered on the floor nearby, like a barbershop. The face was recognizably hers, despite the cuts and bruises and welts that added touches of purple and red and black to her white face, and despite too the jagged slash through her left eye and the ice-pick punctures on her cheeks and her bloodied broken nose and her smashed pulpy lips. Her throat had been cut, ear to ear, but superficially, a mark of torture, not murder. She had lived through most of this.

The red silk housecoat was scorched from the waist down, and so was she, till her legs were virtually charred. So were her hands and arms. Someone had set the housecoat afire—had splashed whiskey on it and set a match to it, it would seem—and she had put the fire out with her hands, or tried to. She'd been somewhat successful, because only the lower part of her was burned, and even the red silk housecoat could still be seen to be a red silk housecoat. But the fire had spread to the carpet, where it met the broken and apparently not empty whiskey bottle and got ambitious. The two nearby walls were black from floor to ceiling, dripping wet from the firemen's hose, the lingering smoke smell still strong, acrid in the room. Not enough to wipe out the smell of death, however, the smell of scorched human flesh. Not enough to smother the memory of a certain foul wind, of dead, rotting flesh, Japs bloating in the sun in the *kunai* grass, charred grinning corpses by a wrecked tank along the Matanikau and then I was out in the hall, leaning against the wall, doubled over, trying not to puke, trying to keep that corned beef platter from Binyon's down where it belonged.

Drury was right there beside me, a hand on my shoulder, looking ashamed of himself. I'd been in there standing looking at Estelle Carey, frozen by the burned sight of her, for I don't know how long, while he got filled in by the detectives already on the scene. Now he was embarrassed, saying, "Damnit, Heller. I wasn't thinking. I'm sorry."

I was breathing too hard to speak.

He said, "I was trying to make a point. This came up, and bringing you along seemed like the perfect way to make a point."

I said, "Don't say 'this came up' to a guy who's trying not to lose his lunch, okay, Bill?"

"Nate. I'm sorry. Shit. I feel like a heel."

I let go of the wall; I seemed able to stand, without any help. "Well, you are a heel, Bill. But . . . who isn't, from time to time?"

"Why don't you go, Nate. Go on home. If you're interested in how this sad affair plays out, I'll keep you posted."

I swallowed. Shook my head no. "I'll stay."

"I was a bastard to use that dead girl like this. I hope my apology's enough. After what you been through overseas, I shoulda had sense enough not to . . ."

"Will you shut the fuck up? Let's go back inside."

Drury, having been one of my partners back on the pickpocket detail, knew very well that Estelle and I had been an item, once. So it was cruel of him to expose me to this. But then he hadn't seen the condition of the corpse yet, when he made the decision; if he had, I doubt he'd have called me in.

He had an excuse though; I was the one who, officially, identified the body.

My lunch was staying down, but I was shaking. We moved through the vestibule into the living room and back into the dining room; it was cold, the windows open to air out the smoky place, letting in the winter chill. Eliot hadn't joined us—he had business at the Banker's Building; Drury had driven me over in an unmarked car. The firemen—who had been the first to the scene, the neighbor across the hall calling in to report smoke seeping out under the front door—had been and gone. The fire had been contained to the one room, only two walls of which were scorched. Present now were two patrol officers, Drury and two detectives; this was Drury's bailiwick, as he was currently working out of nearby Town Hall Station. More police and related personnel would descend soon. Photographers, medical examiner, dicks from downtown. This was a good chance to get a look around before the professionals stumbled over themselves ruining evidence.

I walked into the next room, through a doorless archway, stepping around a shattered glass, which had apparently been hurled against one wall of the compact white modern kitchen. To my left was a small maple table with two maple chairs, one of them pulled away from the table, at an unnatural angle. Against the wall were cabinets and a sink and more cabinets; the cabinets to the far left were blood-smeared; there was blood spattered in the sink, too.

"The most recent thing cooked up in here," I said, "was Estelle's murder. Look at this."

I pointed to the floor where a blood-stained bread knife, a blood-spattered rolling pin, a blood-tipped ice pick and a ten-inch blackjack lay, here and there, as if casually dropped when done. Nearby was a kitchen chair pulled away from a small table, on which was a flat iron, used to batter her, I figured, and a glass ashtray with a number of crushed butts therein; spatterings of blood were on the table, chair and floor underneath.

"This is where it started," Drury said, hands on hips, appraising the chair. Still in his camel-hair coat. He really was too well-dressed to be a cop. Honest cop.

"Not quite," I said. "Take a look."

I stood and pointed to two cups on the kitchen counter. One of them was half-filled with hot cocoa; cold cocoa, now. In the bottom of the other cup was the dry cocoa powder, ready for hot milk to be poured in. The milk was still simmering on the stove, opposite.

"*This* is where it started," I said.

"How do you figure?"

"She was fixing a cup of cocoa for one of her guests, her back turned as she faced the counter. She was already drinking a cup herself. They grabbed her, tossed her in that chair, started beating her."

Drury pushed his hat back on his head; the dark eyes, set so close on either side of the formidable nose, narrowed. "That makes sense, I guess. But why do you assume more than one 'guest'?"

"It's two people. Probably a man and a woman."

"How do you figure *that?*"

"The broken whiskey bottle out in the other room, a glass of which was poured in here and then hurled against that wall." You could see the dried splash it had made.

"So?"

"So Estelle didn't drink. I also don't think it was her practice to keep a liquor cabinet for guests, though I could be wrong."

"You aren't wrong," Drury granted. He said his detectives had already determined that.

"My guess," I said, "is that bottle of whiskey was brought in, by one of her killers, in that paper bag there."

A wadded-up paper bag was tossed in the corner.

Drury went to it, bent and picked it up, uncrumpled it, looked inside. "There's a receipt in here. This is a neighborhood liquor store."

"In the detective business we call that a clue, Captain."

He only smiled at that; we'd been friends a long time. "Well, I'd tend to agree with you that the whiskey was probably brought in by a man. But just because Estelle was fixing a second cup of cocoa doesn't mean the other party was necessarily a woman. Men have been known to drink cocoa, you know."

"It's a man and a woman. The man used the heavy male weapon—the blackjack—and the woman used makeshift female weapons, flat iron, kitchen utensils like a rolling pin, ice pick, bread knife."

He thought about that, nodded slowly.

"Also," I went on, pointing toward the ashtray, "Estelle didn't smoke, either. Yet some of these butts—and there's some heeled-out ones on the dining room floor, too—show lipstick. And some don't. Man and a woman."

Drury smiled in defeat, shrugged. "Man and a woman."

I moved toward the archway, kneeling. "After while they dragged her into the dining room—by the hair, I'd say. There's some strands right here. Red. Hers."

He knelt down next to me. "You haven't forgotten how to be a detective, have you?"

I didn't tell him that the only way I could handle this charnel house was to revert into being a cop; that I was forcing myself, like a man trying to put toothpaste back into the tube, into once again looking at the world from a detached, strictly business perspective. To keep from thinking about scorched flesh, the smell of which was in my nostrils. To keep from remembering the soft pink flesh of a girl I'd loved once.

"They were friends of hers," I said, standing.

Drury stood, too. "Friends? Not hardly!"

"Well—not in the long run, no. But the firemen had to kick down the front door, right? It was night-latched, correct?"

"Yes," he said. "So we can presume she kept it latched, and only let in people she knew."

"And felt secure enough, having let this lovely couple in, to latch it behind her."

"So she knew them. I'll give you that. Not necessarily *friends*, though."

"Friends. They knew her well enough to know she wouldn't have liquor in the place and brought their own. She invited them into her kitchen. She was making one of them cocoa. Friends."

He smiled a little and shrugged. "Friends," he agreed.

"This back door is locked, too," I noted.

"Yeah. We got ourselves a regular locked-room mystery here."

"No mystery," I said, unlocking it, looking it over. "This is a spring lock. The killers went out the back way, the door locking behind them."

Drury gave me a wry one-sided grin. "There's nothing here I wouldn't have figured out for myself, you know."

"Sure," I said, managing to grin back at him. "But I don't mind taking a couple of minutes and saving you two or three hours of brain work."

"You should be on the radio. Cantor could use the help. Want a look at the bedroom? Maybe you can save me from thinking in there, too."

Like the rest of the apartment, the bedroom had been tossed; the mattress had been gutted with a knife, even its pink fluffy spread slit open. The white French provincial furnishings were scattered, occasionally broken.

"What were they looking for?" I said. "They obviously were torturing her, trying to make her talk. What was she hiding? What did she *know?*"

He shrugged. "I'm not so sure they were trying to make her talk at all. I think she was being made an example of."

"Enlighten me."

"Isn't it obvious? It's this grand jury thing, Nate. Nicky Dean was the last to squeal. Bioff went first, Browne cracked next but only recently has Dean loosened up. Only recently has he cooperated at all with Uncle Sam—now that a reduced sentence has been dangled in front of him."

"And killing his girl is a warning from the Outfit for Nicky to clam back up?"

"Yeah. Sure."

"Then why not just kill her? Why torture her like this?"

"This'll have more impact, Nate. This'll smack Nicky between his bushy eyebrows."

"Yeah, right, only Nitti doesn't work this way."

"The old Nitti didn't. But he's been under a lot of pressure."

"Since when?"

"Like the song says, since you went away. There was a big scandal about Nitti-owned linen services having contracts with the public schools. When the press got hold of that, he lost the contracts, which were lucrative, and then Mayor Kelly, to save face, let us crack down on Nitti's bookie joints and night clubs. Even the Colony Club got shuttered."

"Where was Estelle working, then?"

He gestured to the sheared bed. "Right out of here, I'd say."

"What do you base that on?"

"Sergeant Donahoe's already given this room a cursory once-over, and he reports her affects indicate a call-girl operation."

He walked me over to a dresser, on its side; one drawer had been taken out, its contents scattered, bundles of letters, mostly. I wondered if it had been done by the killers or the police. Drury poked around, found a little black address book, which he plucked from the rubble. He began thumbing through it. Smiling as he read.

"Well, well, well," he said, running his finger down a page, then going on to the next page and running his finger down that one. "Some very familiar names. Of some very wealthy men—doctors, lawyers, here's Wyman, the iron construction man. He was involved in a messy divorce not so long ago . . ."

"So she *was* a call girl, then."

"Looks like." He kept thumbing through it. "And get this—some of these other names . . . friends of hers from her twenty-six girl days. High-class hookers."

"What, you figure she was their madam?"

He shrugged. "Of sorts, maybe. Maybe she was a referral service, if you will. But any way you look at it, she was making her living on her back."

I couldn't argue with him.

"Well, then," I said, "you're going to have a merry time sticking this on the Outfit."

His expression darkened. "Why's that?"

"If she wasn't being tortured to make her talk, what does that leave? She was being made an example of, like you say. *Or*—she was tortured by somebody who wanted to see her suffer, for the sheer sweet pleasure of it. For revenge."

"Yeah. So?"

"So what you got here is the torture slaying of a dead call girl who's been seeing a lot of high-hats, and one of her tormenters, one of her slayers, seems to be a woman. Now, off the top of your head, what does that all add up to?"

He grunted. "Jealous wife."

"You got it. See if the papers don't land on *that* with both feet."

"Maybe," he said, giving me his best official look. "And we'll pursue that avenue. I don't rule anything out. You heard, when we came in, the downstairs neighbor say she saw a guy in the alley." Around two-thirty, running, with fur coats in his arms, she'd said. "Well, there's been a series of apartment fur thefts going on in Lakeview for the past three months. So I don't rule that out either, though in my opinion the killer just grabbed the coats on the way out to make this look more like a robbery, not a mob hit. Nonetheless, I smell the Outfit all over this."

I could only smell scorched flesh. My lunch was acting up again. *Be a cop*, a voice said.

"Somebody was looking for something," I said, making myself get back into this on that level. "What?"

Shrug. "Jewels, maybe. Estelle was known to have 'em. That doesn't rule out this being a hit; why shouldn't an assassin pick up a little extra something in the bargain? At the same time confusing the police as to the motive."

That made sense, but then, on cue, Sergeant Donahoe, a heavyset middle-aged detective with a basset-hound mug, came in from the other room with his hands full of obviously expensive jewelry, including a diamond ring and a glittering diamond bracelet.

"We found this in a baseboard hiding place," Donahoe said, "in the living room." His hound-dog expression made the news sound unintentionally woeful.

"So much for jewels," I said.

"That just means the killers didn't find the goddamn things," Drury said, shrugging it off.

"Also," Donahoe said, piling the jewels in one hand, reaching in his pocket with the other, "this was tucked away in there." A little silver .25 automatic with a pearl handle.

Drury took the gun. "Didn't do her much good hid away, did it?" Dropped it in his pocket.

"And there's a sable coat in the front closet," Donahoe said glumly, and went out.

"So much for fur robbery as a motive," I said. "If they weren't looking for furs or jewels, what's left?"

"Money," Drury said.

"A popular item," I admitted. "But Estelle was known for socking her dough away, in banks, in safe deposit boxes. She was notorious for sponging off people; she rarely had a cent on her, or in her place."

"There is a rumor," Drury said carefully, and I had the feeling he had waited till we were alone to say this, "that a fund Nicky Dean was in charge of—something to do with 'taxing' the Stagehands Union members—was emptied just before he was sent up. Dean refuses to discuss it, but the estimate is somewhere in the million-dollar area."

The infamous two percent income tax Montgomery had once told me about.

"Jesus." I finished the scenario myself: "And, I suppose, rumor further has it that Estelle was entrusted with this dough? By and for Nicky, till he got out of stir?"

Drury nodded.

"Then this could have been *anybody*, Bill. Anybody who knew Estelle and knew about the million. They tortured her and she didn't talk. She held on to her dough till the last. Which is like her, the greedy little bitch. Damn her!"

"Nate, I'm sorry I brought you in on this . . ."

"Shut up. Quit saying that."

"Let me ask you something."

"Ask."

"Suppose I can prove Nitti was behind this. Not necessarily in court, 'cause God only knows if that's even possible. You know the department's record where solving gangland murders is concerned. But suppose I can prove to *your satisfaction* that Nitti did this. Would you tell what you know on the witness stand when the grand jury calls you?"

Estelle's death in my nostrils, I said, "Yes."

He grinned and shook my hand; his enthusiasm was not matched by anything of the kind from me. I was feeling weak. *Be a cop,* the voice said.

"What about those letters?" I heard myself say. Working by rote, now.

He went over and bent down at the dresser where the bundled letters lay. One of the bundles was already undone; he read a sample. Skimmed another, saying, "From some serviceman. Love letters. This one's in answer to a letter of hers, so she was exchanging 'em with him. Pretty hot stuff. 'If only I could see and fold you in my arms,' ha. Hey, he's pissed in this one—'Damn your cruel heart.' Jeez, you don't think she was seeing some other guy besides him, do you? Heaven forbid. There's no name on any of these that I can see, just signs his initials—A.D. Year of our Lord? Ha. Anyway, there's a San Diego address for referral overseas. Well, we'll track him down soon enough. Huh, and there's a photo, too." He held it up for me to see, a portrait of a young Marine in dress blues.

"Nate—what's wrong? You're white as a ghost."

"Nothing. I think it's time I got out of here, is all."

I didn't tell him it was a face I'd seen before. The last time had been in a shell hole on Guadalcanal.

D'Angelo.

24

She floated across the dance floor, which was her stage, which was hers alone, graceful as a ballet dancer, naked as the human id but considerably more controlled, a huge ostrich feather fan in either hand, first this fan and then that one, one or the other, strategically placed at all times, granting flashes of flesh at her whim, feathers swooping, fluttering, moving on the toes of her high-heeled pumps, blond hair stacked in curls upon an angelic countenance, no hint of the devil in her smile as her fleeting glimpses of nakedness turned the men in the house into peeking toms and the women into jealous janes.

The music, as usual, was classical—"Moonlight Sonata," her theme song—filtered through the big-band sound of Pichel and Blank's Orchestra, men in white jackets sitting on risers behind her, enjoying the uncensored rear view. The lighting was soft and blue, and from where I sat with Eliot, ringside at Rinella's Brown Derby, at Monroe and Wabash, in "the heart of the Loop!," she didn't look a day older than she had when I'd seen her at the World's Fair almost ten years ago, cavorting with a "bubble," a big balloon she'd temporarily traded in for her ostrich feathers. It had been the second year of the fair and a new gimmick was called for. Even beautiful naked blond women had to keep up with the changing times. Only time wasn't keeping up with Sally, apparently. She was eternally beautiful. Unlike Estelle Carey, fate had been kind. Fate and soft lighting.

And now she was reaching the climax of her act, the moment all had been waiting for, when she unashamedly threw up the feather fans and they loomed over her as she stood like the statue of Winged Victory, smiling, proud, one leg lifted gently, knee up, keeping one small region a secret, a secret she'd shared with me, but long ago. Her smile was regal, her head back, proud of her beauty, her body, her talent. The house went wild with applause.

The lights grew dim and the applause continued but when the lights came back up Sally was gone, and no amount of clapping could bring her back. Once she raised her fans and showed her all, there was no encore possible. For those eager enough for another glimpse of the goddess in the full-figured flesh, there were two more shows tonight. This had been the finale of the eight-thirty dinner show, and as the orchestra began playing schmaltzy dance music, "Serenade in Blue," Eliot and I were working on our third after-dinner drink. Which was beer, as that and wine were the only options; distillers had been banned from producing drinking liquor since last October.

For an ex-prohibition agent—an understated way of describing him indeed—Eliot Ness could really put the beer away. He would have preferred scotch, just as I would have preferred rum. But there was a war on.

"She really brought the house down," Eliot said, latest beer in hand.

"She always does."

"How long's it been since she played Chicago?"

"Last time I know of was in '41. She may have played here while I was away, though."

"Probably not," he said, taking a sip. "The billing said, 'Triumphant Return'—that sounds like it's been a while. You'd think she could play Chicago any time she wanted."

"She could," I said, "if she was willing to play the burlesque houses. But she only plays nightclubs and other classy . . . what is the word she uses? Venues."

"Ha. Uh, how well do you know her, anyway?"

"Not well, anymore. I haven't talked to her in years."

"You knew her well once?"

"I knew a lot of women once. Damn few twice."

He smiled. "You always feel sorry for yourself when you drink."

I smiled. "Fuck you."

A young lady at the table next to us spilled her wine; her older beau glared at me. Both were in evening dress. Both should have been less easily shocked for people who'd bribed a maitre d' for the front-row seat at a strip show.

Eliot said, "You're going to have to watch that mouth."

"Out with soap?" I drank my beer. "Yeah, I know. I'm not fit for the real world, yet. Could you do me a favor?"

"Try to."

"I'd like to track down a service buddy of mine."

He shrugged. "Shouldn't be any problem. In my capacity, I work hand in hand with the military brass, every day."

"You mean, as the guy safeguarding the health and morals of the armed forces."

"That's morale, but yes. I'm well connected."

"You should've shown some of your movies to Capone."

Eliot smirked. "Al and I are fighting syphilis each in his own way."

The young lady spilled her wine again; I waved and smiled as her beau glared.

"Of course," he said, "if your friend is still overseas, it could take a while to track him."

"He should be stateside by now. He was pretty badly wounded. He was one of the guys in that shell hole with Barney and me."

His eyes narrowed. "Oh. You figure he was hospitalized over here."

"Yeah. He might even be out by now. The kind of wound I had, they keep you inside longer."

"What's his name?"

"D'Angelo. B Company, Second Battalion, Eighth Regiment, Second Marine Division."

"Wait a minute, wait a minute." He dug inside his suitcoat and came back with a little notebook and a pen. He had me repeat the information.

"What's his first name?"

"Anthony, I think."

"You think?"

"We weren't much on first names."

He put the notebook and pen away, smiled tightly. "Get right on it, first thing tomorrow."

"Thanks. I'll be in the office."

"This sounds pressing."

"It is. Somebody else will be looking for him, and I want to get there first."

Eliot thought about that for a moment, then smiled again and said, "It's your business. You asked a favor, and it's yours, no questions asked. I don't expect an explanation."

"I know you don't. And I'm not going to give you one, either."

He laughed and finished the beer. Waved at a waitress, cute as candy in her skimpy black and white lacy outfit, who came over and brought him a new bottle. Manhattan brand; the Capone mob's label, forced upon the local niteries by union pressure. I was still working on my previous bottle of Nitti nectar.

"This afternoon sounds like it was pretty rough," he said, pouring the bottle's contents into his glass, meaning Estelle.

"Rough enough. That's something else you could do for me."

"Oh?"

"Keep me posted, Eliot. Now that Estelle's been murdered, the shit's gonna hit the federal fan."

The young lady got up and threw her napkin down and the beau went rushing after her.

"You mean, specifically," he said, "you're interested in how this event affects Nicky Dean and his willingness to testify."

"Precisely, my dear Watson. And my prediction is he zips his lip."

"Do you agree with Drury that it's a mob hit, or not?"

"Why, did Drury fill you in on his views?"

Eliot nodded.

I said, "It could well be. But it sure isn't Nitti's style."

He nodded again. "I tend to agree. On the other hand, a million dollars is a lot of money."

"So you know about that? The Stagehands 'income tax' fund."

"Yes. And that's a conservative estimate. I've heard as high as two million, and the most frequent figure is one point five mil."

"Your point being?"

He lifted his eyebrows and set them back down. "A torture killing is hardly Nitti's style, granted. Estelle Carey was enough of a celebrity in this town to guarantee her murder attracting headlines. Knowing that, Nitti would seem more likely either to have arranged an 'accident' or at the very least brought in out-of-town torpedoes to neatly do the deed. Estelle was running with Eddie McGrath, you know."

"No, I didn't. And who the hell is Eddie McGrath?"

"A New York crumb. Very high ranking in the Joe Adonis/Frank Costello circle. She'd been seeing him down in Miami Beach."

"In other words, if Nitti wanted her dead, he could bring in out-of-town talent and the blame easily be placed on New York."

"Right. He's done it before."

"E. J. O'Hare," I said. "Tommy Maloy."

"Certainly. And others. So I agree that using what appears to be local talent on a torture killing doesn't fit Nitti's pattern. But there are rumors, Nate, that Nitti's slipping."

"Nitti slipping? How?"

He shrugged. "Mentally. Physically. Some say Ricca's more powerful than Nitti, now. Or anyway coming up fast. You yourself mentioned Accardo and Giancana, so you had to have noticed it starting even before you left town, last year."

I shook my head no. "I don't buy it. Nitti slipping? No way. Never."

"He's not a god, Nate. Or some kind of satan, either. He's a crafty, intelligent, amoral human being. But he is a human being. His wife Anna died a year and a half ago, you know."

"I did see that in the papers . . ."

He gestured with two open hands. "He was devoted to her. His family is all to him, they say."

I remembered him showing me the photo of his little boy.

"He's had some financial setbacks," Eliot went on. "He's got this federal grand jury breathing down his neck, and the income-tax boys are after him again. He's been in and out of the hospital for his ulcers and back pain. It's closing in on him."

"And this, you think, might lead to him condoning what happened to Estelle Carey today?"

"Possibly. That money she supposedly had hidden away for Dean was something Nitti might well have instructed his killers to find out the whereabouts of, by whatever means necessary, before finishing the job. A million bucks, Nate! Or possibly even two. Sure it's possible."

"I don't think so."

"You don't want to think so."

"Don't be stupid."

"I'm not stupid. But I think you, well . . . Nate, you look up to the guy, somehow. Admire him."

"Bullshit."

"You just can't remember when this wasn't his town. You just can't accept change."

"I didn't know I had a choice. I tried to buy a pair of shoes, late this afternoon, they told me I needed a goddamn ration ticket. I told 'em I was at Guadalcanal fighting to preserve their way of life, and they suggested I go *back* there and ask for a ration book."

He laughed. "I bet you took that well."

"Funny this is, I did. I started out bad, and was shouting, the guy was shouting back, and then I just sort of faded away. Wandered back out on the street."

"Well, you'd just come back from that ghastly scene at the Carey apartment . . ."

"That was part of it. But I can't handle this place."

He narrowed his eyes. "What place?"

"*This* place. The real world. You know, I thought when I got back here it would be the same."

"And it changed on you."

"Not really, not in any important way. That's the trouble. I came back, and it was the same trivial everyday life waiting for me, my job, credit checks and insurance adjusting and divorce surveillance, and is that what we're the fuck fighting for?"

"Maybe. Maybe it's enough."

"And then there's the killing. The Outfit or whoever, they're still at it, I mean here we are fighting for democracy over there and over here people are pouring whiskey on people and setting them on fire, and cutting them up and . . ."

He grabbed my arm, squeezed. Apparently it had been shaking, my arm.

"Nate."

"I'm . . . I'm sorry."

"Here," he said. He handed me a handkerchief.

Apparently I'd been crying. I wiped my face with it.

"Goddamnit, I'm sorry, Eliot."

Then the head waiter was standing next to me, and I figured I was finally getting thrown out of the joint.

I was wrong.

"Miss Rand would like to see you backstage, sir," he said. Politely. Only the faintest trace of distaste.

I asked him how to get there and he pointed to a door to the right of where the orchestra was playing.

"Eliot, come with me," I said.

"No. This should be a private reunion."

"I'm not up to it. You come along."

Reluctantly, he rose, and we moved along the edge of the crowded dance floor where couples, old men and young women mostly, were clutching each other to "Be Careful, It's My Heart." We went up some stairs and in a hallway we found a door with a gold star; not a service flag, either. I knocked.

She opened the door and smiled at me, looking just a little older, but not much; her blue eyes, the bluest light blue eyes in the world, stood out startlingly, partly due to the long theatrical lashes, partly due to God. She had on a silk robe, not unlike Estelle's but blue, yawning open a little to reveal creamy talcumed breasts; no doubt she was naked underneath it, like Estelle, albeit in better condition.

Then she saw Eliot, and her eyes just barely revealed her disappointment that I wasn't alone, but her smile stayed, and stayed sincere, and she was shaking Eliot's hand without my having introduced her, saying, "Eliot Ness—this is a real treat. I knew you and Nate were friends, but somehow it never seemed real to me till this very moment."

She cinched the belt 'round her robe tighter, and gestured for us to step in. It was a small, neat dressing room with a large lightbulb-framed makeup mirror, a few chairs, and a hinged dressing screen.

"Where do you keep your feathers?" Eliot asked, with a cute wry little smile. He always did well with the ladies, by the way. Except in marriage.

"That's the prop man's department," she said, with her own cute little wry smile. "Union rules, you know."

"Nate knows all about the Stagehands Union."

Sally didn't get the joke. "Really?" she said, looking at me, a bit confused.

"Inside joke," I said. "You were wonderful tonight."

"Thank you," she said. Her smile tried to stay polite but I could sense the ice forming. "You might've told a girl you were coming."

I shrugged. "Last minute. Eliot showed up and invited me out for supper . . ."

"And," Eliot said, saving me, "I'd noticed you were appearing in town, and knew you two were old pals, so I hauled him down here. He, uh . . . he only got back just this morning."

She stood near me, looked at me carefully. Touched my face. "I can see that. You dear. You poor, poor dear."

There was no sarcasm in it.

I swallowed. "Please, Sally. I . . . please."

She turned to Eliot and said, "Could we have a moment alone, please? I don't mean to be rude, Mr. Ness."

"It's Eliot, and don't be silly," he said, and was gone.

"You're still mad at me," she said.

"I don't remember being mad at all."

"Do you remember not returning my phone calls the last two times I was in town?"

"That was years ago."

"I haven't seen you since . . . when was it?"

"Nineteen forty?"

"November 1939," she said. "That night I bribed my way into your apartment. That gangster . . . Little New York . . . he showed up and you pulled a gun on him. Do you remember that?"

"Sure," I said.

"Do you remember how sweet that night was?"

I couldn't look at her. Her blue eyes were just too goddamn blue for me to look at them. "It was a swell night, Sally."

"I wish you'd call me Helen."

"There's no going back."

"What do you mean?"

"It was too long ago. There's no going back."

"Nate, I know it was wrong of me to just leave you a note like that. I should've stuck around, or called you the next day, but it was a bad time for me—I was bankrupt, I was working my ass off getting my business life back together, and my personal life just got lost in the shuffle, and . . ."

"That's not it."

"What is it, then?"

"There's no going back," I said. "Excuse me."

I opened the door; Eliot was standing out there, leaning against the far wall. "We better go," I said.

"If you want," he said.

"Sally, you look great," I said, my back to her. "It was great seeing you again."

I went back to the table. Eliot trailed after, in a few minutes.

"Where have you been?" I said, and it sounded nasty. I hadn't meant it to, really, but it did.

"Talking to a fine lady," he said, angry with me but holding himself back. "She thinks a lot of you, and you should've treated her better."

"What did you talk about, anyway?"

Very tightly he said, "She's concerned about you. Why, I don't know. But she asked me a few questions, and I answered them. Why, is your civilian status a military secret?"

"Hell," I said, getting up, "my life's an open book."

And I got up and walked outside. Stood on the corner and listened to the El roar by. I could smell the lake.

Eliot joined me, after paying the bill. He looked sad, not angry. I felt sheepish.

"Sorry," I said.

"Forget it. You want to get another beer someplace?"

"No."

"Want a lift someplace? I got a car, at the hotel garage. Better still, I got an E sticker."

I laughed shortly. "You and every politician in town, I'll wager."

"For a guy just back from overseas," he said, "you're catching on fast."

"This isn't my first time in Chicago."

"No? Then maybe you could recommend someplace else we could have a beer. What do you say?"

I said, finally, yes, and we walked to Barney's Cocktail Lounge, where Barney's brother Ben hugged me, even though we'd never been friends, really. I was the closest thing he could get to his brother, so I made do for a surrogate hugee. He'd talked to Barney long-distance in Hollywood just today. Barney indeed would be home soon, but Ben didn't know when exactly.

The bar closed at one o'clock—another wartime sacrifice, but as a wise man once said, if you can't get soused by one you ain't trying—and Eliot and I stumbled out onto the street, and he set out toward his hotel, the LaSalle, and I walked home.

I wasn't drunk, really. I'd had six or seven bottles of beer all told, spread well out over the evening. But you would think I'd drunk enough to make me tired. You would think I'd had long enough a day, shitty enough a day, to be sleepy.

But instead I sat at my desk in my skivvies with the glow of the neon night sunning me through the window. I sat there slumped on my folded arms like a kid sleeping on his desk at school, only I wasn't sleeping. I sat there staring at the Murphy bed, folded down, fresh sheets and blankets waiting, that bed I'd slept in so many times, so many years before. Janey. Louise.

I reached under the desk and searched for and found the key I'd taped there, long ago. I removed it and worked it in the bottom drawer. There, waiting for me, was a bottle of rum, and my nine-millimeter automatic, both tangled up in my shoulder holster. I untangled them, left the gun in its holster out on the desk and drank from the rum like it was a bottle of pop.

But I still couldn't sleep. I couldn't even think of sleeping.

Who killed you, Estelle?

D'Angelo, are you back, too? Are you fighting the homefront war like I am? Was Estelle a casualty?

Monawk—who killed *you*, buddy? Bullets flying everywhere, Monawk screaming, Barney pitching grenades, D'Angelo, where are you?

Somebody screamed.

Me.

I sat up.

I *had* slept. Just for a moment. I was sweating, as if from a fever. Neon pulsed over me. I sat there, chilled, wondering if I could ever sleep again without returning to that shell hole. Wondering if I could ever sleep again until I knew what happened to Monawk.

And Estelle. They were tied together in my mind, now, those two deaths, those two murders, and D'Angelo was the knot.

Somebody knocked at the door.

I glanced at my watch; it was after two.

I jerked the nine millimeter from the holster.

I walked slowly to the door and flung it open and pointed it at the person standing there.

A tiny little person, smelling like talcum, wearing a tailored mannish suit with high square padded shoulders, only it wasn't a man. Sally stood with her purse in front of her like a fig leaf and her blond curls piled on her head like a friendly offering to an unfriendly god, and I stood there in my skivvies with a gun in my hand and she smiled, sweetly, sadly, and said, "Please don't shoot."

I dropped the gun to the floor and took her in my arms and held her. Held her.

"Helen," I said. "Helen."

25

The next morning it was snowing, the wind off the lake turning modest flurries into a whistling, swirling near storm. I dug my hands in my overcoat pockets, my hat pulled down, looking down, getting snow tossed in my face anyway, like fine particles of icy glass, as I walked the several blocks from the El to the Linn Funeral Home, for Estelle's services.

The Linn's tiny mortuary chapel was in a low-rise business district in the blue-collar section of Lakeview, two blocks south of Wrigley Field. Only a handful of mourners showed up. I squeezed the hand of Estelle's weeping mother, and shook the hand of her confused stepfather; I'd never met either before, but her mother remembered my name from when I'd dated Estelle, back when she was a girl working the counter at Rickett's. I could see Estelle's pert beauty lurking in the older woman's thin face, those same green eyes, only the mother's were behind wire-rim glasses and lacked the gloss of greed. I shook the hand of an attractive brunette in a fur stole, a cousin of Estelle's; five would get you ten she was a 26 girl, too.

Last night's papers, and this morning's, were already filled with tales of the "queen of the dice gal"'s many suitors; but none of them seemed to have showed. The small colorless chapel wasn't a third full, and the only men present were the stepfather, the undertaker, Drury's boss Chief of Detectives Sullivan, and me. No clergy. Her mother had tried, but no luck: it was unhallowed ground for Estelle. Half a dozen glamour girls in fashionable black, ladies of the evening whose beauty looker harder in the daytime, sat weeping into hankies, or trying to remember how to weep. Those who could were crying for themselves, I supposed, knowing that there but for the grace of God . . .

The functional gray-metal casket was closed, of course. No mortician alive could have restored that face. Atop the coffin lay a simple spray of orchids. The card read: "To a good pal." Unsigned, it seemed to me obviously Dean's work. A real sentimental guy, that Nicky.

I stood there and looked at the casket and tried to believe she was in there. That pretty, greedy little dame. I couldn't. No tears would come to my eyes either, and a part of me was trying. Well, I'd cried for her last night. That was good enough. So long, baby.

The undertaker locked the chapel doors, to keep out the morbid, though the snow had already done the job, for the most part, and walked to a small podium and spoke a few muffled words, made virtually inaudible by the wracking sobs of Estelle's mother.

It soon came time for the casket to be borne to a waiting hearse, only there were no pallbearers. The undertaker recruited Chief Sullivan and me, but six were needed to do the job. Of the handful of the curious who stood in the snow outside—mostly the professionally curious, which is to say reporters—three were enlisted and we carried Estelle to the hearse, which had a C sticker, by the way, like most vehicles used for delivery. The family was being helped into a limo by the undertaker's assistant. A four-car procession, led by the hearse, was all it took to bear the mourners. There was a black limo across the street, parked, its engine going, the windows fogged up; but, oddly, it didn't pull in behind the other cars, as they left for St. Joseph's Cemetery, driving into the blustering snow. But then I didn't go with them, either. I just stood there letting the particles of icy snow flick at my face.

One of the pallbearing reporters was an old friend of mine. Hal Davis of the *News*. Even with a heavy overcoat on, and a pulled-down fedora, his head seemed too large for his body; the bright eyes in his boyish face—he was approaching fifty but looked thirty-five—grew brighter as he recognized me.

"Hey, it's Heller. I must've been walking behind you. For all the men she boffed, you'd think they wouldn't have to resort to strangers to cart her away."

I decked him.

He hit the snowy sidewalk, or anyway his ass did, sending up puffs of powdery white. He hadn't landed so hard, really. He looked up at me, his pride more wounded than anything else, a small trickle of blood at one corner of his mouth.

"What was that for?"

"General principle. You've had that coming for years."

"Fuck you! Help me up."

I did.

He brushed himself off, his coat first; the few other reporters were dispersing, smiling at Davis's fate. He dusted off his hat. "And here I wrote that nice piece about you the other day."

I decked him again.

He looked up, rubbed his face. "Didn't like the piece, huh?"

I helped him up again. "Don't say anything else. I might hurt you next time."

"There's a hundred in it for the personal story of your love life with Estelle. Don't do it! I'll press charges, Heller, I really will!"

"Go away, Davis."

"Goddamn. The war sure has soured you. What happened to your sense of humor? Used to be a guy could depend on you, when a C-note was involved."

"Go away."

He looked at me like I was some weird animal he'd never seen before, shook his head, dug his hands in his overcoat pocket and walked toward his parked auto. It had a C sticker, too. For purposes of delivering horseshit, I would imagine.

I crossed the street, heading toward the El station, when the front door of the parked limo swung open and a uniformed chauffeur stepped out and said, "Mr. Heller. Excuse me, sir?"

I'd never heard "Excuse me, sir" posed as a question before; it was novel enough an event to make me stop in my tracks, and back up, despite the cold and the snow.

The chauffeur was a pallid fleshy-faced man of about forty-five with a bottle-bloodshot nose; terrific choice for a driver.

He said, "Mr. Wyman would like to speak to you."

"Who? Oh. Yeah. Sure."

He opened the back door and I climbed in. A man of medium but powerful build, in his mid-fifties, in a gray suit and a dark tie, his overcoat folded neatly on the seat beside him, sat morosely, staring forward, wet trails on his ruggedly handsome face.

This was Earl Wyman, self-made man, a construction worker who bettered himself, the president of an ornamental iron company with a fancy Michigan Avenue office, now, a man who two years ago had been messily, publicly divorced by his wife, who had named one Estelle Carey as a correspondent in the proceedings.

I got in and sat there and Wyman said, without looking at me, "Could I drop you at the El station?"

"Certainly. It's nasty weather even for a short walk."

He tapped on the window separating us from the front seat and the chauffeur, who responded to the tap by pulling out into the street. We were not headed toward the El station, and I said as much.

Wyman, still not looking at me, said, "We'll just drive for a few minutes, if that's all right. I'd like a word with you, Mr. Heller."

I unbuttoned my overcoat; it was hot in here. The car's heater was a furnace.

"How is it you know me?"

He smiled faintly, just for a second. "I might say from the newspapers. You've had occasion to be in them. Most recently just the other day. And, in passing, last night and this morning. But your experiences on Guadalcanal are quite . . . stirring. You must be a brave young man."

"I'm not particularly brave, and youth, I find, is fleeting."

He looked at me. His eyes were gray. And red.

"A wise observation, Mr. Heller."

"Not really. More like trite. Estelle told you about me. That's where you know me from."

He nodded, slowly. "She trusted you. I'd even say . . . she came close to loving you. Or at any rate I could tell she had been in love with you once. As much as she could love any man, that is. Of course she loved mammon best of all."

Well, that was a little arch, but I couldn't argue with him.

I said, "She loved Estelle, not wisely, but too well. And so did you."

He looked away from me. "I loved her very, very much, for the little good it did me. She could be very cruel. No—that's not fair. She didn't have a mean bone in her body. She was just so very . . . acquisitive."

"Yeah. She was that. What can I do for you, Mr. Wyman?"

He didn't answer. Not directly. "I'm so . . . ashamed of myself. I came here today, full well intending to go in and sit among the mourners, but . . . I came here for the inquest, you know, early this morning, and they continued it till a few weeks from now, so I came out to my limousine to wait, and then the reporters began showing up, and I . . . I was a coward." His head lurched forward and he covered his face and began weeping. "I was a coward. A craven coward. I loved her so. And I didn't, couldn't so much as go in and . . ."

I shifted in my seat. This was the most uncomfortable limo I'd ever sat in, and it wasn't just the heat, and it didn't have anything to do with the seat cushions.

"Look, Mr. Wyman," I said. "She's dead. It doesn't matter whether you went in there and paid your last respects or not. Say good-bye to her in your own way . . . in your, you know, your own heart."

He wiped his face off, with almost frantic swipes of one palm, as if noticing for the first time that tears were there, suddenly embarrassed by them, saying, "I . . . I like to think she knows I came today. That I . . . I did, in my own private way, pay my proper respects. That I did, that I do, still love her. That she's watching, from above."

If Estelle was watching, it probably wasn't from that particular vantage point; if she was watching, it was probably hotter there than this car. Or her apartment had been, at the end. If she'd gone anywhere.

But I said, "Sure, Mr. Wyman. That's the ticket. I'm sure she knows how you feel. Now, uh, the next train leaves in ten minutes. What can I do for you?"

He looked at me, tentatively. "The papers mentioned you were one of the first at the . . . scene."

"That's right."

"Did you happen to have a look around the apartment? Did you aid the detectives in examining Estelle's things?"

I nodded. "Up to a point, yes."

"The, uh, stories said that certain personal effects were found . . . letters from a serviceman, photos, an address book . . . my name was in the latter, though the papers don't have that. Yet."

"I saw all that stuff, yes."

Now he looked at me sharply, intensely. The gray eyes alert. "Did you see anything else?"

"I saw a lot of things, including Estelle herself and various instruments of torture."

He shuddered. "That's not what I'm inquiring about."

It was so hot in this goddamn car, I was sweating; snow storm outside, and I'm sweating. "Mr. Wyman, I appreciate your grief, I share it, but will you get to the fucking point?"

He sighed. "I understand your frustration. I hope you can forgive my, well . . . I'm out of sorts today, Mr. Heller. This has shaken me. This . . ."

"Get to the point. I have a train to catch."

He turned to the fogged-up window next to him, as if looking out. "Did you see a red book?"

"A red book?"

He stared at the fogged window. "With a clasp. Perhaps two inches thick. The book, I mean."

"A diary?"

Now he looked at me. "A diary."

"Estelle kept a diary?"

"Yes. Did you see it?"

"No. There was no diary. And I was one of the first on the scene, as you said."

His eyes narrowed. "Not the very first."

"The firemen were the *very* first. Some patrolmen and detectives after that."

He was quite forceful, now, as he spoke; for the first time, I could see the successful man of business in him.

He said, "I believe that someone stole that diary. Perhaps one of those . . . public servants who preceded you."

I shrugged. "That's certainly possible."

"I would like you to get it back."

"That would be withholding evidence, Mr. Wyman."

He gestured in an open-handed way meant to suggest how reasonable he was. "Mr. Heller, you can read the damn thing if you find it. If what is in the diary should seem to you potentially helpful, in an investigation of her murder, why by all means turn it over to the police."

"After tearing out any pages referring to you, you mean."

Tiny smile. "Of course. You see, I'm about to be remarried. And, I've reason to believe, Estelle . . . recorded personal things about me. About us."

"Sexual things, you mean."

He pursed his lips. Then said, "That is correct. I'll give you two thousand dollars, and expenses."

"I want a grand retainer. No refunds if I can't come through for you."

"Done."

P. T. Barnum was right.

"I'll see what I can do," I said.

"Mr. Heller, I'm engaged to a lovely woman. From a good family. You must help me keep this scandal contained."

"I thought you loved Estelle."

"I did. I do. I was still seeing her, from time to time. I won't deny that. I've admitted as much to my fiancée, and we're working that out. But another public display of my indiscretions could ruin me. Personally. Financially."

He reminded me of Eliot talking about how Nitti was slipping.

I said, "When did you last see Estelle?"

"Sunday."

This was Wednesday.

"That recently?"

"That recently. It was a . . . farewell dinner of sorts. I told her this would be our last evening together, because I was going to be married again. I . . . think I even believed what I was saying. At any rate, I called for her at nine P.M." He smiled, privately. "We wore evening clothes. She was lovely. We spent the evening at the Buttery, where we dined and danced. As usual, Estelle didn't drink and she didn't smoke. She seemed in exceptionally high spirits. She was doing well; she had a lot of money in the bank, she said. I shouldn't worry about her future." Tears were rolling again; God, I felt uncomfortable. It wasn't the heat, it was the humanity. "I don't know where she got her money. She hadn't worked for several years."

He didn't know she was a call girl, then; well, the papers would tell him about it soon enough.

Speaking of which.

"Mr. Wyman," I said, "if a cop or somebody lifted that diary, and didn't turn it in as evidence, then it's going to be sold to the papers. That's the only reason a cop would swipe it. To make a buck in that fashion."

His expression was firm. "Let it be known—let it *quietly* be known—that I will double any newspaper's highest bid."

"Okay," I said. "But you better consider this. The killers themselves may have taken it. If it incriminated them, that's quite likely."

"I've considered that."

"They may even have known about its existence, and its hiding place in the apartment may have been information they tortured out of her."

"I've considered that as well."

"That's just dandy. 'Cause finding Estelle's killers, well—that's something I don't know if I'm up to. I'll be frank. I'd like to find them. I'd like to blow their brains out. But Captain Drury is looking, too, and he's much better equipped than I am. And he's every bit the detective I am, and twice the cop. And there will be dozens of suspects in this thing. Estelle got around. So I'm not promising anything."

He leaned over and touched my hand. I felt even more uncomfortable, now.

He said, quite earnestly, "Estelle had faith in you. I have faith in you, too."

"Swell. I got faith in that thousand-buck retainer. You can make me out a check now, or send it over by messenger."

He looked away, seeming disappointed in me, and in life and the world in general, said he'd send a messenger, and I got out and took the El.

26

I met Eliot for a late lunch at the Berghoff. Just because we were at war with Germany didn't mean I couldn't eat some Wienerschnitzel, if I felt like it. They were even still serving beer in steins, though the menu now described the cuisine as "Bavarian." Also, my serving of schnitzel seemed postage-stamp size, hardly the Berghoff's style. War is hell.

We sat in one corner of the busy open room, where waiters in black tails with long white aprons held trays of steaming food high on upturned palms as they wound swiftly around and through the scattered, clustered tables like acrobats with a mission. It was comforting being in this no-nonsense, wood-and-glass Protestant church of a restaurant, a true Chicago fixture dating back before anybody was alive, a bastion single-handedly stemming the tide of change, despite such minor setbacks as meat rationing and "Bavarian" euphemism. Here I felt at home. Here I felt like I was in the Chicago I remembered.

Also, it was the sort of noisy, bustling room, brimming with people, that provided cover for a private conversation.

"I made those calls first thing," Eliot said, referring to his efforts to track down D'Angelo's whereabouts. "No response yet. Will you be in your office all afternoon?"

"I plan to be."

"If I get word, I'll let you know."

"I'd appreciate that. Sooner the better." Drury, working from the letters signed with the initials "A.D.," that photo and the San Diego referral address, would not be far behind me.

Eliot was eating pig's knuckles and sauerkraut, a Berghoff specialty. Between bites, he said, "You were right about Dean, by the way."

"What d'you mean?"

"He's clammed up, all right. Whether Estelle Carey's murder was a message somebody sent him or not, he sure took it that way."

"So he won't be testifying, then?"

Eliot smirked humorlessly. "Not as simple as that. He'll testify. He'll just have a . . . selective memory."

"Well, you did say Dean was the last to cooperate."

"That's right, and he's only gradually been revealing bits and pieces of this and that. He's never mentioned Nitti or Ricca or Campagna or Capone by name, for instance."

The Capone in question was Ralph "Bottles" Capone, the soft-drink bottler, one of Al's brothers.

"But he has backed up Browne and Bioff's admissions," Eliot went on, "about the Hollywood shakedowns."

"In other words, he's trying to tell just enough to get his sentence reduced."

"Without buying himself a cement overcoat when he finally gets sprung, yes. It's unlikely he'll retract anything he's already admitted; he won't go opening himself up to contempt or perjury or anything. But it's clear he's remembered all he's going to remember."

"What about Lum and Abner?"

He smiled, wryly. "Bioff and Browne? The effect has been quite different. If anything, the boys are going to spill even more, if that's possible." His expression darkened. "Both their wives got anonymous phone calls last night, telling 'em to tell their husbands to keep their mouths shut or 'you'll get *cut*—your kids, too.' This morning, I understand, Willie was raving and ranting—'We sit around in jail for those bastards and they go around killing our families. The hell with 'em.' That sort of thing."

"Those phone calls don't necessarily mean Estelle's murder was a mob hit, you know."

He shook his head, smiled wearily. "You still can't buy that as something Nitti would do."

"No. It just isn't in character. I keep thinking of the Cermak hit, and the lengths he went to, to have his revenge without stirring up the heat. This is a man who had the mayor of Chicago killed, Eliot, and got away with it."

"That was ten years ago, Nate. This is a different time, and Nitti's a different man."

I drank some beer. "You may be right. We'll see."

"Are you looking into this Carey matter yourself?"

"Not officially. Let's just say I'm on the outskirts."

"Those are dangerous outs to skirt. Didn't you tell me once that

Nitti told you to stay out of his business? That was good advice. Drury's a top-notch cop; let him handle it."

I shrugged. "That's good advice, too."

"Take it, then."

"What else do you have for me?"

He shook his head again, smiled with good-natured frustration. "Well, I can tell you that the FBI talked to Estelle a few weeks ago. I don't know if they got anything out of her or not. But I do know they talked to her. So did the tax boys."

"In reference to Dean's missing million?"

"Mostly. And the grand jury investigation in general."

"Would she have been called to testify?"

"Undoubtedly."

"Would she have talked?"

"I don't know. Maybe somebody didn't want to risk she might." He sipped his beer, gave me a crafty look. "There's also a theory that it was her that blew the whistle on Dean."

I sat forward. "Hell, I heard she hid out with Nick, when he was ducking his indictment. That she dyed her hair black and moved into a cheap flat with him, in Cicero."

"Yes, which is where Hoover's finest picked him up," Eliot said. "After somebody tipped them off as to where he was, that is."

"Estelle?"

"That I didn't find out. It's an interesting wrinkle, though, isn't it? Makes Nicky Dean himself a suspect, if it was a contract hit, that is."

"Can't you find out whether she fingered him or not?"

"That information'll likely be given Drury, in good due course. Besides, I can only do so much sniffing around for you, you know. It's got to seem casual, gossippy. If I poke too hard, somebody'll poke back."

"I know that, Eliot, and I appreciate it, what you're doing."

Pig knuckles put away, he used his napkin. Smiled again. "Enjoy me while you can, because tomorrow I'm out of here. It's back to Cleveland."

"To see the wife?"

"Yes, and to check in with the Defense Health regional office there. I'm on a swing where I'm spending a few days at each of our regional offices—there's twelve of 'em, from Boston to San Francisco—giving this co-op workshop with the FBI."

"Gee, do they have VD in Cleveland now? That place is really getting up to date."

"Sure there's VD. It takes the proper stamp out of your ration book to get it, however."

"Which reminds me," I said, standing, throwing my napkin down. "I got to walk over to the courthouse and get mine."

"VD?"

"Ration book."

He shrugged, stood, reached for the bill. "You're fighting the battle of the homefront, now, Nate."

"Ain't we all," I said, and plucked the bill from his hands. "This is my treat. Consider it a payoff."

"When in Rome."

He walked out on the street with me; the snow had let up, but the wind was blowing it around, so it didn't make much difference.

"You take care of yourself," he told me.

"Sure, kid."

He looked at me carefully. "Are you getting any sleep?"

"Some."

"You look like hell."

"You look like shit."

"No wonder we can't get laid," he said, and walked off.

An hour later, ration book in my billfold, I sat in my office, and started making phone calls, working my way down a list of credit checks that Sapperstein had left on my desk. Gladys came in and asked me if I'd like some coffee. I said, sure—blonde and sweet. She said, huh? And I explained that was G.I. for sugar and cream, and now I was sipping it, between calls, slouched comfortably in my swivel chair, as the phone rang.

"A-1 Detective Agency," I said, for the first time in some while.

"Heller?"

It was a hoarse, familiar voice, but I couldn't place it.

"Speaking."

"This is Louis Campagna."

An old chill went up my spine. I sat up.

"Hello, Louie."

"You did pretty good over there."

"Where?"

"Over there with those Jap bastards. You did pretty good. Frank said to tell you he was proud of ya. We're glad you're back safe and sound and everything."

"Well, uh, thank you, Louie."

Silence.

Which he finally broke: "Safe and sound is a nice way to be."

"It sure is."

"You got in the papers your first day back, didn't you?"

"Yeah. How 'bout that?"

"How did you manage that, Heller?"

"Just one of those things. Drury happened to be in my office when he got the Carey call. He was welcoming me back. We were on the pickpocket detail together, you know, in the old days."

Silence.

"So I went along," I said. "I knew Estelle, you know."

"Yeah, we know. That was an awful thing that happened to her."

I tried to find hidden meaning or menace in the voice; I couldn't quite.

"Awful thing," I agreed.

"You ought to stay out of that."

"The investigation, you mean."

"Yeah."

"I have an interest in who killed Estelle, Louie. But I'll leave that to Drury."

"That's smart."

"I can't seem to make myself buy that Frank had anything to do with it."

Silence.

"It just wasn't his style," I said.

Silence.

Then he said: "Frank may want to see you."

"That might not be a good idea. The federal prosecutor knows that Frank and I have met from time to time. I'm going to be questioned about it."

Silence.

"But you might tell Frank that I have a little medical problem left over from the war. I got amnesia over there."

"Meaning you forget things."

"That's exactly right, Louie."

"That's a healthy sickness to have. Frank will like hearing that.

Keep us informed as to the G's interest in you." By G he meant government. "Get a pencil."

I got a pencil.

He gave me a phone number.

"Is this a number I can reach you at?" I asked, trying to understand what this was about.

"The party at that number can reach me," he said. "Reach them, and I'll reach you."

And a click in my ear said good-bye.

I should've been shaken by the call; instead, I felt oddly reassured. Like the Berghoff, Campagna hadn't changed much. Another Chicago fixture, and—judging by the black market talk in the papers, "meat-legging" in particular being attributed to the Nitti Outfit—one unaffected by rationing.

I sipped the sweet creamy coffee, made another credit-check call.

Shortly after three, somebody knocked at my door. A crisp, hard, single knock.

"It's open," I said.

A Marine sergeant stepped inside, shut the door behind him. He was about forty, wore pressed blue trousers, khaki shirt, necktie and campaign hat. The shine of his shoes reflected the overhead light. He stood board-straight, not at attention, not even at parade rest, but his bearing strictly military and intimidating as all hell, anyway.

"Private Heller?" he said, taking off the hat. He had something in his other hand, too; a small dark blue box.

"Yes," I said, standing. He looked familiar. Who was this guy?

He marched over to the desk. "I tried to call before coming, but your line was busy."

"Uh, yes, sorry. Use the phone a lot in my line of work . . . hey, I know you. You're my recruiting sergeant. You're my goddamn recruiting sergeant."

I came around the desk and extended my hand; he accepted it, shifting the hat to the hand holding the little box. His smile was as tight as his grip.

"Welcome home, Private," he said.

"What brings you here, Sergeant?"

He handed me the small square box, the corners of which were rounded off. "It is my honor to present you this, Private Heller."

I opened the little box, half expecting to find a watch inside. Instead I found a medal. A ribboned star of bronze at the center of which a laurel wreath encircled a small silver star.

"That's your Silver Star, Private. For gallantry in action. Congratulations."

"I . . . well, thank you. I, uh . . . shit. I don't know, Sergeant. I feel funny about this."

"Funny?"

"I don't feel I did anything worthy of a medal. I did what I had to and that's all. Only medal I feel comfortable wearing is this." I pointed with a thumb to the Ruptured Duck on my suitcoat lapel. "I did what I had to. But getting medals for killing people, I don't know about."

His mouth was a thin straight line that words miraculously squeezed out of: "Private, the Marine Corps is fucked up in many ways. But one way in which it ain't fucked up is it don't give out medals for killin' people. It gives out medals for savin' people, which is what you and Corporal Ross did over in that hellhole. So if I was you, I would not have nothing but pride for this here medal."

I smiled at the tough old bird. Old? Three years older than me, probably. Not that that made him young. Had he served in the first war? He'd have been a kid. But then a lot of Marines were.

Anyway, I offered my hand for him to shake again; he did.

"Thank you, Sergeant. I appreciate your words."

He gave me another tight smile and turned to go; he was at the door when I called out to him.

"Sergeant?"

"Private."

"Would you happen to know if one of my buddies from B company is back in town? He was in that same hellhole I was."

"Would you be referrin' to Private D'Angelo?"

Another chill shot up my spine; a newer one than the Campagna variety.

"That's right. Is he back?"

He nodded. "Yes he is. He's a brave young man, too. I delivered a bronze star to him this morning."

"I'd like to visit him."

The sergeant's mouth twitched; that was his shrug. "I can give you his address, if you like."

D'Angelo was living with his aunt and uncle in Kensington, a tiny

Italian community at the far south end of the city, right outside of Pullman, just west of Cottage Grove. I took the Illinois Central commuter line out there, passing the Pullman plant where my father had once worked, and Electromotive, both doing war work now, and among Eliot's VD target areas. As the train passed 103rd Street I could see the smokestacks of steel mills against the sky. I sat on the train thinking about unions, thinking about what the unions had meant to my father, about what my father thought the union idea meant, and what sometimes that idea still meant, but how more often greedy bastards like Bioff and Browne and Dean and Nitti and Ricca and Campagna and various Capones and so many others perverted it into just another racket. Is that what we fought to preserve, D'Angelo and Barney and me?

I got off the IC at a little after four at 115th Street, which I crossed—the obnoxious paint odor of the nearby Sherwin Williams plant mingling incongruously with wondrous spicy smells from various hole-in-the-wall Italian restaurants—to Kensington Avenue, the wide, airy street the little neighborhood was named for. This quaint four-block neighborhood was an Italian oasis in the midst of a Swedish and Polish area; it even had its own church. And Kensington was one Italian neighborhood in Chicago with little or no mob taint.

The bottom floor of the narrow three-story brick building was a grocery store; at the top of the second floor stairs was a landing and a single door, with no number. I knocked.

"Just a second!" a voice from within called. Female voice.

When the door opened, a slender, darkly attractive girl of about twenty stood there; she was in rather form-fitting coveralls with her hair covered by a bandanna, knotted in front, Aunt Jemima style.

"Can I help you?" she said, looking at me rather crossly, her thin frame blocking the doorway. What little of her hair was showing under the bandanna was matted from sweat and her face was smudged here and there.

"My name's Heller. I'm a friend of Private D'Angelo's."

She brightened. Stepped back and gestured for me to come in, saying, "Nathan Heller, sure. You're Tony's friend. He told us all about you. Read about ya in the papers, too."

I stepped inside. It was a small living room with nice but not lavish furnishings, overstuffed sofa, some chairs, radio console, Catholic icons.

She gestured to herself, to her coveralls, her bandanna, smiling widely. Her teeth were very white and her eyes were very brown. "Excuse. I just got off my shift at Pullman."

I smiled at her. "Rosie the Riveter, huh?"

"Marie the arc welder. Would you like to see my brother?" She seemed hopeful and sad all at once.

"Sure. He's here, then?"

"Yeah. Sure." She seemed surprised I'd think otherwise. "It's close to Roseland Community." That was a hospital, about a mile from here. She went on: "I think some company might help Tony a little."

She stepped closer; she smelled sweaty, the sweat of good hard honest work. I liked the way she smelled. She was, in fact, a cute kid, and if I wasn't here to see if maybe her brother was a murderer I might have asked for her phone number. I never dated an arc welder before. Or the sister of a murderer, that I remembered.

"Is D'Angelo a little down?" I said. I couldn't seem to bring myself to call him Tony; don't know why.

She stood very close to me. "He's been blue as hell. He was okay when he got home. We were all surprised how good his spirits were, considering. But when he saw the paper this morning . . ."

"The Estelle Carey killing?"

She nodded gravely. "He cried and cried. Don't tell him I told you."

"Look, uh, Marie. Let me give you a tip. Some of your brother's letters and things were found in her apartment."

The skin around her eyes tightened. "Really?"

"They haven't connected them to . . . Tony, yet. But they will. And cops and reporters will be swarming around."

"Oh dear. What should we do?"

I shrugged. "You may want to have him stay someplace else, till it all blows over. I don't mean to suggest you keep him away from the police, but you may want to keep the reporters off him."

She nodded. "Certainly. I appreciate this."

"That's okay. I figure you should be warned. And your aunt and uncle downstairs, with their business and all."

She smiled again. Lovely smile. "It's nice of you."

I wasn't so nice. I was here to confront my old war buddy about a murder. Two murders.

But I owed him this much, this warning. And I liked his sister's smile.

"I'll take you back to him," she said.

"No. You can just point the way."

"Okay. I need to get a bath, anyway."

I didn't want to think about her bathing. I had other things to do.

She pointed me down a hallway, off of which were various bedrooms, and at the end was a small kitchen, with a hoosier cabinet and a table and sink all crowded together. To the left was a bedroom, D'Angelo's, she said.

But I found him sitting out on the enclosed porch, also off the kitchen. It was a little cold, out there. No insulation. But D'Angelo didn't seem to notice. He was at a card table, but turned facing a window looking out on the alley, a half-played hand of solitaire spread out before him like a meal he wasn't hungry enough to eat.

"Hello, D'Angelo."

He turned slowly and looked at me. His face was hollow-eyed, haunted, like the Marines of the 1st Division we'd come to the Island to spell, those wasted scarecrows who'd met us as we waded ashore off the Higgins boats. Only D'Angelo looked even worse. He'd always been razor-thin, and he still was, only now that razor was dull. His eyes were dead.

But something in them came marginally alive when he recognized me.

"Heller," he said. It was cold enough for his breath to show. He smiled, just a little.

I went over to the card table and sat next to him. Just looking at him I knew he hadn't killed Estelle. Monawk was another matter.

"I'm sorry about your girl," I said.

"Hell of a thing," he said. His eyes were full of water. "Hell of a thing." He reached for a deck of Luckies on the card table; shook a smoke out and lit it nervously off a battered silver Zippo lighter from his plaid flannel shirt. "You can't know what it's like to come home and your girl's dead, your goddamn girl's dead. Murdered! Tortured . . ."

I said nothing.

"Want a smoke?" he asked.

"Yeah," I said. He lit it off his—hospital habit—and handed it to me. I sucked the smoke into my lungs and felt strangely alive.

"What the fuck kind of world is it?" he said. "Come home from what we went through, and somebody murdered your goddamn girl!

Your goddamn girl." He didn't want to weep in front of me, I knew, but it was killing him holding all that water in his eyes.

"Go ahead and bawl," I told him. "We all do it."

He covered his face with his hand and tears dripped through his fingers. I looked away. Smoked.

"Who am I kidding?" he said. He rubbed the tears off his face, as best he could; some smears of moisture remained. "She had a lot of guys. Some of my friends wrote me and said she was out with this swell, and that one. She loved money more than she loved any man."

That was true.

He looked at me curiously, all of a sudden. "What were *you* doing there?"

"What?"

"I saw your name in the papers. You were there, at her apartment, with the cops."

"I know the detective whose case it is, is all. Coincidence."

He gripped my arm. "If you find something out, you gotta let me know. If you hear something. If I can get my hands on the bastards that did that to her, I swear I'll wring their fucking necks. How could anybody *do* that to a beautiful girl like her?" He shook his head. "Aw, shit, Estelle. Why'd you have to love money so goddamn much?"

"I remember back at San Diego," I said, "you mentioned you worked for Nicky Dean at the Colony Club. Is that where you met her?"

He nodded. "I was a waiter there. Head waiter. I ran errands for Nicky, sometimes."

"How did you and Estelle get together?"

"She liked my looks. I liked hers. That's all it takes."

True enough.

"I knew her once, too," I said.

"Really?"

"A long, long time ago."

"Did you go with her?"

"Yeah."

"Did . . . you love her, too, Heller?"

"A long, long time ago, I did, yeah."

"So, then . . . I guess you do know how it is to come home to something like this."

"We got that in common, pal."

"We got a lot in common, don't we, Heller?"

We sure did. We both had wounds that would never heal.

I said, "How did Monawk die, D'Angelo?"

"What do you mean? The Japs got him. What else?"

"Did you see it happen?"

"No. No. I was out. I bled a lot, you know."

"Yeah, I know."

I sat there with him for a couple of hours. We talked some, but mostly we smoked. Like in that foxhole looking down on the ridge of *kunai* grass.

When I went out, his sister, wearing a very fresh blue dress with a crisp white collar, her black hair in a shining page boy, greeted me. I think she liked me. I liked her. She smelled like sweet-smelling soap.

"You're a good friend to come see him," she said.

"I'll be back."

"I'd like that."

I wasn't Prince Charming, but there was a man shortage.

She walked me out to the street. The sky was a glowing red. The steel mills.

"Good night, Marie."

"Good night, Mr. Heller."

I didn't think her brother had killed Monawk; I wasn't sure, but my gut, my detective's gut, said no.

Anyway, I knew he hadn't killed Estelle yesterday.

Not on one leg.

CAPTAIN DRURY (WITH CHIEF OF DETECTIVES SULLIVAN)

27

Town Hall Station, a massive faded red-brick building built around the turn of the century, dominated the corner of Addison and Halsted. It was just three blocks west from Estelle's "death flat" (as the papers were gleefully calling it), and within spitting distance of the Salvation Army's national training camp, a baracaded, barbed-wire encampment devoted to saving souls.

Which could not exactly be said for the Town Hall Station, up the steps of which I went, through the main door on Addison, up into the big waiting-room area. It was Friday afternoon, and business here was slow—a few juvies were slouched on the hard wooden chairs lining one wall, waiting for their parents to show, flirting with a bored lone hooker sitting polishing her nails, waiting for her pimp or lawyer or somebody to pick her up. I checked in with the fiftyish flabby Irish sergeant who sat behind the booking counter reading a racing form, and was sent on upstairs. I was expected. Sergeant Donahoe, he of the basset-hound countenance, showed me to the small interrogation room where Drury stood grilling the seated Sonny Goldstone, Nicky Dean's partner from his Colony Club days. A police steno, a plain young woman in matronly blue, sat just behind and to one side of Goldstone, taking it all down.

The cubbyhole was well lit but stuffy. Goldstone's fleshy face seemed expressionless, even bored. He had the sort of soft, bland, unthreatening features—hooded eyes, straight nose, petulant mouth—that so often belong to the truly cold. He was wearing black-rim glasses tinted a slight brown. He was dressed neatly, successful businessman that he was, in a tailored, vested brown suit with a tasteful two-tone brown striped tie.

Drury's usual dapper look was absent; he was stripped down to his vest, sleeves rolled up, tie loosened, working up a sweat. He was as good a man as any at the verbal third degree. On the other hand, you still can't beat a rubber hose.

Drury nodded to me, as I closed the door behind me, and Goldstone's eyes flicked my way once, then stared back into nothing, ignoring both me and Drury, which was a good trick in this closet. I don't know whether Goldstone recognized me or not; we'd only seen each other that once, that night in '39 when Estelle took me up to a third-floor Colony Club suite.

"You were seen going into the apartment building Tuesday afternoon, Sonny," Drury said, matter-of-fact, confident as God. "Positively identified by the manager of Estelle's building."

Looking at nothing, Goldstone said, "She's nuts. She's talking nonsense."

"The woman picked you out of our rogues' gallery files yesterday. And today she picked you out of a five-man lineup."

"I remember. I was there."

"I was there, too, Sonny. I saw her pick you out; no question in her mind."

Shrug. "A lot of people look like me."

"You were in that apartment, Sonny."

Shrug. "I was there before. Not Tuesday. I got twenty or thirty people who saw me elsewhere at the time of the crime."

"Name one."

"I'll wait for the trial. Which there's never going to be."

"Did she talk, Sonny? Did she finally tell you where that million was?"

Smirk. "Why, Drury? You want to borrow some of it to buy some more fancy-ass suits?"

This is where a rubber hose comes in handy.

Drury, unfortunately, was not that kind of cop. Donahoe came in and tapped Drury on the shoulder and said, "Visitor's here."

He nodded toward Goldstone, saying to Donahoe, "Lock that fat bastard up."

"You got nothing," Goldstone said.

Drury pointed at him. "We got bloody fingerprints in that apartment. Think about *that* in your cell, wise guy."

We stepped out in the hall.

"You really got fingerprints in blood?" I asked Drury.

"Yeah, from off a kitchen cabinet," he said, walking toward his office. I followed along.

"You think Sonny's your man?" I asked.

"Maybe. But he was right about one thing—he really does have a common sort of face. Another Nicky Dean associate, Thomas Stapleton, who we're looking for now, could be Goldstone's brother. Ditto for John Borgia, who was tight with Dago Mangano, one of Dean's partners. As for the bloody fingerprints, they belong to a woman or a small man—not Sonny Goldstone. We're in the process of pulling in no less than a dozen Colony Club male employees for questioning, and half again that many working girls associated with Estelle, plus her former roommate. And then there's that Adonis-crowd hood Eddie McGrath being sought for us in New York. And a suspect in the North Side fur thefts we got a line on. That doesn't touch the thirty-plus respectable gentlemen whose names and numbers were in Estelle's little black book."

"Jesus. Why don't you just gather all the suspects in Chicago Stadium and turn off the lights. It works for Charlie Chan."

He stopped just outside his office, the door of which was closed. "It gets worse. But I didn't ask you down here just to hear Sonny Goldstone not talk. There's somebody waiting inside here who might prove a little more interesting."

I followed him inside his private office, which was just big enough to comfortably house his desk, a few files and a couple of chairs, one of which was occupied by a small, dark, attractive but rather frail-looking woman in her late thirties, facing his empty desk, waiting for him to fill it. He did, nodding to her, smiling.

"Mrs. Circella," he said. "Thank you for coming in to see us voluntarily."

"Why shouldn't I?" Nicky Dean's wife said sweetly, with just the faintest hint of an Italian accent. "I'm not a criminal."

She was smartly attired, wearing a black Persian lamb coat over a navy blue suit and a wide-brimmed navy felt hat. The effect of the dark apparel was almost one of mourning. Her oval face was pale, which made her sensual red-lipsticked mouth seem startling, and next to the full red lips nestled a beauty mark, which was enough to make you wonder if Nicky Dean had been crazy or something. Even with a dish as luscious as Estelle Carey, why cheat on this stunning creature?

Greed, of course. Something Nicky and Estelle had in common.

I just stood and listened, leaning against one wall. The police steno filed in and took her inconspicuous place in the corner, as Drury said, "You don't mind going on the record with your statement, Mrs. Circella?"

"Of course not. I'm a good citizen. I always cooperate one hundred percent with the authorities."

If there was any sarcasm in her words, I couldn't find it.

"I came, at your request," she said, "although I must admit I don't understand why you would want to question me in regard to a *murder*. Particularly one committed while I was out of the city."

"Where were you on February second?" Drury asked.

She batted long lashes, innocently; her eyes were wide and brown and lovely. "I was in New York City, of course. I was staying at the Alamac Hotel. To be close to my husband in his hour of need. Nicky and I learned of her death together, you know."

"No, I didn't."

She was twisting a lace hanky in her hands, nervously. "We were sitting outside of the grand jury room of the U.S. Courthouse in New York, and someone brought in a copy of a Chicago paper. The *Herald-American*, I think it was. There was a picture of Estelle on the front page, but at first I didn't recognize it. I recognized the name, though. So I turned to Nicky and said, 'Didn't this girl work for you?' And he looked at her picture and said, 'Yes.' Then he said, 'Let me read that paper.'"

"What did he have to say?"

She lowered her eyes. "'That poor girl,' he said."

"I see. Let's start at the beginning. Did you know about Estelle Carey?"

She shook her head, no. "I didn't know her. I knew who she was, but we never talked. I wouldn't recognize the sound of her voice if I heard it today. Oh, I saw her from time to time—at the dice tables at the 101 Club and the Colony Club, which Nicky owned."

Drury smiled, but his eyes and forehead frowned; this woman was either very naive or very crafty, and, either way, it was getting to him. "Mrs. Circella, I didn't ask if you knew Estelle. I asked if you knew *about* her. By which I mean . . ."

She licked the lush lips. "I heard the rumors that she and Nicky were friendly. I could never verify them, though."

"How hard did you try?"

She smiled slightly, regally. "I didn't. I never tried. I'm a Catholic, Captain Drury. When I married I made a contract with God. None of us is infallible. I am not my husband's judge. Nick has been a good husband to me for nineteen years."

"Have you been aware of how he's earned his living during that time?"

"Yes. Night clubs. But they were no part of *my* life. I spent my time at home, with our two children. I won't pretend I liked his business. It's the one thing we've argued about. But when I've asked him to give up his night clubs, his answer is always the same—that he had to do *something* for a living."

Drury was drumming his fingers on the desk. "Were you aware that Nick was connected with the Stagehands Union?"

"Yes," she nodded. "I know Mr. Browne and Willie. But Nicky resigned from the union before all the trouble started."

"You know nothing of a million-dollar slush fund then?"

She smiled again. "The FBI and the Internal Revenue Service have that same interest. I'm sure if we had a million dollars, I'd know about it."

"And you don't?"

"Of course not."

Drury sighed. "You were in show business once yourself, weren't you, Mrs. Circella?"

She sat up; she didn't seem so frail, all of a sudden. "I met Nicky when I was appearing in a show at the Cort Theater. Each night he'd come and listen to my singing. Then he'd send roses. Finally we met through a mutual friend. That was in 1923; we were married the following year." The past glory faded, and she settled back into the chair, frail again. "Now I can't even sing the baby to sleep, since I had diphtheria. My vocal cords were affected, but that doesn't matter. When I married Nicky, I washed my hands of show business. A wife stays home and minds the children, like Nicky says."

"Getting back to Estelle Carey . . ."

"I was at fault."

Drury leaned forward. "Pardon?"

She gestured with the lacy hanky. "I have been a sick wife for a long, long time. Nick couldn't be blamed for seeking the company of a gorgeous creature like Estelle—and she *was* gorgeous."

Was as in past tense.

She went nobly on: "None of us knows what life has in store for us. We are all in God's hands."

Anyway, Estelle was.

She smiled bravely. "I have only pity for Estelle Carey. She missed everything that is fine in life—home, family, the respect and esteem that are every woman's birthright."

"No bitterness at all, then."

She shook her head no. "I'm sorry for her from the bottom of my heart. Since this has happened, I've gone to church and lit candles in her memory. Her murder was a terrible, terrible thing."

Drury smiled politely, rising, gesturing to her. "Thank you, Mrs. Circella. You're free to go now. Thank you for stopping by."

She rose, smiled politely back at him. Fluttered her eyelashes. Great eyes on this dame. "Certainly, Captain Drury," she said.

"Sergeant Donahoe, in the hall there, will show you out."

She walked by me, snugging on navy gloves, trailing a wake of expensive tasteful perfume. I closed the door behind her.

Drury sat back down. "What do you think?"

I was still standing. "Some classy broad."

"I mean, is she on the level?"

"Yeah. In her way."

"What do you mean, in her way?"

I shrugged. "She's lying to herself, not to you. She's human; she hated Estelle like any good wife would. But she prefers to affect her good-Catholic-wife, stiff-upper-lip, superiority-through-suffering stance. It gets her through the day."

"In other words, her marriage is an arrangement she can live with."

"I'd say so."

"I say if she'd been in town Tuesday, we might have a real suspect."

"No. I don't think so. I can't picture that sweet little thing with an icepick in her hand."

"Sometimes women can surprise you, Nate."

"Hell, they always surprise me. Personally, I wouldn't mind finding a wife like that—beautiful, devoted, expects you to fool around on the side. I didn't know they made 'em like that anymore."

"You want a girl just like the girl that married dear old Nick."

"Maybe. Anyway, I don't think she's a killer. I don't think she even *hired* a killer."

"The papers are going to love her," Drury said, glumly cynical. "They'll fall all over themselves for that 'every woman's birthright' speech."

"You got that right. Anything else you'd care to share with me? Or should I let you get back to your couple of hundred suspects?"

His face narrowed into anger, or at least a semblance thereof. He shook his finger at me. "Yes there is. Why didn't you give me D'Angelo's name?"

"Oh. So Uncle Sam finally ran him down for you, huh?"

"Yes, and we were out to see him this morning. And we discovered you'd been there Wednesday night. What gives?"

I held my hands out, palms open. "He was on Guadalcanal with me, Bill. He was in that same shell hole as Barney and me. We almost got killed together. I owed him a warning of what was ahead for him—cops, reporters. He had that much coming."

"Being in the service together doesn't justify withholding information . . ."

"Yes it does."

He shook his head. "Go on, make me feel like a heel. You been to fight the big war and I haven't. Make me feel like a piker." He thrust his finger at me. "But if you're going to be sniffing around the edges of this case, don't you goddamn *dare* withhold information or evidence from me again; our friendship isn't going to cover that, Nate."

"Understood."

"Now do me a favor and get the hell out of here."

I did.

On my way out, I stopped by Sergeant Donahoe's desk. "You got it?" I asked him.

He nodded and looked around furtively and opened a desk drawer and got out a sack.

"Two gee's?" he whispered, holding on to the thing with both hands.

"Two gee's," I whispered back. "In cash. You'll have the dough tomorrow."

"I better," he said, with his usual hound-dog expression, and handed me the sack.

I took it and walked down the stairs, out of Town Hall Station, in front of which the pretty, petite Mrs. Nick Circella was talking to Hal Davis and some other reporters, halfheartedly shielding her face with a gloved hand whenever a flashbulb went off.

I tucked Estelle Carey's diary under my arm and walked by them.

28

That night I met Sally backstage at the Brown Derby at half past one; she stepped out of her dressing room wearing a white sweater and black slacks and a black fur coat and a white turban and looked like a million. Not Nicky Dean's hidden million, maybe, but a treasure just the same.

"How can you look so chipper?" I asked her. "You just did four shows."

She touched my cheek with a gentle hand, the nails of which were long and red and shiny. "I get a little sleep at night," she said. "*You* ought to try it."

"I hear it's the latest rage," I said.

She looped her arm in mine and we walked to the stage door. "It'll get better for you. Wait and see."

We'd spent Tuesday night together, in my Murphy bed, so she knew all about my sleeping trouble. She knew I would toss and turn, and then finally drop off only to quickly wake up in a cold sweat.

"I go back there when I sleep," I told her. We were walking out on Monroe. It was cold, but not bitterly cold.

"Back there . . ?"

"To the Island."

Our feet made flat, crunching sounds on the snowy sidewalk.

"Did you talk to your doctors about this?"

"Not really. I ducked the issue. I wanted to get home. I figured it would let up, once I did."

She squeezed my arm. "Give it time. This is only your fourth day back. Say. Why don't you see if a change of scenery helps your sleep habits? I've got a room at the Drake, you know."

I grinned at her. "Surely not that plush white penthouse that fairy friend of yours sublet you, way back when."

She laughed, sadly. "No. I don't know what became of him, or his penthouse. It's just a room. With a bed."

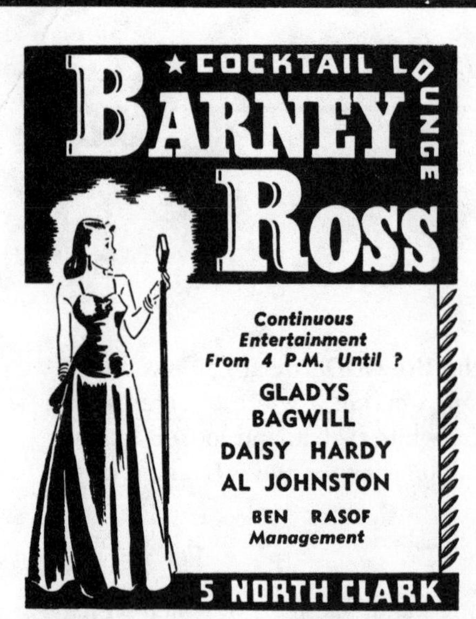
★ COCKTAIL LOUNGE
BARNEY ROSS
Continuous
Entertainment
From 4 P.M. Until ?
GLADYS
BAGWILL
DAISY HARDY
AL JOHNSTON
BEN RASOF
Management
5 NORTH CLARK

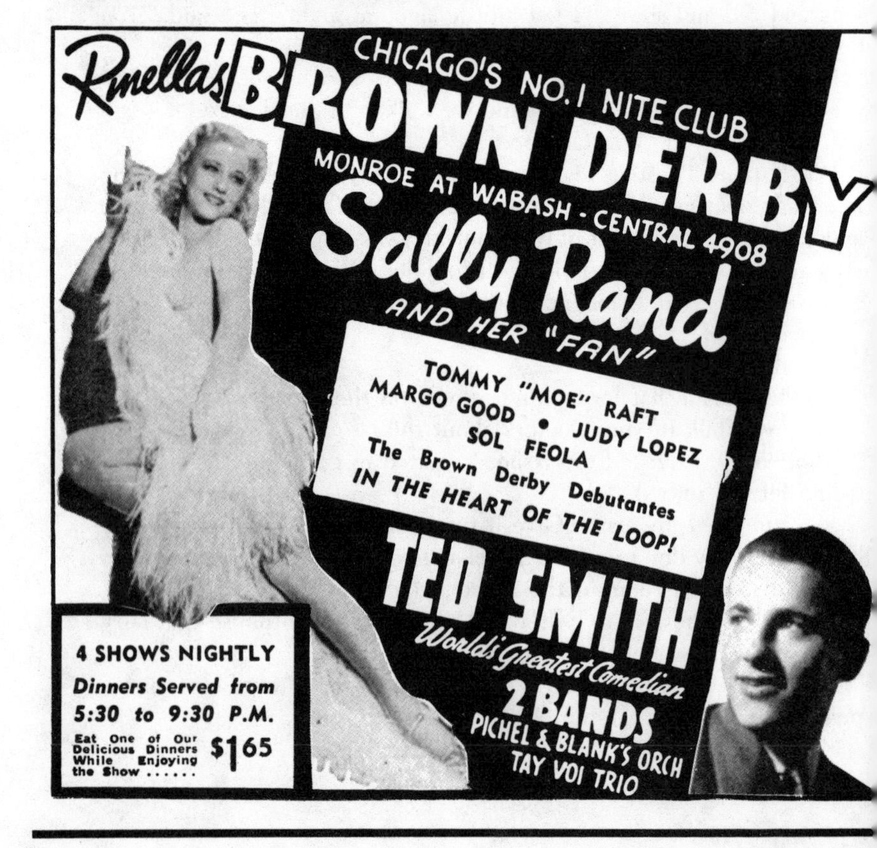
Rinella's BROWN DERBY
CHICAGO'S NO. 1 NITE CLUB
MONROE AT WABASH - CENTRAL 4908
Sally Rand
AND HER "FAN"
TOMMY "MOE" RAFT
MARGO GOOD • JUDY LOPEZ
SOL FEOLA
The Brown Derby Debutantes
IN THE HEART OF THE LOOP!
TED SMITH
World's Greatest Comedian
2 BANDS
PICHEL & BLANK'S ORCH
TAY VOI TRIO
4 SHOWS NIGHTLY
Dinners Served from
5:30 to 9:30 P.M.
Eat One of Our Delicious Dinners While Enjoying the Show ......
$1.65

"You talked me into it."

We crossed Clark Street, heading for the Barney Ross Cocktail Lounge. Traffic was light for a Friday night. Of course, the bars had already been closed for forty minutes.

"Do you know what this is about?" she asked.

I shook my head no. "All I know is Ben asked me to stop by, after hours tonight. I asked him if I could bring my best girl and he said sure, and drinks would be on the house, and we'd have the place practically to ourselves."

"Are you *positive* that's what he said?" she asked.

We were approaching the entrance, from which came the muffled but distinct sounds of music, laughter, and loud conversation. The door was locked, but through the glass a swarm of beer-swilling people could be seen. We stood there basking in the glow of the blue neon that spelled out Barney's name and the outline of boxing gloves, wondering what was going on, and finally Ben's face appeared in the glass of the door, and he grinned like a kid looking in a Christmas window, unlocked it, and we stepped inside.

"What's up?" I asked him, working to be heard above the din.

"Come on back!" Ben said, still grinning, waving a hand in a "follow me" manner, leading us through the jam-packed, smoky saloon. The jukebox was blaring "Blues in the Night" . . . *mah mama done tole me* . . . and the place was filled with guys from the West Side, older ones my age or better, except for some kids in uniform, and a lot of 'em patted me on the back and grinned and toasted me as we wound through 'em, *way to go Nate, you showed them yellow bastards, Heller,* that sort of thing. The rest seemed to be people from the sports world, the fight game especially, including Winch and Pian, Barney's old managers, who I glimpsed standing across the room talking to a young kid who looked like a fighter. I hoped for his and their sake he had a punctured eardrum or flat feet or something, or he wouldn't have much of a ring career ahead of him, not in the near future anyway. A few reporters were present, mostly sports guys, but Hal Davis was there, and he had a bruise on his jaw that looked kind of nasty. The look he gave me was nastier than the bruise.

We ended up at the farthest back booth, around which the crowd seemed thickest, and Ben called, "Step aside, step aside," *when I was in knee pants,* and they did, and I'll be damned if a gray-haired version of Barney Ross wasn't sitting there.

He looked at me with those same goddamn puppy-dog eyes in the same old bulldog puss, only his face was less full than it used to be. Like mine. He didn't seem to have my dark circles under the eyes, though; but his once dark hair, which when last I saw him was salt-and-pepper, was now stone gray. He was sitting next to Cathy, the brunette showgirl he got hitched to at San Diego, but immediately slid out on seeing me, leaning on a native-carved cane he'd brought back from the Island, and stood and looked at me.

"You got old," he said, smiling.

"You're the one with the gray hair."

The music was still loud, *who make you to sing the bloooes,* but we weren't yelling over it. We could understand each other.

"You're gettin' there yourself," he said, pointing to the white around my ears. Then he pointed to his own head of gray hair. "Turned this way that night in the shell hole, just like my pa's did in the Russian pogroms."

"Christ," I said, getting a good look at his uniform. "You're a fucking sergeant!"

His grin drifted to one side of his face. "I see they promoted you, too."

"Yeah," I said. "Back to civilian."

His smile turned lopsided, sad. "Shouldn't have got you into it, should I, Nate?"

blues in the night . . .

"Shut up, schmuck," I said, and he hugged me and I hugged him back.

"Sally!" he said, to the little vision in black and white standing next to me and looking on benignly at this sorry display of sentimentality. "It's great to see you, kid!" He hugged her next, and I bet that was more fun than hugging me. "It's good to see you two back together again."

"Easy," I said. "We're just friends."

"Yeah, sure," he said. "Come on, slide in and sit with us!"

A couple of sportswriters had been sitting across from Barney and Cathy, in the booth, and they made way for us, thanking Barney, slipping their notebooks into their pockets. But Sally didn't join us—Nat Gross, the "town tattler" on the *Herald-American,* stole her away; Sally smiled and shrugged, handed me her fur coat, said "Publicity's publicity," and was soon lost in the smoky throng.

"Reporters," Barney said, shaking his head. "Take those sports guys, for instance. They wanted to know all about me bein' voted boxing's 'man of the year,' which is a crazy stupid thing anyway. I ain't been in the ring since '38! It's supposed to be for the man who did the most for boxing last year, and they give it to *me*. What for?"

"Beats me," I said. Cathy was beaming at him; they were holding hands. "When d'you get back? Why didn't you tell me you were coming?"

"My furlough came through early," he said, shrugging. "I was in New York, getting that 'man of the year' deal, and got a chance last night to hop a military flight here. I called Ben before I left to ask him to round some people up. It was his idea to surprise everybody. Anyway, I got in this afternoon, and spent the evening with Ma and the family. Tomorrow there's going to be a reception with Mayor Kelly and the hometown fans and all; but tonight I just wanted to see my old pals. Damn, it's great to be home!"

"I saw that stupid picture of you," I said, smirking, shaking my head, "kissing the ground when you got off the hospital ship at San Diego. Some guys'll do anything to get in the papers."

He smiled back at me tightly and waggled a finger at me. "I swore if I ever got back home, my first act would be to stoop and kiss the ground. Remember?"

"I remember."

"And I keep my promises."

"You always have, Barney. So promise me you aren't going back over there."

"That's an easy one to keep. I won't be going back, Nate. I got an arm and leg loaded with shrapnel. It'll be months before I can get around without my trusty voodoo stick."

He was referring to his carved native cane, leaned up against the side of the booth next to him. The big head of the cane was a face with mirrorlike stones for eyes. In the mouth were what seemed to be six human teeth.

"Genuine Jap teeth," Barney said, proudly, noticing me noticing them.

"Good, Barney," I said. "It's nice to know you didn't go Asiatic or anything over there."

Cathy spoke up. "Barney's been transferred to the Navy's Industrial Incentive Division."

"That doesn't have anything to do with social disease, does it?" I asked him.

He made a face. "Are you nuts?"

"Yeah, but don't knock it—it got me out of the service." I explained briefly about Eliot's VD-busting role, and how he'd tried to hide behind governmental gobbledygook telling me about it. Barney got a laugh out of that.

"They're gonna send me touring war plants," he shrugged, seeming embarrassed, "telling the workers how the weapons and stuff they're making are helping us lick the Japs. Fat duty. Pretty chickenshit, really."

Cathy looked pointedly, first at him, then at me, and said. "Don't listen to him. The brass told him this was important duty, just as important in its way as Guadalcanal. There's a serious absenteeism at some war plants, and a half-time talk from a hero like my husband can really get those workers off their rears and breaking their necks to beat production schedules!"

She was as full of energy as all three Andrews Sisters, but there was something wrong behind all that pep. Something a little desperate. I didn't know her very well—I'd figured Barney marrying a showgirl was trouble, him being on the rebound from Pearl, his first wife, who I'd liked very much. So I'd resented Cathy, I guess, and never really gave her a chance.

But I could see, tonight, in this smoky gin mill, she really loved the mug. I could also see something was deeply bothering her, where he was concerned.

Barney looked at her, movie-star pretty with her perfect page boy and smart little blue dress, and it was clear he loved her too. "Cathy's turned down two movie roles, Nate, just so she can travel around with me. This war-plant tour's going to mean hitting five, six, sometimes seven plants a day. And we'll be doing War Bond rallies and blood-bank drives . . . I don't mind, of course—we both know how the boys are suffering in those jungle islands, how bad they need guns and ammo."

He'd do fine on the "Buy Bonds" circuit.

I said, "How long will you be in town, Barney?"

"It's an extended furlough. At least a month. And this'll be our home base, after we start the tour." He smiled at Cathy and squeezed her hand. She had on an aluminum bracelet he'd given her fashioned from a section of a Jap Zero.

I said, "Remember D'Angelo? He's here in town."

Barney's smile disappeared. "I know. I had Ben invite him here tonight, but he didn't show."

"He lost a leg, you know."

"He's one up on Watkins," Barney said. "He lost both of his."

"Damn. Where is he?"

"San Diego. I stopped in on him. Still in the hospital, but he's doing pretty good."

"I want his address."

"Sure. Those two Army boys pulled through okay; I've got their addresses, too, if you want 'em."

"You wouldn't know if Monawk had any family, would you?"

He shook his head; his expression was morose. "I checked. No immediate family, anyway."

I just sat there. The Mills Brothers were singing "Paper Doll" on the jukebox now, which somebody seemed to have turned down.

He said, "I'm going out to Kensington and see D'Angelo soon as I can."

"He's getting a raw deal in the papers, you know."

"No, I didn't," Barney said, sitting up.

I explained that D'Angelo had been exchanging love letters with Estelle Carey; Barney knew of the Carey killing—apparently it had been getting some national play.

"They're spreading his love letters all over the damn *papers*?" Barney said. "The lousy bastards!"

"One of the guilty parties is standing right over there."

"Davis, you mean?"

"That's him. The man with the purple badge of courage on his jaw."

"How'd he get that?"

"He earned it."

"You?"

"Once a Marine, always a Marine."

"Fuckin' A told," Barney said, and slid out of the booth and, with aid of his voodoo cane, hobbled over to Davis, and started reading him off, from asshole to appetite. It was a joy to behold.

I slid out and went over and sat by Cathy. I said, "What's the matter, honey?"

"What do you mean?"

"You're worried about that little schmuck, aren't you?"

Her mouth tightened. Then she nodded.

"Why?" I asked.

"He's very sick, Nate. His malaria is flaring up something awful. Chills and fever. And he's having trouble sleeping, and when he does sleep he has nightmares."

Familiar story.

"Hell," I said. "He looks fine. Look at these dark circles under my eyes. He doesn't even have *one*."

My weak attempt to cheer her up had only served to bring her to the verge of tears.

"He's having simply terrible headaches," she said. "He's in so much pain. I want him to put this tour off, but he won't do it."

"That's why you turned down the movie roles. To be at his side if he falls apart."

She nodded. "I'm afraid for him. I want to be with him so I can watch out for him. He really needs a good six months to recuperate, Nate, but he's so stubborn, he just won't hear of it."

"He's a scrapper, honey. I thought you knew that."

"He thinks the world of you, Nate."

"I think the world of him."

"Maybe you could talk to him."

"Maybe I can."

She gave me a kiss on the cheek.

Then she grinned and said, "You thought I was a gold digger, didn't you?"

"Yeah. I was wrong. About the digger part, anyway."

Sally came over with Barney on her arm.

"I caught him bullying the press," she said. "That's no way to run a cocktail lounge, is it?"

"Barney, I'm ashamed of you," I said.

Sally said, "Actually, I don't blame you, the way that little bastard's paper's putting that poor soldier's love life in print for the world to see and salivate over. How do they get ahold of that stuff, anyway? Isn't it evidence?"

"It's supposed to be," I said, and didn't give her the rest of the explanation till later, when we were in bed together, in the dark, in her small but swank room at the Drake, overlooking Lake Shore Drive and the lake that went with it.

"You mean, some police detective smuggled those letters out, and made photostatic copies, and sold them to the newspaper bidding highest? What kind of police officer would do that?"

"The Chicago kind," I said. "Let me tell you a story."

And I told her about the diary. How a high-hat client had hired me to outbid the papers for that juicy little page-turner. And how I'd arranged with a certain police sergeant to pay him two thousand dollars of my client's money for the book, which was now in my possession.

"You're kidding me," she said. "*You* have Estelle Carey's diary?"

"Well. I did."

"What do you mean? You mean, you turned it over to your rich client?"

"Not exactly."

"To Drury, then."

"Not him, either."

"*What*, then?"

"I burned it."

"*What?*"

"I burned it. I read it this afternoon, and I realized that none of the names in it were new ones. That is, they'd already turned up in Estelle's address book or other effects. So there were no new leads, nothing fresh that would be helpful to an investigation, in my considered opinion. But what there *was* was a lot of steamy descriptions by Miss Carey of her love life. Who did what to her, with what, for how long, and how long some of those things were that did those things, and, well, you get my drift."

"Why'd she keep this diary, d'you think? Eventual blackmail?"

"No. That wasn't her way. She was greedy, but she was honest, in her dishonest way. She was a dirty girl, in the best sense of the word. She liked sex. She liked doing it. And, judging from what I read today, she liked writing about it, after."

"So you burned it."

"I burned the goddamn thing. Rather than see it end up in the papers where they'd make her out an even bigger whore and ruin the lives of dozens of men and women who had the misfortune of being attracted to her."

"Am I right in guessing that an earlier diary could well have had a Nate Heller chapter in it?"

"You might be. So, yeah, I can put myself in the place of my engaged-to-be-married high-hat client. I know all about Estelle Carey's charms. So I burned the fucker. What do you think of that, Miss Rand?"

"That's Helen to you," she said, snuggling close to me. "And what I think about it is, hooray for Nate Heller, and let's see if you can't do something with *me* worth writing down, after . . ."

29

Five detectives, Donahoe among them, got transferred and censured after the scandal hit the papers. The other four cops, assigned to back up Drury's investigation into the Carey case, were attached to the coroner's office—"deputy coroners," a job I'd been offered once by the late Mayor Cermak, back before he was late, as a bribe. I hadn't taken it, for various reasons, not the least of which was the company I'd have been in: severely bent cops like Miller and Lang, owed political favors, tended to land the coroner's plum investigative positions. But that was over now.

From now on, the coroner would be required to use county investigators, at a savings to the taxpayers of Chicago of six grand a year.

It seemed that Otto A. Bomark of Elmwood Park, the late Miss Carey's uncle and administrator of her estate, reported many items missing, including several expensive gowns, thirty-two pairs of nylon hose (better than money these days), three dozen fancy lace handkerchiefs worth ninety bucks a dozen, a set of ladies' golf clubs, a camera and, oh yes, photographs of Estelle that had apparently been peddled to the papers.

And then there were the persistent rumors of a diary, which had been "stolen" from Estelle's apartment, possibly by a police officer. But as yet the memoirs of Miss Carey had failed to surface. For some reason.

All this and every other in and out of the Carey case stayed in the headlines of every paper in town for a solid week, except the *Tribune,* which tastefully backed off after a few days and played it inside. Then on the Tuesday after the Tuesday she was killed, Estelle got bumped out of the headlines.

JAPS GIVE UP
GUADALCANAL

MR. AND MRS. BARNEY ROSS

Letters several inches high. Impressive as all hell. But abstract. Remote. Somehow, not real to me.

Yet there it was in black and white:

> New York, Feb. 9.— (AP)—Japanese imperial headquarters today announced the withdrawal of Jap forces from Guadalcanal Island in the Solomons, the Berlin radio reported in a dispatch datelined Tokyo. This constitutes the first admission from Tokyo in this war of abandonment of important territory.

Why couldn't I make it feel real? Why couldn't I make my face smile over this great news? Well, I couldn't. I could only feel weary, on this clear, cool morning, even though I'd had a relatively good night's sleep last night, in Sally's arms, in Sally's room at the Drake. I wouldn't be seeing her tonight, though. She was gone, now, and she took her arms with her. Took the train to Baltimore where she was playing a split week at some nightclub or other. I'd have to try to sleep on my own, again, in the old Murphy bed. Good luck to me.

As I came up the stairs onto the fourth floor, I saw a familiar figure, although it wasn't one I ever expected to see in the building again: my recruiting sergeant, in his pressed blue trousers and khaki shirt and campaign hat. Some of the spring was out of his step, however.

As I met him in the hall, I said, "What's wrong, Sergeant—haven't you heard the news?"

I showed him the headline.

"I have heard, Private. Outstanding. Outstanding."

But his expression remained glum.

"What brings you here?" I said. "Who got a medal today?"

"No one, I'm afraid." He looked back toward my office. "I'm glad you're here, Private. There's a young woman who needs you."

I ran down the hall and threw the door open and she was sitting there, with the telegram in her hands, sitting on that couch I'd caught them humping on.

She wasn't crying. She was dazed, like she'd been hit by a board. Prim and pretty in her white frilly blouse and navy skirt. A single rose in a vase on the desk nearby.

Telegram in her hands.

"The newspapers said we beat them," she said, hollowly.

I sat next to her. "I know."

"You said he'd just be mopping up." No accusation in her voice; just an empty observation.

"I'm sorry, Gladys."

"I don't think I can work this morning, Mr. Heller."

"Oh, Gladys, come here."

And I held her in my arms and she cried into my chest. She cried and cried, heaving racking sobs, and if ever I'd written her off as a cold fish, well, to hell with me.

Sapperstein came in a few minutes later. He was still wearing the black arm band for his brother; it could do double duty, now. I called her mother in Evanston and Lou drove her home.

That left me alone in the office, wondering how Frankie Fortunato could be dead and I could be alive. Young Frankie. Old me. Shit. I wadded up the goddamn newspaper and shoved it in the wastecan. But the crumpled headline, spelling GUADNAL, seemed real enough to me now.

I sat at the desk in the inner office—my office once, Sapperstein's for the moment—and made some calls regarding an insurance investigation in Elmhurst. It felt good to work. The mundane, which when I first got back had driven me crazy, was becoming my salvation. Day-to-day living, everyday working, was something I could get lost in. By eleven-thirty I even felt hungry. I was about to break for lunch when I heard somebody come in the outer office.

I got up from behind the desk and walked to the door and looked out at a beautiful young woman of about twenty-five in a dark fur stole and a dark slinky dress. Suspiciously slinky for lunchtime, but then when it was showing off a nice slender shape like that, who was complaining?

She stood at an angle facing Gladys's empty desk. She had seamed nylons on; nice gams.

"My secretary's out," I said.

"You're Mr. Heller?"

"That's right."

She smiled, and it was a lovely smile; pearly white teeth, red lipstick glistening on full lips. Her big dark eyes, under strong arching eyebrows, appraised me, amused somehow. Her black hair was pulled back behind her head, on which sat, at a jaunty angle, a black pillbox hat. If she wasn't a showgirl once, I'd eat her hat. Or something.

"I don't have an appointment," she said, moving toward me slowly. Swaying a little. It seemed somewhat calculated, or is the word "calculating"? She extended one dark-gloved hand. I didn't know whether she wanted me to kiss it or shake it or maybe crouch down and let her knight me. I settled for squeezing it.

"No appointment needed," I said, smiling at her, wondering why she was so seductively cheerful; most women who come into a private detective agency are nervous and/or depressed, as their business is generally divorce-oriented. What the hell. I showed her into my office.

She took the chair across from the desk, but before I could get back behind it, she said, "Would you mind closing the door?"

"Nobody's out there," I said.

She smiled; no teeth this time. Sexy and wry. "Humor me, Mr. Heller."

"Consider yourself humored," I said, and shut the door, and sat behind Sapperstein's desk.

"I'd like you to find something for me," she said. Hands folded in her lap, in which a small black purse also resided.

"And what would that be?"

"A certain book."

"A certain book."

"A diary."

Okay. I was awake now.

"A diary," I said. "Yours?"

"No, Mr. Heller. Must we be coy?"

"You're the one in the tight dress."

"You're an amusing fella."

"In a tight dress I am. I'm a pip in spike heels."

"Estelle Carey's diary, Mr. Heller. A thousand dollars, and your assurance that you've made no copies."

I cracked my knuckles. "You see, that's why I never got in the blackmail business. There's no way to prove to the customer that you've given 'em the only copy of the goods."

Her smile seemed just a touch nervous, now. "We'd trust you. We hear you're a man of your word."

"Who told you that?"

"A certain Mr. Nitti."

"Gee, I wonder which Mr. Nitti you might be talking about. *I'm* coy? Who are you, lady?"

No smile at all. "I'm someone who wants to recover Estelle Carey's dairy. We've asked around. We know you have it. We know you bought it. If you're intending to sell it to the press, we'll top their best offer. If you're planning blackmail, we'd advise you against it. You made an investment; I'm here to help you make a killing on it. But if you refuse, well, then, there are killings and killings, aren't there?"

"Fuck you."

She stood and she came around the side of Sapperstein's desk and sat on the edge of it and hiked her dress up, legs open a hair, if you'll pardon the expression; showgirl, all right.

"That could be arranged," she said.

I thought about it. Sally was gone again, and this girl had long legs and everything else that went with it; and she smelled like some exotic faraway place. She was also wearing the first pair of black panties I'd seen since I got back in the States—except for one strange guy at St. E's. I could always boff her and then tell her to go to hell. I was born in Chicago.

"What do you say, Mr. Heller?"

"Get your butt off my desk."

She stood; she was clutching the little purse tight in one hand.

"You're a stupid man."

"You're a smart bitch. So what? Go away."

"Name your price."

"No price! Get the fuck out of my office! If you got a gun in that little purse, I wonder if it's as big as the one in my desk drawer." Which from where she was standing she could see my hand was down in.

She sighed. "You're foolish to prolong this. You won't get a better price out of us by making us wait."

"Who's 'us'? You and the Outfit?"

"Five thousand dollars."

"Lady, I burned the goddamn thing."

She winced. "What?"

"I burned it. I was hired by a client who didn't want to be embarrassed by its contents, so I fucking burned it."

"No one would be that stupid."

"I wasn't born that stupid, I admit. I worked at it for thirty-some years. Now get the hell out of here. Go away."

She smiled, only it was more of a sneer. "Why would you even say such a thing? Burned it my ass."

Her ass indeed. Part of me still wanted her; she was a real doll. And in black panties. I bet her bra was black, too. Fortunately, I was thinking with my higher-up head at the moment. Tempered by a sick heart.

"I just learned one of my business partners was killed in the war," I said. "So I'm in a particularly lousy mood today. No mood at all to be fucking around with this chickenshit conversation. I'm about to get up from this desk, take that purse and the gun you must have in it away from you, and kick the living shit out of you. I haven't knocked a woman's teeth out since my second wife left me, by the way, so I'm going to really enjoy this."

Her eyes and nostrils flared; she obviously didn't know what to make of me, or my nonexistent wives.

But she said, "I'll be back."

And left.

The door in the outer office was slamming shut as I dialed Drury at his Town Hall office; caught him going out the door to get lunch.

"I'm going to describe a woman to you," I said.

"This sounds like fun."

"It *might* be fun. That's what the male spider thinks, anyway, when he crawls in the sack with a black widow."

"What are you talking about?"

"Get an earful of this, and then tell me if it matches up with any of your Carey case suspects."

I described her, seamed stockings to pillbox hat, and he said, "That would be so nice to come home to . . . only you may be right about that black widow spider. That sounds very much like Olivia Borgia, John Borgia's wife."

"Borgia? That name sounds familiar. Or am I just thinking about famous women not to go out for cocktails with."

I didn't mention to Bill that the Borgias had turned up in the diary, albeit briefly; mentioned as friends who'd stopped over a few times. No sexual escapades. Whatever the Borgias thought was in that diary, wasn't. Or hadn't been. It was ashes now, after all.

"John Borgia's an Outfit guy who's been around for years," Drury was saying. "Don't you remember, I mentioned him to you as one of our Carey suspects. He looks a little like Sonny Goldstone, only no glasses. He's about fifty. An old pal of Dago Mangano's; connected to Nicky Dean."

"Wasn't there something about a kidnapping, back around '38?"

"Yeah, only it was '37. Some ex-pals of Dean and Mangano grabbed Olivia and held her for ransom. The guys that did it turned up dead in a ditch. Poor bastards snatched the snatch to get even with Borgia, word was—it was for revenge more than dough; these were some guys Borgia had fired at the 101 Club. Which was where Olivia worked, by the way."

"Twenty-six girl?"

"At one time. Also a would-be nightclub singer. Why, Nate? What's this all about?"

"She was just in my office."

"What? What for?"

"She wanted to know if I had Estelle Carey's diary."

"You? Why would she think *you* had Estelle Carey's diary?"

"Yeah, it's nuts, isn't it? I told her I didn't have the thing, and she went away. Only she didn't believe me. She said she'd be back."

"I didn't even know she was in *town*. We've been looking for her, and her husband, from the start. I appreciate the tip, Nate. Every radio car in town will be alerted."

"Don't mention it."

"If they did this, Nate, if they were the last guests your friend Estelle entertained, then there can be no doubt it was an Outfit hit."

"Meaning you'll expect me to be a good citizen and testify against Nitti."

"That's right. Anything else you need? I got lunch to catch."

"Actually, there is. Some bad news. Frankie Fortunato was killed in action."

"Aw, shit."

"Guadalcanal."

"Hell, the papers say we ran those slant-eyed bastards right off that island!"

"We did. It just wasn't free."

We both hung up, and then for a while I sat there staring out the window, where the service flag with Frankie's star hung.

Then around one, Olivia Borgia's promise to return lingering in my brain like a bad taste, I went next door and got the nine millimeter out of my bottom desk drawer and the shoulder holster too and took my coat off and slung it on. Guadalcanal was over. But there were always battles to be fought.

Then I walked around the corner to Binyon's and had the finnan haddie. Meatless Tuesday.

CAMPAGNA

30

I saw my father. He was sitting at the kitchen table with my gun in his hand. He lifted it to his head and I said, "Stop!"

Then Barney's hand was over my mouth; he was shaking, wild-eyed. His .45 was in his other hand. We were still under the shelter half, in the shell hole. D'Angelo was awake, .45 in hand; the Army boys had .45s in hand too.

"You passed out," Barney whispered. "Be quiet. Japs."

Twigs snapping, brush rustling.

Barney took his hand off my mouth; I got the .45 off my hip.

And Monawk woke, in pain, and screamed.

And I shot him. I shot him! *Be quiet, you're gonna get us killed,* but he didn't die, he just looked down at the holes my .45 punched in his chest and his face contorted and he reached for the .45 on his hip and he started firing at me and I sat up in bed, in a cold sweat.

Not screaming, like Monawk. I'd done that a few times, sure. But usually it was like now: jerk awake, dripping with sweat.

I glanced at my watch. A few minutes after 2:00 A.M. I flipped the sheets and blankets off and, wooden floor cold on my feet, padded over to my desk. The nine millimeter in my shoulder holster lay on top of it. The rum bottle was still in the bottom drawer, but almost empty. I sat and, slowly, finished it off, drinking from the bottle, looking out the window at the El. Sitting in the orangeish glow of the neon. Quietly shaking.

Well, this was a new twist. I'd been back in the shell hole many, many times in my dreams. But this time it had been different.

Usually I was just generally back there, mortars landing, machine guns zinging, and the people, why the people weren't necessarily D'Angelo and Monawk and Barney and the Army boys and Watkins and Whitey and me. No, it could be Eliot and Bill and Lou and Frankie and the guy behind the counter in the deli downstairs. Or anybody I knew, or ever knew.

This time, though, it had followed the script. This time it mirrored what had really happened, right up to the moment I fired the .45 at Monawk . . .

Had I done that? Had I really done that? Fired at Monawk, to shut him up? To stop the screaming that was telling the Japs right where to find us?

My dream seemed to be saying so, but awake, I couldn't remember doing it. If the door to the answer had cracked open during my sleep, it had slammed shut again, upon waking.

I couldn't allow that. I forced myself back there, back to the dream and the event it was trying to tell me about, and then I remembered: in the dream Monawk screamed and I fired at him. In life Barney had clasped his hand over Monawk's mouth, but it had been too late, a machine gun opened up and D'Angelo dove for Monawk, as if to strangle him, only Barney stopped him.

"Bastard's gonna get us killed," D'Angelo had said.

Mortar shells, then, bullets zinging.

Beyond that point, I couldn't seem to go.

But I knew one thing.

"I didn't kill him," I said aloud. I put the empty rum bottle in the wastebasket. I didn't know why, exactly, but I'd come away from the dream with the very real feeling, even the certain knowledge, that I had not killed Monawk.

Maybe now I could sleep. I padded back over to the Murphy bed, crawled under the covers and was sliding into sleep when I heard the sound from next door.

Your classic bump in the night.

Funny. The El can go rumbling by and I don't even notice it. The slightest other half-imagined sound and I think the Japs invaded. What the hell. I rolled over and forgot about it and then it bumped again.

I sat up in bed. No cold sweat, this time. Silently as I could, I eased out and went over to the desk and slipped my nine millimeter out of the holster. I listened at the wall, heard muffled sounds, no voices. I put my pants on, and went quietly out into the hall, barefoot, bare-chested, gun in hand.

A light was on in my office. Outer office. Gladys's gooseneck desk lamp, from the look of it. It enabled me to see, through the pebbled glass, the shadow moving around in there.

Frankie Fortunato's voice whispered in my ear: *it worked before*, and I slammed the side of the gun barrel against the pebbled glass and it shattered and I stuck my gun in hand through the opening and there was the beautiful Olivia Borgia, in slacks and sweater and a sporty little beret and a .38 in one hand, the outer office turned topsy-turvy, file drawers emptied, desk drawers stacked, and now cushions of the couch about to be explored. Her lip curled into a sneer and she took a shot at me; the sound of it cracked open the night and I felt it whiz past and shatter the abortionist's glass and I squeezed the trigger and sent one back at her. It knocked her back, onto the couch, with a yelp; caught her in the shoulder.

"Get comfy right there," I told her. I stayed out in the hall, pointing my gun at her through the gaping, spiky hole in the window.

She'd dropped the .38, on the impact of my round; the revolver was on the floor, just out of her reach. She sat clutching her shoulder, blood dripping through the cracks of her fingers.

When she spoke, it was almost a snarl.

"Where's the diary?" she said.

"Why do you want it?"

Sneering smile. "Why should I tell you?"

"Because your gun is on the floor and mine is pointed at your sweet head."

Arching eyebrow. "You want a piece, then?"

"Sure. I want a piece."

Blood oozing. "She had a million dollars hidden away. More than a million."

"And the diary has the answer to where she stowed it?"

Curt nod. "The diary has the answer, yes."

"I read it, lady. I didn't see any answer."

Wide eyes. "It's there! It's in the diary."

"I don't think so."

Narrowed eyes. "If not words, then a key, perhaps—taped inside. *Something!*"

"Why are you so sure?"

Flaring nostrils. "She told us it was."

"When?"

Sneering smile. "Before she died."

The El went clattering by. I had to shout to be heard over it; but

I'd have shouted anyway: "You killed her! Goddamn. You little bitch. You and your husband killed her! Where *is* the bastard?"

Gunfire gave me my answer, four fast blasts that barely rose above the El's rumble, flaming my way from the doorway of my inner office, and, still out in the hall, I hit the deck, glass raining over me.

I stood, meaning to fire again, but he'd ducked back in my office.

His wife hadn't got that far, though. Bleeding shattered shoulder or not, she had gone for the .38 on the floor; her bloody hand was on the gun when I put a bullet in her brain.

Then I dove through the yawning glass-toothed hole where the window used to be, landed on the couch, some pieces of stray glass crunching beneath me, El in my ears, and he was in the doorway, big automatic in hand, .45 maybe, a big man in heavy sweater and trousers, and he did look like Sonny Goldstone, only it wasn't Sonny, it was her husband, John Borgia, whose pockmarked fleshy face fell when he saw his pretty wife on the floor, her head cracked like a bloody egg.

"You killed her!" he said, outraged, white showing all the way 'round his eyes, and he turned to fire at me, but I was off the couch and doing the one thing he hadn't counted on, moving right toward him, and I was on him before he could even react and my gun was shoved in his gut, firing, firing, and I said, "Who the fuck do you people think you're dealing with," and fired again, "who the fuck do you people think you're dealing with," and fired again.

He fell back, on the floor, landed hard, flopping, thudding, five scorched puckered holes in his gut and chest with five slow red leaks, eyes still open and looking up at nothing. The wastebasket, which he'd knocked over as he fell, spilled next to him, the wadded-up paper saying, GUADNAL.

I stood over him and looked down and said, "Who the fuck did you people think you were dealing with?"

But he didn't answer. Neither did she.

I walked out of there, stepping over what used to be Olivia Borgia, a greedy one-time 26 girl who was so much like Estelle Carey it killed them both, walking carefully around the glass shards, as I'd already cut my bare feet in several places, and went back in my office.

I felt strangely calm. The El was as silent as the Borgias, now. I sat there at my desk, soaking my bleeding feet with a cool damp cloth, sorting out my options, wondering if calling Drury was the thing to do. Two dead people in my office. Dead by me. Including a woman. I'd killed a woman. I didn't care.

I just thought of Estelle's burned, tortured body and didn't fucking care.

Why hadn't they found the diary themselves, that awful afternoon? They'd tossed the place, after all. But they'd missed the baseboard hideaway Donahoe had later found, he was a detective, our trusty basset-hound Donahoe, and, besides, Estelle hadn't mentioned the book till *right before she died,* meaning after one of them had splashed whiskey over her and smashed the bottle on the floor nearby to frighten her and lit a match and held it over her to frighten her some more, and maybe then she said it, maybe then she said, *it's in my diary—I'll get it for you,* because Donahoe had after all found a gun in that baseboard hideaway as well, only somebody fumbled the match and the housecoat caught fire, and she was aflame, and she was screaming and there was no more talk of diaries as the fire spread from her to the whiskey to the walls, and the place was starting to burn, smoke was starting to fill the place, and they had no choice but to make a run for it, Borgia grabbing a couple of furs to make it look like a robbery.

That was then. What of now? Had anyone heard the shots over the El's rumble? The building was empty, but for me and those I'd killed. It was the middle of the night. Ten minutes had passed, easily, and no one had come to see what was the matter. No one rushing in. No sirens cutting the night. No nothing.

I dialed a number.

After many rings, a gravelly male voice said, "Yeah?"

"This is Heller. Tell Campagna to call me, right away."

Pause. Then: "It's real late."

"It's later than you think. Tell him."

"I'll ask him."

"Tell him."

Three minutes later the phone rang.

"Heller?"

"Hiya, Louie."

"Are you crazy, Heller?"

"Sure. If I wasn't, I'd still be in the service, shooting people. But I'm finding it easy enough to keep in practice here at home."

"What the fuck are you talking about?"

"I'm talking about John and Olivia Borgia."

Silence.

"They're dead in my office, Louie. I killed 'em."

"Jesus H. Christ."

"They were rifling the place, looking for Estelle Carey's diary. They didn't believe me when I said I burned it."

"You what?"

"I burned it, Louie. Spread the word. The diary is ashes. To ashes. If the secret to her buried treasure was in those pages, it's going to be a well-kept one. Should I call the cops on this? It's not going to do much for business, my killing people in the office. You want a chance to clean up after yourself?"

Silence.

"Borgia was Outfit, Louie. You want to clean up after yourself?"

Silence.

"The Borgias killed Estelle Carey, Louie, but then you know that, right? It was an Outfit hit from word go, just like everybody's been telling me. But I got some outdated notion that Nitti don't work like that. Well, times change, and people change. Take for instance, this is the very first time I killed a woman in my office."

"I want you to go someplace."

"Where, Louie?"

"What's the closest hotel?"

"Morrison, I guess. They don't have any rooms."

"They'll have one for you by the time you walk over there. Don't come back to your office before seven."

The phone clicked in my ear; Louie didn't want to talk to me anymore.

When I got to the office at nine, a fiftyish guy in coveralls was measuring to put in new glass. All the broken glass had been swept up and removed. Bullets had been dug out of woodwork and puttied and touched up with paint.

"I didn't send for you," I said to the guy in coveralls.

"It's all taken care of," he said. He pointed with a thumb over to the doctor's office across the way, where the waiting room and receptionist could be viewed through where opaque glass used to be. "That's being taken care of, too."

The office had been tidied up. File cabinets in order; drawers in desks. No dead bodies on the floor. No bloodstains. Lou Sapperstein was standing in the inner office, looking around, puzzled.

"What happened here, last night?" he said. "The glass is broken, everything's just a little out of place . . . and it smells like disinfectant, and something else . . . what? Paint? Did you have somebody in to clean the place up?"

"Elves," I said. "Tiny Sicilian elves. Lou, I want you to get your things together at the end of the day. I'll be moving back into my office. And I made arrangements over at the Morrison for a room there, till I can find an apartment. You can have the whole big office next door to yourself, till we find somebody to take Frankie's place."

Lou seemed confused, but he said, "Sure. You're the boss."

I went next door and sat at my desk. I'd slept pretty good at the Morrison. Restless, but no dreams about shell holes. Or office shootouts, either.

Midmorning, the phone rang.

"A-1 Detective Agency."

"Heller?"

"Louie."

"No problems, I trust?"

"No. Thanks for the new glass."

"You're welcome. Frank said to tell you he appreciated the opportunity to clean up that mess."

"Well, it was Frank's mess, after all."

"No. It wasn't. They were Outfit, but Frank didn't send 'em to that apartment on Addison Street. And he didn't send 'em to your place, neither."

"Sure."

"You don't have to believe it."

"That's a relief."

"Frank says he owes you one."

"Frank owes me nothing!"

"He says he owes you one. And he's going to pay it right now. Your boxer pal, Ross?"

What in hell could Frank Nitti have to do with Barney?

"What about him?"

"He's got a monkey on his back."

"What are you talking about?"

"He's buying morphine from street dealers."

"What?"

"They must've give it to him overseas to kill the pain and he got a taste for it. He's got a seventy-buck-a-week habit, and it's gonna get more expensive in a lot of ways as the days go by. *Capeesh?*"

I didn't say anything. I couldn't say anything.

"Frank just thought you might want to know," Campagna said.

And hung up.

31

On March 18, a Thursday, the federal grand jury in New York returned indictments against Nitti, Campagna, Ricca and six other top Outfit figures. It didn't hit the Chicago papers till the next morning—I, however, got a preview that very afternoon.

I was sleeping on the couch in my inner office under the photos of Sally and another actress from my past; such cat naps were becoming a way of life for me. Gradually, I'd been sleeping better. The shell hole dreams were easing up. Subsiding. But I'd as yet to have a good, full night's sleep, so once or twice a day, I flopped out here on the couch and snoozed.

And was usually awakened by the phone on my desk ringing, like it was doing right now, and I stumbled over and fumbled for it and the long-distance operator asked for Nate Heller, and I said "Speaking," thickly, yawning, and then somebody else was speaking—U.S. Attorney Mathias Correa, who was spearheading the investigation into the Outfit's Hollywood "extortion" racket.

He was calling from New York; he told me about the indictments that had just been handed down against Nitti and the others, and said, "Mr. Heller, I understand your reluctance to come forward. But we feel your testimony may be valuable. You are a former police officer. You are a decorated soldier—a war hero—and one of the few 'civilians' known to have had considerable contact with Frank Nitti."

"Make up your mind—am I soldier or a civilian?"

"I think you get my meaning. We have Willie Bioff and George Browne's testimony and, in a limited manner at least, Nick Circella's. But both Bioff and Browne lied on the witness stands in their own trials. Their credibility may be called, justly, into question. You, on the other hand, are the kind of outside, reliable, corroborating witness we need."

"I made my feelings clear to your emissaries."

"I'm grateful to Eliot Ness and Bill Drury for paving the way for

RICCA

me. But I'm serving notice on you, Mr. Heller. You're going to testify in this trial. You're being subpoenaed. Whether you choose to perjure yourself on the witness stand or not is, of course, your decision. Good afternoon."

So I called Campagna—or, rather, I called the number Campagna gave me and told the guy I needed to talk to Campagna, and a call from Little New York followed within half an hour.

"They're going to subpoena me," I said.

"What do you want me to do about it?"

"I just wanted Frank to know."

"Okay," Campagna said, and hung up.

I got back to work on some insurance matters and at a few minutes after four Campagna called again.

"Frank wants to see you," he said.

"Is that wise? Surely the FBI is keeping him under tight surveillance. That would just link us further. It plays right into Correa's hands."

"I know. I agree with you. But Frank wants to see you."

"Louie, I'm not in the mood to go swimming forever."

"No Chicago River, no cement shoes. He wants to see you tonight, at his house."

"His house?"

There was a shrug in his voice. "Show of good faith."

"Okay," I said.

"Don't come heeled."

"Don't send me home wounded."

So around seven that night I walked to a parking garage near Dearborn Station and picked up my '32 Auburn. I'd only gotten the sporty little number back out of storage last week; while I was overseas, I'd kept it in a client's garage in Evanston, in lieu of payment for a divorce case. I had the top up—there was still snow on the ground—and my C sticker in the window, and the old buggy was riding well, though I was in no frame of mind to enjoy it. I was on my way to see Frank Nitti, to share a quiet little chat with him in his suburban Riverside home. I turned South on Michigan Avenue, at the Hotel Lexington, Capone's old headquarters, and headed west on 22nd Street, a.k.a. Cermak Road. I drove through Chinatown. After a while I was within a few blocks of where O'Hare had been gunned down, then crossed through the south end of my old neighborhood,

South Lawndale, then Cicero, not far from Sportsman's Park, and across to Berwyn, catching Riverside Drive to Riverside itself. The ride was like having my life pass before my eyes.

I didn't want to park the Auburn in front of Nitti's house, so I left it two blocks up, by a small park, and walked down. It was a cool, clear night, and Nitti's quiet, quietly wealthy little suburban neighborhood, with its large lawns and oversize bungalows and driveways and backyard swing sets looked as unreal and ideal as a street in an Andy Hardy movie. As American as apple pie and twice as wholesome. The smell of cordite was not in the air.

712 Shelbourne Road. A relatively modest brown brick house on the corner, story-and-a-half high, with crisp white woodwork. Car parked in the driveway, '42 Ford sedan, black. A few lights on in the downstairs windows. Shrubs hugging the house; average-size lawn, house well back from the street; postage-stamp patio. Somewhere a dog was barking. Frank Nitti lived here.

Cars parked across the way, turning the narrow street into a one-lane. I wondered if eyes were watching me from those cars. Bodyguard eyes? Federal eyes?

Yes, I was nervous. This was much worse than meeting Nitti in a suite at the Bismarck. His suburban home in Riverside? Wrong. This was wrong.

But, just the same, I walked up the sidewalk, which wound gently up the sloping lawn, to the white front door, over which a light was on. I rang the bell.

The door cracked open, and a sliver of dark attractive female face looked out at me.

Then she was standing in the doorway wearing a Mona Lisa smile and a simple blue dress with a gold broach. A tall, distinctive-looking woman with cold smart dark eyes, wide dark-lipsticked mouth, Roman nose, ironic arching brows. She wasn't as attractive as she'd been a few years ago, pushing forty now and looking it, and she'd always had a certain hardness, but she was still a handsome woman.

"You're Toni Cavaretta," I said. Blurted.

"Mrs. Frank Nitti, now," she said, in her smoky, throaty manner. "Come in, Mr. Heller."

I stepped inside and Mrs. Frank Nitti, the former Antoinette Cavaretta, the former secretary of the formerly living E. J. O'Hare, took my coat.

"I'll just hang this up for you."

She did so, in the closet I was directly facing, and then I followed her around the corner, out of the vestibule.

"Frank just stepped out for a walk," she said. "I'll see if I can catch him."

Then she went out the way I'd come in and left me there.

To my left was a door; directly before me, stairs; to my right, a big open living room, beyond which the dining room could be seen, the kitchen presumably connecting off that. The furnishings seemed new, and expensive, the woodwork dark and shiny; everything was greens and browns, plush overstuffed sofas, dark wood furniture, very masculine, very soothing, a tastefully decorated room. A little boy eight or nine was sprawled on the floor in the midst of it, reading a comic book. He looked up at me through clear-rim glasses. Slight, serious-looking, dark-haired kid; I could see Nitti in his face.

"Hi, mister," he said. "Are you a friend of my daddy's?"

I went over and sat on the sofa near him. "That's right," I said. "How old are you, son?"

"Nine." He closed the cover of the comic book; it said CRIME DOES NOT PAY. He sat Indian-style. "Were you in the war?"

"Yes I was. How did you know?"

He pointed at me. It took me a second to realize he was pointing at the lapel of my suitcoat. His pale blue eyes were alert, his expression serious. "I saw your pin. I got an uncle who has one of those. It's called a Ruptured Duck."

"That's right."

"I want to be a Marine when I grow up. Maybe a Marine flier. My daddy has a friend who was a Marine."

"Really." I nodded toward his comic book. "Do you like to read?"

"Yes, but I like skating better. Daddy says the weather's going to get better soon and I can get my skates out."

Mrs. Nitti came back in, shrugging, smiling, "I'm sorry. I couldn't catch up with him. He must've forgotten what time you were coming by. He often takes an evening walk, and with these winding streets, who knows where he is or how long he'll be?"

I was standing, now, and said, "Well, uh—I could go and come another time, at your husband's convenience . . ."

"Nonsense. Why don't you step into his study and relax. Can I get you a cup of coffee, or some wine?"

"No thanks."

I followed her through the doorway by the stairs into a small unpretentious study—lots of dark wood, a desk, a black leather couch, built-in-the-wall bookcase.

She gestured to the couch and said, "Why don't you sit down? When Frank gets back, I'll tell him you're here. Just relax."

She went back out into the living room, where I could hear her say to the boy, "Up to your room, Joseph, and do some studying before bed."

Toni Cavaretta seemed to be as perfect a housewife as she'd been an executive secretary. And as perfect a mother, too. Well, stepmother, actually. The boy was Nitti's only son, only child, by his first wife, Anna. Whose picture, in fact, was on his desk in a gilt frame: a beautiful Italian madonna with a glowing expression. Nitti had worshipped her, it was said. Yet here he was, little over a year after his beloved Anna's death, married to Toni Cavaretta.

It came rushing back, that business with O'Hare. She'd been Nitti's "man" all the way, keeping tabs on E.J., probably helping set him up for the one-way ride I'd almost taken with him. Planting that note about the feds in his pocket. I'd only checked up on her once, after the hit. I'd asked Stege, probably in '41 sometime, what had become of her. He said she was managing an Outfit racetrack in Florida—Miami Beach to be precise—a dogtrack that had previously been looked after by O'Hare. Seemed she had stock in the Florida track, as well as Sportsman's Park; and some people said she and Nitti were like this. And he held his fingers up in a crossed fashion.

The notion of Nitti having a mistress had seemed crazy to me—everybody knew he kept Anna on a pedestal, that he loved his son, that he was a devoted family man—and I'd dismissed Stege's implication as hogwash. But I also knew Nitti kept a separate home in Miami Beach. And men in his position—particularly men who kept their wives on pedestals—often had side dishes, somebody warm and female and closer to the ground.

Now here he was, beloved Anna gone. Here he was, married to Toni Cavaretta. In his suite at the Bismarck, that time, back in '39, days after O'Hare's murder, I'd heard a woman's voice . . .

I slapped myself. *Knock it off, Heller!* These were dangerous speculations to make. They seemed especially dangerous to be making, sitting in Nitti's own study, even if I *was* keeping them confined to my mind.

I got up and looked at the books on his shelves. A lot of leather-bound classics, whether read or not I couldn't say. Some less fancily bound nonfiction books, on accounting mostly, and a couple of books about Napoleon, seemed well read.

I was tired. I sat on the couch again and looked at my watch—I'd been here half an hour already—and tried to fight my heavy eyelids. At some point, I lost the fight, because sounds in the other room suddenly jarred me awake.

I was stretched out on the couch. The room was dark. Why I'd been left to sleep like that, I didn't know; why the light had been shut off, I couldn't say. How long I'd been asleep was a mystery, too. The room was so dark I couldn't read my watch. But if the film in my mouth was any indication, I'd slept for hours.

Conversation had woken me; and muffled conversation was still quite audible, even though I was sitting on the couch and the door to the living room was across the study from me. Occasionally the pitch of the conversation peaked—in anger? One of those peaks had been loud enough to wake me, anyway.

I got up. Slipped out of my shoes. Crept across the study to the door. I didn't dare crack it open. But I did dare place my ear up to it.

"Frank," a harsh voice was saying, "you brought Browne and Bioff to us. You masterminded this whole thing—and it went sour."

"You didn't complain at the time, Paul."

Paul?

Jesus Christ—Paul Ricca. The Waiter. The number two man. Capone had his Nitti; and Nitti had his Ricca.

And I didn't have a gun.

"There is no point in all of us going down," Ricca said. "Remember how Al took the fall for us, and went on trial alone? Well, that's the way we ought to do it now."

"It ain't the same situation, Paul." Nitti's voice was recognizably his; but something was different. Something had changed.

The strength was gone.

"Frank," Ricca said, "you can plead guilty and we'll take care of things till you get out."

Right. Like Nitti took care of things for Capone.

"This is not that kind of case," Nitti said, voice firmer now. "This is a conspiracy indictment. Nobody can take the fall for the rest of us in this one. We all have to stick together and try to beat it."

Ricca began swearing in Sicilian; so did Nitti. And it began to build. Other voices, in English, in Sicilian, were trying to settle the two of them down. I thought I heard Campagna.

I knelt down. Looked through the keyhole. Just like a divorce case.

I could get a glimpse of them, sitting around the living room in their brown suits, just a bunch of businessmen talking—only among them were Frank Nitti, Paul Ricca, Louis Campagna, Ralph Capone and others whose faces I couldn't see, but, if I could, whose names would no doubt chill me equally to the bone.

Ricca, a thin pockmarked man with high cheekbones, was pale, panting. He pointed at Nitti, as they stood facing each other, Ricca much taller than the little barber.

"Frank, you're asking for it."

Five simple words.

Dead silence followed. Nitti was looking to the other men, to their faces. It seemed to me, from my limited vantage point, that all save Campagna were avoiding his eyes. And even Louie wasn't speaking up for him.

The lack of support meant one thing: Ricca had deposed Nitti. And without the intricate, dangerous chesslike moves Nitti had used to maneuver Capone off the throne and into the pen. Ricca had, through strength of character alone, through sheer will, toppled Nitti.

And Nitti knew it.

He walked toward the front door.

I couldn't see it, but I could hear it: he opened that door. Cold March air made itself heard.

He walked into my keyhole view again.

And, his back to me, gestured toward the outside.

The men looked at each other, slowly, and rose.

I moved away from the door and went back to the couch and sat, trembling. I knew what this meant. Nitti's wordless invitation for his guests to leave was a breach of the Sicilian peasant rules of hospitality they'd all been reared under. It was his way of turning his back on them. It was his way of expressing contempt. Defying them. Ricca, especially.

And Ricca's words—*Frank, you're asking for it*—were a virtual death sentence.

I could hear them out there, shuffling around, getting on their coats and hats, no one saying anything.

Although, finally, when they all seemed to be gone, I thought I heard Campagna's voice. Saying simply, "Frank . . ."

Clearly, I heard Nitti, who must've been standing just outside the study door, say, "Good night, Louie."

I slipped my shoes back on, stretched out on the couch and closed my eyes. Wondering if I'd ever open them again.

The light above me went on; light glowed redly through my lids. I "slept" on.

A hand gently shook my shoulder.

"Heller," Nitti said, softly. "Heller, wake up."

I sat slowly up, sort of groaning, rubbing my face with the heel of a hand, saying, "Excuse me, Frank—oh, hell. Aw. I don't know what happened. Must've dozed off."

"I know you did. I was out for a walk, and I got back and you were sound asleep. Snoring away. I couldn't bring myself to wake you. So I just let you sleep."

He sat next to me. He looked very old; very skinny; very tired. Cheeks almost sunken. His dark eyes didn't have their usual hardness. His hair was the real tip-off, though: the little barber needed a haircut.

"I didn't see the harm," he said, "letting you sleep. Then, to be honest with you, I forgot all about ya." He gestured out toward the other room. "I had some business come up all of a sudden, and I sent my wife and boy over to the Rongas, and she said now don't forget about Heller, and I went and forgot about you, anyway." He laughed. For a man who minutes ago had heard his own death sentence, and who had in return thrown down the gauntlet to Ricca and the whole goddamn Outfit, he was spookily calm.

"When I first got back from overseas," I said, "I had trouble sleeping. But lately I catch myself napping every time I turn around. I'm really sorry."

He waved that off. He looked at me; his eyes narrowed—in concern? Or was that suspicion?

"I hope my business meeting didn't disturb your sleep," he said.

"Nope," I said, cheerfully. I hoped not too transparently cheerfully. "Slept right through it."

"Why was it you wanted to talk to me, Heller?"

"Uh, *you* invited *me*, here, Frank."

"Oh. Yeah. Correa called you. That prick."

"He's going to call me to testify. I guess they were keeping tabs on you, when we were having our various meetings over the years. They're going to ask about those meetings, and . . ."

He shrugged. "Forget it."

"Well, that's what I intend to do. What you and I talked about is nobody's business but ours. Like I told Campagna, I got some convenient after-effects of my combat duty—they treated me for amnesia, while I was in the bughouse. I don't remember nothing, Frank."

He patted my shoulder. "I'm proud of what you did over there."

"What?"

"I brag on you to my boy, all the time. You were a hero." He got up and crossed to an expensive, possibly antique cabinet and took out a bottle of wine and poured himself a glass. "This is a great country. Worth fighting for. An immigrant like me can have a home and a family and a business. Some vino, kid?"

"No thanks, Frank."

He drank the wine, pacing slowly around the little study. "I never worried about you, kid. You coulda gone running off the mouth about Cermak, and you didn't. You coulda done the same thing where Dillinger was concerned, but you didn't. You understand it, *omerta*, and you ain't even one of us."

"Frank, I'm not going to betray you."

He sat down next to me. "You seen Ness lately?"

"Yeah," I said. "Last month."

"You know what he's doing these days?"

"Yeah," I said, and smiled.

Nitti sat there and laughed.

"Al coulda used his help," he said, and laughed some more.

When he stopped laughing, he finished the glass of wine and said, "That's another secret you kept."

"Frank?"

"You knew about O'Hare."

I swallowed. "You mean, you knew . . ."

"That you figured out I . . ." He gestured with one hand, as if sculpting something. ". . . sent Al away. Yeah. I saw it in your eyes, kid, when we talked that time."

He meant that night in '39 in the suite at the Bismarck.

"Then why in hell am I alive?" I said.

"I told you to stay out of my business. You stayed out, more or less. I trust you. I respect you."

"Frank—I'm right in thinking you didn't have anything to do with Estelle Carey's death, aren't I?"

"Would I invite such heat?" His face tightened into an angry mask. "My bloodthirsty friend Paul the Waiter sent those"—and then he said something in Sicilian that sounded very vile indeed—"to hit her. He was afraid she'd talk, this grand jury thing. I believe her killers took it on themselves to try to make her talk." He laughed without humor. "To make her lead them to money she never had."

"Money she . . . what?"

He got up and poured himself some more wine. "The Carey dame never had Nicky's dough. He didn't trust her. He thought she'd fingered him to the feds. That million of his, well, it's really just under a million, the feds exaggerate, so they can tax you more . . . anyway, that million is stashed away for Nicky when he gets out. He's being a pretty good boy. He's talked some, but not given 'em anything they didn't already have. Willie and Browne, well . . . don't invest in *their* stock."

Nitti's openness was startling. And frightening. Was he drunk? Was he telling me things he'd regret telling me, later?

"You killing that bastard Borgia and his bitch was a good thing," he said. "And then calling me so we could clean up, that I also appreciate. Think of what the papers woulda done with that; talk about stirring up the heat. Do you know how many of the boys have been pulled in over the Carey dame? Shit. That's Ricca for you. Anyway." He sipped his wine. "I owe you one."

He'd said that to me before, more than once. More than twice.

"Hey, you have some wine, now," he said.

I had some wine. We sat and drank it and I said, "If you feel you owe me one, Frank, I'd like to collect."

Nitti shrugged. "Sure. Why not."

"You know about my friend Barney Ross."

He nodded. Of course he knew; I'd heard it from him. Or from Campagna. Same difference—before tonight, at least.

He said, "Have you talked to him about this problem of his?"

"Yes I have," I said. "And he claims he can handle the stuff. He needs it for his pain, he says. To help him sleep. He acted like it was no big deal—then made me promise not to tell his wife, his family."

"He's a good man," Nitti said. "He shouldn't have this monkey on his back. It will ruin him."

"I know."

It seemed to anger Nitti. "He's a hero. Kids look up to him. He shouldn't go down that road."

"Then help me stop him."

He looked at me; the old Nitti seemed to be home, if only briefly, in the hard eyes.

"Put the word out," I said. "Nobody in Chicago sells dope to Barney Ross. Cut off his supply. *Capeesh?*"

"*Capeesh,*" Nitti said.

We shook hands at the front door and I walked out into the wintry air, wondering how many eyes other than Nitti's were on me.

32

Drury drove. We left his unmarked car on Cermak Road, near Woodlawn Cemetery, and walked along the railroad tracks, south. A light drizzling rain was falling. These were Illinois Central tracks, freight, not commuter; at this time of afternoon, just a little before four, there would be little or no train traffic, not till after rush hour—Cermak Road was too major a thoroughfare to be held up by a train, this time of day.

We were out in the boonies, really. To my left a few blocks was downtown Berwyn, but just due north was a working farm; and right here, the tracks ran through a virtual prairie—tall grass, scrub brush and trees. Up at right was a wire fence, behind which loomed the several faded brick buildings of a sanitarium. Some uniformed cops were gathered there; three men in coveralls, railroad workers obviously, were being questioned over to one side.

I followed Drury down the gentle embankment from the tracks through brush and tall grass to where the cops stood by the wire fence. One of the cops, a man in his fifties, in a white cap, walked to Drury and extended a hand and the men shook, as the white-capped cop said, "Chief Rose, of the Riverside P.D. You'd be Captain Drury."

Drury said he was.

"Thanks for getting out here so quickly. We need you to positively ID the body. And we could use a little advice about where to go from here . . ."

Drury didn't introduce me; everybody just assumed I was another cop. This time I'd been in *his* office, when he got the call. Correa had asked him to talk to me again, and as a courtesy I'd taken the El over to Town Hall Station. I was sitting there being scolded by him when his phone rang.

Now here we were, in a ditch next to an IC spur between North Riverside and Berwyn, in the midst of a bunch of confused suburban

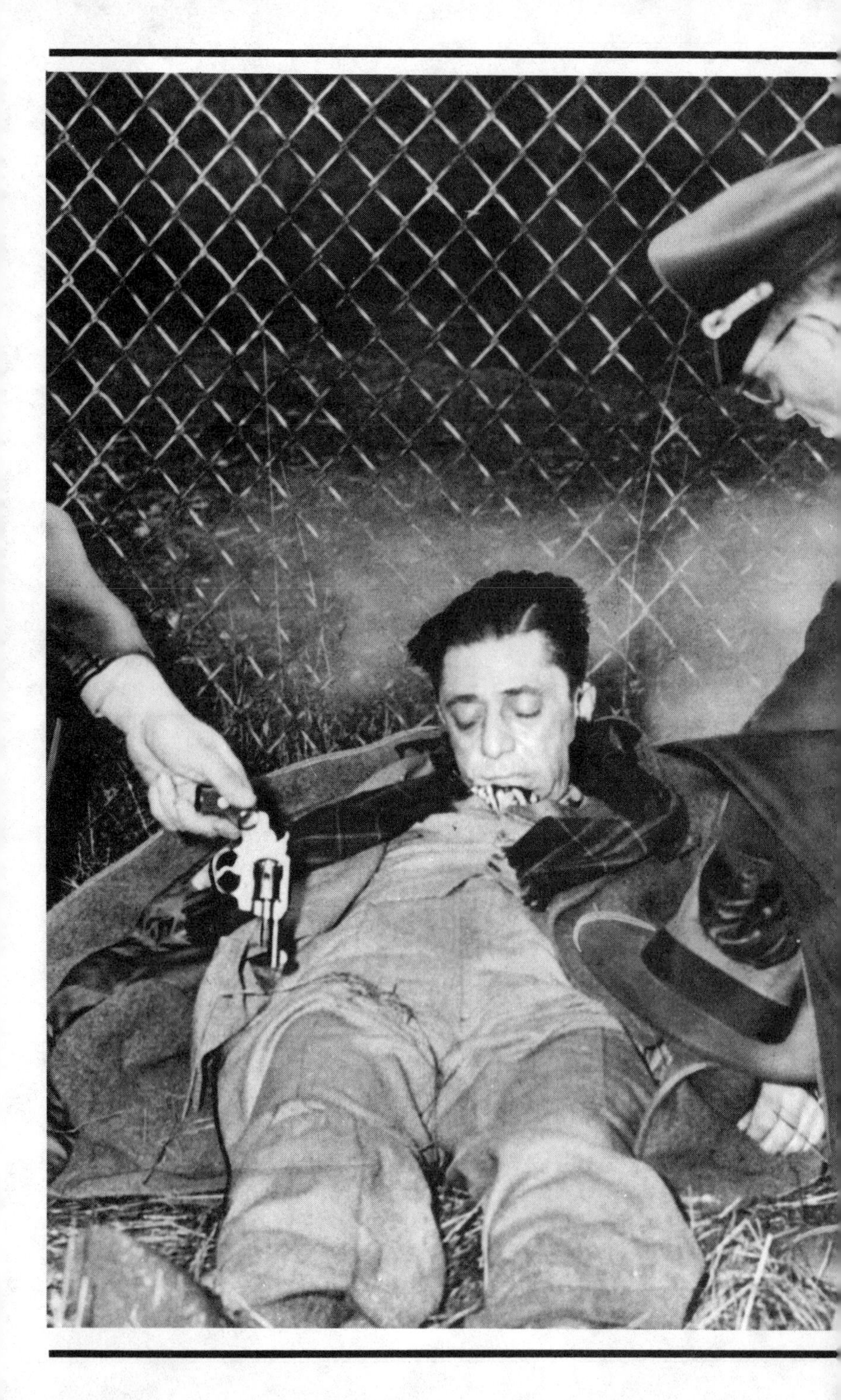

cops who'd drawn a stiff who was just a little out of their league—although very much a resident of their neck of the woods.

He sat slumped against the fence, parting the tall grass around him, brown fedora askew on his head, which rested back against a steel post, eyes shut, a revolver in his right hand—a little black .32, it looked like—and wearing a snappy gray checked suit, expensive brown plaid overcoat, blue and maroon silk scarf. On his shoes were rubbers; some snow was still on the ground, after all. Above his shoes stretched the off-white of long woolen underwear. Behind his right ear was a bullet hole; above his left ear was the exit wound.

Both Drury and I bent over him, one on either side of him. The smell of cordite was in the air.

"He must've got his hair cut this morning," I said.

"Why do you say that?" Drury asked.

I hadn't told Drury that just yesterday I'd seen this man. And I wasn't about to.

"Just looks freshly cut, that's all. You can smell the pomade."

"I can smell the wine. He must've been dead drunk. Well, now he's just dead."

Drury stood. He said to Chief Rose, "That's Frank Nitti, all right."

"His driver's license says Nitto," Rose said.

Drury shrugged. "Nitto's his real name." He laughed shortly. "He thought 'Nitti' sounded more American, I guess."

I was still bent over Nitti's body. I carefully lifted the hat off his head. The brown fedora had several bullet holes in it. Five, to be exact.

"Bill," I said. "Take a look at this."

I showed him the hat. "How in the hell does one bullet through the head put five holes in your hat? From the angle of the fatal shot, there should be only *one* hole, about here . . ." And I put my pinky through that very hole. "What made these others? Mice?"

Drury took the hat and turned it around in his hands, studying it, frowning.

Chief Rose said, "We've got witnesses. Maybe they can help explain."

He took us over to the three railroad workers. Two of them were skinny, in their forties, and looked uncannily alike, although they proved not to be brothers. The third was heavyset and about thirty-five.

Drury identified himself, and one of the skinny ones stepped forward and said he was William Seebauer, conductor; he and the other men, a switchman and a flagman, were on an IC switch engine when it started. He wore wire-frame glasses—which was about all that distinguished him from the other skinny man—and as he spoke he occasionally removed them and rubbed the drizzle of rain off the lenses, nervously.

"It was around three o'clock," he said, "and we were backing the train south, caboose in front. After we crossed Cermak Road, I saw a man about a block and a half down, going the same direction as us, south, walking on the tracks just over from us. He was staggering. I thought maybe he was drunk."

"How fast were you going?" Drury asked.

"Not very. When we got up close to him, I was on the platform, and hollered, 'Hi there, buddy,' and at that, the guy raised his hand and there was a revolver in it. He fired at me, and I ducked."

I asked, "How many shots did he fire at you?"

"Two," Seebauer said. The switchman and flagman standing nearby both nodded at that.

"What happened then?" Drury asked.

"The man was wavering around and I didn't think his aim was good. He staggered down the embankment"—he stopped and pointed at the fence and Nitti's body—"and ended up there. Sat down, or fell down. I couldn't say."

"And?"

"Well, I ordered the train stopped and we got off and walked back toward him. He was sitting there with his eyes closed. I told the other boys, 'Watch this guy—he's nuts. He may be making believe he's passed out just to take another shot at us.' So we moved slow. We were maybe sixty feet of him when his eyes opened, and he looked at us. Kind of rolled his eyes." The conductor swallowed. "Then he raised the gun to his head. He didn't miss what he was shooting at that time."

Drury had the other two tell their stories, individually. While that was going on, I went back to the body. I knelt over him. It.

"Shit, Frank," I said.

A cop nearby said, "What?"

"Nothing," I said. I got a handkerchief out of my pocket and carefully lifted the gun from his hand; I shook open the cylinder. Three bullets remained. Three had been fired.

Soon Drury came over. "Their stories all match, pretty much."

"Three bullets fired, Bill." I showed him the revolver.

He took it, and my hanky.

"That makes sense," he said. "He fires two shots at the caboose boys, and put one in his head. Two plus one makes three in my school."

"Really? Tell me, Bill, the day you graduated—how many bullet holes did you have in your mortar board?"

His mouth distorted as he thought that over. "Maybe he wasn't shooting at the boys on the train. They just heard shots and thought he was."

"Who or what was he shooting at, then?"

"His own head, of course!"

"And he *missed?* And his hat didn't fly off when these mis-aimed bullets flew through?"

Drury shrugged. "There are always anomalies in a case like this."

"Anomalies my ass! Is that how you explain evidence that doesn't suit you? Dismissing it?"

"Heller, you're just a civilian observer here. Here at my discretion. Don't cause any trouble."

"What do *you* think happened here, Captain Drury?"

He put his hands on the hips of his expensive black topcoat and smirked. "Gee, I'm trying to work up a suitable theory that makes sense with what little we got—namely, three eyewitnesses who saw a guy shoot himself in the head, and a guy with a gun in his hand and a hole in his head. I'm just leaning the slightest little bit in the direction of suicide. What do *you* make of it, Heller?"

I motioned around us. "Look at these clumps of bushes; the high grass, weeds. He was running, staggering. Drunk? Sure, from the smell of him he'd been drinking. Granted. But mightn't he been running from somebody?"

"Who?"

"People trying to kill him, Bill. Maybe he was out walking and somebody took a shot at him from those bushes, and he started running away. He was known to take regular walks, you know."

"No I don't," he said. He eyed me suspiciously. "How do you?"

"Never mind. He did take walks. Maybe he walked a regular route—this route. We're only a few blocks from his house—he was headed home. Somebody took a shot at him, possibly using a silenced gun, and when he returned fire, those caboose crawlers thought he was shooting at them."

Drury smiled humorlessly and shook his head. "And then an assassin in the bushes shot him in the head just as the railroad boys were approaching, I suppose?"

I looked up at the sky; let it spit on me. "No, Bill. Nitti shot himself. I don't question that."

"What do you question, then?"

"The circumstances. I think he fell, fleeing would-be assassins—knocked himself out. Maybe he was blind drunk and fell, what's the difference? Anyway, when he opened his eyes he saw the hazy image of three men walking toward him—sixty, seventy feet away—and rather than give Ricca the pleasure, he raised his gun to his head in one last act of defiance and ended it all."

"Ricca?"

I shrugged. "There's a rift between Ricca and Nitti—and the Outfit's sided with Ricca."

"Who says?"

"Everybody knows that. Get out of your office once in a while. Let's say Ricca put a contract out on Nitti. His torpedoes tried to kill Frank, today, along these tracks, and when the switchman and flagman and their conductor jumped off the train, the torpedoes headed for the hills. Unseen. Only Nitti didn't know they'd gone. And he mistook the IC men approaching him for his assassins."

Drury thought about that. "That's where the bullet holes in his hat came from? They shot at him and missed, these torpedoes of yours and Ricca's?"

"Yeah. Or Nitti hit the high weeds himself, when the first shot rang out. And then stuck his hat up on a stick or on his finger, to draw their fire. Maybe." I shrugged again. "Who knows?"

"Anomalies, Heller," he said. "These things never sort out exactly right."

"So what do you think?"

"I think he shot himself in the head."

"Cornered by Ricca's gunmen, he did."

"What's the difference?"

I couldn't answer that. I walked away from him, my hands in my topcoat pockets. Why did it matter to me? Why did I want to believe Frank Nitti's final act was one of defiance, not despair?

I felt a hand on my shoulder.

Drury.

He said, "When we get some more cops out here, some more *real* cops, I'll have these ditches combed. If we find any more spent shells, I'll give your theory some thought. Okay?"

"Okay."

"You liked the man, didn't you?"

"I wouldn't say I liked him."

"Respected him, then."

"Let's just say I knew him."

We walked back toward the suburban cops and Nitti's body. Chief Rose approached us. He said, "I never heard of one of these big gangsters killing himself before. Isn't this a little unusual?"

"Frankly," Drury said, "I'm not surprised. Nitti's been in ill health. He probably figured he was due for prison, and that he couldn't get the express medical care he desired there—so he took the easy way out."

That was the way Bill wanted it to be. He hated the gangsters, and he loved the idea of making a coward out of Nitti. Bill was a fine cop, a good man, a better friend; but I knew my reading of how Nitti had died would be lost in the shuffle. Maybe it was wrong of me to look at the facts and investigate wanting to prove Nitti died defiantly; but it was just as wrong for Drury to do the same wanting to prove Nitti a coward. Bill was in charge, though; and the way he saw it would be the way it went down.

Then, suddenly, in a black coat and a black dress, already in mourning, automatically in mourning, there she was: Antoinette Cavaretta. The current Mrs. Frank Nitti. The widow Nitti. The steel woman. On the arm of a uniformed cop who'd gone to get her, at Chief Rose's request, as it turned out.

She walked falteringly to the fence where Nitti lay; she knelt by him and held his hand and made a sign of the cross.

She stood.

"This was my husband," she said.

Her usually dark face seemed pale; she wore very little makeup. The uniformed man escorted her a ways away from the body.

Drury went to her; I followed.

"I'm very sorry, Mrs. Nitti," Drury said.

"Don't be a hypocrite, Captain Drury," she said. "We both know you hated my husband."

I said, "Where were you when this happened?"

She looked at me sharply. "Praying for my husband."

"Really," I said.

"Frank left about one o'clock and said he was going downtown to see his lawyer. I was worried. He's been sick, and then this grand jury trouble came up. So I went to church, to Our Lady of Sorrows, and made a novena for him."

Drury shot me a look as if to say this news proved that Nitti had set out today to commit suicide.

She said, "You people have always persecuted him. Poor Frank! He never did a wrong thing in his life."

Drury said nothing.

"Do I need your permission," she asked, bitterly, "to make the funeral arrangements? To have my husband removed to a mortuary?"

"I'm afraid that won't be possible," Drury said. "Due to the circumstances of his death, it's the county morgue for him."

She gave him a look to kill. "You're so superior, Captain. Don't take such a death so lightly. You and my husband played in the same arena; such an end could well be yours one day."

"Is that a threat, Mrs. Nitti?"

"No, Mr. Drury. It's the voice of experience. Now, I'd like to go home. I have a little boy who'll be coming home from St. Mary's in half an hour. There's difficult news I must share with him."

"Certainly you can go," he said, not unkindly.

"Why don't I walk her?" I asked him.

"It's not necessary," she said.

"I'd like to," I said.

Drury didn't care.

Mrs. Nitti said, "I would appreciate an arm to lean on, Mr. Heller, yes."

I gave her my arm and we walked back up along the tracks toward Cermak Road; it was the opposite direction from her house, but the closest street that crossed the tracks.

"My husband was fond of you," she said.

"Sometimes he had funny ways of showing it."

We walked.

"That was Frank," she said, as if that explained everything.

"Mrs. Nitti—or should I call you Toni?"

She took her arm from mine. Stopped for a moment. "Mrs. Nitti will be just fine. Do I sense a touch of disrespect in your voice?"

"I must say you're taking your husband's death well, Mrs. Nitti. You're a rock, aren't you?"

"What do you mean?"

"I mean, that the first time I saw you, you were in the presence of a dead man. Oh, he didn't know he was dead, or at least he didn't like to think he was. But with your help, his faithful secretary's help, E. J. O'Hare got dead. Good and dead."

She looked at me coldly, impassively; but she was pulling breath in like a race horse.

"A few years go by, and then you turn up again. At Frank Nitti's front door. His loving wife. The wife of a dead man. That was the difference between Frank and O'Hare—your husband knew he was dead. When I spoke to him last night, I could tell he knew he was very near the end. He was a brave man, I think."

"Yes he was," she said.

"I wonder," I said, "if you were keeping tabs on Frank for Ricca, like you kept tabs on O'Hare for Frank."

"You're a fool."

"Am I? How's this for foolish? Frank Nitti, unknown to all but a handful—said handful including you and E. J. O'Hare—betrayed Al Capone to the feds."

Her eyes flickered.

"It's so obvious," I said, "but no one ever thought of it . . . even though key Capone witness Les Shumway was still employed at Sportsman's Park. *Of course,* Nitti arranged Capone's downfall. *Of course,* Nitti moved the chess pieces until he was king himself. In a way, I admire him for it."

"So," she said, "do I."

"But then his wife Anna dies. She was the love of his life. She, and his son, were everything to him. And he begins to slide. He goes into the hospital, for the old back trouble from the wounds Mayor Cermak's boys caused. And for the ulcers that developed after he was wounded."

"His heart was also bad," she said. "And he was convinced he had stomach cancer. I wouldn't want you to leave anything out, Mr. Heller."

"Stomach cancer. Perfect. I bet you don't even know why he had that notion."

"Certainly I do," she said. "The assassin who killed Cermak believed he had stomach cancer."

"That's right. Joe Zangara. The one-man Sicilian suicide squad who pretended to shoot at FDR so that your husband could bring Mayor Cermak down without . . . I can almost hear Frank saying it . . . 'stirring up the heat.'"

"My husband was a brilliant man."

"Once," I said. "He was—once. He began to slip, though, didn't he? Despondent over his wife's death, he took long solitary walks. He even began to drink a little—not like him, not at all like him. His memory began to falter. That's where you come in."

"Really? In what way?"

"A marriage of convenience. A business arrangement. You ran a dogtrack in Miami; you helped run Sportsman's Park. You'd been Frank's inside 'man' with O'Hare. Frank had a son he loved very much, who needed a mother—a strong person who could look after little Joseph's interests after he was gone. A mob insider like you, that was perfect. And, maybe, it was a way to keep you from ever spilling what you knew about Frank setting up Capone. Hell, maybe you blackmailed him into marrying you."

She let out a long breath, and began to walk again. Quickly. I walked right alongside her.

"You know what I think, Mrs. Nitti?"

"What do you think?"

"I think you've had practice being a widow. After all, you've been a black widow for years."

She stopped in her tracks, next to the tracks, and she slapped me. Hard. A hard, ringing, stinging slap.

"What do you know?" she said. There was bitterness in the throaty voice, but something else too: pain.

But I pressed on, my cheek flaming, like Estelle Carey in her final moments. "You want me to believe you weren't keeping tabs on him for Ricca? That you didn't send him out to meet his death on his regular walk, today?"

"I don't care what you believe."

She slowed. She stopped. She turned to me.

"I loved Frank," she said. "I loved him for years. And he came to love me. He worshipped Anna, but he loved *me*."

"Goddamn," I said, stopped in my tracks now. "I believe you."

She shook her head slowly, lecturing with a jerky finger. "Perhaps some . . . *some* . . . of what you said is true . . . but know this: I was *never* in Ricca's pocket. I *never* betrayed Frank. I didn't blackmail him into marriage. I'm no black widow! No black widow." She sat down, on the slope, by the tracks. "Just a widow. Another widow."

I sat next to her. "I'm sorry."

It was still raining, a little. Still drizzling.

She was breathing heavily. "I understand. You felt something for my husband. That's what caused your anger."

"I guess so."

The pain was showing on her face now. "It's hard to lose him like this. Death by his own hand."

"My father committed suicide," I said.

She looked at me.

"He put a bullet in his head, too." I looked at her. "It's something you learn to live with, but you never forget."

"Perhaps you've lost another father today."

"That's putting it a little strong. But I am sorry to see the old bastard go."

Then I looked at her again and she was weeping. The steel lady was weeping.

So I put my arm around her and she wept into my shoulder.

When I left her at her door, the boy was just getting home.

MRS. NITTI (WITH EDWARD O'HARE, JR.)

33

I had supposed the final favor Frank Nitti promised me was one he'd been unable to keep. After all, I asked him Thursday night; and Friday afternoon he was dead.

But Saturday morning a pale, shaking Barney Ross, in civvies for a change, brown jacket, gray slacks, and a hastily knotted tie under a wrinkled gray raincoat, came into my office, around eleven, slamming the door behind him.

I was standing at Gladys's desk, handing her my notes on an insurance report.

"We gotta talk," he said. He was sweating. It was starting to look and feel just a little like spring out there, but nobody was sweating yet. Except Barney.

Gladys seemed thrown by this uncharacteristically sloppy, angry Barney Ross. And it took quite a bit to throw a cool customer like her.

"Forget this last report," I told her. "Go ahead and take off a little early." We only worked till noon on Saturday.

"Sure, Mr. Heller," she said, rising, gathering her things. "See you Monday." And, with one last wide-eyed glance back at us, she was out the door.

"Step into my office," I said, gesturing, smiling.

His one arm hung at his side, hand shaking; the other leaned against the wooden walking stick, which trembled like a coconut palm in a storm. "Did you do this, Nate?"

"Step into my office. Sit down. Take a load off."

He went ahead of me, as quickly as his walking stick would allow; sat down. I got behind the desk. He was rubbing his hands on his trousered thighs. He didn't look at me.

"Did you do this thing to me?"

"Do what, Barney?"

Now he tried to look at me, but it was hard for him; his eyes darted around, not lighting anywhere. "Nobody'll sell me anything. I need my medicine, Nate."

"You mean you need a fix."

"It's for my headaches, and earaches. The malaria relapses. Goddamn, if you don't understand this, who would?"

"Go to a doctor."

"I . . . I used up the doctors the first three weeks, Nate. They'll only give me a shot, once. I had to go to the streets."

"Where you've found your supply has suddenly dried up."

"You did it, didn't you? Why did you do it?"

"What makes you think I did?"

His sweaty face contorted. "You've got the pull with the Outfit boys. You coulda gone straight to Nitti himself. That's what it would take, to dry this town up for me like this."

"Don't you read the papers, pal? Nitti's dead."

"I don't care. You did it. Why? Aren't you my friend?"

"I don't think so. I don't hang around with junkies."

He covered his face with one hand; he was shaking bad. "You can't stop me. I'm going back out on the road tomorrow. Back on the war-plant circuit. I can find what I need in any town I want. All I got to do is find a new doctor each time—they'll give it to me. They know who I am, they'll trust me. They know I'm traveling with a Navy party on this tour . . . they got no reason to think I'm looking for anything but just one shot of morphine for a malaria flare-up."

"Sure," I said. "That'll work. And when you run out of doctors, you can go back to the street, to the pushers. But not here. Not in Chicago."

"Nate . . . I live here."

"You used to. Maybe you better move to Hollywood with your movie-star wife. You can go make your connection out there. I can't stop that."

"Nate! What are you doing to me?"

"What are you doing to yourself?"

"I'll get past this."

"That's a good idea. Get past it. Get some help. Kick this thing."

He screwed his face up, sweat still beading his brow. "You know what the papers'll do with this? Look what happened to D'Angelo—all that poor bastard did was write some love letters, and they *ruined* him."

I shrugged. "I talked to him a couple of days ago. He's fine. They're fitting him a leg. He'll be working someplace, before you know it. He understands that this thing we went through, we got to put it behind us. You got to put the Island behind you, too, Barney."

He was almost crying, now. "How could I ever face people? How can I tell Cathy? What would Ma say, and my brothers and my friends? What . . . what would Rabbi Stein think? Barney Ross, the kid from the ghetto who became champ, the guy they call a war hero and the idol of kids, a sickening, disgusting dope addict! The shame of it, Nate. The shame . . ."

I got up from behind the desk and put a hand on his shoulder. "You got to do it, Barney. You got to check in someplace and take the cure. You can keep the publicity down to a minimum if you go into a private sanitarium, you know."

"I . . . I hear the best place is the government hospital at Lexington. But then everybody'd know . . ."

"They'd understand. People know what we went through. They don't understand the extent of it. But they'll forgive you."

"I don't know, Nate."

"You could start with forgiving yourself."

"What . . . what do you mean?"

"For killing Monawk."

He looked up at me, the tragic brown eyes managing to hold still long enough to lock mine. "You . . . you know?"

"Yeah."

He looked away. "H-how long have you known?"

"A little over a month. The night some people broke into my office, it was. Like you, I'd been having nightmares. I dreamed I killed him myself, in one, that night. But when I woke up, I knew I hadn't. After I thought about it, though, I knew *why* I'd dreamed that—you killing that poor son of a bitch was the same as me killing him. It was as hard for me to accept, to live with, as if I'd done it myself. That's why I blocked it, pal. You been sticking a needle in your arm to forget. I managed to forget without any help."

He was shaking his head. "God, God. I didn't mean to."

I squeezed his shoulder. "I know you didn't. He was screaming, giving us away; you had the forty-five in your hand, and you put a hand over his mouth like you did before, only this time the gun just went off. It was an accident."

"But I killed him, Nate."

"Not really. The war killed him. You were trying to save all us poor wounded bastards, him included."

"I didn't know anybody else saw it happen."

"I don't think anybody did, but me. We were all hurting so bad we were floating in and out of it. But if anybody did, they'll never say a word."

He was looking at the floor. "I . . . I should have reported it. Admitted it. I let them hang this hero shit on me . . . what kind of man would do that?"

"That's just it. You're just a man, Barney. And fuck, you *were* a hero that night. I wouldn't be here if you hadn't been."

"I killed him. I kill him over and over in my dreams . . ."

"The dreams will pass."

"You shouldn't have done it, Nate. You shouldn't have cut off my supply."

I patted the shoulder. "Someday you're going to have to learn to live with it. Until that time, go on from town to town selling bonds by day, and scrounging up your fix by night. But don't do it in Chicago."

"This is my hometown, Nate—my family's here . . ."

"They'll be here when you decide to come back, too. And so will I."

He stood, shakily. "I know you did this out of friendship . . . but it was still wrong . . ."

"No it wasn't," I said.

He and his voodoo cane stumbled out of the inner office; I didn't help him.

"You might try the abortionist across the hall," I said.

"You bastard," he said. But some of the old fight was in his eyes. Barney was still in there, somewhere, in that shell. Someday maybe he'd crawl out.

Barney wasn't the only local boy to make it big in the papers as a war hero. There was also E. J. O'Hare's son, "Butch"—a.k.a. Lieutenant Commander Edward Henry O'Hare, a combat pilot who in 1942 received the Congressional Medal of Honor for shooting down five Jap bombers. He died in aerial combat in 1943, and in '49, Chicago's International Airport was renamed O'Hare, honoring the son of the proud father who had died eight years earlier, in combat of another sort.

Antoinette Cavaretta, Mrs. Frank Nitti, looked after her stepson well. She managed her late husband's finances, battling (and winning) various IRS assaults; and she continued receiving payments from an Outfit source, namely her old Sportsman's Park crony Johnny Patton. In 1955 she requested mob banker Moe Greenberg turn over the capital of a trust fund Frank had set up for his boy Joe. The boy was twenty-one, now, and it only seemed fair. Greenberg refused. The Outfit sided with Mrs. Nitti. Moe Greenberg turned up dead on December 8, 1955.

The boy, Joseph, grew up to be a successful businessman.

Les Shumway, incidentally, was still working at Sportsman's Park as late as the early sixties. How his charmed life extended beyond Nitti's death, I never knew; perhaps the widow Nitti's fine hand was at work there as well.

As for the others, many are dead, of course. Jack Barger, in '59, having branched out from burlesque into pioneering the drive-in movie business. Johnny Patton. Stege. Goldstone. Campagna. Wyman. Sapperstein. Sally. Eliot. When you get to my age, such lists grow long; they end only when your own name is at the bottom—and you're not alive to put it there, so what the hell.

Pegler had quite a run, for the ten years following the Pulitzer he won for the Browne/Bioff expose. But he grew even more arrogant, once he'd been legitimized by the prize. His anti-Semitism, his hatred for the Roosevelts, his blasts at the unions, at "Commies," became an embarrassment. His off-kilter opinionated writing grew increasingly self-destructive, until finally he met his downfall when he libeled his old friend Quentin Reynolds. In the 1954 court battle, Louis Nizer—your classic New York Jew liberal lawyer—skewered him; it was never the same after that. By the end—June 1969—he'd lost his syndicated column and was reduced to contributing monthly ramblings to a John Birch Society publication.

Montgomery, of course, continued to star in motion pictures through the late forties; but he began directing, as well, and was a pioneer in the early days of TV. His interest in politics and social concerns never abated; he was the first TV media advisor to a U.S. president (Eisenhower) and was a vocal critic of the abuses of network TV, being an early advocate of public television. He also continued to be outspoken on the subject of the mob's influence on Hollywood; his Chicago contact in such matters was Bill Drury.

Bill waged his war against the mob for the rest of his short life, despite largely trumped-up charges of misconduct that finally lost him his badge. He was fighting for reinstatement, and preparing to testify to the Kefauver Senate Crime Investigating Committee, when he was shotgunned to death in his car on September 25, 1950.

On October 5, 1943, Paul "the Waiter" Ricca, Louis "Little New York" Campagna, Phil D'Andrea, Frank Maritote (a.k.a. Diamond), Charles "Cherry Nose" Gioe, and John Roselli were found guilty in the federal court in New York. Each was sentenced ten years and fined $10,000. A co-conspirator, Louis Kaufman, head of the Newark, New Jersey IA local, got seven years and a $10,000 fine. I did not testify against them; with Nitti no longer a defendant, and after a discouraging interview with me, Correa declined to call me.

Ricca, Campagna, Gioe, and D'Andrea walked out of stir on August 13, 1947, having served the bare one-third minimum of their sentences that it took to make them eligible for parole. Nobody in history ever got out of prison on the very day they became eligible for parole—till Ricca and company. The fix, obviously, was in—and it stretched clear to Tom C. Clark, Attorney General of these United States, who (it was said) received from Ricca, by way of payment, the next open seat on the Supreme Court, in 1949. Of course, it was actually President Harry Truman who nominated Clark—Campagna's lawyer, by the way, was St. Louis attorney Paul Dillon, Truman's "close personal friend" and former campaign manager.

I don't know, exactly, what became of Nick Dean, his wife, and (I presume) that fabled hidden million Estelle Carey never had. The government tried to deport him, back in the early fifties, but it fell through. Last I heard of him, he was in South America. He may be there still.

Browne simply faded away. For a time he had a farm in Woodstock, Illinois, near Chicago; and I heard he moved from there to a farm in Wisconsin. I hear he died of natural causes. If so, he managed that by keeping out of any further union and Outfit business, after his release from prison.

Bioff was the Outfit's prime target, but he too, for a time, was spared. While still in prison, Ricca was said to have ordered contracts on both Bioff and Westbrook Pegler, but was talked out of it, having been advised that killing them would only create martyrs, and public opinion would be so against Ricca and company that their paroles (already in the works) might not go through. A low profile was needed.

That was advice Bioff might well have taken. But in 1948 he helped the government again, testifying in a tax case against the Outfit's Jake Guzik and Tony Accardo. Then he belatedly took the low-profile route, settling with his wife and kids on a farm outside Phoenix, Arizona, where he became a stockbroker. He called himself Al Nelson, and got chummy with Barry Goldwater, to whose campaign for U.S. Senate he'd made a political contribution of $5,000.

But, gradually, Willie's itch for action got him back in the mob's domain. By early 1955 he was trying to worm his way into the gambling scene in Nevada, specifically a joint in Reno, using the same old strong-arm tactics he'd perfected as a pimp. And in the winter of that same year he was hired by Gus Greenbaum to be in charge of entertainment at the Riviera Casino in Las Vegas; Greenbaum was discouraged by his Outfit friends from hiring Bioff, but Gus felt Willie, with his Hollywood contacts, could "persuade" big-name acts to work cheaper. Labor man Willie had no problems working for management.

Two weeks after his latest airplane ride with Senator Goldwater (the senator, in his private plane, from time to time chauffeured Bioff and his bride to various parties around the Southwest), Al Nelson, a.k.a. Willie Bioff, strolled out of the kitchen door of his luxurious Phoenix home on East Bethany Road and climbed behind the wheel of his pickup truck. He waved to his wife; she was waving back, from the kitchen window, when he put the foot to the starter, which was followed by an explosion that blew the truck and Bioff apart, showering Mrs. Nelson/Bioff with glass from the window where she'd been waving. Every window in the house was shattered. And parts of Willie and his truck lay glistening in the desert sun. The former panderer's charred former finger bearing a $7,500 diamond ring was found in the grass two hundred feet from the house.

Willie's Vegas mentor Greenbaum was killed in 1958; he and his wife were trussed up in their home and their throats slashed.

Such deaths were typical of the post-Nitti Outfit's style; the headlines were often bloody, the heat was frequently stirred up. Not until the 1960s did the style revert, somewhat, to Nitti's lower-key approach.

The Chicago local of the IATSE, by the way, continues to be linked to the Outfit; in 1980 the Chicago *Tribune* reported that the feds had identified twenty-four men with mob ties as members of Local 110. And the second-highest-paid labor leader in the entertainment industry, *Variety* said in 1985, was the business manager of that local, who took home nearly a million in salary and expenses over the latest ten-year period.

As for me, from time to time I had dealings with Nitti's successors, but never again did I come to know one of the mob bosses in the way I knew Nitti. My agency, A-1, is still around; but I retired years ago.

Barney? On January 12, 1947, he was released from the U.S. Public Health Service addiction hospital in Lexington, Kentucky, where he had admitted himself voluntarily three months earlier. He'd gone that route because (he told me later) he heard "those private sanitariums ain't tough enough." Also, by going to a government hospital, he'd make a clean breast of it, publicly; he might encourage others with the same problem to come forward, too. It was also a gesture to his wife, who had recently left him, of his sincerity about quitting the stuff. Cathy was there for him, when he got out of Lexington.

"The withdrawal gave me the miseries," he told me, "because the reduced dose of morphine wasn't enough to kill the cramps and the sweats. I learned quick enough where the expression 'kick the habit' come from. When they gradually cut down my dope, I got spasms in the muscles of my arms and my legs actually *kicked*. And then I was back there again, Nate. On the Island. I kept fighting the Japs in that muddy shell hole, over and over again. But now I don't have to go back there no more."

I hope nobody does.

I OWE THEM ONE:

Despite its extensive basis in history, this is a work of fiction, and a few liberties have been taken with the facts, though as few as possible—and any blame for historical inaccuracies is my own, reflecting, I hope, the limitations of my conflicting source material, and the need to telescope certain events to make for a more smoothly flowing narrative. The E. J. O'Hare and Estelle Carey cases are complex and, in order to deal with them both within this one volume, the use of compressed time and composite characters was occasionally necessary. While in most cases real names have been used, I have at times substituted similar or variantly spelled names for those of real people, when these real people—particularly, more minor, non-"household name" historical figures—have been used in a markedly fictionalized manner. Such characters include Nate and Barney's fellow Marines and soldiers in the Guadalcanal section; Sergeant Donahoe; the Borgias; and Wyman. All of these characters did, however, have real-life counterparts.

While numerous books and newspaper accounts were consulted in the writing of the Guadalcanal section of *The Million-Dollar Wound,* several books proved particularly helpful. *Semper Fi, Mac* (1982), by Henry Berry, a Studs Terkel–style oral history of the Marines in the Pacific, was far and away the most valuable resource for that section, and is highly recommended to any readers interested in exploring this subject further. Very helpful as well (and recommended reading) were (are) two Marine memoirs: *With the Old Breed* (1981), E. B. Sledge; and *Goodbye Darkness: A Memoir of the Pacific War* (1980), William Manchester. And, of course, the autobiography of Barney Ross (written with Martin Abramson), *No Man Stands Alone* (1957), provided the basis for Barney and Nate's story; it should be noted that the death of a Marine by "friendly fire" in this novel is fictional, although it grows out of an admission in the Ross autobiography that such an event *nearly* occurred. Otherwise, the account of Barney Ross's experiences in that bloody, muddy shell hole is a true one.

The portrait of Westbrook Pegler is drawn primarily from two biographies—*Pegler: Angry Man of the Press* (1963), Oliver Platt; and *Fair Enough: The Life of Westbrook Pegler* (1975), Finis Farr. Also consulted were Pegler's own writings, including the collections *'T Ain't Right* (1936) and *George Spelvin, American, and Fireside Chats* (1942), as well as his newspaper columns pertaining to Bioff and Browne. The anti-Semitic behavior of Pegler depicted here is reflected in these biographies to an extent, as well as in Louis Nizer's *My Life in Court* (1961); but is based also upon an interview with an acquaintance of Pegler's who was on the receiving end of the columnist's prejudice.

As was the case in *True Crime* (1984), the portrait of Sally Rand herein is a fictionalized one, though based upon numerous newspaper and magazine articles, and especially drawing upon Stud Terkel's oral history *Hard Times* (1970); but I feel I must label it as fictionalized, as I know of no historic parallel in Sally Rand's life to her relationship with Nate Heller. Her portrait in these pages is also drawn from a 1939 *Collier's* article by Quentin Reynolds. The portrait of Robert Montgomery is largely drawn from another *Collier's* article by Reynolds of approximately the same vintage (it is typically Heller-ironic that two articles by Quentin Reynolds, whose libel suit against Westbrook Pegler spelled the beginning of the end for the feisty columnist, served as major reference sources for this novel). The Montgomery portrait was further drawn from *Current Biography* (1948) and *Contemporary Authors*, his own book *Open Letter From a Television Viewer* (1968), and various other magazine articles and books.

Other books that deserve singling out include *The Legacy of Al Capone* (1975) by George Murray—the only comprehensive study of the post-Capone mob era, and a very valuable reference to the writing of the Nitti Trilogy; *The Tax Dodgers* (1948), a memoir by Treasury Agent Elmer L. Irey (with William J. Slocum); and *The Extortionists* (1972), a memoir of Herbert Aller, business representative of the IATSE for thirty-six years.

The portrait of Antoinette Cavaretta, the second Mrs. Nitti, must be viewed as a fictionalized one. Although the basic facts of her business involvement with Nitti, working as E. J. O'Hare's secretary, marrying Nitti, etc., are accurate, few interviews with her exist (and these brief interviews were at the stressful time of her husband's death); my imagined portrait of her is largely drawn from the newspaper accounts of the day, and from material in Murray's *The Legacy of Al Capone* and Ed Reid's *The Grim Reapers* (1969). Also consulted (in regard to Antoinette Cavaretta and other mob-related figures in this book) were the transcripts of the Kefauver Senate Crime Investigating Committee hearings. Nate Heller's speculations about Cavaretta's personal relationship with Nitti prior to their marriage—including her possible role in O'Hare's murder—should be viewed as just that: speculation; and speculation by a fictional character in a historical novel, at that. It should be noted, however, that the Kefauver investigators explored the same area in the questioning of various Chicago crime figures.

Several hardworking people helped me research this book, primarily George Hagenauer, whose many contributions include helping develop the theory regarding Frank Nitti "setting up" Al Capone, and exploring the suspicious circumstances surrounding Nitti's death. In the previous two volumes "from the memoirs of Nathan Heller," *True Detective* (1983) and *True Crime* (1984), which with this novel comprise the Nitti Trilogy, theories regarding the assassination of Mayor Anton Cermak, and the substitution of a "patsy" in the FBI-sanctioned shooting of John Dillinger, were respectively explored; these theories, however, had been discussed and developed, in part at least, by previous crime historians. To our knowledge, no one has ever before questioned and explored the circumstances of Nitti's suicide, or seriously suggested that Nitti engineered Al Capone's fall; these theories are new to this volume. Despite their presentation within this fictional arena, we offer, and stand behind, these as serious theories and invite further research by crime historians, which we feel will only serve to demonstrate the legitimacy of our claims. (We have, for example, visited the Nitti death site, the terrain of which tends to confirm our notion that a gunman or gunmen may have been firing at Nitti just prior to his suicide.)

Mike Gold, another Chicagoan who is a Chicago history buff with an eye for detail, provided his usual help and support. My friend John W. McRae, a Marine through and through, was kind enough to read the Guadalcanal section and make some suggestions, all of which I took. My friend and frequent collaborator, cartoonist Terry Beatty, also lent his support and editor's eye to this project. And I would like especially to thank Dominick Abel, my agent, who has done more for me than these few words can indicate. Ruptured Duck awards for combat duty are due Tom Dunne, my editor, who has believed in Heller from the beginning; and his associate Susannah Driver, whose hard work on these books was well above and beyond the call of duty. Thanks also to editorial assistants Susan Patterson and Pam Hoenig. And a big thanks to Ed Gorman and Connie Sisson of Media Consultations. Thanks also to Jane Crawford, of AAA Travel Agency, Muscatine, Iowa; and Chris Dobson, American Airlines historian. Thanks to Chicago's Bob Cromie for sharing his Pacific experiences in an interview (and whose original *Tribune* articles were invaluable). And a tip of the fedora to three suspense masters: Andrew M. Greeley, Howard Browne, and Mickey Spillane, for help, suggestions, and support.

A special thanks to my aunt and uncle, Beth and Paul Povlsen, who shared with me their wartime experiences as nurse and corpsman, respectively, at St. Elizabeth's. Some of the medical treatment described herein (including the use of hypnosis in treatment of amnesia) derives from John Huston's classic documentary *Let There Be Light* (1948).

Photos selected by the author for use in this edition are courtesy AP/World Wide Photos and the Chicago *Tribune;* the rest have been selected from the personal collections of George Hagenauer and the author, the bulk of them having been culled from long out-of-print "true detective" magazines of the late thirties and early forties—a few others are U.S. Marine Corps photos. Efforts to track the sources of certain photos have been unsuccessful; upon notification these sources will be listed in subsequent editions.

Hundreds of books, and magazine and newspaper articles (from the *Tribune*, *Daily News*, *Herald-American*, and other Chicago papers of the day), have been consulted in researching *The Million-Dollar Wound;* among the magazines are issues of *This Week in Chicago*, a publication that provided background on Rinella's Brown Derby (where Sally Rand did indeed appear in 1943), the Barney Ross Cocktail Lounge, and the Rialto Theater. I am particularly indebted to the anonymous authors of the Federal Writers Project volumes on the states of California and Illinois, both of which appeared in 1939. A few other books deserve singling out: *Hollywood Babylon II* (1984), Kenneth Anger; *Maxwell Street* (1977), Ira Berkow; *Cleveland: The Best Kept Secret* (1967), George E. Condon; *This Was Burlesque* (1968), Ann Corio (with Joseph DiMona); *Captive City* (1969), Ovid

Demaris; *Time Capsule: History of the War Years 1939–1945* (1972), John Dille; *Pacific Victory 1945* (1944), Joseph Driscoll; *Dining in Chicago* (1931), John Drury; *Gone Hollywood* (1979), Christopher Finch and Linda Rosenkrantz; *The Art of Detection* (1948), Jacob Fisher; *Mafia USA* (1972), Nicholas Gage, editor; *The Battle for Guadalcanal* (1963), Samuel B. Griffith II; *The Homefront: America During World War II* (1984), Mark Jonathan Harris, Franklin Mitchell, and Steven Schechter; *WW II* (1975), James Jones; *Capone: The Life and World of Al Capone* (1971), John Kobler; *Chicago Confidential* (1950), Jack Lait and Lee Mortimer; *World War II Super Facts* (1983), Don McCombs and Fred L. Worth; *Guadalcanal Remembered* (1982), Herbert Christian Merillat; *The Mob in Show Business* (1973), Hank Messick; *People to See* (1981), Jay Robert Nash; *The Untouchables* (1957), Eliot Ness and Oscar Fraley; *The Great Battles of World War II, Volume I: The Pacific Island Battles* (1985), Charles E. Pfannes and Victor A. Salamone; *The Green Felt Jungle* (1963), Ed Reid and Ovid Demaris; *Since You Went Away* (1973), Donald I. Rogers; *The Man Who Got Capone* (1976), Frank Spiering; *The 100 Greatest Boxers of All Time* (1984), Bert Randolph Sugar; *Encyclopedia of American Crime* (1982), Carl Sifakis; *Syndicate City* (1954), Alson J. Smith; *The Good War* (1984), Studs Terkel; *Guadalcanal Diary* (1943), Richard Tregaskis; *Yank: The Story of World War II as Written by the Soldiers* (1984), *Yank* editors; and *The Guadalcanal Campaign* (1949), Major John L. Zimmerman, USMCR.

When all the debts have been paid, or at least acknowledged, one remains: this book could not have been written without the love, help, and support of my wife, Barbara Collins—Nate's mother.